P9-DEL-310

I LOVED A ROGUE

❧ The ❧ Prince Catchers

KATHARINE ASHE

AVON
An Imprint of HarperCollinsPublishers

AVON BOOKS
An Imprint of HarperCollins*Publishers*
195 Broadway
New York, New York 10007

Copyright © 2015 by Katharine Brophy Dubois
Excerpt from *The Devil's Duke* copyright © 2015 by Katharine Brophy Dubois
ISBN 978-0-06-222985-4
www.avonromance.com

First Avon Books mass market printing: March 2015

Avon Trademark Reg. U.S. Pat. Off. and in Other Countries, Marca Registrada, Hecho en U.S.A.
HarperCollins® is a registered trademark of HarperCollins Publishers.

Printed in the U.S.A.

10 9 8 7 6 5 4 3 2 1

To the circle story girls,
co-authors of my (our) first (insane) romances ~
Jill, Kate, Kathy, Susan, Susie, & Tenny

Y se alegre el alma llena
De la luz de esos luceros.

And his heart is filled with rapture
At the light in those lights above.

CHARLES G. LELAND,
The Gypsies

"*Every person pretending or professing to tell*
fortunes, or using any subtle craft, means, or device,
by palmistry or otherwise, to deceive and impose on
any of his Majesty's subjects; every person wandering
abroad and lodging in any barn or outhouse, or in any
deserted or unoccupied building, or in the open air,
or under a tent, or in any cart or wagon . . . and not
giving a good account of himself . . . shall be deemed
a rogue and vagabond."

VAGRANCY ACT OF 1824

The Gypsy Boy

By a Pond in a Wood in Cornwall
September 1807

Taliesin Wolfe had tasted blood before. At least twice a year his uncle split his lip with the flat of his palm. That made thirty-four split lips to date.

He'd tasted mud before too. When a man spent most of his time with horses, it couldn't be avoided.

He had never before tasted them in the same mouthful. Hot blood. Warm mud. Anger hovering precariously between the two. And a fog in his head he'd definitely never known. Squire Shackelford's son had not used his palm.

"What's wrong, Gypsy boy? One jab and you're already face down?" Shackelford jeered from behind him. Snickers came from the other boys.

"Five attempted jabs," he corrected through gummy lips. Thomas Shackelford looked stupid, but Taliesin had always supposed he could count. He ran his tongue over his teeth. None broken. Small miracles. "You only struck me when those three bounders held my arms."

Hard footsteps. "Why, you insolent—"

"Tommy, leave him be, why don't you?" This from the stranger boy who'd stood back while the others had grabbed Taliesin. "It looks like he's had enough, and I don't know that your father would approve." An uncomfortable chuckle. "Don't you agree, Freddie?"

"I'd like to see you trounce him good, Tom," young Freddie Shackelford mumbled. "But Rob's right. Father won't like it, you mixing it up with a Gypsy. Says every time you do it they filch another dozen fence posts."

"Father should have driven them off his land years ago."

"Filthy thieves," grumbled one of the boys who'd held him still so Shackelford could connect his fist with Taliesin's jaw.

"This one's the vicar's favorite," Freddie supplied.

"The one that cuts the verge in the cemetery?"

"Does odd jobs around the vicarage too. Mother says he runs tame over there, but she can't say it's wrong because the vicar calls it charity."

The world stopped spinning and Taliesin pressed his palms into the mud. He pushed his face and then his shoulders off the ground.

"Whichever one of them he is," Thomas Shackelford

said, "he's done more than steal a fence post this time. Haven't you, peddler boy?"

"Not a peddler." Taliesin coughed on blood, his vision spotty. He blinked hard but saw only a blur. For a poor shot, when Shackelford did connect, he did so with mighty force. "Horse trader, you dolt."

Footsteps again. Quick.

Boot.

Ribs.

Pain. *Pain.*

Shackelford stepped back. Taliesin rolled onto his side. Fought for air. Sunlight cutting through the trees burst like stars.

"Come now, Tom," Stranger Boy said in a constricted voice. "You don't know that he did anything untoward with the girl. Why don't you ask him first?"

Shackelford laughed. "They're liars as well as thieves, Rob. He wouldn't tell me the truth even if I asked him."

"Ask him. If he lies"—another strained chuckle—"then you can trounce him as heartily as Freddie likes."

Coward. Stranger Boy knew Shackelford should back off, but Englishmen never raised a hand to help a Rom. Except the Reverend.

Sucking in air, agony slicing his insides, Taliesin pushed himself up again. This time he got his feet under him.

"All right." Shackelford made a sound like a pig. "I'll ask him, Rob. Then you'll see how he couldn't tell truths from lies if you spelled it out."

Them, not *it.* Truths. Lies. Plural. Not singular. Didn't they teach grammar at fancy schools? How porridge-for-brains Thomas Shackelford got to be heir to the biggest landholder in St. Petroc, Taliesin would never understand. Even if he were lucky, Taliesin knew he'd never own more than a horse and the clothes on his back. Reverend Caulfield always said a man must rest content with the lot God gave him. The Apostle Paul, Colossians, chapter three: *Servants, obey in all things your masters . . . knowing that of the Lord ye shall receive the reward of the inheritance.*

Paul had obviously never been a Rom horse trader.

Fighting back the pain in his side, ignoring it like he'd learned to ignore taunting from Englishmen as a child, he straightened his shoulders. Black fogged his vision. He struggled on broken breaths. Broken *ribs.* Years ago he'd been kicked by a horse. He knew this pain.

"What of it, Gypsy boy?"

He blinked and Shackelford's scowl came into focus, the beads of sweat on his upper lip delicate, like dew, a high flush in his cheeks. Behind him, Stranger Boy's eyes were like bluebirds, bright, free.

"My shirt." Slurred, but it couldn't be helped. His lip was starting to swell.

Shackelford's pale brow puckered. Minutes earlier, when Taliesin had brushed off his attacker's feeble attempts to hit him and went after his shirt tangled in the reeds at the edge of the pond, Shackelford's friends had jumped him. Now he wouldn't give them another chance like that, back turned, vulnerable. He had to have that shirt, though. He couldn't don it now—didn't think he could lift his arms. But he had only one shirt, and damn if he'd lose it because of imbecile Squire Shackelford's imbecile son and school chums.

"Give him his shirt," Shackelford grunted. One of his henchmen went to the bank, splashed in the mud, and cussed. But he snatched the shirt off the reeds and tossed it to Taliesin.

He wouldn't ask for his coat or neck cloth, or his

boots. They were behind the reeds on the other side of the pond. He would return later to retrieve them. If he could walk later.

Shackelford sneered. "Well, boy?"

"I don't know what you want," he said, rougher than he intended. No air for words. Pain everywhere.

"Liar," a henchman said, but limply now. Taliesin almost sympathized. The heat hung so heavy, his bare skin wore it like a sleeve.

"What were you doing with the vicar's daughter?" Shackelford demanded. "We saw her walking away from this copse not ten minutes ago."

Ten minutes. Barely long enough to wrest control of the havoc she'd roused in him—*that she always roused in him*—before these louts had appeared.

"Vicar's got three daughters," he said, and this time the words came out strong, like the Reverend always told him to speak: humble before God but equal to any man.

Shackelford squinted. "Huh?"

"Which daughter did you see?" He lifted his chin, squelching a wince. "Whichever one it was, next time I'm at the vicarage I'll make certain to tell her not to go wandering around alone." He narrowed his eyes. "Never know who she might encounter."

He'd gone too far. Too impudent. Too unwise. He knew it before the words slipped over his torn lip. But he was tired of Shackelford and every other boy in St. Petroc being allowed to talk to her in public—in the street, churchyard, shops, at the fair—when all he could ever hope for was a smile from a distance. Now he'd tasted her. Now he knew she wanted him.

He'd finally had enough.

"You insolent son of an Egyptian whore." Shackelford gaped. "I gave him a ch———, Rob. You heard me do it." His pasty face flamed as he stripped off his coat. "Now, Gypsy boy, you'll pay."

Taliesin braced himself, the pain and heat nothing now to the anger surging in him, furious and fast. "Give me your best."

Like a dog, Shackelford snarled and came at him.

He gave Taliesin his best.

Chapter 1

The Prodigal Son

Combe Park
Home of the Duke and Duchess of Lycombe
February 1819

"**Y**ou're a ghost."

This comment came at Eleanor Caulfield's shoulder, quietly. Eleanor ignored it and tried to concentrate on the echoing glory of the pipe organ, whose music filled the chapel.

"A living human's cheeks cannot be so pale," her youngest sister insisted below the hymn. Not whispered. Ravenna didn't know how to whisper. "Yours are chalk."

"They aren't." Eleanor did whisper. She'd nearly perfected the art. "Now, hush." But she lifted a hand to her face. Clad in silk-lined kidskin fastened with tiny buttons fashioned from oyster shells—gloves borrowed from her other sister, Arabella, the Duchess of Lycombe—her fingertips pressed at her cheeks.

Cold. Like death.

The death of life as she knew it.

"Really, Ellie. You look like a princess," Ravenna stripped off her shawl and covered Eleanor's shoulders. "But you'll catch a chill in this frigid sepulcher."

The ducal chapel was hardly a sepulcher, rather, a lovely little space of honey-colored limestone and clear windows that allowed the winter sunlight to warm the assembled wedding guests one pale ray at a time. Still, she pulled Ravenna's shawl over her bosom. With her hair cascading about her shoulders, Ravenna didn't need it, and everyone always assumed Eleanor did. Thirteen years had not yet erased from her family's memory the time when every wisp of air stealing through an open door had tipped her closer to death. The inflammation of the lungs she'd taken in her fourteenth year had lingered so long that no one ever thought she would fully recover.

No one, except one.

Today her bloodless cheeks had nothing to do with ill health or the February chill. At the foot of the chancel her beloved papa appeared sublimely happy as he wed a woman ideally suited to him.

Neat and subdued in a modest gown of dove gray cotton, the Reverend Martin Caulfield's bride lifted a serene face to her groom. Intelligent, interested in theology, moved by his sermons, and honestly pious, the widowed Mrs. Agnes Coyne was the perfect wife for the long-widowed vicar of St. Petroc. The moment she had moved into the village everybody agreed.

Eleanor rejoiced that her papa would find happiness in marriage again; his first wife had perished even before he discovered her and her sisters in the foundling home. But Agnes's willingness to assist him with his work and her experience running a gentleman's household pointed to one damning certainty: Eleanor was now superfluous.

Her heart beat at too quick a tempo, and so hard it seemed to drown out the hymn rolling from the pipes. Her papa's newfound happiness did not cause this. That her life was upon the verge of changing dramatically did.

After years of silence on the issue, Papa had spoken: his eldest daughter should marry. Joy! Happiness! He was to find contentment in wedded bliss, and he wished for her the same blessing.

Agnes had concurred, compassionately, so that Eleanor could not but love her for it. No woman grown wished to live in another woman's house, she'd said. "My son admires you quite sincerely," she added, then with a smile: "How could he not?"

Now Mr. Frederick Coyne stood behind Papa on the opposite side of the chancel steps, ogling her without subtlety. Subtle ogling wouldn't have impressed her either. His coat buttons as large as tea plates made her giggle. But his brilliantly orange spotted waistcoat and matching stockings actually turned her stomach. How sensible Agnes had spawned this specimen of ostentatious exuberance, Eleanor couldn't fathom.

Frederick waggled his brows, then shifted his eyes to the exit, suggesting . . . *what?* That she steal off with him for a quick assignation in the middle of their parents' wedding? Or perhaps he intended for them to elope entirely.

He'd said as much that morning when he found her alone at breakfast. " 'Spect you're at wit's end now that Mum's taking over the roost, m'dear. Nothing to do for it but get leg shackled right away. Now, there's an idea! Why don't we skip this dull hash, El, and show the parents how to do it right? Border's only three or four days' ride, if the weather holds. What say you?" Perusing her bodice, he'd waggled his brows then too.

If he looked at her breasts now, in church, she might laugh aloud.

And there was the trouble of it. Her palms were sticky-cold with nerves but she *wanted* to laugh.

She wanted to *sing*. Not as she sang on Sundays in church, but as loud as the lark that woke her each morning through her bedchamber window with its abandoned song.

She wanted to *dance*. Not decorously like she had danced at her sisters' weddings attended by ladies and lords, but freely, wildly, gloriously, like the Gypsies who camped each winter in St. Petroc danced at the May Day festival.

She wanted to tear off her bonnet and feel the dangerous joy of wind in her hair and blazing sunshine upon her face while she galloped her horse along the edge of the cliffs. To suck the cold, salty air into her nostrils and fill her hungry lungs.

Quite simply, she wanted an adventure.

She had *always* wanted an adventure. Ever since as a girl she'd first read the books in her papa's library, curled up in a window seat as the Cornwall winters blustered and batted the windowpanes, she'd made herself the heroine in the tales of knights and dragons and demons. Dreaming, always dreaming, while the world beyond the cozy safety of the vicarage—a world of workhouses and blisters and cruelties and starvation—no longer touched her.

Now she could have it. Finally, nothing held her back. Not the vicarage, or the needs of the parish, or her papa. Agnes would care for those.

Nothing stood in her way.

Accustomed as she was to quiet, studious restraint, this abrupt freedom to abandon herself to the unknown both terrified and excited Eleanor.

Frederick adjusted his wide lapels and smiled invasively.

She should be flattered. Poor vicars' spinster daughters weren't often ogled by fashionable young gentlemen, or proposed to, even offhandedly, she suspected. Frederick wasn't a trial to look at, with that thick swipe of hair over his forehead and hooded eyes. She'd even seen him reading a few of times. She could bear a husband's fashion excesses if he read good books.

It was tempting . . .

His gaze slithered down her bodice.

Not tempting enough.

Then again, she'd never been tempted by any man. Not by any *man*. Only a boy. Young and naïve at the time, she would have left the comfort and safety of the vicarage for him. She would have gone anywhere for him.

But that was ages ago and didn't bear recalling, except that he had helped her to learn the inconstancy of the male heart.

Not her papa's, though. Papa would never demand that she leave the vicarage. Neither would Agnes. If she remained in St. Petroc, she would settle into a life of their endless kindnesses, and her own pathetic superfluity would choke her to death. She had lived modestly for years. But she had never been a milksop. The one moment in her life when she had been on the cusp of becoming so, a wild Gypsy boy had shown her a much better alternative. *An adventure.*

Then he'd broken her heart.

The medieval tales she loved were full of unexpected pitfalls and disasters, of course. That was to be expected. She could have an adventure now, only different in one crucial detail. An adventure that *did not* involve a man could be ideal.

Drawing a slow breath to bank the fledgling excitement that curled through her now, fire licking at kindling, Eleanor turned her eyes away from the happy couple to the chill winter day beyond the chapel window.

And ceased to breathe entirely.

A horseman rode up the drive from the house toward the chapel. The great black beast, powerful in neck and legs, thundered forward, its hooves marking the earth upon impact. The rider controlled the animal with ease, his greatcoat flaring out over the horse's haunches. Eleanor could not see his entire face; his hat brim masked it. But she knew him from the confident grasp of his gloved hands upon the reins and from the manner in which he rode, as though he might command the world from that horse, and could.

She knew him because every day from September through April for seven years of her young life she had watched him ride. She had memorized him.

That boy.

The co-author of the single real adventure of her life.

Taliesin Wolfe.

Long ago she had trained her heart to take no notice of anything concerning him, not the infrequent letters he sent to Papa, nor her sisters' accounts of seeing him in London occasionally. Now that heart betrayed her: it leaped into a gallop faster than his horse's.

Beside the chapel he dismounted. A groomsman appeared and took the reins, but the beast swung its head around and bared its teeth, and the groom stumbled back. Taliesin placed his hand upon the thick ebony neck and the animal swiveled its face to him. With horses he had always had a rare magic; a natural wisdom and potent touch, like the wizard of Arthurian legend after whom he had been named: Taliesin the Merlin. This magic still seemed to be his. Lowering its head, the mighty beast went docilely with the groom.

Alone on the drive, Taliesin stood still for a moment as he removed his gloves, his black hat and dark overcoat making him a roguish shadow against the pale gray day. He seemed entirely out of place and yet perfectly at ease. *As always.*

Any moment he would look to the window and see her gaping. She must look away. As he'd always done as a boy, he would sense her attention upon him and he would—

He didn't. With the loping grace that had characterized his movements as a youth, he went forward and out of her sight. She'd barely time to register the raucous thud of her heartbeats before the door to the chapel opened and he entered.

In the building.

Mere yards away.

After eleven years.

The brisk chill of the day seemed to cling to him in the high color upon his cheeks and the tousle of his satiny black hair.

And the kindling within Eleanor burst into flame.

Eleven years of modesty. Eleven years of careful reserve. Eleven years of regretting the only adventure she'd ever had. Now he stood before her again, dark and lean and staggeringly virile. And like a sleeping princess in a fairy tale brought back to life by magic, every morsel of her maidenly body awoke.

"Tali!" Ravenna exclaimed below the swell of the organ.

"I told you he would come," Arabella murmured from her other side.

She *had*?

"Good heavens, Ellie," Ravenna said in her ear. "Now you look positively fevered. Are you sure you're well?"

The music ended on a single, dramatic chord. In the sudden silence the prodigal Gypsy's boots clunked on the church floor. Eleanor's papa turned his head around, and his face opened in happiness.

"In the name of God above," the priest began, and everybody looked at him. But to Eleanor, even the impact of her papa entering into marital bliss could not now compare to the sudden appearance after so many years of Taliesin Wolfe.

In the last of several rows of empty pews, he stood imposingly erect, still, and dark, his presence making shadows where none had been before. With a lift of lashes, dark and thick like a starless night, he met her gaze directly. Slowly, the corner of his mouth tilted up.

Confusion. Indignation. Anger.

Heat.

All tangling together in the pit of her stomach and down to her fingertips. He had always done this to her—turned her insides out and her outsides quivering. Now after years of absence he was doing it again with no more than a mocking semi-smile.

She refused to succumb. The years had taught her. They had changed her.

Clearly they had changed him too. All sharp jaw, long limbs, sunken cheeks, and deep eyes as a boy, when he began to grow into his bones he had become an impossibly handsome youth. Watching him at a distance or walking beside him, she had found it difficult not to look too long at him, like a hunger that refused to be satisfied.

In appearance he was no longer that boy. His taut jaw and too-long hair and the silver rings in his ears were the same, but all else had changed. Fine clothing, broader shoulders, and the hardness in his black eyes marked him as a stranger now. And yet still she could not look away.

He bowed.

To her.

He *bowed*.

When had he learned how to bow? When had he thrown off the urchin who teased her and competed with her and made her crazy? When had he become this gentleman? And when had God decided that after a life of maidenly quietude she had sinned so greatly that she deserved to again meet the single person who could make her sin again?

HER CHEEKS FLOWERED with pink and fire lit her eyes as she returned his stare as though he'd no business in this place.

Taliesin had not expected this. He should have. Just as he should have expected the grinding ache in his gut now. Her pull on him.

Golden, like a summer morning, with a quick glimmer in her eyes. That's what he had remembered about her, the contrast between her fragile body and strong mind. As a boy, it had enthralled him. Often he'd goaded her only to see her ivory cheeks turn rosy and her golden green eyes flash. Always he'd sought to draw her gaze, to command her attention even if only to scold him for impertinence or arrogance or any of the other sins of which she believed him guilty. He would have done anything then to secure her notice. Anything.

Now he had merely walked through a door and

she gave it to him. Voluntarily, thoroughly. She hadn't ceased staring since he crossed the threshold. He hadn't craved the touch of her gaze in years. But, God's blood, he liked having it now.

A cool mist of displeasure slipped over her features, rain shrouding a spring garden. She turned her attention to the vicar and his new wife.

Satisfaction. Already he'd gotten under her skin. She hadn't changed in that manner. Nor in loveliness. As a girl Eleanor had never been a blatant beauty like Arabella nor naturally vibrant like Ravenna. But she had been graceful and quick-witted and so lovely that for years she had commanded his waking thoughts, and sleeping.

Not only his thoughts.

"Before God I declare you husband and wife," the churchman pronounced to the pair before him. "Go and make fruit of your union."

A muffled chuckle from Ravenna—the vicar taking his bride upon his arm but his gaze coming swiftly to the back of the chapel again—applause from everyone—organ pipes exploding into sound— Arabella smiling at him, diamonds around her neck.

And Eleanor's averted profile, pure and perfect, with cheeks abloom like roses.

Chapter 2

The Challenge

T

"*H*e hasn't gone."

Eleanor snapped her attention from the drawing room door. "Who hasn't gone?"

"Taliesin," Ravenna replied. "I only say it because you've been staring at that door for the past half hour."

"I haven't." *She had.* "I've only been waiting for an opportunity to subtly elude our new stepbrother." Her lips twitched. Much better than the nervous tremors she'd been biting back for hours. Taliesin *had* gone, disappearing after the ceremony to leave her in a state of agitation throughout luncheon and now in the drawing room where the modest gathering of provincials were disposed in clusters, taking tea. Gone as though he'd been a vision, like in medieval dream tales, an incubus sent to tempt her into harrowing emotions.

Rather, sent to temp her into sins. Anger. Lust.

She sank her cold palms into the skirts of the gown that Arabella had insisted she wear today. The Duchess of Lycombe's eyes had gleamed with an intentional, determined light when she instructed her own superior maid to make up Eleanor's hair with a silk net of tiny pearls. Then she had fastened a pearl choker about her neck and declared Eleanor's toilette perfect.

"Oh, of course," Ravenna said with a sideways grin. "Brother Frederick."

Standing before the mirror above the hearth, Frederick adjusted his striped cravat between shirt points that rose to his ears. Then he pursed his lips and blew a kiss to his reflection.

Ravenna's eyes danced. "Has he come to the point yet?"

"This morning he suggested we elope to Gretna Green."

"How intrepid of him. Did you hear that he has royal blood? Agnes told me this morning. On his father's side, generations back. Six centuries."

"I don't believe it."

"But you must. Our stepbrother is only three hundred and fifty-seventh in line from the throne. Isn't that splendid?" Ravenna's grin widened.

Abruptly, the intentional gleam in Arabella's eyes earlier—the gown, the pearls—all of it—made sense. Arabella still believed in the Gypsy fortune from their childhood: one of the three sisters must wed a prince if they were ever to learn the identities of their real mother and father. Despite her marriage to a duke, Arabella would not give up the hope that someday they would learn the truth. Now that Ravenna had wed, Eleanor was to be the sacrificial lamb upon that altar.

As there were no princes presently at Combe, she'd felt at ease on that account. But *this*?

"One drop of royal blood or one hundred, Frederick Coyne is not a prince. Bella has become desperate." Eleanor paused. "Ravenna, does—"

"Does he intend to return? Yes. Shortly, I think."

"Who?" But she knew.

"Tali, of course. He had a horse to see today in the county, but he told Arabella he would return. His business is spectacularly successful, you know."

"I wasn't going to ask about him."

"Oh," Ravenna said cheerfully. "My mistake. Our new stepmama is heading our way. I think I hear my husband calling."

"What? Why—" But it was too late. Ravenna always moved like a wild creature, preternaturally still at times and quick as a hare at others. And she wasn't overly fond of Agnes; all that kneeling and praying made her start to throw out spots. With a swirl of tumbling locks she darted away, abandoning Eleanor to greet their new mother with a sincere smile and pattering pulse.

He would return. To apologize for abandoning their family without warning more than eleven years ago? In the smattering of letters he'd sent Papa since then, he had never apologized. Arabella and Ravenna had seen him occasionally over the years, but he had never returned to St. Petroc, neither to the Gypsy camp nor to the vicarage.

"Eleanor dearest," the bride said. "Your cheeks are violently red. Are you unwell?"

Eleanor smiled. Falsely. "How could I be unwell when the occasion is so happy?" He'd been back in their family's life mere hours and already he was inspiring her to lie again.

"Dear daughter," Agnes said. "For today I delight in calling you daughter. I don't expect you ever to call me mama, but if you should like to, I would be honored."

Mama. She hadn't had a mama since the age of four, and remembered only vaguely the woman who had sent her daughters across an ocean, then disappeared.

"Thank you."

"Eleanor, although this is a difficult subject I feel I must speak of it to you plainly. Today I have learned the reason that you are reluctant to respond to my son's courtship."

Guilt propelled her brows upward. "You have?"

"I understand that your sisters have not explained matters to you sufficiently, which is only proper of modest young ladies. And they are your juniors, of course, so it could not have been expected of them." Agnes lowered her voice to an intimate whisper. "Thus it falls to me, with the most sincere and affectionate duty, to fill the gap in your feminine education."

Feminine education?

This could not be good.

"When we are finished speaking of this, I assure you," Agnes continued, "you will no longer be afraid of marriage. With the right man—a man of good character and immaculate morals—even the rigorous act imposed upon a woman with the sacred mantle of marriage can be rendered innocuous, even mildly pleasurable, if only a woman knows what to expect."

Jaw slack, Eleanor stared. Perhaps her mouth even hung agape.

"Oh, dear." Her stepmother's lips crinkled. "Arabella said you might respond in this manner."

"Arabella? My sister spoke to you of *this*?"

"She warned that you would not like me to speak

to you of your greatest fear." She took Eleanor's hand. "You are innocent and frail, as is to be expected of a young woman who has passed so many years convalescing, and with a scholarly bachelor father too. But you needn't fear marriage any longer. Once we have had a little tête-à-tête, you will be glad to take a worthy husband to wed, and—in the interests of honest concern I must be frank—to bed. The marital act mustn't distress you. I will explain it so that your concerns over your inconstant health will no longer deter you from marrying. Nothing, dear Eleanor, must stand in the way of your future happiness."

This could not be happening.

The *marriage act*? Her *inconstant health*? Her past would never leave her be. Even Agnes, who hadn't been in St. Petroc thirteen years earlier, imagined her frail and fearful. None of them knew that she was precisely the opposite—not the helpless sleeping maiden waiting for a prince to wake her. Rather, she was the maiden dragon sleeping beneath the mountain, roused now and finally ready to spring into the sky spewing flame and roaring.

If she ever took an adventure, she would roar. And set fire to things, perhaps. That would be vastly entertaining.

She swallowed over the swell in her throat. "Agnes, I hardly know how to—"

"Thank me?" Her fingers tightened about Eleanor's. "You needn't. It is all to ensure my dear Frederick's happiness. Can you not see how smitten he is with you?" She looked fondly toward her son.

He winked at himself in the mirror.

Eleanor caught a bubble of laughter with a cough. "I am honored by his admiration. But—"

"Ellie." As though summoned by an angel—or perhaps the devil—Arabella appeared at her side, gorgeous in azure silk with tiny puff sleeves and an overskirt of white tissue. She looked every bit the duchess, gently rounded from recent childbirth, glowing, stunning. Her eyes passed over the heavy shawl wrapped around Eleanor's shoulders, and one delicate line marred her forehead.

Agnes released Eleanor's hand and gave her a private smile of sympathy. "We will finish this conversation later."

When hell froze over.

"I'm terribly sorry to drag my sister away, Agnes," Arabella said, "but I should like her company in the library. I've something of interest to show her."

A manual on the marriage act. Or a genealogy of the Coyne family going back six centuries. Eleanor didn't protest. She needed privacy for what she must now say to her sister.

Agnes looked pointedly into Arabella's eyes. "I am always happy to aid in the wishes of such beloved sisters."

"Thank you, Stepmama. You are beyond generous." With a glittering smile, Arabella took Eleanor's arm and swept her from the room.

"What do you wish to show me?"

"That was an excuse. What on earth were you speaking with her about? You looked as peculiar as I've ever seen."

It wasn't to be wondered at. "I need a cup of tea." And several hours of quiet. *To plan.* Maiden dragons shouldn't leave the lair without a plan.

"Or a brandy, I daresay. Is she still threatening to marry you off to Frederick?"

"Rather, encouraging. She's far too kind to threaten. I think she means well. But I don't understand, Bella, did you speak to her about my . . . my . . . ?" Her cheeks went hot as a fireplace poker again. Some things she could not say aloud, even to her sisters. Some things she had only ever shared with one person.

He hadn't deserved it.

Arabella closed the library door. "Your what?"

"Oh . . . My mind is wandering today." To incubi and maiden dragons and adventures that her sensible sister would never understand.

Arabella went to a table upon which a tea tray had been laid. "Agnes is a good-hearted soul. But she thinks excessively highly of her son. I suppose that's natural, of course." She carried her teacup to a tall window that overlooked the drive and peered out. "Perhaps if you leave the vicarage at once, it will not appear to be an insult when you refuse him. You must come live here. I would adore that, and Luc would too. I will send a maid and footman to fetch your belongings to Combe."

To Combe? Where every month Arabella would produce another prince for her inspection?

A prince. . .

The idea came upon her suddenly. Clouds parting. The maiden dragon racing from darkness toward the light.

"Bella, I want to find our parents."

Arabella pivoted in a swirl of azure. "You do?"

She did? "Why not? I've been content to let you search for them. But now you have a baby and a husband, and this house and your household in London too. I have nothing to do and I need occupation. I may as well take up your quest." *And have an adventure.*

"You know that the investigator Luc hired found no record of three sisters sailing from the West Indies for England twenty-three years ago."

"Hundreds of ships probably visited those ports each year. Perhaps the records were lost during the war." She moved to her favorite bookshelf, filled with tales of valiant knights and demonic villains. Tugging off her gloves, she passed her fingertips across the bindings, all of them stories of glorious adventures. She plucked one out. "But perhaps the answers we seek are not in the West Indies. They could be in Cornwall where the ship wrecked. Wreckage can take years to wash up after a ship founders."

"I never thought you were interested in searching for our parents."

"It seems I am now."

Arabella was quiet for a moment. "Perhaps the man we hired simply didn't know what to look for. You could be the key. You remember little of our parents, I know, but perhaps if you see clues that our investigator saw, they will mean something to you."

"We can hope." The tingle of excitement in her belly grew. The last time she'd felt it she'd been fifteen, recently recovered from her illness and learning how to ride a horse in secret from everyone—everyone except a Gypsy boy. His adventures traveling with his family's caravan each summer had always seemed to her so wild and free and wonderful and frightening. Even as she'd clung to the comfort of the vicarage, she had envied Taliesin his travels. "It's certainly worth a try."

Arabella clapped her hands. "Ellie, I am beside myself. What do you need from me? Tell me your plan and I will do whatever you need to make it a reality."

She hadn't a plan. Yet. "Well, I have little experience of travel, of course. We must find a traveling companion for me. Someone with experience of the road."

Her sister beamed. "An excellent idea. Luc's and my acquaintance is extensive. It shouldn't be difficult to find the ideal person for the task."

"Here you are." Ravenna entered the library in a froth of wrinkled skirts.

Her husband, Vitor Courtenay, followed, a pair of dogs at his elegant heels. At the tea table, Ravenna plucked up a powdered cake and popped it into her mouth. The dogs sat at her feet until she fed them cakes too. Another cake disappeared between her own lips. "Bella, these are positively delicious. I'm taking a plate of them to my bedchamber tonight for a bedtime snack."

"Vitor," Arabella said, tucking a cup of tea into Ravenna's hand, "do you never feed my sister?"

His eyes smiled. "Her nourishment is the sun, the wind, and the rain, of course."

"And him," Ravenna said, depositing another cake upon her tongue. "As to the weather, thank goodness the snow has melted now and we can be on our way home tomorrow. It isn't that I dislike your house, Bella," she said, perching upon the arm of Vitor's chair with teacup *sans* saucer. "It's splendid. But I don't think I can abide another day in the same residence with the besotted couple. They're so . . . *staid*. Agnes is far too pious. Even for Vitor." She offered her husband a sparkling grin.

Vitor, once a monk, smiled at his wife from beneath lowered lids.

"Honestly, Ellie, I don't know how you will endure it," Ravenna said.

"She won't have to," Arabella said. "She intends to set out on a journey to the coast of Cornwall to find our real parents."

Ravenna's eyes popped wide. "She does?"

"I do." Lip caught between her teeth, Eleanor drew from the shelf a volume bound in faded red leather. The gold embossed letters of the title were worn thin from handling.

"It will take her away from the vicarage," Arabella said, "and she can do what I haven't yet been able to. It is the perfect solution."

Temporary solution. But temporary suited well enough. Eleanor turned a page. *Aha*. Perceval. An impetuous hero.

Medieval chroniclers had always seen signs in everything. Perhaps *this* was a sign. Perceval had set out on a quest to find the Holy Grail. But before he achieved his goal he met a succubus who pretended to be his beloved. Laying herself down on a sumptuous bed, she tried to tempt him into sin.

A smile tugged at Eleanor's lips. At least she needn't worry about that peril on her journey.

"Tali!" Ravenna exclaimed. "You came back."

Eleanor nearly dropped the book. Her head snapped up. He stood in the doorway, tall and broad-shouldered and looking directly at her. As always.

Arabella went to him and grasped his hand. "It's such a pleasure to welcome you here. I'm glad you could return so swiftly."

"It is my honor." He smiled at Arabella, but only slightly, a familiar, subtle lift at the corner of lips that Eleanor had once thought the most perfect lips in Christendom. He bowed with great ease, just as he had bowed to her in the chapel. "Duchess." His voice was smooth and deep, like a woodland well in summertime, deeper than the last time Eleanor had seen him. Of course it was. Now he was a man.

"Good heavens, you mustn't tease," Arabella laughed. "I'm not the queen."

"Yet I never doubted that you would rise in the world."

Ravenna went to him and bussed him on the cheek as she had always done as a child. "You're looking fine, Tali, like you're attending a wedding, I guess. Be glad you arrived too late for the endless hymns."

"I will count my blessings, mite."

"You mustn't call me that anymore. I am a lady now. And there is my lord to prove it." With a spark in her eyes that were as black as Taliesin's, she pointed to Vitor.

Vitor stood and bowed. "I am glad to make your

acquaintance, Mr. Wolfe, though I don't know that I should be. I understand that you once threatened to break my arms."

"If I had known what an imposing fellow you are," Taliesin said, eye to eye with the nobleman, "I certainly wouldn't have done so."

"I sent you an invitation to our wedding last summer," Ravenna said. "I wanted you there. Why didn't you come?"

"Forgive me," he said, and nothing else.

Arabella moved toward the tea table. "And here is Eleanor, of course," she said, gesturing. "I think it's been quite an age since you've seen each other."

Throat thick with her heartbeat, Eleanor offered him a shallow curtsy. Bereft of the smile he had offered Arabella and Ravenna, his eyes were like dusk, all shadows and mysterious quiet. This time he only nodded.

"There now," Arabella said overbrightly. "We have accomplished that awkward reunion and can all be at ease. Won't everybody take a seat and have some tea?"

"Really, Bella." Ravenna chuckled. "They both look like rigor mortis has set in and you're asking them to sit?"

"Wolfe, I understand you've spent hours in the saddle today," Vitor leaped smoothly into the gathering maelstrom of Eleanor's silence. "Why don't we investigate the sideboard in Lycombe's study for more substantial refreshment?"

"No. Wait," Arabella said. "You mustn't go away yet. I've just had a marvelous idea. Ellie, you wish to search out clues to our parents' identities, but you haven't familiarity with the travel needed to accomplish such a thing." She pivoted about. "But Taliesin does. Taliesin, could you help us? Eleanor will need to visit the northern coastal villages of Cornwall, nearest where the ship wrecked."

Eleanor choked. "Arabella—"

"It shouldn't require more than a few weeks to retrace the steps that our investigator traveled. My sister is so clever, in that time I'm certain she could find anything that he mistakenly overlooked, stories of the wreckage or even pieces of it, I imagine. Ravenna told me yesterday that it's still some weeks until the foaling season, so I think you cannot be too busy this month. Can you?"

Eleanor disbelieved her ears. But this was her sister, the former governess who, penniless and alone, had sailed to France in search of a prince to wed. "Arabella—"

"I am not at liberty to leave my son now, or I would go." Arabella still spoke to the man she'd barely seen in a decade. "And Ravenna has all those animals she can never leave for long."

"Arabella—"

"You know how it is." Arabella said to him as she walked toward Eleanor. "Bits of old ships are always washing up on shore years later. And we've never really searched." She grasped Eleanor's hand tightly and whispered, "Unless you wish me to continually throw princes at your head, this is an ideal solution." She turned again to him. "Will you do it, Taliesin? You know the West Country thoroughly, and you are travel-wise where my sister is not. With your assistance, Eleanor could find what we are looking for."

"No." The word popped from her mouth, propelled by raw panic—in her lungs and veins, crowding out the confused, jittery heat his black eyes put there. Only one person in the world was entirely unsuitable to assist her in this adventure, and he was it.

"I'll do it," Taliesin said.

Arabella beamed. "Will you?"

"There's nothing to be lost in such a search. And it so happens that I have time to do so now."

He had time for *this*?

Hands outstretched, Arabella went to him. "Thank you! Oh, thank you, Taliesin. You are too good."

Ravenna dropped into a chair, her skirts flouncing this way and that. "Well, I cannot pretend to believe that this silly quest will amount to anything. But you're splendid to agree to it for the sake of affection, Tali. I do worry about your horses, though, when you abandon them to go off searching for a shipwreck."

"They will be well cared for." He smiled, sincerely, honestly, like a thousand candles illumining midnight.

Eleanor felt dizzy.

Arabella's face shone. "Then it is settled. If you leave from here, Ellie, it shouldn't require more than a few days to reach the coast and you can begin your search immediately. The weather is beginning to turn already, but the roads should still be passable for several weeks. Taliesin, have you any objection to departing within the sennight?"

"I am at your disposal, Duchess."

"Wait." Panic pressed on Eleanor's lungs. "I haven't yet agreed to this."

Taliesin looked at her. "You needn't."

And there it was, familiar, as though she'd last seen it yesterday: the provoking curve at the corner of his mouth that said he had the upper hand already. It was the same challenge he had leveled at her every day of their childhoods. That he could best her at anything. And would.

Except not exactly the same. He *had* changed. Now his shadowy eyes told her that he wouldn't only win, he would eat her for breakfast if she gave him the chance.

He turned to Arabella. "I will travel more swiftly alone and make every inquiry you wish without trouble. Your sister needn't be disturbed."

Without trouble. As though she would be a hindrance to her own family's interests?

"I cannot allow you to burden yourself with the concerns of my family," she said tightly.

"I would not consider it a burden." He almost purred the words. Rather, he growled them, like some feral beast. A warning growl. "As I said, you needn't come." Again he looked to Arabella. "Write out what I must know, and give me all correspondence from the man you hired. As soon as you've done so, I will depart."

Arabella nodded. "I will gather what you need and have it sent to the inn in the village. I wish you would accept my invitation to stay here tonight."

"I have business to attend to and should be a poor guest," he said with comfortable nonchalance, as though Gypsy horse traders received invitations to stay at duchesses' homes every day.

Arabella glanced swiftly, uncertainly at Eleanor. "Then it's all settled."

"No." Her damp palms slid against her skirts. "It isn't settled. I . . ." She battened down on the panic and moved toward her sister. She could not allow him to win. *Never again.* "If you wish it, Bella, I will agree to this. I will go on this quest. With him."

Arabella grasped both of her hands. She kissed her on the cheek and said quietly, "You won't regret it."

"She already regrets it." Languid laughter rumbled in his voice.

Eleanor swiveled around. "You are generous to offer your assistance in this endeavor. But do keep in mind that you do so upon my sufferance."

"I will keep it in mind. For I certainly shouldn't like to see you suffer," he said, without a hint of teasing now. Then he bowed, without a trace of mockery.

Eleanor could only stare and hope that he saw the dragon in her eyes and not the helpless maiden.

Chapter 3

The Vow

She pivoted to face Arabella, presenting him with the graceful line of her back and her hair like spun gold. God's blood, how could she be lovelier now than she'd been as a girl? The merest tilt of her chin stirred hard hunger in him.

But he recognized lust well enough. He'd learned it with her. The contours of her lips, the swell of her breasts, the curve of her hips had driven him mad for years.

Apparently they still did.

Over her shoulder her gilded eyes cast a javelin at him. She said to her sister, "We shouldn't tell Papa."

Of course.

"No?" Arabella said.

"He could be hurt, imagining I was betraying him to go in search of our real father."

"You know him best. Let's go now and speak with my butler so that he can make arrangements. The sooner you set off, the better." She offered Taliesin another grateful smile.

Eleanor left the room without looking at him again, the same crease in her brow that he knew well. At one time, he'd known every detail of her face. And her hands, her wrists and arms and hair, her voice and laughter and quick, unguarded smile that turned his world upside down.

He had loved her. With every breath in him, every sinew and bone and feeling and deed. Even after he'd left St. Petroc. For more than a year after that spring morning, miles and worlds away from the vicarage, he'd lain awake at night aching with longing. And anger.

Hard labor and near starvation had buried the anger beneath screaming muscles and a howling belly. After a time, he'd put aside the longing. He had cast off the past. And he'd made a vow: never again would he allow himself to fall into that darkness.

She didn't want his assistance with this mission. That was clear enough. But he was no one's servant now, and he'd made a promise he would fulfill.

Ravenna grabbed up a biscuit and chewed around a smile.

"Well, I suspect you'll find nothing, but it should give Bella some satisfaction." Trailed by her dogs, she went to the door. "I'll leave you two to drink brandy or whatever you must do to feel unassailably masculine. I'm going to look in on your horse, Tali." He watched her go with a twirl of unkempt skirts and dogs in her wake. Even now in their elevation to the aristocracy, she and Arabella were the same girls they'd been long ago.

In his life he'd held few people dear. His cousins with whom he had traversed the West Country for fifteen years of his life. Evan Saint, his traveling companion after he departed St. Petroc. And Martin Caulfield and his daughters. Years ago, if he'd held one of those daughters considerably less dear, he would still be traipsing across Devon and northern Cornwall in his family's caravan. He would have passed the last decade of his life like any Rom.

A man entered the room, a strip of cloth tied across his brow concealing one eye and part of a scar. Yet even half blinded he walked with authority. "Gentlemen," he said.

"Lycombe," Courtenay drawled, "This is Wolfe, who has just agreed to the most ill-fated mission I've had the pleasure to hear."

"As you've considerable experience with missions, Vitor, I trust you in this." He assessed Taliesin, and Taliesin returned the assessment. Powerfully built, like a Percheron, the duke stood no more than an inch taller than him but could boast at least a stone more of sheer, imposing brawn. Arabella had chosen a man of wealth, status, and presence. He suited her, just as Courtenay's air of contemplative assurance suited Ravenna.

A servant shut the door and Taliesin was alone with two lords in a ducal mansion. A first, though not by much. He bowed. "Your grace."

"Should I trust you, Wolfe?" Directly to the heart of it. Taliesin liked him already.

"You should."

"My wife mistrusts most men. Yet you are exempted from this."

Taliesin could say nothing to that. He'd never doubted that Martin Caulfield, a quiet, retiring intellectual, had invited a Gypsy boy into his home in part as protection for his daughters. In return for shelter and lessons, that boy had provided it. Until he had become the threat.

The duke still studied him. "Arabella tells me you were like a brother to them."

To two of them. Taliesin nodded.

"I understand that when you left years ago, you did not return to St. Petroc again."

"Not to the vicarage." Nor anywhere near it. "Is this an interrogation, your grace?"

"Lycombe will do," the duke said. "What took you away so precipitously from these people who called you family? Was there a woman involved?"

Taliesin nearly laughed. But he didn't. "There was."

"You don't deny it?"

"Why should I? I charge you to show me a man who hasn't made a mistake because of a woman. If you yourself haven't, then they should crown you king. Rather, saint."

Lycombe grunted. "Hnh. Right." Then his eye narrowed. "I accept your loyalty to my wife and her sisters when you were young. But why should I trust you now?"

"Because if they asked, I would do anything for them." Once upon a time he had vowed that if one of the sisters should call upon him, he would come to their aid. From across England, Arabella had called.

Lycombe stared fixedly at him. "Arabella believes in the prophecy of the prince. Do you know of it?"

"I do." Ravenna had once told him their secret. Clearly Lussha the Seer had performed at her finest on that occasion.

"Do you believe in it?" Lycombe asked.

"I am a horse trader, not a soothsayer. I believe in good pasturage, fine bloodlines, and an honest price."

Finally the severity eased from the duke's face. "An honest price?"

"When prudence dictates it."

"I daresay." Lycombe ran his palm across his scarred brow. "The trail has gone cold on this shipwreck, as it does on most lost boats. I've little confidence in this quest. But my wife will not admit defeat, no matter how I attempt to reason with her." His gaze hardened anew. "If Eleanor comes to harm on this wild-goose chase, be assured, Wolfe, I will see you hanged."

"She will be safe." He would protect her. Always.

"Then we understand each other," Lycombe said.

"It seems we do."

The duke thrust out a hand. Taliesin grasped it. Englishmen rarely took his hand, as though they feared that if they allowed him too close he would steal their pocket watches. And Rom avoided shaking hands with a *gorgio*. But he'd been so long straddling the two worlds, he'd learned to live in both.

"I will send you in my traveling carriage," the duke said, then paused. "Or have you . . . Have you a traveling carriage of your own, or . . . ?"

Or a wagon?

"I've no need of a carriage. I travel alone or with assistants, and always on horseback."

"Ravenna tells me you own property."

"Not all Rom are vagabonds, your grace."

The duke's face darkened. "I told you to call me Lycombe."

"When you are ready to see me as a man and not merely a Gypsy," he said, "I will be ready to call you by your name." He strode toward the door.

"I'm beginning to understand how it is that you

rubbed along so comfortably with that family," Lycombe said behind him. "May good fortune go with you on this journey, Wolfe."

Fortune had nothing to do with it. He should have declined. It was an enormous mistake. He should tell Arabella that he couldn't help with her search, and depart. Fifty horses and a house crumbling from decades of neglect required his attention elsewhere.

Ravenna appeared in the corridor, her cheeks red from the cold. "Your horse is magnificent. I want to keep him. Why are you staring at the drawing room door? Who do you hope will come walking through it?"

A woman with the grace of a meadow buttercup and the pride of a lioness. "She wishes me to the devil."

"She always did." Ravenna's grin laughed. "Did it ever stop you?"

Never.

He would do Arabella's bidding and assist in this task. Then, vow fulfilled, he would say good-bye. One final time.

Chapter 4

The Maiden Dragon

In her sister's carriage, a footman placed a heated brick beneath Eleanor's feet and covered her lap with a rug.

Luxuries she was not accustomed to for a mission just short of folly.

Like naïve Perceval, who set off on his knightly adventure with only a sharp throwing stick, she was taking nothing on this quest, no experience at hunting for anything except theological minutiae in scholarly tomes and inspiring quotes in Scripture—all for her papa's work. Now she was armed only with a cheerful coachman, a young maid, and a Gypsy horse trader she hadn't spoken more than one sentence to in eleven years.

Impetuous, yes.

Maddened butterflies in her stomach, yes.

Daunted, *no*.

Arabella pressed a small pouch into her hand. Eleanor knew its contents not by the weight or shape, but from the plea in her sister's eyes. It was the ring upon which the soothsayer had told three orphaned girls their fortune. A prince would recognize it, Lussha the Gypsy had said that day in the tent. He would know who they were.

"Take this," Arabella said. "Please. I don't know why, but I think you will need it."

"Our sister, the fortune-teller in disguise." Ravenna laughed, and blew a kiss to Eleanor.

Tucking the ring into a pocket, Eleanor watched her maid mount the carriage steps, ginger curls around her temples and eyes large as constellations. Young and farm bred, Betsy peered about the carriage in wonder.

"Have you ever ridden in such a carriage, Betsy?"

"Never, miss," she said in a hush, then looked toward the men on the drive and her face pinched like a dried apricot. Taliesin spoke with Vitor and Ravenna as he walked his huge black horse from the stable. He mounted with such ease it seemed he made himself a part of the animal rather than its rider. With a nod to Luc and Arabella, he rode off.

The coach started forward and Eleanor lifted a hand to wave to her family. As the drive became woods and woods became fields, Betsy pressed her face to the window and peered ahead.

"I'm glad he isn't riding in here with us," she said with a squinting eye. "Beg pardon, miss, but I don't think you should trust him."

Eleanor had little experience with personal maids, but she didn't think this was typical. "Why not?"

Betsy's arms banded across her chest. "He's got a dark look about him."

"He is well known to my sisters. A trusted friend." *Not hers.* "Betsy, do you worry because he is a Gypsy?"

Her teeth fidgeted with a truculent lower lip. "Is he, miss?"

"He is a gentleman." He looked like one now. Mostly. Except for the earrings and those smoldering black eyes. And he was far too masculine to really be a gentleman. Too raw. Watching him ride ahead, she felt his ownership of the road, the ambling grace of power in his seat upon the stallion, the imposing breadth of his shoulders. He rode like no Gypsy she'd ever seen, nor like any Englishman, rather, like a knightly hero from medieval tales—tales that years ago he'd read as eagerly as she.

Arabella had been wise to insist he escort her on this journey. His dark presence alone would deter danger.

Eleanor's skin felt tight, stretching over her bones like linen bound too tightly around swelling dough. Rain began to patter on the window, and the wood through which they passed loomed gray and ominous. In the shroud of it, darkness seemed to cling to the Gypsy. The gentleman.

Once upon a time, his eyes had not been so shadowed. And he had not been a gentleman. Far from it.

He'd been there since the day her new papa brought her and her sisters home, working in the vicarage, scrubbing floors, chopping wood, keeping the churchyard neat for Sundays. When after a time she realized that no other family in the parish had a Gypsy boy for a servant, she asked her papa about it.

"When Taliesin was no more than six years old, his aunt came to the door selling baskets," Papa said. "I needed no basket, but a servant of the Lord cannot turn away a destitute soul. The woman did not want the work I offered. Taliesin did. He has returned each autumn since then."

"Why do you let him sleep in the barn?"

"All of God's wild creatures need a place to rest their heads."

Eleanor wanted to point out that wild creatures did not need barns. Afraid to displease her papa, though, she closed her lips.

A sennight later she found the boy sitting in her chair by her new papa's side, bent over a paper with a pen.

"Very good, Taliesin. If you continue to study, you will be able to write out all the Psalms by Christmastime." Her papa had bestowed upon him the smile of pride she thought he reserved for her alone.

"Papa," she asked him later, her cold, damp palms against her apron, "why are you teaching Taliesin to write?"

He placed his warm hand on her head and stroked her hair. "His people are an ignorant race. It is my Christian duty to help him become a responsible member of society. And I see a natural intelligence in Taliesin that deserves cultivation, so that one day he might fully flourish as a vine in the Lord's garden."

That night upon her cot she wept scalding tears. She'd had a papa for only six months, and she did everything she could to please him. To take second place in his heart so soon swamped her with fear. What if her papa decided to keep the orphan Gypsy boy not as a servant but as a son? Every man wanted a son. And the vicarage had only one extra bedroom. The dread of being returned to the foundling home where her hands bled from scrubbing floors and peeling turnips for hours, and where the headmistress beat their backs, made her heave great, choking sobs into her pillow.

But by morning she had dried her eyes and squared

her shoulders, resolved to win first place. She did her chores swiftly and studied every extra moment. She excelled. Upon her tenth birthday, her papa presented her with a notebook of blank pages in which she was only to write Latin. She worked hard, and each day he smiled and called her his little scholar.

Then one day, conjugating "to be" aloud as he wrote his sermon, it happened.

"*Sum, es, est, sumus, este—*"

"It's *estis*." The boy stood at the edge of the doorway, a shadow in torn shirt and trousers, his feet wrapped in only rags despite the December frost.

Her papa lifted his head. "Continue, Taliesin."

"*Sum, es, est, sumus, estis, sunt.*"

Her papa had barely noticed while she recited, but pleasure now covered his face. "How have you learned this?"

"Begging your pardon, Reverend. I found this." He pulled a tattered primer from his pocket.

"That's mine!" she cried. "Papa, he filched my book."

"Your old book," he said, surly. "A month ago you left it on the well and forgot about it."

"Why did you keep this from me, Taliesin?" her papa said.

"I wanted to learn it, sir." He looked directly into her papa's face, as though he had the right to. When she had looked squarely into the face of the headmistress, she'd had her palms flogged. "I was afraid you wouldn't like it," he said.

"I do not dislike that you wished to learn Latin. Indeed, I am pleased. But I do not like it that you withheld your possession of the primer from me."

"He *stole* it."

"Daughter, if you cannot contain your lack of charity I will ask you to remove to a private chamber where you can bring your conscience into a more regulated state."

She bit her lips together. But she saw the gleam in the black eyes of her challenger, and she was ready to surpass anything he flung her way. To her papa, Taliesin Wolfe might be worthy of charity. To her, he was a usurper. No lanky boy with hair falling over half his face would steal her papa's affection.

His hair still fell over his brow, unconfined and satiny black as it had been in his youth. He was handsomer now. Much. She wanted to hate him for it, and for hurting her then. But she was no longer a child and she had learned to temper her emotions. To restrain them. It shouldn't matter that beneath her skin surged unbearable heat. She would not allow Taliesin Wolfe to get the best of her ever again.

TALIESIN RODE EACH day. Rarely speaking to her, he arranged for her meals and lodgings yet said no more to her than the innkeepers did. Oftentimes less.

In the carriage she read and talked with Betsy and tried not to stare when he came into view through the window of the closed carriage. Occasionally he had company, a farmer or tradesman riding alongside. It seemed that every innkeeper knew him, every stable hand extended his palm for the generous coin he would offer, and every ostler spoke to him with respect.

The first day of the journey became the second, then turned into the third, then the fourth. Slowly, with nothing to look at but shapeless wintry landscapes—*and him*—and nothing to think about but vexing memories—*of him*—and no one to speak to except a simple country maid, when the person with whom she had shared every book and every secret till she was nearly seventeen *barely spoke a word to her*—Eleanor went mad. The luxurious carriage became a prison, her innocent maid a jailer, and the man on his ebony stallion an incubus tormenter. Medieval morality tales were full of such stories: a virtuous woman was visited by a powerful eagle who, upon alighting, transformed into a handsome knight, only to be revealed later as a demon in disguise sent to tempt her into sin.

Clearly, she was losing her mind. Desire to *do* and *see* and *touch* and *taste* all that she hadn't for so long clogged her head with wishes. Suffocating in the dark, she was the maiden dragon seeking freedom from her barren lair.

When the coach halted as day waned on the fourth evening, and the coachman, Mr. Treadwell, opened the door, she burst out of it and nearly fell into a heap on the road. Stumbling to right herself, she headed blindly toward the door to the inn.

"There now, miss," Mr. Treadwell called after her. "Take care. Morgan le Fay stepped into a rabbit hole on the road not a quarter mile back. I wouldn't want you to do the same."

She swiveled around. "Who is Morgan le Fay?"

"That fine mare there, miss." He pointed at one of the carriage horses. "She's not nearly as clever as Lady of the Lake. But Lady's a leader, so she's got to have smarts."

Arabella's coachman had named his horses after characters from medieval Arthurian legend. How was this to be believed? "What are the others called?"

"Guinevere and Pendragon, miss."

She lacked thought even for laughter. Dazed, she looked around and all about them saw nothing. No trees. No houses. No shrubs. Not even fields. In the falling mist she saw only dark stretches of undulating land, tufted with moss like seared emeralds and sprinkled with rusty scrub, rising in gentle hills like enormous waves. And all around, complete silence.

Not even a hen's cackle or dog's bark marred the soft stillness. They had come to the moor, but deep in the moor where she had never before been, a place of unrelenting, silent solitude.

Like her soul.

Taliesin came out of the inn. In the settling dusk he looked like a great black shadow, a lord of darkness who might seize her silent soul and lock it away forever.

A shiver ran along her spine.

This, of course, was how madness began.

"The inn is nearly emp—" he began, but she ducked around him and hurried inside.

Within, lamps lit the papered walls in a cozy glow, and the scents of roasting meat and freshly baked bread tickled her nostrils. But Eleanor had no appetite.

Tea. She would drink tea. She'd read too many medieval tales full of dark demons and magical knights and unhappy ladies swept into scandalous adventures. And the monotony of travel was bound to make her fanciful. Tea would calm her.

Empty except for a pair of old men in a corner and a woman of comfortably middling years serving them dinner, the taproom was just the sort of place Eleanor liked. Yet she couldn't sit. She'd been sitting absolutely still for four days. *And a decade.*

"Well now, miss," the woman said with a smiling nod. "Do take a seat over by the fire and I'll bring you—"

"Have you any chocolate?" She never drank chocolate. *Ever.* Ravenna did. Ravenna adored chocolate. But Ravenna had few inhibitions. "Have you?"

The woman's bushy brows went up. "Well, now, miss . . . Come to think of it, I do. Mr. Hodges, you see, he likes to bring me treats from Exeter when he can. It just so happens that at Christmas last he brought me a tin of the dearest—"

"May I have some?"

"Well, I don't know how I would be fixing it—"

"I'll show you." Throwing her cloak and bonnet over a chair, she took Mrs. Hodges's arm and guided her toward the kitchen. "Have you milk? Sugar?"

The tin of cocoa was found, milk set on the stove, a sparing spoonful of sugar added, and the chocolate was heated. Chuckling, Mrs. Hodges said she'd never learned a new receipt from a lady.

Eleanor held the porcelain cup to her lips and inhaled until she felt it in her toes.

Mrs. Hodges plunked her hands on her hips. "Well, aren't you going to drink it?"

"I am reveling." Her lips could nearly taste it. Nearly. *Temptation*. The waiting teased. *Deliciously*.

"You're an odd duck, aren't you, miss?"

"Not usually." She tilted the cup upward. "Usually I am entirely predictable. Reserved. Modest." Her words were muffled by the rich liquid so close, heating her flesh. *Heady sensation*. "Usually I am very"—she let the chocolate wash against her lips—"very"—and a ripple of pleasure went through her—"good." The sweet, thick milk stole around her tongue. Decadent. *Sinful*.

She sighed.

Taliesin appeared in the kitchen door.

She choked.

"Well now, sir," Mrs. Hodges said, wiping her hands on her apron. "Miss was just teaching me here how to make chocolate like they do at all the big houses."

He leaned a shoulder into the doorpost and crossed his arms. His shadowy eyes scanned her from toe tips to brow, finally coming to rest on her lips. "Was she?"

A thick droplet of chocolate clung to her bottom lip. Eleanor felt it there like a beacon. She should wipe it with her kerchief.

The tip of her tongue stole between her lips and licked up the droplet. Another shiver wiggled through her.

What was she doing?

"Now then, miss," Mrs. Hodges said, "you'd best go and leave the kitchen to me, and I'll fix up a nice dinner for you."

Clutching the cup in both palms, Eleanor went to the door. Taliesin stepped back but with so little space she had to shift sideways to move past him. She darted a glance upward.

Immobility. His. Hers. She could see every line, every whisker that had not been on his face eleven years ago. *Not* the same boy she'd known. A man now. Her pulse fluttered. Then it fluttered harder as his scent mingled with the flavor of chocolate upon her tongue. Horse. Leather. Him. *The same.* It tangled in her nose, in her head, a memory barreling through her, while he watched her eyes from inches away.

She slipped past him.

The taproom was empty now. Mr. Treadwell was probably in the stable seeing to his Arthurian characters and Betsy must be in their room seeing to mundane tasks Eleanor was accustomed to seeing to herself.

"Chocolate?" the incubus behind her said. "Missing the luxuries of the ducal mansion so soon, are you?"

She swung around to him and the chocolate sloshed in the cup. "Is that what you think? That I have grown spoiled by my sisters' good fortune?"

"No." His black eyes hooded.

"No? Is that all you can say?" Her tongue, it seemed, was an unbridled thing. Too much prison. Too much *feeling* to swallow again and again. "We've not seen each other in eleven years, and now for four days you have said nothing to me."

Again he leaned his shoulder against the doorpost in an attitude of sublime nonchalance. "You made it clear you did not wish my escort. I am respecting that."

She didn't believe it. He had never respected her. He had teased her endlessly. "You could at least speak to me."

"What would you have me say?"

"Anything. How do you go along these days, Eleanor? How is the parish? Is it still the same as eleven years ago when I departed so precipitously, without warning, without word?"

His face grew still, planes of dark beauty like hewn marble. "Ah," he said in a low voice. "You wish for empty pleasantries. Or perhaps an apology? I regret that neither is in my lexicon."

"I don't wish for pleasantries or apologies. I don't care why you left as you did. But you hurt Papa. Do you even know how deeply you hurt him?"

His lips were an unbreakable line.

"He wouldn't even speak of you." Locked behind bars for years, Eleanor's words now tumbled forth. "He said nothing except when Ravenna mentioned you. She did not understand why you left either, but she accepted it in her way. She always thought you would return. But Papa didn't. And it wounded him."

"I wrote to him," he said after a moment.

"Rarely. So few letters that the pages grew thin from folding and unfolding. He never said a word about them or read a line to us, but do you know where he kept them? In his Bible, tucked in Luke, chapter fifteen. The story of the prodigal son."

His eyes had become hard obsidian. But he remained silent.

Her hands clenched around the cup. "Why won't you speak?" she exclaimed.

"Seems like you're speaking enough for the both of us." His perfect lips barely moved.

"Can't you even be civil? Or did you leave those lessons behind too when you left St. Petroc?"

"Listen to you. As righteous as you always were."

She threw the chocolate at him.

She didn't know quite how it happened. One moment strange, frantic panic coursed through her, straight from her heels to her throat. The next moment a demon possessed her, seizing her arm and forcing it to jut forward and disgorge the contents of her cup at him. Chocolate spattered everywhere—on the wall, the doorpost, and on the dark, handsome man from her past for whom she had wept months of tears.

"What in the—" But he didn't finish. Instead he came at her. Her foot dropped back but he grabbed her wrist and jerked her hand with the cup up between them. "What do you think you're doing?" Chocolate dripped down her wrist and along his cheeks and lips. He stared down at her in astonishment.

"Wasting my chocolate." She tugged. His grip tightened. Arm to arm, he held her close, and he did not look into her eyes. He looked at her lips. The shadows in his eyes were deeper, but now limned with fever brightness, so bright that she could see the flecks of brown there that she had discovered as a girl.

"How do you go along these days, Eleanor?" His voice was rough.

"Wh-what?"

"How is the parish?" His gaze never left her lips, his fingers strong around her wrist. "Is it still the same as eleven years ago when I departed?"

"Precipitously," she whispered. "Without warning. Without word." The syllables trailed into the silence of her raucous heartbeat.

"Precipitously. Without warning."

Through his hand she felt him. Her skin, her bones, her blood felt him.

"You are poking fun at me," she said. "Don't."

"What will it be, Eleanor? You demanded my attention. You have it now. Do you want it or not?"

She wanted to taste the chocolate on his lips. She wanted to remember the danger and delirium she'd felt the last time she had been entirely alive.

"You are holding me." She saw only his eyes, so close she could count each ebony lash. "Why are you holding me?"

"Hot beverage. My face. Sound familiar?" His lips and jaw were bathed in sugar. Parted lips. Uncompromising jaw. "But if this counts to you as holding, *pirani*, you've clearly missed a lot of life shut up in that vicarage."

She could not speak to confirm or deny it. For the first time in eleven years he had called her his pet name.

Black eyes scanned her features slowly. The groove between his brows deepened.

"Damn it," he growled, and released her. He crossed the room in hard strides and went out. Cool air swirled around Eleanor, bathing her fiery cheeks. She peered into the cup in her quivering hand. Breaking every rule she had ever learned about comportment, she stood alone in the taproom and licked the cup clean.

BETSY SNORED. THE innkeepers and Mr. Treadwell had long since gone to bed, and Eleanor supposed Taliesin had washed his hands of her—and chocolate—for the night and now slept too. But her thoughts spun and the blood in her veins seemed whipped up with fire. She needed air, and space. *To breathe.*

She dressed quietly and tucked her feet into her shoes. Drawing her cloak about her shoulders, she slipped from the bedchamber and out of the inn. Between the clouds, the full moon struggled to illuminate the moor, wind twirling across the hills like dancers in a ballroom. The air smelled of snow. When she lifted her face, an icy mist settled on her hot skin.

She crossed the road and walked out onto the moor, wrapped in her cloak but buoyed by strange excitement.

"Do you have a death wish?"

She pivoted around. Taliesin walked toward her. He carried a lamp. The light cast him in a glow, not of comfort or warmth but of mystical, dangerous things—faeries and fire demons and elven kings.

"You needn't be here," she called to him.

"If you're wandering alone on the moor at night, I'm thinking I need to be here."

"There is no one around for miles. There is no danger."

"There is more on the moors than men, *pirani*."

"If a stray sheep accosts me I will defend myself like a knight of old against a dragon. Have you a sword that I can borrow?"

"Not at present." Almost, he smiled.

Her stomach did pirouettes. "I don't need a protector."

He halted two yards away. "All evidence to the contrary."

"You are only here because Arabella would not agree to fund this journey unless I allowed you to come. Did she tell you that? She forced me to accept this arrangement. But I don't need you here, and she won't know if you leave now. Mr. Treadwell has a pistol. Once we come to the coast tomorrow I am familiar with the country and can manage without your help."

"I am not your protector. I am your guide only. Your sister asked this favor of me and for the gratitude I bear your family I agreed to it."

"You agreed to it because you knew I didn't want it."

"What do you want, Eleanor?" he asked, an edge of darkness in his deep rumble. "To take to the road on this quest like a peddler without assistance and hope for the best? I've been there, and I can assure you it's no holiday. Not even for a few weeks."

"I'm not naïve. I know the challenges I face." Tiny, icy pebbles from the sky layered the earth, covering the darkness with sound. Bits of frozen rain clung to her lashes. "You don't think I can do this, do you? Find my parents."

"I think you could do anything you put your mind to."

He always had.

"Is that—" Her words stumbled upon feeling. "Is that a challenge?"

"A challenge?"

Shame like nit bites prickled her skin. What a fool she was to imagine that their shared past meant anything to him. "You don't remember."

"Remember what, exactly?" he said warily.

"When we were young, all you wanted was to prove that you were better than me, superior, smarter, more daring and adventuresome, that you could best me at any challenge," she said. "When we—"

"When we were young, all I wanted was you."

Her limbs were butter. *But it wasn't true.* He had not wanted her. He had wanted to win.

"Fortunately, youth passes," he added. He lifted a hand and rubbed the back of his neck. The gesture was so familiar, she must have seen him make it hundreds of times—the last time on that last day, when she had been buttoning her gown and he'd stood in the middle of the pond up to his hips in water and watched her.

"I heard that after you left St. Petroc you went to jail," she blurted out.

"Ah. But which occasion?"

"It's true? What did you—what did you *do* to merit it?"

"Vagabondage. Roguery. Nothing worth the telling." He stepped forward. "Is that it? Is this journey about proving your daring? Your foolhardy courage?"

"Of course not."

"No. I see now." He spoke slowly, watching her face so closely that she felt touched. "It's about proving your strength, isn't it? But to whom, I wonder."

A thousand unspoken words clogged her throat. Black satin locks falling over his collar and the lamplight glinting off the silver loops in his ears made him look like a pirate—or how she always imagined a pirate, save for the peg leg, of course. Taliesin's horseman's legs were long and sharply muscled beneath fine, clinging wool. She felt hot and unsteady. Wild inside. Like she'd never seen a man's legs in breeches before.

She dragged her attention up. Looking into the eyes of the single person who had never once doubted her strength, she lied, "No one." Her whisper threaded through drops of falling ice. "I don't wish to prove anything to anyone."

The year after her illness, when she was still weak, she had been bursting to leave the house, to capture on her skin not only the sunshine in the garden but the wind on the cliffs. Her papa cosseted and fretted over her, and she reveled in the attention. But the moment he left the vicarage, she'd stolen out and gone to the Gypsy camp, where Taliesin had taught her how to ride. She met him every day and neither of them told anyone.

"I simply want to find my parents," she said.

Now he walked to her until he stood just before her. He seemed so large, so powerful, and certain of himself.

"You are trying to convince yourself that you are afraid," he said, his deep voice coated the icy stillness of the moor.

"I am not."

"You aren't afraid." Then he touched her. Just like that, skin upon skin, flame to flame. He stroked her cheek with the backs of his fingers and she did not move, did not flinch, did not turn away. The weight of all the stars hidden behind the clouds held her immobile.

"You are a wild bird, caged too long and desperate to be free," he said. So close, his skin and scent. His mouth. Dear God, *his mouth*. If he kissed her, she would let him. She would fall to pieces. "You have believed every word they've said about you, Eleanor. You have accepted the cage, despite your nature. Even now when you are freed, you have allowed them to tie the jesses tight to ensure your return."

"I— What jesses?"

"Ducal carriage. Lady's maid." His shadowy eyes, glittering gold, caressed her lips. "But they chose the wrong man for the job of bodyguard, didn't they? Only you and I know that."

"I'm not trying to convince myself that I am afraid," she forced past the clutter of emotions in her throat. She had loved her life. He'd been the one to abandon the vicarage, not her. "There is no cage. No fetters."

"Prove it."

Prove it.

"P—" Her tongue fumbled. "Prove what?"

"Prove that this isn't about fear. You aren't in St. Petroc now. Your family is miles away. Do what you wish," he added upon the purring growl that was wholly new and alarming. And intoxicating. She felt drunk.

She stared into his black eyes, but now they were not hard. They were hungry. He was suggesting something more than a journey, more than a simple adventure. As he had years ago, he was suggesting him.

He couldn't be. Memories were playing tricks on her, making her imagine. And wish.

"I—I don't need to prove myself to you."

He shrugged and began to turn away. "As you wish."

"I don't want to make this journey in the carriage," she said upon a reeling breath. "I would like to ride."

He paused. Assessed her. Made her knees tremble again. "It's a long road."

"You're riding. Why can't I?"

A suggestion of the provoking grin appeared. "I suspect I'm more accustomed to the saddle than you."

"Hire a horse for me and I will prove you wrong."

"And if you don't?" he said, turning fully to her, and she knew she'd won. He would do this for her.

"Then I will repay you the expense of it."

He laughed. "I don't want your money." He walked to her, the lamplight casting his features in halos of heaven and hell. "What do I get from it?" His gaze dropped, slipping down her body, then slowly back to her face.

He *was* suggesting what she imagined. What she wished.

She tugged her cloak tighter. "The satisfaction of knowing you're right."

A slow smile curved his lips. "While that's tempting, if I am to engage in this wager I'll want more than that."

"Name your terms."

"For each challenge, the winner chooses the prize."

It was like they'd never been apart. Eleven years, he stood there a man, she a woman, but nothing had changed.

"This isn't a game, Taliesin." Her words quivered but she couldn't care. "You don't believe me, do you? You think I'm being willful."

"I believe you wish it. I don't believe that you are convinced you're up to it."

"I am. I will prove it to you." Memories crowded her chest, warning of danger, jumping onto her tongue. "Or you could go, as I said."

"I'm not leaving you to this, *pirani*. If you imagine I would abandon you alone on the road, then I suggest you employ that imagination otherwise." He started back toward the inn. "Now, before I haul you over my shoulder and carry you inside where it's warm and dry, come."

"I'm sorry," she said.

He looked back. "That you've made me come into the frozen rain in the middle of the night? I accept your apology."

"About the chocolate."

Not quite a smile.

"But don't imagine I won't do it again if you provoke me," she said.

"Believe me, I will. And, yes," he said into the frigid night.

"Yes?"

"I can be civil."

"You're not doing a particularly good job of it." She went toward him now, her steps more certain upon each tuft of moss. When she came beside him he grasped her wrist and halted her.

"You will lose this challenge, *pirani*. You know that, don't you?"

The girl beneath her skin, the girl who eleven years ago had packed away her desire, now whispered that losing and winning this challenge wore the same face. "As ever," she said aloud, "you are wrong."

He gestured toward the inn. She went because she believed he would in fact haul her over his shoulder if she defied him now. For all his fine clothing and gentlemanly airs, he was still a wild, unpredictable boy at heart. And she did not trust him.

Chapter 5

The Quest

*H*e shouldn't have done it. He should not have allowed the arrogant boy confined beneath his ribs to best him. And he most assuredly should not have touched her after she threw the chocolate at him. Her wrist had been so slender in his grasp, her strength a revelation he was a fool to have forgotten.

Then he'd made the grave mistake of looking at her lips. He'd gotten lost in contemplation of those lips too many times in years past to have made such a blunder now.

He'd gone off, berated himself for a fool, changed his clothing, and gone to the stable to see to his horse. Then he'd seen her walk onto the moor at midnight, a willow sylph with golden tresses.

And he'd done it again.

She drove him insane. She had always driven him insane. Now, however, he'd no business making wagers with her. He was no longer a lad, wrapped around her finger and hungry for her beyond even his understanding then. Yet she could still make him do what he must not.

He still hungered.

"I heard you send Hodges's boy off," Treadwell said as he fastened the final line to the carriage. "Fetching a saddle horse for the lady?" He lifted a yellow brow.

Even Arabella's coachman thought he was insane.

"If she wants to ride," he growled, "I'll let her ride." He'd have the horse by sundown, and after a day in the saddle she would regret it. He ran his hand along Tristan's withers, seeking steadiness. He hadn't been so surly in years. Ten or so.

"She's a taking little thing, isn't she?" Treadwell said.

Taliesin snapped his head around. Betsy walked toward them, the coachman's attention fixed on her like a dog on a meat bone.

"She's sixteen, Treadwell." But Eleanor hadn't been more than sixteen all those years ago. Sixteen and in thorough control of him.

"A man can look," Treadwell said with a chuckle.

And yet, on the moor last night, Taliesin had dared Eleanor to do more than look. Did she understand that? He doubted it. She'd never had any idea what her eyes shimmering with longing did to him. Had always done to him. She thought he'd wanted to be wild, but she had it entirely wrong. He'd come by his wildness naturally. Learning to control it had been his greatest challenge. He'd done it for her.

But this time he didn't need help from her or anyone else to maintain control of the situation. This time he knew how to approach the challenge. Forget about the fire in her eyes in the darkness. Forget how it felt to touch her. And completely ignore his need to show her what she might have had if all those years ago she had waited for him.

THE WIND WHIPPED harder as they approached the coast, the carriage dipping to a lull in the valley before ascending the final hill. Abruptly, the ocean appeared, frothing gray and white beneath February's weak sun.

"Coming to the crossroad soon, sir," Treadwell called from the box.

The foundling home where Martin Caulfield had discovered the three sisters was tucked in a crevice two miles beyond the northern edge of the village that they headed toward now. They would avoid the orphanage. Nothing could be found there. In that fishing village where the little girls had washed ashore twenty-three years ago, Eleanor intended to begin her search.

A bell on the wharf rang, and a trio of weathered old fishermen lifted their heads as the carriage drew to a halt before the inn at the base of the village. At the feet of the buildings layered two deep along the rise of the coast, a strip of sand glowed silvery-gold in the late-day sun, stretching to a wharf where fishing boats that had already returned for the day were securely moored. Gulls circled overhead, white and gray against the pale sky. The place was quiet now, a sleepy wintertime village that, come summer, would be bustling with traders and merchants.

"A prettier spot I've never seen," Treadwell exclaimed as Taliesin dismounted. "Now you take care there," he said to the boy who'd come from the mews alley toward the carriage horses. "Morgan le Fay will take a bite out of your arse if you snag the rein."

Taliesin walked forward and gave his mount into the boy's hand. "This is Tristan," he said with a hand on the stallion's back. "Care for him as you would for your own mother."

"Don't have a mother, sir. Just me ol' da, an' he's out on the boats all but one Sunday a month."

"Then care for him as you would care for a gold coin, and I will see that you have a gold coin in return for it."

The boy's eyes flared and he led Tristan away carefully.

Taliesin went to the coach, but the door burst open before he reached it and Eleanor flew out. Eyes bright, she scanned the beach.

"I remember this place," she said, the wonder of a girl in her face. "But how could I remember it? I wasn't but four at the time."

Her maid poked her head out of the opening. "Well, I'll remember it for the rest of my life, miss, that's for sure."

Eleanor smiled, and Taliesin's throat thickened.

"Will you, Betsy?"

"Yes, miss. It's the first time I've ever seen the sea."

"How perfectly delightful for you." Her eyes were soft now in honest pleasure. "Then I am glad we set off on this journey after all." Then her gaze came to him. It darted away swiftly. She was shy today of the challenge he had offered her the night before, apparently. But then her shoulders straightened beneath her cloak and her jaw set, delicate lines of bone and flesh he had once longed to caress. "Let us be about our task then, shall we?"

No ONE HAD anything to tell her. While the maid dozed in a corner of the taproom, Eleanor walked from shop to shop, emerging from each with a firmer step and averted face. From the base of the street, Taliesin traced her progress until she reached the end of the long row of buildings. She returned to him.

"Nothing," she said as she drew near. The breeze lifted the shimmering locks peeking from beneath her bonnet, and ruffled the hem of her cloak. "Some of them recall our wrecked ship, but no one has memory of a man searching for his three tiny daughters."

"Did you expect it?"

"I did not. Of course. Don't be smug."

"I'm not being smug." Rather, he was having trouble ordering his thoughts. He'd never in eleven years imagined he would be alone with this woman again. He had never imagined he would want to be, and that he would want to touch her with the intensity with which he wanted to touch her now. "I hope you will find what you're searching for."

She stared at him for a stretched moment, her brow creased in concentration. So familiar. So many times she'd looked at him like this, her eyes upon him but blind to him, her thoughts traveling elsewhere.

Then abruptly she walked toward the barricade that ran along the top of the beach. Grabbing up her skirts under her elbow awkwardly, she set off across the rocks. She stumbled and slipped.

He moved forward. "You will—"

"No!" she called over her shoulder, her fingers tangling in the ribbons of her bonnet. "Don't."

"Don't what?"

"Don't stop me." The ribbons flailed in the wind, and the bonnet jerked from her head. It tumbled away along the rocks. She took no notice, instead continued on.

"I don't know what you're doing to try to stop you from it," he said across the wind.

Strewn with rocks above, the crescent beach stretched to the water, a cove of lapping waves protected from the force of the sea by the wharf. She walked straight for the water's edge, slipping and tripping on the stones, her skirts billowing out in the cold wind.

He crossed the rocky border and followed at a distance. The sun was dipping low over the ocean, setting the water aglow in bronze and pink. Gulls overhead called as though urging her on.

Two yards from the water she paused to throw off her shoes. Then she rucked her skirts to her knees and strode into the water. She yelped, and laughed, and continued walking.

That water had to be half a man's body heat. At best.

"What are you doing?"

"There is a shallow rocky shoal a few yards ahead," she called back, her ankles entirely submerged, steps fumbling. Her lips were pulled back from her teeth. "You can see it from the inn." Her skirts dipped into the ocean. She grappled with them and her knees peeked out. "Since the tide is now low, I'm going to stand on it. I've never waded in the ocean before." Her voice pitched high. The frozen water, no doubt. "I have gotten very close. I've sat on beaches for hours. But never once in my twenty-seven years have I waded." She cast him a glance of wide-eyed mischief that went straight to his gut. "And now you must too."

"Yet I have waded in the ocean before, and in fact I mustn't now. It's February." Pleasure collected in his chest. This was the girl he'd known, the girl of erratic modesty and absolute delight.

"Oh." She took another unsteady step deeper into

the frigid sea. "You poor thing. I suppose you're only brave when it comes to safe little ponds."

His throat caught. *Safe little pond.* Years ago. Temptation and torture and pleasure so acute he could practically feel it again now. *Safe?* No. Not with her. Never with her, he was beginning to see.

Clearly she was not shy today of the wager they'd struck.

"The climate is somewhat different now than on that occasion." That occasion that had changed his life. And now she teased, as though it had meant nothing to her. But he'd long since known that.

"Don't tell me you're worried that I will take a chill and perish?" she said without turning. "You never were before."

Before, she hadn't been curved in every place he wanted to put his hands. Some. But not all. And there hadn't been tiny lines of laughter at the corners of her eyes. Before, he'd been a boy, driven by a boy's devotion. Now a man's desire drove him. God's blood, she was beautiful with the wind whipping at her tightly bound hair, threatening to tear it free of its bonds. More beautiful than she'd been as a girl, with her sharp nose and gentle lips and laughing eyes that sought him with such longing. And her legs—legs he'd only seen glimpses of before, slender and long—legs that had fed his fantasies night after night.

She stood like a flame, vibrating with daring, the gentle waves lapping around her knees. "Frightened?"

The same taunt he'd thrown at her eleven years ago.

"Not on your life." He pulled off a boot, then the other, then his stockings. By God, even the rocks were cold. But she had never shied from a challenge. He'd known that when he goaded her last night on the moor. He had known, and he'd done it anyway.

The icy water bit at him like pins. She had reached

the shoal and was climbing onto it, her feet sinking deep into the rocky sand that abraded the soles of feet. He went swiftly into the surf, soaking his breeches and biting back on the pain.

She slipped and yelped again, louder—in fear—releasing her skirts as her arms flailed.

He reached forward and caught her. She gasped. Grabbed for him. He dragged her against his chest.

This.

For eleven years he had been wanting this: her face uplifted to his, her body pressed to his, her lips parted and his hands on her. Often he'd told himself that his memory exaggerated how good it had felt to hold her.

It felt infinitely better.

He held a woman now, her full breasts crushed to his chest and long legs trapped between his. Frigid water and frozen feet be damned. If he stood here with her hips and thighs pressed to his for long, she would swiftly discover how decidedly cold he was not.

But he couldn't release her. Not yet. Her wide eyes, green from the ocean's reflection, stared at him as though she had never seen him before. Her hands clutched his shoulders and her breaths came fast. Gilded silk whirled about her cheeks.

"It—" Her throat constricted, a ripple of smooth ivory. "It *hurts*," she groaned, and hopped up on one foot. "I cannot bear it another *moment*." She broke away. Grabbing up her skirts, she splashed through the water toward the sand.

Yes, it hurt. But not his feet.

He followed slowly. On the beach she ran to her shoes and threw herself onto the sand to tug them over her soaked stockings. She hadn't removed her stockings that time long ago either, and he'd seen a gentlewoman's stockings for the first time in his life. Now sodden skirts tangled about her shapely calves, cling-ing, revealing, and he stared like the boy he'd been. She struggled with the shoes.

He pulled off his coat, knelt, and snatched the shoes from her hands.

"St-stop that. Wh-what are you doing?" The words came from lips the color of wax, trembling and caught between her teeth. "Give them back."

He wrapped his coat around her legs and feet. "Accept this gracefully, *pirani*," he said, holding her feet between his hands and willing the wool to do swift work. He'd seen his cousins lose toes. The winter of 1799 had been especially brutal on Rom living in caravans. If not for the Reverend Caulfield's barn and the warmth of the goats and horse, he might not be whole now. Or alive.

"Look what you have done to your fine coat," she said. But she wasn't looking at his coat around her legs. She was staring at his shoulders.

"It's nothing." His voice sounded hoarse. Her ankles were so narrow, his fingers spanning them even through the coat. The fabric of her skirts encased her knees haphazardly. Without allowing himself to think, he let his hands follow his gaze upward.

"But—"

"There are other coats." But there were no other women. No women like this. No women he wanted to both goad into daring and rescue from danger, and touch everywhere, as he was doing now, her calves a new paradise, a discovery of pure feminine perfec-tion. No women who made him hot as hell with a mere blink of her lashes, with her parted lips as he slid his palms higher, curving his fingers beneath her knees. No women that drove him as mad as she had appar-ently become in the decade since he'd last seen her by a pond in a copse, barely clothed, sunlight in her hair and a mischievous smile on her lips—a smile that coaxed him into the sea in the midst of winter.

Her breathing was fast, faster than moments earlier, her eyes wide as sunlight.

Ice-pale lips. Pink tongue. Lashes long as eternity draping themselves downward as his hand climbed. His fingertips strafed the underside of her thigh, salt and sand and pure beauty against his skin.

She gasped. Fear shone deep in the gilded green of her eyes.

Chest constricting, he released her.

Dragging her legs free of his coat, she scuttled back like a crab, scrabbled to her feet, and ran.

Taliesin's blood pounded, a tide he'd no power to control. He bent his head and stared at his empty hands.

Chapter 6
The Whiskey

She couldn't stop looking at him.

Neither, apparently, could Betsy.

"I don't trust him, miss." Brow crunched, Betsy shook her head and sipped tea.

Beyond the window, on the cobbles just above the stones that bordered the beach, the stable boy led Taliesin's great black horse to him. He took the reins and spoke to the boy for a moment. He had changed into dry clothes, and wore now both hat and greatcoat. Except for the silver rings in his ears, he looked like a gentleman. Earlier, on the beach, he had behaved like one. Until he hadn't.

"Why don't you trust him?" Eleanor said a little breathlessly.

"I saw how he stole your shoes." Betsy glared through the window.

"Then you also saw how he replaced them with his coat."

Betsy leveled her a challenging eye. "Has he given the shoes back to you, then?"

"Well. No." She hadn't really given him opportunity. The wind on the beach had pressed the very fine shirt linen to his shoulders and arms, revealing muscles she'd been too naïve to even dream of. Then his big, strong hands had slipped from her feet up her calves, and she'd lost a little bit of her mind. "I thought perhaps he gave them to you."

Betsy wagged her head anew. "I've heard tell Oriental princes don't let their womenfolk wear shoes. Their men like to keep them trapped in the house at their ravenous mercy, you see."

Betsy, it seemed, had an overly active imagination. They were well suited.

"And they have more than one wife," Betsy added. "Dozens of them, I've heard."

"That may be. But it has no bearing on my shoes. Mr. Wolfe is not an Oriental prince, of course, and I am not a member of a harem."

"Then what's he done with your shoes?"

Mr. Treadwell walked from the mews alley. Taliesin spoke to him, impossible to hear through the glass, then mounted and rode away.

Eleanor flexed her toes in her dress slippers. "I shall have to ask him when he returns." She'd no idea where he was going. He could not possibly be leaving her in this little fishing village with only a maid and coachman, not on the verge of nightfall.

But on the moor she had asked him to leave her

alone. Then, the challenge. Since then, she had taunted him into the frigid ocean, and when he'd gone to his knees in the sand before her and touched her like he should not have, she'd fled like a frightened girl.

Mr. Treadwell entered the taproom. "Ma'am." He touched the brim of his cap. Beneath it was a tangle of straw-colored hair. His face was long, and he wasn't above twenty-five, despite his weathered skin. He turned to Betsy with a shy smile. "Good day, miss."

Betsy's cheeks flared rusty pink. She looked down into her teacup.

"Mr. Treadwell, where has Mr. Wolfe gone?"

"He said he's got a parcel to retrieve a distance aways, but he won't be no more than a few hours."

"What sort of parcel?"

"I shouldn't be saying, ma'am. But he wouldn't hear of me going and fetching it for him. I'd have done it too. Guinevere, you see, doesn't mind being saddle rode by a good man every so often. Just like her name-sake, I suppose."

Eleanor cracked a laugh. Then slammed her palm over her mouth.

Betsy's freckles became one large splotch of pink.

"Beggin' your pardon." Mr. Treadwell's cheeks had grown ruddy too. He twisted his cap between his hands. "There's times when my tongue runs away from me."

"Do not fret, Mr. Treadwell. You've caused no trouble for me." Queen Guinevere of legend had ridden the wrong man, Lancelot, despite how dangerous it had been. She'd done it simply because she wanted him and the temptation was too great to withstand.

But Guinevere had been a fool. From the comfort and safety of her queenly throne, she had stepped straight into the fire.

Eleanor suspected she ought to take some lesson

from this. With the memory of Taliesin's hands on her like a wicked dream, she could not.

Taliesin did not return in time for dinner, nor did he return by the time she changed into her nightclothes and crept under the covers of her narrow bed not unlike the bed she'd slept in for twenty years of her life. While he had slept in a barn. And elsewhere, she supposed.

What had he done with his life since he'd left St. Petroc? Ravenna said his business trading horses was successful. Where had he made that business away from his uncle's family? Gypsies didn't often leave their families. And how had he the time now to escort her on this quest? Or was he simply still the wild boy she'd once known, a nomad by blood, up to a lark if it meant travel, even if it meant playing escort to an aging spinster?

An aging spinster whose legs he had caressed with hands that made her dizzy.

With the sounds of the sea in her ears she couldn't sleep. Her blood pounded quick, pulsing, every moment lying abed a moment wasted. She'd wasted too many moments of her life already.

Today she had waded into a frozen ocean, with nary a sniffle to show for it. Only a pressing need to be *alive* bubbled in her now.

Donning her cloak, and once more stealing out of her shared room, she made her way down to the taproom. Betsy's shoes were large and clomped on the stairs. No one else lodged at this inn now; she didn't fear encountering anyone.

The taproom was dark, not even the kitchen dog anywhere to be seen. She drew her feet out of the heavy shoes and padded to the window on bared feet, her toes exploring each floorboard like an exotic landscape. The clouds had departed. Now the moon shone brilliantly, silver-white amidst clusters of thousands of stars, illumining the cove.

She lifted her eyes to the moon and sighed. She *sighed*.

She had never sighed before in her life.

In the morning, with a head heavy and aching from lack of sleep, she would not be sighing. She would be grumbling.

Moonlight allowed her to peruse the bar. The inn-keepers were trusting people; two bottles sat atop it. Her papa sometimes shared with her a finger of sherry as a nightcap. Not, however, since Agnes had begun to join them after dinner. A girl of Eleanor's delicate constitution, she had kindly suggested, should not be drinking sherry before sleep. Warm milk would serve her better.

A girl of Eleanor's delicate constitution should not be wading into a frozen sea or daydreaming of the infidelities of a medieval queen either.

She reached for the whiskey and a spoon.

The first spoonful caught in her throat and made her sputter. She waited and felt nothing. She stared out at the sea in which he had held her to his body and looked down at her with eyes that had grown hot even as her feet had grown numb, and she felt no stirring of heat from the whiskey like the heat he had stirred in her that afternoon. No sleepiness either.

The second spoonful of whiskey curled across her tongue and into her chest like a living thread of fire.

The third spoonful worked its way into her lips and her belly, and into her head in warm clouds.

The fourth spoonful made her eyelids droop, her head tilt back, and her heels seek the chair opposite.

The fifth spoonful—what was left of it after she spilled some on the table—caused her fingers to unbind her braid and made her breaths long and slow and deep as she remembered his hands sliding up her calves. Then higher.

Upon the sixth spoonful she thought, perhaps, that

she was coming to understand Guinevere remarkably well indeed.

TALIESIN FOUND HER in a pool of moonlight, her cloak cast off, her nightclothes bright like the robe of an angel, her hair cascading in ripples down her back. Bare feet propped up on a chair, hands folded over her waist, and eyes closed, she slept in the middle of the public room like a princess reclining in her own boudoir.

But perhaps she did not precisely sleep. A half-empty bottle of Irish whiskey and a spoon rested on the table beside her.

Not a cup or glass. A spoon.

Instead of loosening the cords that had been wrapped around his chest since she'd run from him on the beach, that spoon cinched the tension tighter.

For months she had taken medicine by the spoonful. Never complaining, always obedient to the doctor, by the strength of her will alone she had survived an illness that should have killed her.

He remembered the moment he had first been allowed to see her during her convalescence. Emblazoned on his soul, it would never leave him.

She had not stirred from her bedchamber in months. The disease had left her lungs, but she could not walk well, Ravenna had told him with the blithe perplexity of a girl who'd never known a day of poor health in her life. Eleanor's knees buckled when she tried to walk; she fell over, her sister reported. She ate little, and she had no strength. So she remained in her room, away from his eyes. Every day that he came to the vicarage to work and take his lesson, all the while knowing she was mere yards away, beyond the closed door of her bedchamber, was another day of purgatory for him.

The Reverend went about with shadowed eyes. One

day, when Taliesin was scooping ash from the grate to scatter over the garden soil, the Reverend looked up from the sermon he was writing. In a bruised voice, he told Taliesin that his eldest daughter would not read. Her weakness had turned her despondent. She possessed enough strength to lift a book, but she hadn't the will for anything more. Devastation had marked the vicar's haggard face.

Several days later, entering the house by the back door, Taliesin met Ravenna in hot pursuit of her monstrous black dog.

"Tali!" she gasped, pausing in her full-tilt run out the door to shove a book against his chest. "Beast is after the squire's pointer bitch again. I simply must catch him before he catches her! Take this to Ellie, I beg of you. Papa wants her to have it immediately. He'll be cross with me if she doesn't." Flashing him a wild grin, she flew out the door after her dog.

He didn't need a second invitation. The vicar's study door was closed. He wouldn't know.

Taliesin knew it was wrong, that he should not enter a girl's bedchamber under any circumstances.

He did it anyway.

He went with his heart in his throat. Then that heart fell to his feet.

Standing in the doorway of her bedchamber, he stared at the fourteen-year-old invalid wrapped in blankets and shawls, a wraithlike shadow of the girl he had loved since the moment he'd set eyes on her five years earlier, and the backs of his eyes prickled painfully. He'd never in his life wept. But this wan specter was not the girl he knew, not the sharp-tongued tormenter who drove him mad with her nose-in-the-air superiority and her sudden, unguarded smiles.

Sensing his presence, he supposed, she had turned her head. Her eyes, dull and listless, were ringed with black.

"Go away," she whispered.

"No," he managed to choke out. The single, rough syllable sounded harsh in the confined space.

"I don't want you." Her voice was barely a breath.

"I've brought—" His throat felt thick. "I've brought a book the Reverend wants you to read."

"I don't want it."

He stepped into the room. "Then what do you want? To die? Because I can't think of anything stupider than making it through the worst of it just to waste away afterward."

She turned her face from him and her eyes stared like glass at the drawn draperies. "Go away."

Crossing the tiny chamber, he pulled wide the curtains, allowing the pale winter sunlight to enter. He sat down on a stool before the window and opened the book.

"All right," he said, trying not to touch the pages with his fingers that were filthy from the barn. Usually before he came indoors for lessons he made certain to wash his hands. "If you don't want to read it, I will. I don't suppose you're smart enough to read this one, anyway. Don't know what the Reverend was imagining to think you were."

"Are you laughing at me?" Her words came forth crackly. "I can't see your ugly face to tell. The sunlight is behind it."

"I can see yours. You look awful."

"You are"—she pulled in a shallow breath—"a beast."

"And you're a miserable invalid. Which is worse, do you think?"

"I can read it."

"I'll wager you can't."

"I *can*." A puff of air came out of her mouth upon the word, the most she'd worked her beleaguered lungs in months, he guessed.

"Prove it," he said.

That day she read a page. When her fingers slipped on the binding and the book tumbled from her lap, he caught it. Leaning her head back on the pillow, she closed her eyes and said, "Will you . . ."

He waited. But weakness—or perhaps pride—did not allow her to complete her request.

"Listen here," he said, opening the volume across his palms. "This next part is where Abelard gets charged with heresy for applying philosophical methods to Scripture." He read aloud but soon she slept, and he departed itchy under the collar and out of sorts.

The next day when he opened the door to her room, her face was turned toward him. The book rested beside her on the counterpane. Her eyelids cracked open and she drew a stuttering inhalation. "Come for more proof, stupid boy?"

He couldn't suppress his smile. "Sure have, Princess Invalid."

Every day after that he went to her and teased her into reading. Some days she was sullen, exhausted, especially at the beginning. But eventually when he came into her room he would find her sitting up in bed, her hair combed or tied beneath a cap, her eyes cautiously eager. Ravenna told him that Eleanor was eating more now, and that she was able to walk as far as the parlor.

When the Reverend learned of Taliesin's visits to the sickroom, he did not object. His little scholar was reading again, studying. The grief left his eyes.

The morning that Eleanor met Taliesin in the garden instead of in her room, he nearly crowed aloud. Sunlight dappled her drawn face and sparkled in her eyes. As he closed the gate behind him, a soft smile of triumph shaped her mouth. He picked strawberries from the patch and she ate them, carefully, one by one in tiny bites, and read aloud from Malory's *Le Morte d'Arthur*.

Occasionally she lapsed into silence, but when he looked up from pulling weeds, she would still be reading. Lost in the story, she'd only forgotten his presence.

Shortly after that, his family packed up their tents and left St. Petroc for the summer. Never had the wandering season lasted so long. Never had he wished so acutely to be somewhere he was not.

When he returned to St. Petroc that fall, the first day, as his family was still pitching camp by the squire's north wood, she came to him. A surge of pleasure had gone through him, from the soles of his feet right into his head. Still far too thin, with purple smudges beneath her eyes and sallow cheeks, she had greeted his aunt and Lussha and the other women with a quick curtsy. Then, without even saying hello to him, she demanded that he teach her how to ride a horse.

Now he walked into the center of the taproom, not quieting his footsteps. But she did not wake. Her breathing remained deep, her folded hands rising and falling slowly with the movement of her ribs. He took his time enjoying this vision of her, from bared feet and slender ankles, up the length of a nightgown so thick he could use it as a saddlecloth, to the buttons that cinched the fabric snug about her neck. Then to her face.

No longer gaunt, but soft, her skin shone luminescent in the moonlight. Her lips, parted and pink, drew him down to the chair beside her. He could stroke the rippling gold satin so close to his hand now and she would never know. Years ago he'd done so often enough in his imagination.

But years ago he'd been a fool of a boy, infatuated with a girl far above his station. And he didn't touch women who did not invite it. Not as he wished to touch her now.

And if by some miracle she did invite it, there was no way in Hades he'd take her up on it. The feeling of her in his hands on the beach would not leave him, the old insanity back in his body and—worse yet—in his head, from even that brief touch. She turned him inside out and made him forget who he was, a man who lived according to his will only, and who damned well liked it that way. An aching chest and endless nights of seeking satisfaction—in bottles and troublemaking—yet never finding it had taught him an excellent lesson: a man alone was a man free to make something of himself. He wasn't about to let lust drag him into hell, no matter how tempting. He'd made a vow to himself never to do so again.

As she had on that day thirteen years ago, now she stirred, drew in a quick, sudden gasp, and her lashes fluttered up. She seemed not to see him for a moment. Then gradually the golden green jewels grew aware. The familiar pucker appeared between her brows.

"Why are you in my bedchamber?"

"This is not your bedchamber. You are in the tap-room of the inn at Piskey."

She blinked and turned her head, squinting. Her feet tipped inward to cross her toes over each other. "I fell asleep," she said in an airy mumble.

"It seems you did."

"I was dreaming. There was a horse . . ." She blinked again and snapped accusing eyes to him. "I wanted to ride it and Papa would not let me. I begged. But he gave it to you."

"Your father never gave me a horse, *pirani*."

"I was jealous of you."

"They were not my horses. They were my uncle's."

"Not of your horses." She pushed herself up, dropping her feet with a thump to the floor. "Of Papa's attention."

"You are intoxicated," he said, because the linen had caught and was tugging across her thighs and he couldn't keep his attention on her fogged eyes. "You must return to your bedchamber now."

"I am intoxicated." She gripped the seat of the chair beside her knee. "But I'm speaking the truth. He always wanted a son."

Perhaps. But not him. Not as she believed.

He stood and offered his hand. "Come now."

She swung her head from side to side. "No." She climbed to her feet without assistance, pushing her hair from her brow when it fell like shimmering summer before her eyes, and swaying. She reached out and he caught her arm. Gripping the back of the chair with her other hand, she drew away from his hold.

"I don't think you should touch me," she said to the floor.

"All right. But I will follow you up the stairs."

"I would like you to," she mumbled, and plunked onto the chair again with a jointless lack of grace. "That is, not follow me. I would like you to touch me. Like you did on the beach without permission. But of course that would be an immeasurably bad idea."

Immeasurably bad. Yes. Her nightgown cinched under her knee, exposing her foot, ankle, and entire shapely calf, and Taliesin's brain was shutting down. Like a boy who'd never seen a woman's naked legs before. But he'd seen plenty of women's naked legs.

Not this woman's. On the beach he had put his hands on her legs and she had allowed it for a full ten seconds before bolting. But she'd remained still long enough for him to imagine urging those legs apart while she moaned his name. Long enough to imagine her eagerly wrapping those legs around his waist.

He swallowed across his pounding pulse. "Right." What had she said? "Of course." *Years.* It had taken him years to get over her. Years of struggle and hard labor. He should not have touched her on the beach. She was right. *Immeasurably* bad idea.

"But . . ." Her eyelids fluttered and she leaned her

head back against the chair. In her neck, the slow throb of her heartbeat beneath pale skin taunted him to touch it. "I should like . . ." She breathed deeply, her breasts tightening the simple fabric, a contrast of purity and voluptuous temptation. "I should like you to touch me, you know. No one has since you. That time." She whispered, "I wish . . . you would."

He acted then without thought, with only the instinct that had saved him dozens, perhaps hundreds of times in dangerous situations: he scooped her up in his arms and strode toward the stairs.

She was soft and light, and urgency made him quick. He ascended the narrow risers before he'd time to think, to alter his course. Setting her on her feet with an arm around her, he reached for the door handle. Honeysuckle and sage hovered about her unbound hair, filling his head, and his hand brushed the underside of her unbound breast. For a moment—barely a moment—he succumbed. He pulled her close, fitting her body to his. He bent to her, sank his nose into her hair, and breathed her in. Sweet and musky and silken soft. The scents and sensation of lust. Of longing. Of everything he'd fought so hard to forget.

God's blood, *what was he doing?*

Against his neck she murmured words, or perhaps only sounds of pleasure. His hands found her shoulders, her back through the linen, spreading, touching— after eleven years waking to the memory of her.

He opened the door.

He would regret this. *Of course* he would.

In a single stride he carried her to the bed, untangled her arm from about his neck, and left before the maid could rouse from sleep. Closing the door, he descended the stairs to the taproom and the unfinished bottle of whiskey.

Chapter 7

The Prince of Night

Someone had dropped every book of Holy Scripture on her skull from a very great height. Or an anvil. Eleanor's head throbbed, and a pudding that had been stored in the chicken coop had wrapped itself about her tongue.

The whiskey had put her to sleep. That she'd no memory of returning to her bedchamber she must now store away in her private room of shame that no one else ever entered.

She dragged her head and then the rest of her body from bed. Sunlight cut a long, sharp angle through the shutters. Betsy had gone, leaving clothes laid out on a chair, including a pair of boots fashioned of soft, rust-colored leather with delicate silver buckles. The traveling boots Taliesin had taken from her on the beach were not to be seen.

She dressed with fumbling fingers, then slid her feet into the new shoes and with an aching head left the inn. The sleepy little village boasted only a dozen shops and few cottages. She'd spoken to people in every one of them the day before, with no luck. One woman had suggested she search in the church records, but her husband said the church flooded in a storm in '08; all the records had been carried out to sea.

Eleanor went toward the archway to the stable, her borrowed boots making each step a pleasure.

The clopping of shod hooves upon cobbles sounded nearby, and Taliesin appeared beneath the archway, leading a horse by either hand. The stallion jerked its head at her. The other horse, a sleek young chestnut mare with four milky socks and a blaze between her eyes, tilted her face to the man guiding her as though seeking his attention, or perhaps approval from him.

Eleanor's breaths left her in tiny bits of memory. Seeing him like this, years ago beneath the shadow of tree cover, she had invented a story.

In some ancient past, the moon had wagered the sun that she could bear a son of such dark beauty, with hair black as a Saracen's and eyes like shining opals, that forever after all who saw him would be jealous of the night. The moon's boast came true; the Prince of Night was born to her, black-eyed and handsome as the stars. Conceding defeat, the regal sun gifted the boy with wisdom and strength, so that every creature would be drawn to him and find happiness.

For his part, the prince loved only one maiden, as fair and frail as he was dark and strong, and as ordinary as he was beautiful. Confined in a bower of twining vines that she could not escape, the maiden waited for him, and each day he would come. She knew she was loved and, never fearing to lose him, she rejoiced in his visits, however brief they were. But secretly she hoped that one day he would destroy the vines and take her with him.

A fanciful tale written by an infatuated girl the season before Taliesin had left St. Petroc without a word.

He halted. "Good morning." It seemed a question.

"When did you return?"

"Late."

Where did you go? "I'm looking for Betsy."

"She has gone to the cobbler's to demand that he return your old shoes."

"Demand? Why? Did—" A jolt of understanding. "Did you purchase these?" She poked a toe out from beneath her skirt. "I did not ask you to."

"You left your shoes in my keeping. I found them in need of replacement."

"I . . ." She had not precisely left them in his keeping. In panic she had fled him. Unprecedented lack of care. But he had always made her do things she'd never done before. "These are very fine shoes. Too fine for me."

"Your sister is a duchess."

"And yet, remarkably enough, I am not."

A smile crooked the corner of his mouth. It pained her that after all these years he could simply show that confident humor and her eyeballs became glued in place staring at him. His lips were too fine, his smile too provoking.

He started forward again, drawing the horses into the sunlight. "Betsy confronted me at breakfast to demand that I return your shoes. She believed that I stole them." He looked over his shoulder. "You have a valiant guardian. My compliments to your duchess sister."

But she had the suspicion that Arabella had not intended Betsy as her protector. Rather, the opposite. Arabella had been too eager in urging Taliesin to assist in this journey.

Her sisters had never understood how it was between her and Taliesin. How it had been. They didn't know. No one knew but them.

"Betsy doesn't like you," she said.

"I think I had noticed that."

"Taking my shoes didn't help."

"I will remember that the next time I seek to ingratiate myself to a sixteen-year-old lady's maid."

"You should not have taken it upon yourself to buy me new shoes."

He turned, the horses' hooves clacking on the stones. "You did not tell me that your shoes had been ruined by your walk in the rain on the moor two nights ago."

"Why should I have?"

"Perhaps you prefer to go about barefoot."

"I don't."

"Last night in the taproom was an exception, then?"

The taproom? *Good heavens.* "I was . . . foxed."

The grin deepened at the side of his mouth. "First chocolate. Then whiskey. What will it be next, I wonder?"

Him. She wanted to drink him, to pour him into her mouth and taste him on her tongue and get drunk on him. Her cheeks felt as hot as the flames of hell, where she was surely headed. "You are impertinent."

"If I had a shilling for every time I've heard you say those words to me . . ."

"You would be a rich man. But you seem well off enough without those extra shillings." If he cut his hair and removed the silver rings in his ears he would look like any other comfortably settled gentleman, dressed with easy elegance. His skin would mark him out, of course, and the spark of danger in his black eyes—the spark that coaxed something buried deep in her to the surface. "Still—"

"I wasn't the one drinking whiskey alone in a taproom last night." His horse snorted as though chuckling.

"Did I do anything that . . . well, that I should not have? Say anything?" Vague recollections tugged at her. But they must have been dreams. She would never have said anything like that to him in reality, even foxed.

"What would you have said that I have not heard before, do you imagine?" He said it like a caress.

Her face was hot. "It isn't right that you bought shoes for me. I will repay you."

"You owe me a prize."

"A prize?"

"You ran from the water first yesterday."

"But I was in the water longer than you." But she had fled from the beach. When he had touched her, she had not been up to the challenge. And he knew it. "All right. I concede," she said. "But if the prize goes to you, then I should be buying you shoes."

"My prize will be that you are comfortably shod."

"But—"

"Enough arguing. It is my prerogative to choose whatever prize I like."

And then she remembered: A boy's bare feet stained with ash and dirt, and cracked from the cold of winter. Her papa's oldest shoes, and his instruction to cut them into scraps that could be used to mend book bindings. But she had not done as her papa asked. Instead, in secret, she gave the village cobbler all the pennies she had saved. Three days later she left the repaired shoes in the barn.

"Thank you." She could not look at him. "Where is the carriage?" She turned to the mews and marched forward. "It's nearly nine o'clock. Shouldn't we be off soon if we are to make any headway toward the next village today?"

"Treadwell is harnessing the team now. I thought you wished to ride." He drew the mare forward and the animal sidestepped, keeping her head close to his arm. The horse wore a lady's sidesaddle.

Her eyes rounded. "Is she what you went to fetch last night? But I didn't think— That is to say, I thought . . ."

"You thought that you could not have what you wished. You were drinking whiskey in a public room at midnight last night. Nothing holds you back from mere riding now."

Stifling the smile that wanted to tear open her lips, she put her hand beneath the horse's nose. The mare's snuffle tickled her palm. Taliesin proffered the leathers and her fingers itched to grab them.

"Where did you hire her?" she said, barely above a whisper.

"I didn't hire her." He grasped her hand and placed the reins in it, then released her. He drew his horse into the sunlight. "And before you add your accusations to your maid's, I didn't steal her either."

Fingers curling around the leather straps, Eleanor swung her head around. "When did you purchase her?"

"I sent the Hodges' boy to retrieve her yesterday."

"From where?"

"A stable I know of to the south." He swept her toe-to-shoulder with a swift glance. "Have you suitable garments for riding?"

"Yes, but—"

"Are you unhappy to be able to ride?"

"I am not." It was his business, of course, to buy and sell horses. She mustn't think anything of it. "Did you purchase her so that I could ride? Because I said that I wished to?"

Releasing the reins of his horse, he walked toward her, the giant black beast remaining where he left it like a dog ordered to stay. Taliesin came to her and she forced back the urge to retreat. This close, he made her feel weak, unsteady, tangled inside, and overflowing with happiness.

"Two nights ago you claimed that you wished to break free of your bonds." His dark gaze moved across her features. "Was that all bravado?"

Her heart rattled like Gypsy tambourines. "I can ride as well as you. For an hour or for a day."

The corner of his mouth curved upward. "I suppose we'll see, won't we?"

Betsy appeared from a shop along the lane. "The cobbler has already dismantled your shoes to use for other purposes. The *gentleman* here told him to do so." She set a narrow eye on Taliesin.

Eleanor looked at him. "You told him to?"

"If you are to do this, there's no turning back," he said.

No turning back. He meant more with these words. He meant no going back to the girl with the cage around her life.

"No turning back," she said.

In his smile was both danger and beauty.

THE SUN SHONE brilliantly over the wind-battered road that curled around hills fronting the ocean, meandering between farms quiet in this season, dotted with sheep and cows and scrubby winter green. The mare's gait proved smooth and even. Taliesin would never acquire a horse of inferior quality.

He rode behind her, the carriage far back on the road. She suspected she was fanciful to imagine it, but she felt him watching her. It made her giddy, her nerves singing from the sunshine on her cheeks, the reins in her hands, and the beautiful horse beneath her. And the man.

He'd bought her a horse. To use on this journey only, of course.

But he'd bought her a horse.

She looked over her shoulder and her heart flipped upside down. Taliesin lifted his gaze without any show of discomfort at having been discovered staring at her behind. She knew she should be offended; any modest woman would be. But she was not modest, only pretending for years. Her hands conveyed her pleasure to the mare. The animal sidestepped.

"Certain you can handle her?" he said with a lifted brow.

"Most assuredly." She bit her lip. "Like Eleanor of Aquitaine handled her mount while leading the Crusaders on to victory." Legends told of the queen going bare-breasted to inspire the army.

Taliesin knew this. Eleanor knew he knew this. They'd read of it together when she'd been far too young to understand the significance of it.

"I should like to see that," he said.

"Should you like to see the dirt that this mare tosses up at you as I beat you to the crest of that hill?" She pointed.

"Are you challenging me to a race?"

"Of course."

He laughed. "You're challenging *me*? To a race on horseback?"

"I am. Are you up to it, Mr. Wolfe?" She gathered the reins. With salty wind tugging at her bonnet and the road stretching like a twisting band of possibility, she took off.

HE WAS UP to it. After appreciating every nuance of the curve of her behind settled in the saddle, and blessing the thinness of her cloak that defined those nuances, he was up to much more than a ride on a horse. How a woman in a plain dress and unremarkable cloak, with her hair bound in a prim knot beneath a bonnet suited to a country spinster, could rouse him as she did . . .

But he knew her to be more than she allowed herself to appear. She had never been perfect. She had been willful and proud and prone to secrecy and far too intrigued by a poor Gypsy boy than a vicar's daughter should be.

He pressed his heels into Tristan's sides and started after her. The road was even and hard and her pace quick. Astonishingly quick. He'd known the mare could run, but he hadn't quite realized the woman still could. As a novice years ago she'd ridden superbly. He should have anticipated this.

She pulled away swiftly, her cloak billowing and her laughter tumbling through the sea wind. A gust swept across the hill, her skirts billowing to the side. With a snap, the prim little bonnet went flying. She did not release the reins to grab for it, or slow. The mare's gallop remained steady, fast, directed. They were halfway to the crest of the hill already. Eleanor intended to win.

Tristan shook his mighty head, playing the bit, impatient to be off.

"Can't let the ladies have it, can we, my friend?" Taliesin murmured to his horse.

The mare proved no match for the stallion. In a scant

quarter mile he passed her. Taliesin looked over his shoulder and Eleanor was laughing.

Laughing.

On the hill's apex he pulled his horse to a halt, dismounted, and turned to watch the woman and mare come. Breaking to a canter, Eleanor lifted a hand and swept sunlit locks from her cheeks. Her eyes glittered above flushed cheeks and her lips were parted, every feature brilliant with exhilaration and joy. And in the moment it required Taliesin to draw a single breath, he was right back where he'd stood when he first knew that he would always love her.

He'd spent the winter and spring teaching her how to ride—she not even a woman at fifteen, he barely a man. Galloping one day she fell off, but with wisdom and sufficient experience to direct her fall into a hill of fresh straw. Her landing proved easy. Gasping for air and eyes alight, she had laughed and laughed at her failure, tears of mirth dribbling down her cheeks as his heart raced. He'd said she'd grown too bold. She replied that it was because of him, that she would not have left the house all winter if he had not promised to teach her how to ride.

At that moment, he had known that whatever came—wherever his wandering life took him, and whatever she did to push him away as she always did—he would never stop loving her.

Stammering, he'd told her she was pretty. She laughed harder, called him an idiot, and lifted her hands for him to help her from the straw. He took her up and never wanted to let her go.

That night at the May Day festival, beneath the old oak in shadows cut by slivers of moonlight through branches, he kissed her for the first time. Years of dreaming and finally he found the courage. She did not shy away or object, but offered up her lips, pure and sacred, as the altar upon which he might worship. He'd known he shouldn't, that miles separated him from a gentleman's daughter, that she was his superior in every way. And yet she allowed him to kiss her, simply, briefly. Afterward, the promise in her eyes and playful smile on her lips carried him through the summer traveling through Devonshire with his uncle's family.

He'd been a fool. A young fool who'd known the absolute folly of his hopes, yet had hoped them anyway.

Watching her now he could force no words to his tongue, no taunt or even praise. He hadn't been tongue-tied in eleven years. Only this woman could do it to him.

"Well?" Gold dusted her eyes. "Aren't you going to gloat over your victory?"

He released Tristan and went to her horse's side. "Would it suit you if I behaved unsportsmanlike now?"

She unhooked her knee from the pommel to dismount. He lifted his arms and as naturally as if it hadn't been a decade since she'd last done so, she came down into his hands. Her waist was slender, the curve of her ribs soft.

She looked up into his eyes, her cheeks rosy with life. "You might marvel at what a bruising rider I have become."

"I might, if I ever used such a word." He held her beneath her arms and she did not seek to disengage herself.

"Bruising?" She laughed. "Isn't that word in your Gypsy lexicon?"

He spent so little time with other Rom now, he barely knew. He knew nothing, in fact, with her so close. The sunshine tangled in her hair that had come loose. His brain was shutting down, her body in his hands and her scent of wind and sea and honeysuckle all he knew.

"What a bruising rider you have become, Miss Caulfield." His voice scraped.

"I think I learned it so that I could gallop away from the life I was living if ever I wished to. I have done that, leaving my family to come on this ridiculous quest. I am doing that now." Her eyes widened. "Why have I told you this?"

"Because you know that I won't condemn you for it. I want my prize."

"Your prize?"

"For winning this challenge."

"Oh." Her breaths were swift. "But you have the stronger mount, and I am riding sidesaddle. This contest was not fair."

"Excuses? It seems you are shrinking from this adventure already."

Her eyes flashed. "I will win the next challenge. All right. You won this time. What prize will you claim?"

No single pair of pink lips should be so tempting.

"I claim a kiss."

The pink lips parted. Her gaze darted back and forth. "Wouldn't you rather I rub down your horse when we come to the next village? Or perhaps conjugate a few dozen Latin verbs?"

"That wouldn't be very courageous of you, would it?"

"No one said the prizes must require me to be courageous, only the challenges." She spoke breathlessly, her eyes everywhere but on his. "And why you imagine that allowing you to kiss me would require courage of me, I haven't the foggiest."

"You are afraid." God's blood, he hoped she was too afraid to meet this challenge. Because he was quite certain that he was now stepping into the biggest mistake he'd made in eleven years.

Chapter 8

The First Kiss

"**I**'m not afraid," Eleanor whispered. The wind swirled about her, whipping her skirts about his long legs where he trapped her between the horse and temptation. Her cheeks were fire, her hands ice. A half grin of brazen male confidence curved Taliesin's lips and she could no longer look away from them. They were perfect and she wanted, finally, to feel them against hers one more time. If she died an old spinster, at least she would die having kissed the most perfect lips in Christendom twice. Thrice, if she found the courage now.

"You aren't up to it," he said. "All dreams and no daring, is that it, *piran*—"

She pushed onto her toes and pressed her mouth to his.

There she thought it would end. But before she even had time to register the softness of his lips, the scent of his skin that she had remembered every night of her life for eleven years, his hand came around the back of her head, and he held her mouth to his and truly kissed her.

Coming home. Thrilling. Frightening. His lips upon hers the only reality.

He kissed her without haste, briefly first, and then again, as though tasting her. Warmth spread in her belly. Shame warred with it, and she could not look at him. *She wanted this too much.* Her eyes closed. Voluntarily blinded, she allowed herself to feel his strength and taste his flavor and know the closeness of him that she had dreamed about for years. She fed on sips of him and longed to feast.

She didn't entirely remember how it should be done; she had never really known. But he made it easy. Caressing her lips slowly, softly, he let her feel him. Then he took more. With his mouth he guided hers open and she felt all the heat of a summer day. She sank into him, touching him with only her lips as he held her securely with his hands, and she wept inside that *this* was the only thing he made easy for her. This caress. This intimate touching of lips and, fleetingly, tongues.

His hand came around her jaw and he urged her lips farther apart, and the kiss changed. His fingers threaded through her hair, his tongue her tormenter now, giving then taking away. He made her seek him, licking, drinking, *drinking him*, but never enough. Heat and need were everywhere and she felt as stripped and vulnerable as though she stood upon the hill naked, yet as powerful as a goddess. He *wanted* this. He wanted to kiss her.

The pad of his thumb passed along her cheekbone, his breath upon her lips, his lips touching hers again, claiming deeply, powerfully, as though he needed this too. Needed her.

Through the moan of the wind, the clatter of hooves and carriage wheels came from a distance. He released her.

Her eyes popped open to see him stepping back.

"Acceptable winnings," he said in a low voice.

"That wasn't an agreed-upon prize," she said, biting his flavor with her teeth.

"There were no agreed-upon prizes." He pivoted slowly on one fine boot heel, turning to his horse. "But if you're worried you will continue to lose, feel free to cancel this game at any time."

"I told you it isn't a game." There were no steady words in her throat. "And I will win next time."

"Then I will look forward to you claiming your prize." With a crooked grin, he took up the reins of his horse.

She sucked in salty wind, feeding now on the distance from him. "How am I to mount again?"

"There is a farmhouse ahead. We will walk there and stop for luncheon." He drew his horse from the grass beside the road. "It isn't far. It will allow you time to still your shaking knees before attempting to ride again."

"My knees are not shaking." *A lie.*

He offered her a skeptical brow and started up the road.

Fumbling with the reins, she drew them over the mare's ears. "This horse is a splendid runner. What is her name?"

"Iseult," he said over his shoulder.

A prickling tingle went up the back of her neck where he had held her. "And yours?"

"Tristan."

Her throat closed, but the wind separating them now as he walked ahead like he owned the road made it difficult for her to respond anyway.

Iseult, a princess of medieval tales. Tristan, a knight of Cornwall devoted to her, whose love was thwarted by a powerful king.

Somehow the scandalous adventure story of passion, magic, and betrayal had found its way into her papa's collection. She and Taliesin read nearly every book in his library, competing to prove which of them could read them all before the other. The story of Tristan and Iseult had been Taliesin's favorite. At the time, young and naïve, she hadn't understood why.

A shout came from behind. A boy rode a pony toward them. Passing the carriage, he raced forward.

"Miss!" he called. "Sir! Hold up!" He reined in, pulling off his cap to bow from the saddle. "Beggin' your pardon, miss, but my pa got to thinking today about what you asked him about that wreck. He sent me to tell you he'd remembered something you might like to know."

"You are the smith's son, aren't you? What did your father remember?"

"He said that a year or so back he had a visit from a fellow over at Drearcliffe who wanted him to break open an old box he'd found washed ashore. The thing was solid lead and soldered shut and he couldn't make heads or tails of it all sealed up like that."

"Drearcliffe? I don't know that village. Where is it?"

"Not a village, miss. It's old Sir Wilkie's place, 'bout four miles inland by the crow. Pa says you could go lookin' there. Sir Wilkie might have more old boxes like the one he wanted opened."

"What was in the box?"

"Papers and such." He wagged his head sorrowfully. "No treasure, miss."

Papers. From a box sealed in lead. Ships carried such boxes to protect the contents from water.

"Thank you. You have been very helpful." She smiled. But the boy's face only lit when Taliesin put a coin in his palm. The boy doffed his hat again, turned the pony about, and spurred it toward home.

Taliesin turned his attention upon her and quite abruptly she found her tongue useless. Her tongue that wanted to taste his again.

He bowed elegantly. "I await your command, my lady."

"Don't call me that. It's silly."

He laughed. "You really haven't changed, have you?"

If he meant that his teasing still drove her insane, and that she always wanted his black eyes upon her, then she had not in fact changed.

"To Drearcliffe?" she said. "Can you find the way?"

A hint of a smile showed again at the corner of his mouth. "I can find my way anywhere, princess. That is, after all, what I'm here for."

To help her make her way along the coast in the footsteps of Arabella and Luc's unsuccessful investigator. But Drearcliffe was not on the investigator's itinerary, just as kisses atop windswept hills weren't on hers.

Gathering the mare's reins and drawing her hood up about her ears, she ducked her head into the wind. Eyes on his shoulders, she followed him.

SHE HAD NEVER wanted to touch another man.

Years ago the squire's son, Thomas Shackelford, had tried to kiss her, the first time when she asked him to teach her how to drive his curricle. He let her drive them out of the village, then he'd taken the reins and slowed the carriage before putting his arm around her shoulders and his mouth on hers. She had pushed him away, and he had stiffly begged her pardon. But the following week he tried it again. At Christmas that year, after too much punch at his family's caroling party, he made another attempt.

Once one of her papa's tutoring students visiting St. Petroc for the term break from university had taken her hand while walking in the garden. He had tried to draw her near. She'd never regretted rejecting him.

Only once in her life had she ever wanted a man to touch her. Only once had she ever wanted to touch him too.

Late in her seventeenth year, a wave of heat beset northern Cornwall that had every window closed and everybody indoors in the cool shade of stone. The harvest was due in shortly, but the sun beat down on that September like a flogging to the earth. Not a soul stirred in fields or pastures.

Not a soul except the Gypsy boy who had worked at the vicarage every day of every autumn, winter, and spring since Eleanor had lived there. Sitting beneath the cherry tree heavy with fruit, writing in her notebook and trying not to drift off to sleep in the heat, she looked up and saw him walking toward the garden gate. She hadn't seen him since the night of May Day four months earlier when he kissed her. She hadn't even known that his family had returned to St. Petroc.

He did not open the gate, but halted on the other side of it and said, "Come for a walk."

No greeting. Nothing except what she had wanted for four months and what frightened her the most—to be alone with him again. Nerves spinning, she set down her pencil and notebook and went.

They walked for hours, talking and laughing, a little

flushed, each of them uncertain, she thought. They had known each other for years, doing chores and studying side-by-side, and he'd taught her to ride. But they had never done this. They had never simply been together for the sake of that alone. When she looked aside at him as they walked, she felt like she was tumbling through air.

Indeed, she could not stop looking at him. Something had changed in him over the summer. His hair was still far too long, his eyes still like coal, his jaw steeply angled and skin darker than ever from the summer sun. He didn't look like an Englishman and yet she thought he was the most beautiful creature she had ever seen. She had never wanted to stare at Thomas Shackelford. She had never wanted to walk forever with him, or with any other boy.

The woods with their shadows beckoned and they found themselves in a clearing with a pond. The day sweltered, heat radiating in the dapples of sunlight between the trees, flowers in riotous bloom in the humid air, bees buzzing about and dragonflies speeding between water reeds.

"That water looks heavenly." She dabbed moisture from her brow with a kerchief. She wanted to dab her neck and lip too, but she was not allowed to touch any intimate part of herself in a boy's presence, even if she was dripping.

He looked at her for a moment, a peculiar study she did not understand. Then he unfastened the top button of his coat.

"We may as well cool off." One button after another loosened until the coat hung open and her mouth hung agape. Gypsy men always went around bundled up to their chins with shirts, waistcoats, coats, neck cloths, overcoats, and hats. Taliesin rarely wore a hat, preferring to turn girls' heads with his satiny black locks, she supposed. And she'd seen his poorly shod feet plenty of times. But she had never seen a Gypsy man remove so much as a kerchief from his pocket.

Now he removed his coat entirely. Then he pulled off his boots.

She stared. She knew she should not watch him undress, but desperate curiosity seized her. She resisted it, turning away as if to study the pond and clamping her attention on it.

"Cool off in that?" she said with forced skepticism.

"Where else?"

She heard something drop to the ground. A garment? She peeked. His waistcoat lay on the grass with his coat. He was unknotting his neck cloth.

"I suppose it would be refreshing to dip my toes in." The thought of removing her shoes in his presence made her heartbeats thump. And Papa would scold if she caught a chill. Her lungs could not endure it. But the day sweltered, and her shoes pinched dreadfully. Cooling her feet would feel spectacular. "For a minute, perhaps."

"Not only your toes, *pirani*." She could always hear it in his voice when he laughed at her.

"What?" She looked around at him. "Do you think I should wade all the way into this pond? As though I were bathing at the sea?" She'd been to the seaside but was never allowed to bathe. The water was too cold, Papa said, and her constitution too weak. Still, she longed to. But this was just a puddle, really. In such heat it couldn't possibly harm her.

"I do." His neck was exposed, dark and sinewy with strength, his hair falling around his shirt collar.

"With you?" Dragonflies alighted in her belly now. "At the same time as you?"

He smiled slightly, provokingly. "Frightened?"

She laughed derisively. "Of three feet of water?"

Slowly he shook his head.

"Of you?" She gulped. Then she jerked her chin away and crossed her arms. "Never."

"Then why not? Nobody's around for miles. No one will know."

No one will know. Like no one knew anything of this. Of them. Of the time they spent alone together. The winter and spring before, she hadn't told anyone about him teaching her how to ride—not her papa or Ravenna or even Arabella, who wasn't shy with boys. Her sisters cared for Taliesin like a brother, and Papa held him in great affection. Still, she couldn't tell them, and not only because Papa didn't want her exerting herself.

When she'd gone out in Thomas Shackelford's curricle along the village lane, nobody thought anything of it. He was the squire's son, and she the vicar's daughter. The tailor had tipped his cap from the doorway of his shop and the draper smiled at them fondly as the dust rose behind the carriage wheels.

But none of the church ladies or shopkeepers of St. Petroc would understand *this*.

His family's rules were just as strict. They sold trinkets and horses to the residents of St. Petroc and the surrounding villages, but they only truly mingled at the May Day fair. The smith was friendly with them, and Papa, of course. Otherwise, the Gypsies kept to themselves and the people of St. Petroc obliged them. Everyone abided by the invisible barriers.

If anyone discovered they had gone walking today, there would be a price to pay on both sides. Both of them were breaking the rules. But that was not the reason she'd hidden it from her family. Now, with her heart dancing in her throat, she could not deny the reason. Doing this—being with him—felt wrong.

It felt wrong because it felt too right.

"I don't wish to go in." She tilted up her nose. "It will sully my gown and Papa would scold." And ask questions. Questions she could not answer truthfully.

Taliesin didn't respond. Finally she turned her head. He wore only his shirt and trousers. "Then take it off," he said.

"Take it off?" she uttered dumbly.

"Your dress." The provoking smile returned, but something else shone in his black eyes that made her heartbeats stumble. "You are afraid," he said with complete assurance.

Not afraid. *Terrified*. "I am not."

"Prove it."

"I don't have to prove it to *you*." She gave him the scoff she'd been perfecting on him since she was nine.

The intensity left his eyes and he shrugged. "Suit yourself. But I'm going in." He climbed down the bank to the water's murky edge. She watched him close his eyes, long dark lashes dropping, and his face registered perfect pleasure as he walked into the pond without tripping or slipping on the rocks. He moved now just like he mounted a horse, with confidence and ease, the way he did everything. He was as comfortable in water as anywhere.

Jealousy and frustration and yearning gathered in her breast.

"It looks like tepid broth," she said, trying not to stare at his shoulders. Threadbare at the seams, his shirt pulled from one side to the other. They'd gotten wider over the summer—his shoulders. She didn't know how she knew this, except that when he'd stood near earlier, she'd felt small beside him for the first time ever. "How is it?"

"Feels like that heaven you mentioned," he said, wading into the middle of the pond, the water rising to his knees then higher, soaking his trousers. He glanced over his shoulder at her. "The one your father's always preaching about."

"How would you know? You don't go to church."

"It may be that I don't need to go to church to know what heaven is." The tail of his shirt dipped in the water. He lifted it out and squeezed it, and silvery sparkles leaped on the pond's surface. "Are you coming in or not?"

"I already said I'm not. I don't wish to."

He looked up at her. "You sure about that?"

Beneath her shift, moisture trickled between her shoulder blades and down the gully of her breasts. The boy in the pond who had become a man over the summer looked cool as autumn rain.

Then in one fluid movement he pulled his shirt up his waist and over his head, and tossed it onto the reeds by the bank. He shook out his hair, and a slow, goading grin lifted the side of his mouth.

"Come on, *pirani*. Now it's your turn."

She couldn't breathe and the oppressive heat was not the cause. She had never seen such a thing and knew she should not be seeing it now. But she could not tear her eyes away. Lean and muscled from shoulder to belly, he stood before her without shame. He swept up a handful of water and splashed it across his chest and she stared like a pauper at a shiny guinea. As she watched his palm slide down his tawny skin, her knees went wobbly.

Only one wish battered at her: to be next to him, as close as possible to that raw maleness that was thoroughly alien yet belonged to the boy she had known for years. She *needed* to be near him.

She had to go into that water.

But what if a chill took her lungs and she had to explain how it had happened?

She couldn't.

Taliesin's grin penetrated her panic: pure goading deviltry. She could not refuse this challenge, no matter the consequences.

With sticky-hot fingers it took her some time to unfasten her sweat-dampened gown and the ribbons of her petticoat. Wearing her stockings, shift, and simple cotton corset, she half walked, half slid down the bank into the water. He came forward and when she slipped on the slimy rocks, he grabbed her hand and steadied her, and the muscles in the enthralling landscape of his chest shifted. Eleanor's lungs ceased to function.

He released her as soon as she found her footing. The water soaked through her skirts to her skin, her legs, cool and secret. He did not move away, but stood right before her as if challenging her to acknowledge that something was happening here.

So she did.

"I have never before seen a man's bared chest."

"I don't suppose you have."

It looked smooth. Firm. Vital. *Touchable.* Longing curled in her, urging her to get closer still. He was everything familiar, known her entire life it seemed, always there, always plaguing her, and yet now something entirely alien too, male and thrilling. "I . . . I want to touch . . . it." *Him.* Her mouth was dry. She licked her lips to wet them. "May I?"

His gaze seemed fixed on her mouth. "Not such a good idea."

Pique pricked at her. "You made me come in here, leave my clothing on the bank, and you removed your shirt. Now you're turning craven?"

"Didn't exactly expect you to say you want to touch me, *pirani.* Didn't think you were that kind of girl."

What kind of girl? At his family's summer camps did he know other girls? Other vicars' daughters? Did he teach them how to ride and walk with them in the woods? Did he remove his shirt and make them wild to be closer to him?

"Don't you want me to?"

"I want you to." His breathing sounded rough. "Too much."

She barely touched him, brushing her fingertips across his chest, his heat and the taut softness of his flesh a sudden revelation. He was so strong and beautiful and free and perfect, and he made her want to be beautiful and free and wild too. He always had. Stroking her fingertips along the ridge of bone that cut from his shoulder to his chest, her hands started to shake.

And quite abruptly she understood that everything she had ever wanted was standing right in front of her.

This boy. She didn't want to best him. She simply wanted *him.*

Overwhelmed, filled with feeling and confused, she dropped her hand and sank it beneath the water's surface, ashamed that he might think she trembled because of fear.

"My turn," he said in a low voice.

"Your turn?"

With the grace of physical strength she had always envied in him, he cupped his broad palm, dipped it into the water, and took up a glimmering handful. His hand tilted and the water drizzled over her shoulder. She gasped from the sudden freshness, and sighed upon a smile. Then he did it again, this time over her breast. It was cool and felt miraculously good as it trickled beneath the shift and dampened her nipple. Alive with sensation, from her lips to her fingertips and oddly in her belly, she giggled.

For once he did not laugh. With utter reverence he brushed the backs of his fingers along the side of her breast. Eleanor's breaths stole from between her lips in little stutters. Delicious, quivering weakness eddied through her. The expression of worship on his face and the tingles in her body made her gulp back more sighs. Then he cupped his hand around her breast.

"Aren't you going to tell me to stop?"

"I should." She couldn't seem to get enough air. "Do you want me to?"

With heavy, uneven breaths he squeezed her breast gently. It was not unpleasant—rather, astonishingly pleasant. *Pleasurable*. Her eyelids felt thick, the damp heat of the day and the quiet sounds of trickling water and birds all around, and his hand touching her as he should not, making her wish he would touch her *more*, making her feel wicked. Wanton.

"I like it," she whispered. "I think that makes me a bawd. Or perhaps a Jezebel."

He dropped his hand. "It's best we go now," he said tightly.

"I'm still hot." *Mesmerized*. "Aren't you?" She slid her fingertips along his forearm corded with strength. He was made so differently than she, his skin thicker than hers and taut over muscle and big bones. Strong. Every bit of him drew her, fascinated her, made her weak with a strange sort of yearning. How many times she had sat beside him laboring over texts without noticing anything except how much more quickly he was accomplishing a task? Now she wanted to memorize him, to know every part of this new Taliesin, the muscle and sinew and new depth of his voice. Her fingertips reveled in him, in his texture.

"Eleanor," he said deeply, his chest rising. He never called her Eleanor. Sometimes he called her Vicar's Girl, but mostly that Gypsy word.

She ran her fingers along the water's surface, then smoothed them over his shoulder wrapped with muscle. The streak of moisture glistened on his skin.

As if in response, jittery heat darted all through her. She did it again and an animal sound came from his chest. It didn't repel her. It made her feel good. It made her ache. *Deeply.* The need to explore him, to know him, swelled beneath her ribs and in her belly. She trailed her fingertips down the hard center of his chest to his waist.

"*Eleanor.*" He reached forward, grasped her behind the neck with his big, callused hand, and brought their mouths together.

She had always assumed that a kiss satisfied a need. It didn't. It made the need greater. From the first fumbling meeting of lips, through the learning, the knowing of shape and pressure, and tasting, to the melding of mouths in frantic rhythm, she discovered that kissing him once was not enough. Kissing him twice made her want even more. She'd been waiting for this all summer and now she couldn't get enough. He must feel it too, this longing that surged with each meeting of lips, each breath drawn from the same air.

His hands came around her face, sinking into her hair and holding her close as their mouths consumed. Their tongues met. Retreated. Met again. Twined together. Tongues. Lips. Hands. He licked her teeth like he was licking preserves from them, and it felt astonishingly wonderful. Everything was real, natural, and desperate for more. The more he kissed her, the more of his kisses she wanted. The more she wanted *him.*

This *could not* be right.

She broke free, gasping for air. "I—"

"God's blood, *pirani,*" he blasphemed, wrapped his arms around her, and in one movement brought their bodies together, and their mouths.

Chest to chest, thigh to thigh, arms around her, he held her tight and she let him kiss her. And she kissed him. She clutched his back and wicked, torrential thrills crashed through her along with the certainty that nothing could feel so right as the hard length of his body pressed to hers and her mouth under his. Nothing could *be* so right. Nothing.

He dragged her off him and backed away, water eddying out around him. His chest heaved, a tawny rippling of shadows and sunshine that made her tender lips fall open in awe.

"You've got to go."

"I know." Dazed, panting, she stared at him. "I do? Why?"

"Men aren't built to stop once it gets going. And I don't want to stop with you. I'd never want to stop with you." His eyes looked feverish. "But I know I can't have what I want."

She nodded. Everything inside her seemed to be rushing forward. Toward him. "What happens now?"

"You go, and I cool down."

"And we talk later." She attempted a little smile. "When we're dry and dressed again?"

"If that's what you want."

She wanted him to kiss her again. She wanted it with a sweet sort of desperation she'd never before felt. She wanted more than anything to press her palms to his smooth, hot skin and feel his heartbeat pounding as quickly as hers. She wanted him to put his strong arms around her and make her feel not weak and vulnerable, as everyone except him seemed to think she perpetually was, but powerful. Powerful that she could inspire this fever in his black eyes. But she said, "All right."

He remained in the pool while she climbed the bank, took up her clothes, and donned them as best she could. The wet shift clung to her legs as she dressed in a haze. She didn't realize until later that he must have seen everything there was to see of her through the soaked linen. She didn't realize it even the following day, after he did not come to the vicarage, and after he was not at the horse corral when it came time for her afternoon ride.

Instead she went about with her head in the clouds and her toes two inches above the ground, a jumble of nerves in anticipation for the next time they would meet.

Tonight? Would he kiss her in the moonlight as he had the first time? Or tomorrow morning would he take her to the old oak and kiss her there again? Now that this *thing* had happened between them, they would have to tell Papa. Wouldn't they? Or would they keep it a secret from everyone? When no one was watching would they hold hands and steal kisses that made her knees weak? She wanted to shout her feelings to the world. She couldn't imagine her feet ever touching the ground again.

Then she heard her papa telling Ravenna that, since Taliesin had gone, he expected her to see to the task of scooping out the ashes from the grate.

"I don't know why he had to leave so soon," Ravenna complained, "when he'd just arrived."

"Gone?" Eleanor stood in the parlor doorway, her stomach a knot. "The Gypsies have gone?"

"Only Taliesin," Papa said distractedly, opening a book upon his knee.

He had *gone*? After only three days back in St. Petroc? Without telling her? "To where, Papa?"

He turned pages. "North, I believe."

Had he come and told Papa he was leaving, yet not said good-bye to her? Everywhere was north from Cornwall. Her chest felt too tight for full breaths, as though the sickness in her lungs had returned but *so much worse*.

"Has he gone for a short trip?" She didn't care that

her words might reveal her. She'd never before felt such longing and joy and perfect aching. She wanted to see him. She must see him or she would burst with this feeling. He needn't kiss her if he couldn't. She could be content with speaking with him, feeling his ebony eyes upon her. That would be enough. It *had* to be enough.

"He is unlikely to return until the spring," her papa said. "His uncle has interests that he needs Taliesin to see to in . . . where was that? Bristol, perhaps. Fetch my spectacles, child. I can never make out Professor Hinkle's writing without them."

The spring? An eon away. A *lifetime*.

Yet he had said nothing of it. Instead, without a word he had abandoned her in a strange confusion of yearning. Indeed, he had encouraged her to it, seeking her out immediately upon his return to St. Petroc, inviting her to walk with him, urging her into that pond, then kissing her and bringing every bit of her to life.

A more measured mind—a mind as measured as everyone believed hers to be—would have tucked away her longing, to retrieve again when he returned. A more sanguine character would have gone on with her usual modest amusements and her work, and brushed off the niggling suspicion that he had teased her to a purpose. Because Taliesin Wolfe had never *not* taunted her into doing things she shouldn't do. Since she could remember, he had taken pleasure in challenging her. Simply to prove that he could best her.

This time he had succeeded. With her head flying above the clouds, she couldn't deny it. Eager to see him again, with warm cheeks and memories of their forbidden adventure, she'd been thinking of nothing except him for days, combing her hair, cleaning her teeth, dressing in her finest frock. All for him. She'd even found his favorite book to lend him, the story of

Tristan and Iseult he liked so much even though it was so tragic. She'd done all this thinking of him.

While he had gone off to Bristol without a single word.

But he would not best her for long.

With that intention, she spent the winter translating Latin texts for her papa, riding the old cart horse every day, and avoiding the copse where a Gypsy boy had coaxed her into the pond, kissed her, then told her to go. And she planned for spring. On holidays when Tommy Shackelford came home, she asked him to teach her how to drive his curricle so that in the spring she could drive it right past Taliesin with her nose in the air and prove that he didn't do everything better than her after all. He knew how to drive a wagon, but she didn't think he'd ever driven a curricle. Two could play at this game, and she wasn't about to let him win.

It was the longest winter of her life.

When finally he returned, even taller and broader and more bone-meltingly beautiful than eight months earlier, she was ready for him, entirely prepared to hold her own against any challenge he could throw at her, and so eager for more kisses she trembled with anticipation.

She saw him first at the May Day fair. Across the field crowded with people, in the trading corral he was mounted on one of his uncle's half-broken horses, handling it as easily as a knight on a charger. Nerves a-kindle, she waited for her opportunity to get the best of him.

Then, nothing.

No visit to the vicarage. No finding her when she was alone and teasing her or walking with her or holding her hand or kissing her. Nothing.

The day after the fair, the Gypsies departed.

It was only later, much later—after he did not return

that fall, instead sent a letter telling Papa that he'd found permanent work up north and would not be returning to St. Petroc again—that she knew she had mistaken it. After the pond he had not been trying to challenge her. He had gone without saying good-bye to her not because he thought he would get the best of her, but because he simply didn't think of her at all. When he'd taught her to ride, walked with her, kissed her, he had merely been a boy passing the time, and she meant so little to him that he'd swiftly forgotten her.

Unaccustomed as she was to her new feelings, and not comprehending how longtime admiration could turn to indifference, it took some time for her to understand it all. But eventually she did. As months passed and she realized what it meant to truly miss him, to be forced to accept that he was never coming back, it seemed certain that this time she had been the only one playing the game. The only one foolish enough to fall in love.

Chapter 9

The Dungeon

*D*rearcliffe sat on the flank of an ancient wood, a dark, ominous hulk of ivy-encrusted stone fashioned into imposing gables decorated with Gothic pinnacles, and all of it surrounded by a high wall. To the west, a hill rose steadily to an apex topped with a lonely church tower.

A pack of dogs rushed to the gate, snarling and gnawing at the bars as if they meant to chew through to mount their attack.

Taliesin's horse looked down his long nose and offered them a contemptuous snort. But the less seasoned mare was restive beneath Eleanor. Guiding her mount to a pile of toppled stones, she slid out of the saddle and onto the stones awkwardly. Anything to avoid his hands on her again.

The coach drew up behind them and Betsy alighted.

"Glory be, miss," she said, her eyes as wide as Eleanor had yet seen them. "We're not going in *there* to look for clues, are we? We'd more likely find ghosts."

"We are going inside, Betsy. But you needn't fret. I'm certain Sir Wilkic is perfectly amiable."

A servant with patched elbows, faded knee breeches, and torn stockings came from the house and calmed the dogs by scattering a handful of biscuits on the pebbles. With a beleaguered air and a ring of keys larger than at least two of the dogs, he unlocked the gate and swung it wide on rusted hinges.

"This rabblerash won't bite," he said in the thick roll of the coast. "They pretend they're fierce, but every one of them is a cowardly varmut."

"Thank you. I am—"

"No need to tell me." He waved impatiently. "Won't remember anyway. Come to see the master, and I'll take you to him. He's in the dungeon, it being Tuesday. The boy there'll take your beasts. They'll be well cared for. If they're not, the master'll flay the whelp alive."

The stable boy, a lad of no more than eight, took the mare's lead from Eleanor's hand and gave her an enormous wink.

Betsy cowered close as they approached the door. "Do you believe in ghosts, miss?"

"I don't believe that anything from the past can harm me unless I allow it to, Betsy." Stealing a glance at the man beside her, she found his eyes quite serious upon the building's facade.

"Very wise," he said.

Sir Wilkie's servant ushered them forward. Within, all was cold and damp and stuffed to the ceilings with objects. To one side of the foyer, chairs of all sizes and fabrics were stacked one on top of another. The other side seemed decorated by a mad artist, with easels and half-finished paintings and palettes of paint all cluttered together, cups of paintbrushes and old rags like mismatched rainbows scattered throughout.

"This way. This way." The servant gestured past the stairwell and to a door at the rear of the foyer.

Betsy dug her heels into the floor. "I'm not going down into a dungeon, miss. I'll stay right here and wait for you, if you don't mind."

"Why don't you find the kitchen and call up some tea for us all? I think it's likely we'll find there isn't a mistress here."

Betsy nodded, cast Taliesin a narrowed glance, and disappeared through a door behind a stack of chairs.

Taliesin held the door open for her and she went before him into the bowels of Drearcliffe Manor. The space darkened swiftly as she descended and her feet sought each steep step more slowly than the last. The glow of firelight came behind her. Taliesin passed a candle to her.

"Ah," she said, accepting it. "You have been in dungeons before, I assume."

"You assume correctly."

At the base of the stair she halted. The air here was dryer than above, smelling of dust and resonant of glue. The candle illuminated piles upon piles of books. Stacked against the walls, books by the hundreds made a narrow corridor of brown and red and blue and green that glimmered with dull gold.

"Sir Wilkie is an avid reader, it seems," the man at her shoulder said.

"He is a hoarder." She ran her fingertip along the

closest bindings and brought it away dusty. "He keeps things, even things he does not wish to keep, because he cannot rid himself of them. Even though he might try, it is too painful for him to let them go."

"I can understand that well enough."

She turned her face up to his. Deep eyes. Sculpted mouth. Satin hair. Her hands wanted to touch all of him. Longing lashed her thoughts and strapped her belly.

"You should not have kissed me," she whispered.

He leaned in, surrounding her in the tight space. "Actually." His eyes scanned her features, resting finally upon her lips. "You kissed me."

"I—"

"Ussel now, miss! Sir!" Sir Wilkie's manservant called from beyond the books. "The master's waiting."

She pivoted and followed the corridor between the stacks, glad of the dark that hid her fiery cheeks. Gradually the stack to her right descended from the ceiling to head height, then lower, revealing the thick bars of a jail cell against which were piled yet more books on the other side.

An opening appeared to her left. Sir Wilkie's servant stood just within.

The cell was not terribly large, and decorated with more stacked books. A squat, coal-burning stove was the source of the dry air. Beside it was a small writing table and a large, comfortable leather chair with a gentleman of advanced years ensconced in it. Scraggly gray hair topped with an old wig and tied with a ribbon framed a face lined with wrinkles. A pair of shrewd, bespectacled lapis lazuli gems peered at her.

"Who are you and what do you want?" His voice was rough and as aged as his velvet coat and breeches.

"I am Eleanor Caulfield." She curtsied. "This is my traveling companion, Mr. Wolfe."

His sharp blue eyes focused tighter. "A Gypsy, eh?" He made an impatient gesture to his servant. "Mr. Fiddle, lock up the silver. Can't be too careful with a Gypsy in the house."

"Yes, sir," Mr. Fiddle said, and departed.

"I don't suppose it would relieve you to know that I haven't any interest in your silver." Taliesin glanced about. "Your books, on the other hand, would make quite the library in my house. I've just the room for it."

"Aha, speak like a gentleman, do you? Dress like one too. But I've seen my fair share of cozeners, young man. I'll not be bamboozled by a wolf in sheep's clothing." Sir Wilkie scowled. "Well. Speak up, missy. I'm a busy man. I can't be bothered by every pretty young thing that comes calling. What is it you want? If it's to poach in my wood, I won't have it. Smelled shot smoke yesterday beyond the ford. I've never heard of a Gypsy hunting with a firearm. More likely to eat what's already dead and call it the Almighty's blessing. But if it was some other menfolk of yours"—he pointed a bony finger at her—"then you'd best tell them to hare off my land or I'll send Fiddle with the Manton to flush 'em out."

"I'm sorry to hear that you must endure poachers, Sir Wilkie," she said. "But I can assure you we have only just arrived at this hour. I understand that you collect odd objects, and have in your possession items that have washed ashore. Items from shipwrecks." She didn't know why she should be clutching her fingers together tightly now, nor why the ring that Arabella had given her seemed especially heavy in her pocket.

"Interested in a shipwreck, are you?" His eyes narrowed. "Which one?"

"Unfortunately, I don't know. It happened twenty-three years ago. I don't suppose you've been collecting items since then?"

He scowled. "I've been collecting since I was a lad, and I'm not a day under seventy."

"Could I perhaps see the items that you have collected from the sea, sir? I would be tremendously grateful."

"I don't give a sow's ear for your gratitude, missy. I haven't got the time or the patience to gather every scrap of wreckage in this house for your perusal."

"But, sir, I—"

"Don't 'But, sir' me, missy. I've said no and that's an end to it." He stood up. "Now where's Fiddle gone to? He'll show you out. Did you ride? Come in a carriage? He'll make sure your animals get what they need."

"Sir Wilkie." She moved toward him. Where her skirt brushed against his writing table it pressed the ring into her thigh. "If you would be so kind as to let me look about your house a bit before we leave, I would—"

"Look about my house? What'll you be demanding next, I wonder? Peeking in my drawers while I'm still wearing them? Aha! That's made her color up when her nosy presumption didn't."

"Oh." The notion of Sir Wilkie's drawers strangled her. "I don't think—"

"Sir." Taliesin's voice was deep. He did not step forward or move, but all at once his shadowy presence seemed to fill the small space. "Miss Caulfield has the most benign interest in your house and belongings, and she has requested your assistance without demanding that you disturb yourself unreasonably. She deserves your apology."

Sir Wilkie's bright blue eyes bulged. "Well . . . I . . ."

"I agree." The voice came from behind her, clear and firm. A young man stood in the opening of the doorway, his guinea bright hair making a contrast with the gloom of the dungeon library.

"Sir Wilkie has spoken atrociously, madam," he said with an easy smile. "And he must apologize at once or I shan't remain."

"Young jackanapes." Sir Wilkie glared. He cast an agitated glance at Taliesin, and bowed. Then with another glare at both men, he slumped back down in his chair. "She's welcome to look. But if she removes a single item, I'll run them both off my property." A defiant jaw jutted toward Taliesin.

"And that, I'm afraid, is all that he is likely to oblige us," the stranger said to Taliesin. A rueful grin spread good humor across his chiseled features.

"Thank you, sir," Eleanor said. "You are kind to help."

Taliesin remained silent, his attention intent upon the newcomer.

"I understand you have only just arrived," the stranger said. "Why don't we all go upstairs and enjoy some refreshments while Fiddle collects the items you wish to see?"

"I should like that." The ring burned against her leg. "But who, may I ask, is proffering the invitation?"

He stepped forward into the lamplight and made an elegant bow. "Welcome to Drearcliffe, Miss Caulfield." His bright blue eyes upon her were appreciative. He nodded to Taliesin. "Mr. Wolfe." His attention returned to her. "I am Sir Wilkie's grandson. My name is Robin Prince."

Chapter 10

The Prophecy

T

*R*obin *Prince.*

Eleanor stared. Rather, she gaped. She had never fully believed nor disbelieved in the Gypsy fortune that she and her sisters had heard years ago. But *this* . . . this coincidence was too remarkable.

The ring seemd to want to burn a hole in her pocket.

"Thank you," Taliesin said and touched his hand to her lower back.

It was the slightest connection, barely contact at all, only to direct her toward the door. But Eleanor's heartbeats fell over themselves. He had never before touched her like this, in public, familiarly. Possessively.

Her face snapped up to him.

The black eyes were again shadowed. "After you," he said quietly, on the edge of the growl she'd heard only once.

"Yes." Her throat was empty. "Of course."

Mr. Prince's smile slipped. He turned his back to them and led them upstairs.

She drew away from Taliesin's hand and followed Mr. Prince, a confusion of fantastical notions cluttering her head.

Could Arabella have understood the fortune wrongly? Had the soothsayer obscured its meaning intentionally? Was their identity to be discovered not through marriage to royalty but to a man *named* Prince? None of them had ever met a man with such a name. It seemed too incredible that she would now, while searching for their parents, within reach of the answers she and her sisters had sought for so long.

And yet, even with this astonishing turn in her quest, all her thoughts were upon the man behind her and the sensation of that slight touch that had, for the briefest moment, declared to the other two men in the room that she was his.

"GRANDFATHER ISN'T THE troll he seems." Robin Prince smiled at Eleanor and accepted a cup of tea from her hands. "He's shut up here in this house most of the time, with only old Fiddle and his dogs for company. He forgets how to speak to people. By tomorrow he'll have improved his manners."

She poured another cup, all the while her golden green eyes fixed on Prince. "By tomorrow? Really?"

Prince chuckled. "In truth, no. But I shouldn't wish

you to call off your project in fear of his crotchets. He's got a good heart beneath it all, and I don't think he likes his house like this any more than I do. Why, he's just had his library renovated, every book rebound and the entire collection organized. If only he can empty the actual library of all the clutter so he can use it for the books, that will be a true victory." He laughed and sat down on the sofa close to her. "Now, do tell me more about your research project, then I will see what Fiddle can do to help."

To reach the drawing room he'd brought them through a dining chamber cluttered with dishes and a parlor lined with stacks of yellowing journals tied with string. The drawing room housed a dusty collection of stuffed and mounted animals, from fox to birds to heads of deer. But the chairs were clear of objects, and the table upon which the serving man had set refreshments boasted only one upright hare, arranged on its stand so that its whiskered nose pointed at Prince. As though it were sniffing him. As though it had reason to.

Taliesin had traveled the breadth of England, and most of Wales and Scotland. He had forgotten few people he'd met along the way. That he remembered Robin Prince as though he had encountered him the day before, however, was certainly because that encounter had happened on the most memorable day of his life. The day he had both won and lost the girl he loved.

That girl, now a woman, was staring at Prince as though he had descended from the heavens upon wings. Not angelic wings. Rather, the sort that fell from the heavens abruptly. The familiar crease in her brow had become a notch at the bridge of her nose, her jaw taut. Her hand had slipped into her pocket and bunched into a fist outlined by the cloth.

"Twenty-three years ago," she said, "my two sisters and I washed up on shore not far from here."

"Washed up? Good heavens." Prince leaned toward her, his brow now mimicking hers.

"Our ship wrecked and we were the only survivors. We were saved by my infant sister's cradle and our cot, and a portion of the cabin wall to which our cot was attached. Our rescuers told us that the pieces had remained stuck together and made a sort of raft. If a fisherman had not happened upon us, we would not have survived."

"How glad I am for that fisherman," Prince said earnestly. He seemed to mean it. He was an ingratiating man, and Taliesin didn't think that attitude was false. "I must send him a message of thanks straight off," Prince added with another smile.

She dipped her lashes. Pleased. Perhaps flustered. Prince dressed like he'd just rolled in from Brighton, with style but without undue ostentation. He looked exactly like an old school friend of Thomas Shackelford's would: comfortably prosperous and modestly fashionable.

He had given Taliesin nothing more than the perusal of one man to another. Prince did not recognize him. Of course.

"Thank you, Mr.—Mr. Prince," she said with halting breaths that lifted her breasts in gentle jerks. Prince's attention descended, then snapped back to her face when she continued.

"We left the village soon after our rescue. The officers of the village could find no other trace of our ship, or even hint of its destination. They sent to London, but no one was looking for us."

"Your parents perished in the wreck, I presume," he said with great concern. "I am terribly sorry for it."

"They did not. Our mother had sent us with our

nurse, and we were to be met by our father, I think. But at which port or on what day, we never knew. We don't even know our real surname."

"You must have been very young, for you say this happened twenty-three years ago? You say your sister was an infant, but you must have yourself been one as well."

"Not at all. I am the eldest. I was four at the time. I've just told you all I remember of it."

The bald flattery had passed her by. Taliesin almost smiled.

Beyond the window, a carriage entered through the open gate and approached the house.

"Your sisters have burdened you with this task of uncovering your past?" Prince asked.

"Not entirely. My sister who is one year my junior is now the Duchess of Lycombe, and my youngest sister is now wed to the son of the Marquess of Airedale. They are both busy, as you might imagine, while I have little to do. I was glad to take up this quest and make myself useful."

Prince's eyes widened almost imperceptibly, but he masked his surprise. Leaning forward, he took the empty teacup from her hands and set it on the table.

"I will be honored to assist in your search to the utmost of my ability. My grandfather's house is filled with trinkets fished from the ocean or discovered on beaches the length of this coast. I'm certain that with thorough application we shall find a clue from your ship that will direct you toward your parents. In fact I have every confidence."

"Thank you." She stood up. "Shall we begin now?"

He rose to his feet with a bemused smile. "Wouldn't you like to settle in first? Perhaps take a stroll about the park before dinner?"

"Settle in? Dinner? Do you mean here? Oh, I don't think—"

"You must stay at Drearcliffe while we are investigating your shipwreck." The *we* slipped off Prince's tongue naturally. "I will not have it otherwise. The closest inn is miles away. Far too distant for convenience." He turned to Taliesin. "Have you made other plans, Mr. Wolfe?"

"I haven't."

She turned her face to him, a mingling of fear and hope in her eyes that twisted the knot in Taliesin's gut.

"But—" she began.

"No. It's settled," Prince said. "You will be our guests at Drearcliffe until we have uncovered the mystery of your past." He smiled warmly. "I insist."

"Thank you," she said with odd hesitation. "You are very kind."

With a squeal of hinges, the drawing room door burst open and two women entered.

"Good gracious, Robin. You rode like the wind was behind you," the woman in front said brightly, wiping her gloved fingertips with a kerchief. "But I suppose it was! Wretched Cornish wind. In the five yards from the carriage to the door it positively destroyed my coiffure, and I had maintained it splendidly all day in the carriage." She patted the hat atop her curls and made a pretty scowl. Her eyes, two spots of blue, alighted upon Eleanor. "Hello!" She extended her hand. "I am Mrs. Upchurch and this is my sister, Miss Henrietta Prince. Who are you?"

"Miss Caulfield and Mr. Wolfe," Prince said to Eleanor, "I am pleased to make you acquainted with my sisters."

"We are here to celebrate Grandfather's birthday, or we shouldn't have come to this dark and dingy house in this wretchedly cold season," Mrs. Upchurch said gaily, grasping Eleanor's hand. She perused Taliesin with a quick flutter of lashes and curtsied. "How do you do, sir?"

Her sister, barely more than a girl, stared at him, colored up, and dropped her eyes to the floor.

Mrs. Upchurch turned to Eleanor. "My brother, the tease, did not tell me we were to have company on this visit. But I am ever so glad he kept the secret or I should have been impatient on the drive. Now we shall have an excuse for a party and Sir Wilkie will not be allowed to scold."

"I held nothing back from you, Fanny. Upon my honor," Prince said with a smile for everyone. "Miss Caulfield and Mr. Wolfe have come to search Grandfather's collections for items from a shipwreck that occurred years ago. It is our good fortune that they happened to visit Drearcliffe while we are here."

"Good fortune, indeed!" his sister said. "Ever since my dear Henry perished on that horrid battlefield, I have had to fill my lonely hours with projects to busy my hours. Whatever your task, Miss Caulfield, I shall be an avid, experienced assistant."

"Thank you. I will be glad for your help." She said it simply, honestly. In character she had changed little. And yet, lovelier now, matured into a quiet elegance in company, she looked more like a fine lady than the daughter of a poor village vicar. But her manners and speech with others were much the same as they'd been years ago. And she tasted the same.

He should not have kissed her. But he'd never done what he should with her.

He wanted to kiss her again, if only to confirm that her lips still tasted like honeysuckle and her breaths upon his skin still quivered from her pleasure.

"Oh, dear, Miss Caulfield, you mustn't call me Mrs.

Upchurch." Prince's sister pouted. "It makes me feel like an old widow, which I suppose I am. But there is so much of life yet to be lived," she said brightly, putting the lie to her lonely hours of grieving. "However much I adored my Henry and miss him dreadfully, I cannot bear the idea of being known as the Widow Upchurch. You must call me Fanny and we will be great friends, I think."

"I shall be honored." She did not offer the use of her Christian name in turn. But the Prince siblings seemed not to notice, already speculating on where in the house they would begin the search. When they sat again around the table with the hare and the tea, Eleanor sat too, appearing as though she listened. But now an abstracted glimmer lit her eyes.

Abruptly she turned her face to him. Her cheeks were pale, her lips unsmiling. Her fist remained tightly crunched in her pocket against her leg.

Encountering Prince disturbed her.

Years ago she'd found a stack of maps among the vicar's books—maps of the faraway islands of Britain's empire and places close to home too. She had spread them on the floor and together they studied them. Stroking a fingertip along the coast of Cornwall on one map, she'd said that while to be truly happy she only really needed her sisters, Papa, and books, she thought it would be great fun to travel—to have an adventure like he had each summer. To the boy he'd been at the time, traveling had not been glamorous or adventuresome; it meant hard work and absence from her. He had watched her study the maps and wished she would add his name to her list of needs.

Then the vicar had discovered them, gently reprimanded her for sitting on the floor, and stored the maps away at the back of a cabinet, saying they were from his "distant past" and best left there. Taliesin and

Eleanor had never looked at the maps again, and eighteen months later he'd taken to the road permanently. Until then, she had been his entire world, his single compass point.

Prison had cured him of that. And Evan Saint, the friend he'd met in one of a series of fetid jail cells. Saint had taught him that a man who lived by his own will alone was the only truly free man.

He had also taught Taliesin something he'd never learned in the vicar's household: how to fight. More importantly, he'd taught him how to win.

Since leaving St. Petroc at age eighteen, Taliesin had fought and beaten men like Robin Prince plenty. Those wins had satisfied him. He could make Prince finally pay for the thrashing he had allowed Shackelford to deal him that day in the wood. But he wasn't interested now in fighting for revenge. He'd left his own distant past behind. He had other interests to attend to.

Eleanor returned her attention to Prince, her face still taut.

Falling into the bittersweetness of the past again, as he had unwisely done for a moment on that hill when she pressed her mouth to his, would not serve him now. But if Robin Prince harmed her, he would kill him.

Chapter 11

The Storm

I

"*E*leanor." Fanny bent to peer into a box of trinkets. "How is that you come to be traveling with Mr. Wolfe? It isn't quite regular, of course." Slender chestnut brows arched high, she peeked over the stacks of old shoes and mismatched furniture stuffed into the tiny parlor. "Oh, but do you mind that I ask? Robin says I am far too intrusive. Henry used to say the same. But I like to know everything, you see."

Fanny's curiosity about everything certainly aided in this task. This hopeless task. Every corner of Sir

Wilkie's mansion seemed crammed with flotsam and jetsam.

"I don't mind that you ask, Fanny." Except that she didn't have an answer that wouldn't make her blush to the roots of her hair. *Because she had accepted the gauntlet he'd silently thrown down before her in the library at Combe. Because she had hurled herself impetuously into a quest in order to escape her life. Because a dragon must have a handsome knight to battle.* None sufficed. "My sisters and their husbands were not able to travel with me. Mr. Wolfe is a dear friend of my family."

Fanny's lashes beat once, swiftly.

"He is vastly handsome," she said quite bluntly, as if women who barely knew each other said such things.

Eleanor pretended to study the contents of the crate before her. "I daresay."

"Is he . . . That is to say . . . The rings in his ears are so distinctive, of course, and he is as dark as a sailor. I think he is a Gypsy. Is he?"

"He is."

"You will think me everything impertinent, Eleanor, I'm sure. But I ask because . . . Well . . . He doesn't quite look like a Gypsy, does he? His dress and speech mark him as a gentleman."

Not only his dress and speech. He had never quite looked like a Gypsy, at least not like his uncle's family. But that was to be expected. He was an orphan, just as she and her sisters were, taken in by his uncle and aunt out of charity.

She met Fanny's curious stare. "Perhaps you should ask him."

Fanny's lashes fanned out. "You put me in my place, Miss Caulfield. I am now ashamed to have spoken."

"I did not intend to put you in your place. I'm making an honest recommendation. He can certainly tell you more about himself than I can." She knew next to nothing about him now, only that he had been to jail. That he owned many horses. That his eyes had taken on the shadows of midnight. That his kiss could still make her think of little else, even the purpose of her journey.

"Thank you." Fanny seemed chastened. Her lashes batted again. Eleanor was coming to see those lashes as an indicator of their mistress's temper. "But would he share anything? He seems more the strong and silent sort than talkative."

Hardly silent.

"He isn't shy." Rather, the opposite when he wanted something. "He knows three languages." Four, including the language of his people. "You might feel perfectly at ease engaging him in any of those tongues."

Tongue. Lips. Scent. Heat.

Her cheeks flamed.

She had so little experience of life that a single kiss preoccupied her entirely. She should be focused on the sudden appearance of a man named Prince. But the memory of Taliesin's hand touching her back carved an aching heat through her, like moonlight dancing through darkness.

Today he had departed early, leaving word that he would return by nightfall. Where he had gone she hadn't an idea. But his absence suited her. With the gold and ruby ring burning in her pocket and Lussha's prophecy whispering like a ghost, she couldn't seem to meet Taliesin's gaze without her cheeks erupting in fire.

That wretched kiss. That perfect kiss.

It was contrary. She was contrary. If Robin Prince was the fulfillment of the Gypsy prophecy, then *he* should be making her cheeks burn. His charm seemed unrehearsed, his conversation intelligent, and his manners without pretension. He and his sisters were normal people, well spoken and amiable. And he was attractive. Betsy had rhapsodized on his blue eyes and square jaw the entire time Eleanor dressed that morning.

But it was all ridiculous. Prince was not the same as *prince*. For heaven's sake, if she allowed that logic, Sir Wilkie could be the fulfillment of the prophecy. Ravenna would laugh herself silly over that.

But Arabella . . . Arabella would take one look at Sir Wilkie's handsome grandson, his firm jaw and twinkling blue eyes, and pronounce Eleanor betrothed on the spot. Then on the wedding day her duchess sister would produce the ring and demand that Mr. Prince tell her all he knew about their past. Bella was just mad enough to do it.

"Three languages." Fanny's lashes were butterfly wings. "I should be thoroughly intimidated if I had any thought of making an impression on him myself."

Eleanor's stomach twisted. "Making an impression on him?"

"My sister, Henrietta, has just turned eighteen. She will make her debut in London next month." Fanny poked into a box. "But already she has become acquainted with any number of eligible gentlemen in Bath." She drew forth a packet and began to untie the string. "I have never once seen her as tongue-tied as she was last night at dinner."

"She is not usually timid?"

"Not at all! She is more talkative than me, if you can believe it." She chuckled. "After dinner I asked her what cat had caught her tongue, and she said, I quote, 'Mr. Wolfe is quite, quite wonderful, isn't he?' She would not say another word after that, though I begged her to elaborate." She set the half-opened packet in her lap.

Fanny had donned what she called a "work dress" for the day's dusty activities. It was finer than the gown Eleanor wore to church on Sundays. Sitting amidst the chaos of this parlor, her cheeks smudged with dirt, and her curls sparkling in the light of lamps they had arranged throughout the gloomy room, she looked positively taking. While pretty enough, Henrietta was a pale reflection of her elder sister.

"So, you see, I must know more about him to assure myself that my sister does not lose her head over a man unsuited to her," she explained. "To that end, my brother invited Mr. Wolfe out shooting this morning."

Shooting? *Taliesin?* "Did he go?"

"Robin said that he declined then rode off without taking breakfast. I suppose I must interview Mr. Wolfe directly. I have no scruples about it, you know, Eleanor. There is nothing in the world I wouldn't do to ensure my brother and sister's happiness." She smiled quite like her brother, identical lapis eyes twinkling. She opened the parcel in her lap. "A china doll. I don't suppose this came off a wrecked ship, do you?"

A rumble of thunder shuddered the windowpanes.

"Oh," Fanny exclaimed. "I hadn't an idea that it would storm today. I wonder if Henrietta has returned?"

"Where did she go?"

"For a ride about the park. Grandfather keeps the prettiest little mare for her. He spoils us all atrociously. I hope she has returned." A flash of light from beyond the windows illuminated her in white. A hard crack of thunder followed.

Eleanor dashed the dust from her skirt. "Let us go find her downstairs. Then we can all have tea and congratulate ourselves for being inside during this storm."

"I like the way you think so positively." Fanny linked their arms. "I absolutely abhor dark and gloomy people. And dark and gloomy houses. I loathe visiting Grandfather, though I am deeply fond of him. But Robin likes to make certain he's well. As I have nothing else to do, I come too."

They walked companionably to the landing, and Eleanor liked Fanny's arm in hers. It reminded her of time with her sisters. Arabella would like Fanny. Ravenna too.

"It's really extraordinarily tedious being a widow, Eleanor." Fanny sighed. "I should much rather be married, with children to spoil and a husband to amuse. Bath—that is where we live now, you know— Bath is horridly unfashionable these days, filled with rheumatic people drinking the wretched waters and being generally crotchety." She laughed. "But I like gossip and there's plenty of that." She squeezed Eleanor's arm. "Oh, I do like you, Eleanor. When my tongue trips along like it always does, you don't make me feel in the least bit foolish. I think you are quiet by nature."

Quiet, bookish, and with too many thoughts. While Fanny, like her brother, was entirely charming. Sitting beside her at dinner the night before, Taliesin had certainly seemed charmed. Every time Eleanor had looked at him, he'd been speaking with Fanny.

As they stepped onto the creaking wooden planks of the foyer, the front door flew wide. Mr. Prince entered in a gust of rain and wind. He struggled to shut the door against the wind, shook his coat, and came to them across the foyer.

"Henrietta has returned, I trust? Without her horse?"

Fanny went to her brother and took his dripping hat. "What do you mean, without her horse?"

"She cannot possibly be out in this storm. Yet her horse is not in the stable. Has she returned on foot? Perhaps she lost hold of the animal somehow. That little mare's temperament is flighty."

"Oh, dear. Henrietta is not here. We haven't seen her

since breakfast." Fanny hurried to the corridor. "Mr. Fiddle!"

Mr. Fiddle, Betsy, and the housemaid were all questioned. Only Betsy had seen Henrietta.

"Having a right close chat with that stable boy this morning, she was, sir."

"Perhaps he recommended a new trail for her and she simply got lost." Donning his hat again, Mr. Prince went out the door in a swirl of rain.

"Eleanor," Fanny said, her voice tight, "do you think she is stranded in the midst of this horrid storm?"

Eleanor grasped her hand. "Your brother will find her. You mustn't worry."

Mr. Prince returned shortly. "The stable boy is gone. The pony too. I suspect he and Henrietta are holed up in a farmer's cottage waiting out the storm."

"What if they aren't? The ford overflows during a storm, Robin." Fanny's brows twisted. "What if they tried to cross it and met with misfortune?"

"Now, Fanny, you mustn't imagine the worst." But his mouth was tight. "We will wait, and when the rain lets up I will ride out again. Has Wolfe returned? I should like his assistance in this."

"*That* gentleman is not in the house," Betsy said with an arch sniff.

Mr. Prince and Fanny exchanged glances. "Well," he said, "let us all go into the drawing room. Tea will restore our spirits. Fiddle?"

An hour passed before the storm abated enough so that Mr. Prince could again take his horse into the rain. From the drawing room window, Eleanor and Fanny watched him ride to the gate. Another horseman appeared there in the rain. They spoke, and then Mr. Prince rode to the front door and leaped down from his mount. Fanny ran into the foyer to pull the door wide.

"She is safe," Mr. Prince said upon a heavy exhalation.

"Oh! Thank heaven! Who was that man, Robin? Where did he come from?"

"Wolfe's house. It seems that Henrietta took herself farther from Drearcliffe than she intended. She became lost trying to find her way home. Wolfe came upon her, and as the storm was breaking and they were closer to Kitharan than here, he brought her there." He turned to Eleanor. "Neither of you mentioned that he was my grandfather's neighbor, Miss Caulfield."

"In truth, I did not know it until this moment."

"Ah!" Fanny said with a delighted clap of her hands. "A man of mystery. I like that. And now he is a hero too. I am immensely relieved Henrietta is safe. As soon as the rain abates, we will drive over there and collect her."

"That won't be possible today." Mr. Prince's brow was sober. "The ford has overflowed. The fellow Wolfe sent over said he was obliged to ride all the way to the footbridge to cross the river, and it was a hairy business. We must wait until tomorrow when the river has quieted."

"What about on horseback? You could ride over and bring her back."

"It will be dusk within an hour. Henrietta is safe. Tomorrow will be soon enough to bring her home."

"Robin. Our sister cannot stay overnight in the home of an unmarried man. She will be ruined."

"Fanny, we haven't a choice in the matter. No one will know of it but us," he said with a deep frown. "If Wolfe is a man of honor, he will tell no one. And I suspect Miss Caulfield won't either."

"The servants will talk," Fanny said. "You know they will. The news will spread to Gillie that our sister spent an unchaperoned night with a man, then it will spread farther. She will be barred from every polite drawing room in London before we even reach town this spring."

"As there is nothing to be done about it at present," he said shortly, "I suggest you try to calm yourself and tomorrow we will make the best of it." Removing his gloves seemed to steady him. "Miss Caulfield, I understand that Mr. Wolfe is well known to your family. They must trust him to have allowed you to make this journey with his escort alone."

She tried to breathe. Succeeded only marginally. "They do."

"There it is, Fanny. We must trust in his honor and hope that, if it comes to it, he will do the right thing by Henrietta. Now, I am soaked to the core and must change my clothing. I will meet you shortly for dinner."

Without a word to Eleanor, Fanny walked silently to the drawing room. Eleanor stood in the foyer, her heart beating hard enough to break through the prison of her ribs.

Chapter 12

The Gypsy Lord

*T*hey spoke to him with respect and deference. Taliesin had visited this house no more than a dozen times in five years, most of those visits in the last six months. He had given the people in his employ no warning that he would be in residence now. Yet when he rode up the long drive that was no longer overgrown with grass and brambles as it had been months earlier, they led his horse to the stable, took his wet coat and hat, and welcomed him home.

Servants. A novelty with which he was not yet comfortable.

Deference. A thing he had never expected to receive from anyone.

Home. A reality that he did not feel he truly deserved. And yet it was apparently his.

His uncle and aunt had often told him that he was peculiar to want a house, even a parcel of land. Rom who settled in one place year-round were unusual, to be sure. He argued that up north it was common enough, but they shrugged; the winters there were especially hard, so why not have a house for a season? But such property only fettered. They had not understood that he preferred the barn at the vicarage to the wagon, and stone walls to canvas. They said he was not one of them, in truth. Yet they had shared their tent with him, their food, and the shillings they earned for clothes. Generous and kind, clever and compassionate, they had treated him as one of their own even though he was not.

When on the cusp of eighteen he announced that he was leaving, they were unsurprised. Giving Taliesin a new coat and pair of shoes swapped for a set of knives at the fair, his uncle kissed him on the brow and wished him well. Lussha the Seer—who saw more than she ever said aloud—put her hand on the back of his neck and told him that he must never forget from where he had come. She liked to tease him, and that particular touch and those words had only stoked his anger. He thought probably she intended it.

At that time, angry and directionless, he had never imagined he would be the owner of acres of land and four dozen horses.

For three years after he purchased Kitharan, the decrepit house remained empty and the pastures overgrown. The land required work: fields drained, brambles cleared, fences built. The house itself needed a practical gutting to be habitable. He hadn't the funds or the time. But he needed the land. His business had grown. The animals required a home. After ten years of vagabondage, he did too.

Finally he hired a stable master and a hand. Then he hired three servants: a general manservant, a cook who kept the kitchen and garden, and a housekeeper who kept all four men in order.

He now understood how she accomplished that. Within minutes of his arrival, Mrs. Samuel led him on a tour of the improvements made since his last visit: the mended windows in the parlor, the new floor in the master bedchamber, the rebuilt chimney in the kitchen, and the roofing that had been delivered and awaited installation.

Several hours later he understood even better what a powerful ally he had in his housekeeper when, after bidding her good-bye for another month, he reappeared in the foyer of his house with a sodden girl of eighteen in a state of high agitation. Like a stern mother hen, Mrs. Samuel took Henrietta Prince into her care, banishing him to his parlor.

He sat there for some time, dripping on the faded upholstery, staring out at the rain falling in diagonal sheets across the hills and shallow valley that, remarkably, he owned. Then he walked to the stable in search of a messenger. Miss Prince would be missed; word must be sent to Drearcliffe.

In the stable he discovered that his housekeeper had already sent off the stable hand, although not to Drearcliffe: to Gillie, the village a mile away. Instead, Taliesin sent his stable master to Drearcliffe. Then he sat down atop a pile of straw with the stable boy from Drearcliffe, who had appeared at Kitharan during the storm. After an informative conversation, he returned to the parlor and waited as the rain eased.

Within an hour a one-horse gig could be seen creeping through the misty dusk up the drive toward the house. Before the door it disgorged a matron of portly frame and gimlet eye. She marched inside and curtsied crisply to him.

"I am Mrs. Amelia Starch," she said, looking him up and down thoroughly and nodding. "I'm glad to finally make your acquaintance, Mr. Wolfe. Now if you'll direct me to the maiden's chambers, I'll see to matters."

Martin Caulfield had been a widower for years, and Taliesin knew little about wives of men of the cloth. But Amelia Starch, wife of the vicar of Gillie, was quite as good as her word. He neither saw nor heard Henrietta Prince until the following morning. At that time, accompanied by her new duenna, she joined him for breakfast in his sparsely furnished dining room.

Neither woman seemed to note the spartan appointments. Mrs. Starch made conversation with the stuttering girl. Miss Prince threw him giddy glances over the lip of her teacup while the cook served them with the assistance of Pate, the manservant. Never particularly fond of girls without speech, and even less comfortable being served breakfast by anyone, Taliesin swiftly escaped to the east pasture and his animals. Today the sun shone in a sky dotted with white and silver clouds. The earth had drunk up the rainfall from the night before and his stable master had returned from Drearcliffe an hour after dawn. The girl's siblings would arrive soon.

They did. Her brother came riding, followed closely by his traveling carriage that slogged along the muddy road. From the stable, Taliesin watched Mrs. Upchurch descend from the carriage. Then Eleanor appeared upon the step. She lifted her astonished face to the facade of his house, and her cheeks were white.

Mr. Pate ushered the visitors inside. Without removing

his coat or changing from his muddied boots, Taliesin went to his parlor to greet the first guests he had ever greeted in his life. He stood at the door, entirely stymied and wishing he were anywhere else. On the back of a horse many miles away would be ideal. A wagon would even suffice if necessary.

Eleanor saw him first. She said nothing, only stared at someplace twenty feet beneath his ribs.

"Good day, sir," Prince said. "Tell me straight off if you will: is my sister well?"

"To my knowledge she is. Since yesterday afternoon she has been in the care of my housekeeper, Mrs. Samuel. Last night she was attended by Mrs. Starch, the wife of the vicar at Gillie. I recommend that you apply to them, or indeed to your sister herself, for details."

The girl appeared beside him. She cast him a quick glance, then went swiftly to her sister.

"Henrietta, how could you have strayed so far from Grandfather's estate?" Mrs. Upchurch said. "This must be two miles away, or more."

"I am ever so sorry, Fanny," she said, stringing together the most words Taliesin had ever heard from her in one sentence. "The storm confused me and I must have gotten turned around. Then my horse took fright and bolted. But"—she turned dazed eyes upon him—"Mr. Wolfe rescued me."

In another time, another place, he might have laughed. But Eleanor's eyes were like a specter's.

"Mr. Wolfe, my brother and I are grateful for your assistance." Mrs. Upchurch moved toward him. "You were excellent to arrange a chaperone for my sister. Thank you." The natural animation she had shown at dinner two nights earlier had dimmed. "And I am thrilled to know that Kitharan has a master again. The man who owned it before left it moldering for a decade at least. He had other property, in Kent, I believe. But I always wished he would take this house in hand and restore it to what it must have once been. Now I see you are doing that. How delightful. When you are finished the repairs, you must open your doors to the county and have a grand party. And we shall come from Bath to welcome you." An air of disappointment hung about her.

"Would you like to see the house now?" Was that what one offered? Or did they expect tea? His aunt and Reverend Caulfield had always offered tea to visitors. But he'd no idea if his cook or housekeeper anticipated this sort of thing. He'd never given it a thought. He'd never considered that he might have callers here. "I suspect my housekeeper would be glad to give you the tour." At least he'd no doubt of that.

"Oh, yes, Fanny," her sister said. "Let's do. I have only seen the bedchamber I slept in with Mrs. Starch, and the dining chamber. But Mrs. Starch told me stories of secret passageways and a rose garden overflowing with riotous blossoms. And of Mr. Wolfe's beautiful horses too." She cast him a shy smile.

"There are no roses in this season, Henrietta." Mrs. Upchurch turned to him. "Thank you, Mr. Wolfe. We would enjoy a tour."

Mrs. Samuel led and he followed. Eleanor's eyes grew wider in each room but she did not turn them upon him again. Finally in the room at the top of the stairs, furnished with only an ancient desk and a single chair, and flanked by white marble hearths and empty bookcases built into the walls, she pivoted to him. The others had moved on, and in the light from the window that had no draperies her golden green eyes accused.

"You meant this room. Didn't you?" she said like the rumble of a swollen stream. "When you admired Sir Wilkie's books and said you had a library you wished to stock, I thought you were having a bit of fun. But it was this room you spoke of. This actual room. Wasn't it?"

It was not incredible that this was the first thing she said now. She had changed so little.

He nodded.

Snapping her face away, she swept from the room. The air went with her. Now he understood himself. Since the first time he'd visited Kitharan he had imagined her in this room. Not empty like this. Instead, lined with books, and she disposed in a chair by the window with a volume between her hands. Her spirit in this room. Her presence.

In his imagination, of course, sparks had not flown from her furious eyes.

He moved onto the landing and words drifted up to him from the foyer below, fully audible in the semi-dome of the ceiling.

"They call him the Gypsy Lord, Fanny! He has such a way with horses that half of them think him some sort of wizard. His servants say he is wonderfully undemanding and generous, and Mrs. Starch says that everybody in the village is positively astonished by him."

Eleanor had paused halfway down the stairs, still as marble. In a rush, she descended and followed the others into the parlor.

"Fanny," Prince was saying as Taliesin came to the door. "I know you wish to smooth over this awkwardness, but it must be addressed."

"Robin—" She saw him in the doorway and broke away from her siblings to come to him. "Mr. Wolfe, you mustn't mind my brother. He was worried senseless when Henrietta went missing yesterday. We all were. But now all is well and we thank you."

"We do," Prince said firmly. "But Fanny, you cannot ignore this. Wolfe, do you intend to do the right thing by my sister?"

It seemed extraordinary to him, standing here in a three-hundred-year-old house that he had purchased with money he had earned, that even in these circumstances an Englishman still believed he could dictate his actions.

"I have already assisted your sister to the extent that I am able, sir."

"You are perfectly correct, of course," Mrs. Upchurch said hastily. "Mrs. Samuel was here every moment and the vicar's wife too. Isn't that so, Henrietta?"

"Yes, Fanny," she said in a small voice. "After coming here."

"You see, Robin? He saw to everything."

"You said it yourself, Fanny. Servants talk. Everyone in Gillie already knows that our sister spent the night here alone."

"Suitably chaperoned."

"It hardly matters. The truth won't even be considered once the gossip reaches London."

"As my part in this is finished," Taliesin said, "and as I have business to attend to, I will leave you to yourselves." He had little to attend to; his employees had his house and stables in perfect order. But he went to the stable where the night before he had rubbed down Tristan himself, as he always did, because he was not a lord of any sort, Gypsy or no, but a poor man who had barreled into a spot of exceptional good luck and made the most of it.

The building had been restored completely, his first investment at Kitharan when he'd scraped together the funds. Tristan gave him a hard nudge to his chest in greeting. He ran his hand over the horse's back. Proud, powerful, and unwilling to bend to any man's hand but his. He'd bought him as a foal with the first guineas he had ever saved. Guineas saved to prove that he could deserve a gentlewoman's hand. Guineas that, in an instant, had become dispensable.

A footstep sounded on the floor, soft and quick, graceful but not hesitant. Eleanor Caulfield had rarely been tentative about anything. Once roused, she held the bit between her teeth. Somehow he had forgotten that. He'd forgotten how the moment he had finally found the courage to touch her, she had followed him eagerly into that recklessness.

"Why didn't you tell me about this house?"

And direct. She had always been direct. Especially when displeased with him.

He turned from the horse. "You didn't ask."

"I didn't *ask*?" Her eyes blazed, and a spike of hard, hot need shot straight through him. What this woman in a passion did to him. God's blood, as a boy he had been damned and eleven years later he was still damned.

"What have you been doing for the past decade?" she demanded. "Robbing banks, for heaven's sake? Don't laugh at me! Answer me."

He moved from the stall and she stood her ground. Good. The closer the better. When she stood close, her scent of honeysuckle and sage made him insane to touch her, an insanity he had deprived himself of for too long. Perhaps it was time to finally take what he wanted. Perhaps if he got some satisfaction from her, the deprivations of the past would no longer haunt him.

Or perhaps he should walk off a cliff now and save himself the certain misery to come.

Insane. She made him insane. Insane to smell her, hear her, touch her. And the greatest insanity of all: he wanted her to like his house.

"Some years ago I found myself regularly lodging in public facilities."

Her eyes clouded. "Public facilities?"

"Jails. After one such sojourn I had the good fortune of being allowed to defend myself against the charges against me."

"Let me guess. Vagabondage? Roguery?"

"And theft. And before you ask, no, I hadn't stolen anything."

"I know that. I made the robbing banks remark facetiously." Anger flared again in her eyes, as though she believed the best of him and expected him to understand that. Despite all.

"According to my accusers," he began, but his tongue would not obey him. He had been wise to remain distant from her for years. She made him believe that people existed who trusted. That people were trustworthy. And she made him want to kiss her senseless, until she couldn't argue or question or even speak, until she just stared up at him as she had after he'd kissed her so briefly on that hill, like he was a god. "According to my accusers I had disturbed the peace."

"Had you?"

"If it's disturbing the peace to walk along a high street in a surly humor, with a head heavy from drink the previous night"—and a heart filled with anger—"most certainly."

"They threw you in jail for that?"

"I had been incarcerated for lesser offences." And greater. "But on that occasion, I was brought before a lord magistrate for judgment. This was a new experience for me, and I swiftly understood the import of it."

"What was it?"

"They intended to deport me."

Her eyes flew wide, and her delectable pink lips parted. "Deport you?"

"The common cure for vagabondage in England. Send your vagabonds elsewhere and you will not find yourself bothered by them again." Send them away. Far away. Send him away, and you will not have to worry for your daughter's welfare again. Yet she stood before him now, every ivory and golden inch of her quivering in indignation for him.

He wanted to touch her now even more than he'd

wanted his freedom then, with an ache so deep it bit at his bone.

"What happened?" she said.

"I quoted Saint Augustine to the magistrate."

She blinked. "You quoted Augustine?"

" 'He that is good is free, though he is a slave; he that is evil is a slave, though he be a king.' "

Her lips curved. "How clever of you."

"*Legem non habet necessitas,* however, convinced him."

"Necessity knows no law." Her pleasure now, each feature softened from anger, made him feel drunk. How clever of him indeed. How clever of him to read and memorize ancient texts for years, all for the purpose of impressing this girl. She had saved him that day. If not for what she had inspired him to accomplish, he would long since have rotted to death in jail.

"What did the magistrate do?" she asked.

"He exonerated me. But the municipal law refused to be placated. So the lord placed a ban on my entrance into that shire, and four more shires in which I had previously been jailed, for the duration of my miserable vagabond's life."

"What would happen if you entered those shires?"

"I would find myself on the ocean."

"Exile?"

"They don't use the word *exile* for Rom, *pirani*. That word is reserved for gentlemen."

Her smile faded and Taliesin felt like he'd taken a punch to the belly.

"How did you come to be . . ." She chose her words. "A gentleman?"

"I am not a gentleman. I am a vagabond and a rogue, just as they believed. Just as I have always been." Tied to no one. Bound to none. Unfettered and unbreakable, no matter what this house said of his life or what his thundering heart said to him now.

"You haven't yet told me how you came by this house."

"After my trial, I was set free. But the lord magistrate was not finished with me. He said that he had never before encountered a Gypsy with a classical education."

"Are there any others?"

"Not to my knowledge. Nor to Lord Baron's. But he suspected that with assistance and reform my people could be made into responsible, hardworking subjects of Mother England." Englishmen, even those with good intentions, understood little about Rom, that the vast majority of them would rather die than settle. "He decided to use me as an experiment. He owned a small property in the West Country. He never visited it but had reports that it was falling to ruin, both the house and grounds. He said it was on a parcel of grazing land and that the locals had taken to pasturing their sheep and cattle on it, and suggested that a wise man might make good use of such a place. He offered it to me for fifty pounds and two fine horses."

Her eyes were wide. "Extraordinary."

"Wasn't it? Who knew that a fourth-century bishop still had such influence?"

For a moment her sweet lips twitched. "Papa always said Saint Augustine was infinitely wise. But that was when he was trying to teach us to be modest girls."

"Trying?"

Her eyes glimmered, and he saw again in her the girl he had held in his arms, standing waist-deep in a pond. He wanted to take her into his arms and touch her now as he had then.

"Did you have fifty pounds and two fine horses?" she asked.

"Two years later I did." Two years of exhausting work and blinding starvation. He had gone without food and sleep many days and nights to save the money.

"And his offer still stood?"

"We are standing on that land. This is the house."

"It is a . . . a beautiful house. It is wonderfully comfortable inside."

"In the rooms that have been renovated."

"Fanny—that is, Mrs. Upchurch—quizzed me about you yesterday." Her voice turned diffident. "She asked me if you would be a suitable candidate for her sister's hand."

"What did you tell her?" His heart beat too swiftly.

"I told her that I don't know, that she should ask you. But it seems as though her brother is more interested in the answer now. What will you do?" The crease in her brow was deeper now than it had been as a girl, but just as expressive.

"What will I do?"

"Mr. Prince is right. When the scandalmongers take hold of this story, Henrietta's prospects will be ruined."

"You have lived in a hermitage your entire life. What do you know of scandalmongers?"

"Little from my own experience, it's true. I haven't the advantage of years of vagabondage to give me vast knowledge of the world not to mention arrogant confidence, like some." Her eyes snapped. "But Arabella has known plenty of cruel gossip, and she has been hurt by it. Rumors that our mother was a woman of ill repute plague her, and it worries her for the sake of her child. Even a duke is not immune to cruelty. Don't you see? It is the very reason she sent me on this foolish quest, the reason I accepted the charge—aside from your provoking willingness to do it, of course."

He knew not whether to laugh or scowl.

Spots of agitation lit her cheeks. "Servants will talk, and the villagers too. Henrietta will find every door in London closed to her."

"Eleanor, I have no intention of wedding Henrietta Prince."

Her breaths seemed to stutter from her. "But— but a solution must be found. She is an innocent girl—"

He stepped forward and the space between them became inches, so close that he could taste her honeysuckle scent upon his lips. "That innocent girl paid the stable boy to follow me from Drearcliffe yesterday, and then to guide her here just as the storm broke. He proudly showed me the penny he earned for it, though he said that given how he and his pony had been soaked through, he thought he deserved an additional penny. So, you see, she is not quite as guileless as you would have her be."

"Did . . ." Her throat jerked upon an awkward swallow. "Did you pay him the additional penny?"

"That would have made me complicit, wouldn't it?"

"I don't insist that she is guileless," she said. "I am barely acquainted with her."

"You know nothing else yourself, I think, and so you expect it of others." All the books in the world had not taught her that the world was full of manipulation and betrayal.

"She is like—like the Cropper twins." Her lips were parted, revealing a glimpse of her rosy tongue, and his rational mind was going to hell again.

"The who?"

"Those girls in St. Petroc. The twins that followed you around for an entire winter, hoping you would notice them, until their father threatened to beat you for it."

"You knew about that?"

"Everyone knew about it. The twins adored you so much that they denied themselves the sight of you to protect you from their father. I think they considered it a noble sacrifice on your behalf." The pulse in her throat above the modest neckline of her gown beat swiftly. He needed to touch it, to feel with his hands how he affected her.

He laid his fingertips along the arc of her throat. She gasped softly and turned her head aside. But she did not retreat. He spread his fingers. Silken skin. The beat of her heart beneath his fingertips. Faster.

"No doubt you thought they were fools," he heard himself say.

"I am guileless," she whispered. "I wish I weren't. I wish I knew how to secretly plot in order to get what I want. But I haven't really the temperament for dissembling or the humor for effective teasing."

A single lock of gold lay against her neck. He twined it around his finger, stroking her skin. A fantasy he'd had forever. "At one time you teased me plenty simply by walking into a room."

She turned her face to him. "I didn't intend that. I never intended that." The jewels of her eyes seemed uncertain. Then, lashes shrouding her gaze, she reached up and laid her palm on his chest.

God's blood. He dropped his hand. "Eleanor—"

"Acting directly is more rational," she said. "Like those medieval heroes who set out on quests to achieve what they desired."

Her touch scalded, a branding that had long since scarred over, he'd thought, fool that he was.

"Reason had nothing to do with it. Faith drove those knights," he uttered, warning, threatening. He wanted her. He had always wanted her. Only hurt would come of it. Years ago he had imagined that hurting her would heal his wounds. But when he had believed that, her hand hadn't been on his chest. *This.* Now. All had changed. He could have her and find the satisfaction he ached for. "Most of them failed," he said.

"I don't intend to fail." Her voice was soft and pebbly, yet laughing, at once playful and quivering with intention. She tilted up her chin and her fingertips pressed into his chest. "Gypsy Lord, I challenge you."

Chapter 13

The Fire

*I*er lips, pink and ripe, were a breath away. He wanted them beneath his. He wanted her entirely beneath him and his name upon those lips. He wanted her pleasure in his hands.

"Eleanor, you are playing with fire." He grasped her wrist and held her palm tight against his chest. "I am not a boy of seventeen anymore. It won't be like that kiss the other day on the hill. Not for long. Don't start this unless you are willing to get burned."

"Actually, you started it. Or do you touch women like you just touched me in the regular course of things? Perhaps only in stables?"

"Nowhere." No one else. Only her.

"Are you— Could you be *afraid*?" A single brow rose. "Am I to win this challenge with so little effort?"

Yes. If they began this battle he would lose it. And when he left her again it wouldn't require a decade to wipe her from his senses, but a lifetime.

But a man could endure only so much temptation. He needed her hand to remain on him. He needed her hands all over him.

"I haven't been afraid a day in my life, *pirani*." Not for himself. Only for her.

She met his gaze squarely. "Then touch me again."

Gripping her waist, he dragged her against him. Their thighs met, and hips. A soft moan escaped through her parted lips. One breath—two—three— her breasts pressing at her gown with each sharp inhalation. Startled, but not reluctant.

Her hand upon his chest traveled upward, to his face, her fingers strafing his jaw, tentative at first. Then exploring. Her fingertips stole over his lips, the light kiss of her curiosity and desire tearing him apart inside. Her eyes opened wide.

"Eleanor? Mr. Wolfe?"

Eleanor stepped back, out of his hands, swallowing over the heartbeats thumping in her throat. She pressed her palms to her cheeks. "Fire," she whispered.

Light footsteps came toward the stable. "Eleanor?"

Taliesin turned away and walked the length of the stable, passing through the stripes of sunlight slanting through stall windows, his broad shoulders rigid, his boot steps firm. He could walk perfectly upright, with an even stride, while for her standing in place was like battling a cyclone.

What had she done? She'd seen his house—all sprawling golden brown Elizabethan elegance gracefully set into a hill overlooking a velvety valley, horses in the pasture and pheasants poking their heads from the long grass—and upon hearing Mr. Prince's demand that he wed Henrietta, desperation had consumed her. It made her follow him to this stable. It made her challenge him. Boldly. Brazenly. But to *what*?

He knew. He knew so much more of the world, of real men and women, than she did. More than stories in books. He had always seemed to know more.

Except about her. He'd never known that she had watched him just like the Cropper twins, that she had waited for him to come to the vicarage each day with her nerves in a twist, that she didn't understand him and hated his teasing, but that he compelled her like no one else did. And he had no idea that for every single day for eleven years she had wondered where he was, if he was alive, well, and why he had never returned. He had no idea that when he left she hadn't wished to live, that she hid her grief in books and studying; that since he had appeared in her sister's house less than a fortnight ago, her heart had not ceased its hard beat; and that she wanted nothing more than to throw herself into adventure and suffer the consequences, even if it meant getting burned.

That this was all much easier to admit to herself since she'd spent a night believing he would marry Henrietta Prince made her want to tear her hair out.

Thrusting her quivering hands into the folds of her skirt, she turned to the doorway.

"There you are!" Fanny paused on the threshold to squint into the shadows, then came forward. She had dressed stunningly today, in a gown that clung to her petite figure and dipped over her rounded bosom so that it was just on the edge of modesty. The colorful ribbons of her straw hat enhanced the twinkle in her eyes. She was the perfect combination of elegance and carefree ease, and she had been married. She would know exactly what a man meant when he warned her that she was playing with fire.

"Where is Mr. Wolfe? Did you find him? Oh! There." She smiled as he came toward them. "I am so happy you haven't gone off somewhere, though I would not blame you a bit for it. My brother was boorish, and I'm sorry."

Taliesin said nothing. Not even a muscle flexed in his jaw. Strong and silent, indeed.

Eleanor's mouth was dry, but Fanny seemed to expect a response. She looked between them eagerly.

"Your brother said only what he believes is right," Eleanor said.

"Perhaps," Fanny said. "But I think Henrietta has been even more ill-behaved than Robin. Vastly more. And I apologize for it, Mr. Wolfe. I am to blame. I have been negligent in her upbringing since our mother died. But I have now had a stern conversation with her and I believe she is aware of the trouble she has caused you, and chastened."

"I have suffered no trouble," he said.

"Oh, but I am terribly afraid that you will. Henrietta tells me that your servants hold you in the highest esteem, and that the vicar's wife condemned her for being a fool. But others could easily see it differently." She moved toward him, the swish of her skirts on the stable floor mingling with the music of the delicate glass bracelets tinkling on her wrist. "I should be devastated were my sister's girlish misstep to cast any doubt upon your character in the neighborhood, and you so recently arrived. If anyone should take uncharitably to you because of this incident, I would never forgive myself or Henrietta."

Fanny did not say aloud that already he faced a battle to gain the respect of the local families simply because of who he was.

"I have no concern on that account," he replied.

"On the contrary, you must," Fanny insisted. "But I have had the most marvelous idea that should silence all gossip and turn this mistake into a triumph. We will throw a party at Kitharan. Rather, Mr. Wolfe will throw the party, and you and I, Eleanor, will help. We will invite everybody in the county and it will be a grand celebration to welcome you to the neighborhood. Kitharan has been closed up for ages and everybody will come to see it again and to meet its new master. Isn't it the most wonderful idea?"

"A fine idea," Mr. Prince said as he walked into the stable. "Welcoming a new neighbor by demanding that he host a party. No one will suspect anything amiss about it."

"Well, we cannot have it at Grandfather's house. He would scold all the guests. And anyway, the purpose is to show everybody that we think the world of Mr. Wolfe." She swung back around to face Taliesin. "You have acted gallantly and mustn't be punished for it. I beg you to agree to this plan. Miss Caulfield and Mrs. Samuel and I will make all the arrangements."

"You need only open your wallet and pay for it all, Wolfe," her brother said, but the twinkle had returned to his eyes and he seemed again in his usual good humor. He offered Eleanor a warm smile.

"And while the preparations are going along, we can continue to search for clues to Eleanor's shipwreck in my Grandfather's collection. Please, Mr. Wolfe. Do say yes."

He only nodded.

But it was enough to send Fanny into transports of delight. Grabbing her brother's arm, she declared, "Come, everyone. We will make up a guest list and then Eleanor and I will meet with Mrs. Samuel to determine what needs to be done to prepare the house. Oh, I do adore a party, and I haven't thrown a truly grand party in years. This will be such fun."

Eleanor watched them go, aware with each of her senses of the man standing silently behind her. Finally he moved past her and into the light.

"Have you ever thrown a grand party?" she called after him.

He paused and looked at her. "What do you think?"

Meeting his shadowed gaze was falling into confusion. "I don't know. Until two hours ago I didn't know that you owned a grand country house. So how am I to imagine I know anything about you now?"

"You will help me with this, as she said."

"Me? I don't know anything about hosting a big party either. I've been living in a hermitage my entire life, recall. And I have another project to see to, for which I came here in the first place."

He walked to her. "This is not a request. You will help me with this." There were endless dark nights in his eyes. Countless sufferings. Eleanor didn't know why she was seeing this now, and her heart ached. Where had he been in all these years? What had those jails done to him?

"Why must I?" she whispered.

"Come, you two!" Fanny called from the drive. "We mustn't waste a minute."

"Consider it the next challenge." The corner of his mouth lifted ever so slightly, cracking her heart open.

"You haven't met the previous challenge yet." She didn't know where she found the courage to say it.

Taking the step that brought her close again, he bent his head. His words brushed her ear. "Take care what you wish for, *pirani*. Not every wish is fulfilled in the manner one hopes." He moved away before she could speak. But she hadn't words anyway, or even coherent thoughts, only gelatinous knees and a heart saturated with desire.

For a single day Fanny Upchurch cheerfully combed through a room full of objects that Sir Wilkie had found on beaches. But her conversation was all about the party plans at Kitharan. She had urged Taliesin to remain at his house so that he could give all his attention to preparing it, assuring him that Eleanor would be well cared for at Drearcliffe in his absence. Eleanor could find no reason to object—none that she could say aloud. Without discussion he removed entirely to Kitharan.

Fanny seemed especially satisfied with the arrangement; Henrietta was less likely to throw herself at him if separated by miles, she said.

But Eleanor suspected he hadn't left Drearcliffe because of Henrietta. She had thrown herself at him and he rejected her. That his rejection had included a warning should not heat her in excruciating places each time she thought of it, except that she was a sheltered spinster—raised in a hermitage—only now learning the true meaning of adventure and freedom, and not yet accomplished at managing either.

"Fanny departed for Kitharan nearly as soon as the sun rose this morning," Mr. Prince informed her at breakfast. "She is anxious to ensure that the party will go off smoothly. She has tasked me with aiding you in your search, and I am eager to assist. Dispose of me as you will." He bowed handsomely.

Eleanor wanted to like him. She *did* like him. She couldn't help but admire his manners and his kindness to his sisters.

Now as he turned from her to the sideboard she noticed the breadth of his shoulders and curl of gold hair over his ears. A frisson of warmth stirred in her belly.

Then she thought of Taliesin, his legs when he sat astride a horse, muscular, taut, and the scratch of whiskers on his jaw that her fingertips had explored, his perfect lips that made her sigh, and his hands—*his hands*. And her entire body went weak and loose with heat.

"Thank you, Mr. Prince." Taliesin didn't want her. Not as she wished. "You are kind." And attentive. Interested in her. "The blacksmith's son who told us of your grandfather's collection mentioned a box sealed in lead. Might that box and its contents still be here?"

"Certainly. I was the errand boy that saw to the task of having it opened, in fact. I know precisely where it is to be found now, unless my grandfather has moved it since then, of course."

They soon discovered that Sir Wilkie had indeed moved it. The refurbishment of his library had upended several rooms at Drearcliffe, including the room in which Mr. Prince had stored the small casket and its contents.

"They were nothing remarkable, I think," Mr. Prince said with a downcast air. "At the time they seemed to me old documents of no particular interest."

"And yet your grandfather sent all the way to Piskey to have that casket opened. Why?"

"He is peculiar that way. He cannot bear to have anything he's taken out of the sea not studied thoroughly. Perhaps he hopes to find a pirate treasure." He smiled, but his face sobered again swiftly. "I am sorry the papers have gone missing."

"Are there other such boxes in the house?"

"I don't recall. Shall we ask him?"

"I would like that."

His face lightened, the distress falling away from his

features. "You are so refreshingly sensible, Miss Caulfield."

Not always. Not lately. Not concerning one man.

"Am I?" she said distractedly.

"I admire that in you." Mr. Prince's voice had grown
warm. "But not only that."

She blinked.

"You mustn't doubt that I admire you, Miss Caulfield." He paused before the door to the dungeon.
"Quite a lot. Is it too soon to say such a thing? I realize
we've only been acquainted a few days, yet your character speaks so strongly to me. I cannot be mistaken in
it. And . . . forgive me for expressing myself so frankly,
but not only your character inspires my admiration."
His appreciative gaze passed over her hair. Betsy had
taken special care arranging it that morning. Betsy
liked Mr. Prince.

"Thank you, sir."

"I wish you would call me Robin."

"And yet I cannot."

"You call my sister by her Christian name."

"She begged it of me."

"If I begged it of you, would you relent and allow me
the honor?"

"Mr. Prince, you begin to make me uncomfortable."
And yet Taliesin had demanded a kiss of her and now
she only wanted more.

"I beg your pardon. I could never want that." And
he left it at that.

Sir Wilkie fussed and harrumphed, but he led them
to a room cluttered with boxes of all sorts.

"There you are, miss. Not a one of the lot offered
up anything more interesting than old clothes and
papers."

"May I know where those clothes and papers went,
sir?"

"I suspect in the fire," He waved it away and shuffled off, muttering that young people were too full of foolish questions.

"Should we ask Mr. Fiddle?" she said.

"Yes. My grandfather often forgets that he orders Fiddle to save things. Fiddle could very well have those clothes stored in a corner somewhere about the house. The papers, however . . . Grandfather probably spoke the truth about those. Fiddle keeps the journals, of course, but I've never seen another bit of paper in the house."

The manservant was nowhere to be found, and Mr. Treadwell told them he'd gone to the village. They returned to the room of boxes and Eleanor studied each, opening lids and finding them all empty.

"What exactly do you hope to find, Miss Caulfield?" Mr. Prince said as he examined the broken lock on a jewelry box.

"I don't know. Anything." She sat on a closed traveling trunk. "It seems a hopeless task, but my sister is devoted to the idea that we might someday find my parents."

"And Mr. Wolfe? What is his interest in this quest?"

"He hasn't one."

"Except, perhaps, the quester?" His face was quite serious.

She dropped her eyes to the floor. "You have misunderstood it, Mr. Prince."

"Have I?"

She looked up at him. "He isn't here now, is he?"

"No," he said. "I am."

The ring made a lump in her pocket. She could show it to him. She could know now if he recognized it and waste no more time searching. Lussha had said that no man must see the ring until one of them wed a prince. But Eleanor had always thought that a ridiculous prohibition. Still, she couldn't make her hand draw it forth now.

"What are you thinking, Miss Caulfield?"

"I am thinking of my sister's wish to find our parents. And that I might never satisfy that wish."

His hands gripped his knees and emotions crossed his features in quick succession: frustration, doubt, then determination. "I will not rest until they are found."

"Really?"

"Yes. I give you my word."

Here was a man any woman could give her heart to. If she still possessed a heart to give away.

She dipped her gaze and it alighted on a casket of a size that she could hold in her arms. A captain's safe box? Painted on the side in faded red were the words "LADY VOYAGER," and below that in smaller letters "JAMAICA CANE CUMPANY."

She squinted her eyes and shook her head. The faded words remained at the edge of her memory, but starkly familiar. She'd seen these words before. *This box.*

"I beg your pardon, Miss Caulfield," Mr. Prince said. "I've done it again—made you uncomfortable. I—"

"No." She fell to her knees before the box. "You haven't misspoken." The fasteners and lock had long since been broken. She put both palms to the lid and pried it open.

"What is it?" He came to her side. "What have you found?"

"Nothing. That is, probably nothing." Carved of cedar, the box showed no signs of having been soaked through, no rotted or misshapen boards. The cloth lining inside was not water stained or damaged. She studied the edges of the lid and found traces of lead where it had once been soldered shut.

"Jamaica. Isn't that where you embarked for England?"

It couldn't be the captain's box of their ship. It would be too fantastic.

Lady Voyager. Familiar yet frustratingly distant. "It might have appeared on a beach any year since then," she said.

"And yet I know it did not."

She tore her attention from the box. "What do you mean?"

"Some years ago I hoped to invest in a sugar venture on Jamaica. I studied the companies and came close to making a commitment, only to learn that my funds were insufficient for the venture. But I did learn that the company I was interested in, Jamaica Sugar Incorporated, had until a decade earlier been called the Jamaica Cane Company. It was in operation under that name for only a few years."

"Heavens." She could hardly draw breaths. This could not be happening. She had believed until this moment that her quest was futile, the journey merely an excuse to indulge in an adventure. Now, with an actual clue before her and the ring burning against her thigh, she saw the lie she'd told herself: She had agreed to this mission so that she could be with Taliesin. Only for that reason.

She swallowed back the revelation. "Do you recall the years during which the company operated under this name?"

He stood. "No, but I could discover it easily enough. I will send to London, to Lloyd's insurance market. I first learned of the company there. They will have records."

She rose to her feet. "I could not ask you to go to that trouble on my account."

"You haven't asked. I have offered."

Taliesin had offered too. He had offered to make this

journey without her. He'd nearly insisted upon it. Had she imagined the challenge in his eyes that day? Had she misread him so thoroughly *again*?

"Thank you, sir." This man could be her future. Here was admiration and companionship without the confusion of memories and lust to hopelessly tangle her reason.

"It will be my honor," he said. "It should only require several days. In the meantime we will scour the house for the papers that came from these boxes."

"I am grateful for your assistance."

He stepped toward her. "I wish that someday you will want more than my assistance. Then I will insist that you call me Robin." There was no playfulness about him now. She thought he would touch her. Part of her wanted him to, and yet she prayed he would not.

Chapter 14

The Suitor

Fanny returned as dusk fell. She swept into dinner with glowing cheeks and full of news about the impressive industry of Mr. Wolfe's servants.

"Fanny, your concern for Henrietta's reputation is admirable," her brother said as he lifted a spoonful of soup to his mouth. "But shouldn't you have some concern for your own reputation as well?"

"Oh, pish tosh. Mrs. Starch was present all day as well as Mrs. Samuel, who is a veritable gorgon, it turns out. And of course I am an old widow lady. I haven't a tender reputation to be besmirched by silly gossip."

At no more than twenty-six she was the prettiest, most vivacious widow Eleanor had ever met. And she had expressed quite clearly that she did not like being a widow.

"Pretty girls are always up to larks." Sir Wilkie scowled over his boiled lamb. "You'll never keep her in line, Rob. You ought to find her another husband right quick."

Mr. Prince chuckled. "I will give it my first consideration, Grandfather." His eyes came to Eleanor and he gave her a private smile, as though they shared a special secret.

"Eleanor, you must come with me to Kitharan tomorrow," Fanny said. "There is so much to be done and it's all so diverting."

"I'm certain you are much more capable than I of planning a party." She felt no duty to assist. That Taliesin had ordered her to help meant nothing. He had deserted her here to discover her past with Mr. Prince. That the moment she'd found the box she had wanted to tell him about it was her own weakness.

"No, no," Fanny said brightly. "I insist." She continued to insist throughout dinner, and Eleanor finally agreed to it. Fanny clapped in delight and said Mr. Wolfe would be thrilled. Eleanor doubted it.

But when morning broke rain was falling again, though not as heavily as the day of the storm. It was sufficient, however, to postpone the trip to Kitharan. Fanny declared that instead they would search Sir Wilkie's collection with renewed vigor. Hearing of the captain's safe box from *Lady Voyager*, she dimpled in delight and offered her brother a speaking look that Eleanor had no idea how to interpret.

Two hours of leafing through piles of yellowed London journals in the hopes of finding ship's documents led nowhere. And however much she enjoyed

Fanny's company, Eleanor didn't think she could bear hearing another detail about Mr. Wolfe's gorgeous house and his beautiful horses and party plans. Asking Mr. Treadwell for his escort, she took Iseult for a ride.

The woods beside Sir Wilkie's house were thick and dark, with a single path layered with pine needles through the center. She rode, staring into the shadows at the bracken between the trees. Sticks littered the ground. Despite the rain, everything beneath the tight-woven canopy was dry. Sir Wilkie and Fiddle had no need to burn paper for kindling. They had bushels of kindling at the doorstep.

Paper was dear. It would not be discarded foolishly at Drearcliffe, especially not by a man who sat in his dungeon library day after day reading and writing. Sir Wilkie wasn't poor like Martin Caulfield, but he didn't seem to be particularly wealthy either.

Something niggled at her mind . . . Some piece of information that she was forgetting . . . Like the letters on the captain's box, the name of the ship, nearly recalled but not enough . . .

Papa had reused paper whenever possible. The blank notebook intended for her Latin lessons had been a precious gift.

Then it came clearly to her.

Urging Iseult through the trees, she raced back to the house, threw the reins into Mr. Treadwell's hands, and hurried inside. Tearing off her hat and pelisse, she went toward the dungeon door.

"Miss Caulfield?" Mr. Prince called behind her.

"Is your grandfather below?"

Mr. Prince came swiftly to her. "I believe so. What has happened?"

"Nothing yet." She tripped down the stairs into the cavern of books. Pulling the first that she saw off a stack, she ran her fingers across the newly stretched cloth binding. Cloth. Not leather, despite the obvious age of the crumbling pages within. The cloth was a marker of Sir Wilkie's economy.

Mr. Prince came behind her.

"You said that your grandfather had restored his library collection recently," she said.

"Yes. It must have taken him a year. Rather, the fellow he hired. A student from somewhere or another in need of a repairing lease, I think." He chuckled. "Grandfather said he was always tucking into the wine cellar after dinner, but that he did a fine job of the work. He went through hundreds of books, of course."

She flipped open the cover and tried not to think how the last time she'd stood in this spot the man she hadn't seen in eleven years had told her—quite rightly—that she had kissed him. Or how, contrary fool that she was, she wished he were here now instead of Robin Prince so that she could kiss him again. And again. Until she had kissed him enough to satisfy her need.

Her fingers skimmed the inside binding of the book. *Paper.* Not vellum or cloth or leather. Paper. But plenty of bookbinders bound with paper.

Ink shone through the thin sheet.

She pried the binding away from the edge of the inside cover and with her fingernail scraped at the glue that attached the sheet of paper to the cover board.

"May I ask what you're doing?" Mr. Prince said close to her shoulder.

"In the fifteenth century," she said, struggling to preserve the paper intact as she worked it away from the board, "the great scholars who served as clerks in the Vatican decried a common practice in Rome at the time." The glue held too tightly. Tucking her fingertip beneath the page, she tore it gently from the board. "It seems that artisans and the owners of memento shops regularly disassembled ancient codices that they found in abandoned buildings throughout the city. They used the pages of those codices to make pilgrim emblems. The emblem for Rome, of course, was the Veronica Veil, an image of Christ's face on a woman's handkerchief. The demand for them was huge and codices from crumbling, neglected libraries throughout Rome were decimated to provide materials to make them. Thousands of pilgrims left Rome with bits of Pliny, Cicero and Aristotle pinned to their hats and scrips. Marvelous, isn't it?"

"I—I daresay."

"But it wasn't only pilgrim emblems. Scriptoria and eventually printers also used the pages of ancient texts as bindings for new books." She pulled the inside cover lining fully free and turned it up to the light. "Humanist scholars searching for any copy of ancient texts they could find thought this practice a travesty, of course. They were forever finding partial pages of lost ancient manuscripts in the linings of new, cheaply produced books." Lines of writing crossed the page. "They complained about it in their private letters to each other, and I'm terribly grateful to them for that, or I never would have thought of it." She displayed the twice-used page with a satisfied smile. "This, Mr. Prince, is where the papers from all those boxes have gone."

"Miss Caulfield." He was not looking at the paper. His bright blue eyes were wide. "You astonish me."

"I do?" Taliesin would not be astonished. He would smile that provoking half smile and call her something impertinent. But she would see the pleasure and pride in his eyes, the same way he had looked at her after their horseback race, before he kissed her.

"You do," Mr. Prince said. "I am speechless over your erudition and ashamed at my ignorance."

"Useless erudition in most cases. Living with a vicar and surrounded by books, I've had little else to do but study." And fantasize about having grand adventures.

Grabbing another book off a stack, she opened it and studied the lining. This one came away more easily, as did the next and the next. After a dozen similarly loosely bound books, the tight glue on the first book seemed to be an anomaly.

"These seem to be bits of letters," Mr. Prince said, peering beneath the linings as she passed him books to restack. "Ah. Here is one from a sailor, I think. Or perhaps a soldier. 'My dearest Eliza, How I long to return home to you and our five dear—' How disappointing. It breaks off there. What do you suppose they had five of? Canaries?" He smiled.

"Children." She plucked another book down. "You shouldn't laugh, Mr. Prince. These letters did not reach their destination. Who is to know if the senders ever saw the recipients again?"

Contrition blanketed his features. "I am forgetting the tragedy your family suffered. Forgive me, Miss Caulfield."

"Gentlemen are always begging forgiveness of silly girls these days," Sir Wilkie croaked from behind her. He lifted his lamp. "What are you doing there, missy? Tearing apart my new books, are you?"

"They aren't new books, Grandfather. Only new bindings that the fellow you hired last year put on. But Miss Caulfield and I have discovered the most remarkable thing, you see."

"I don't care what you've discovered, jackanapes." He grabbed the book from Eleanor's fingers and the volumes in his grandson's hands, and clutched them to his chest. "If you destroy one more of my books, young man, when I'm dead I'll give the whole lot of them and the rest of Drearcliffe to that sister of yours instead of to you."

Mr. Prince cast Eleanor a swift glance. "Yes, Grandfather. Of course we shan't disturb your books."

Panic crimped Eleanor's stomach. "But—"

"Miss Caulfield, shall we go inquire of Fiddle after dinner? It's nearly six o'clock, I daresay." He nodded toward the stair.

At the top of the stairs he closed the door and his shoulders drooped.

"I am wretchedly sorry." He shook his head. "My grandfather is a queer one."

"Is there no way around it, then? Perhaps he might change his mind?"

"Unlikely, I'm afraid." He looked truly miserable, but he said nothing more and she had to wonder about Sir Wilkie's threat. Mr. Prince and his sisters seemed affectionate with each other, and they certainly didn't appear pockets-to-let; their clothing was considerably finer than most of hers and their horses and carriage were respectable. But appearances could deceive. No one in St. Petroc had ever guessed that a poor Gypsy boy received the education that a boy at Eton or Harrow might. If they'd been told point-blank, they still would not have believed it.

But the key to her past could be hidden in one of those books.

By the time Mr. Fiddle brought dinner to the table, Mr. Prince had returned to his usual good spirits. "Why don't we all go over to Kitharan in the morning and offer our help to its master?"

"Splendid idea," Fanny replied. "You, Henrietta, will remain at my side every moment."

"Oh, Fanny, don't scold," her sister said. "I know you find him as wonderfully intriguing as I do, or you wouldn't be running over there at every opportunity."

Fanny frowned. "You will remain with me, and that

is an end to it. Betsy will come with us to make certain Henrietta does not escape, won't she, Eleanor?"

"I don't like it," Betsy said later, "you going over there to see *that* gentleman when there's a perfectly fine gentleman *here* who admires you." She fluffed Eleanor's pillow with extra emphasis.

"I wish you wouldn't speak of Mr. Wolfe disrespectfully."

"I'll speak of any man as he deserves, miss. And *that* gentleman having unmarried ladies to visit his house every other day is a scandal waiting to happen. Mark my words."

"Betsy, does the duchess know you are this impertinent?"

"I expect so, miss. Mama told her grace I'd be a shambles of a lady's maid, though I was trained for it since the time I was four." Eleanor's hair whipped through her deft fingers as she fashioned it into a braid. "Both of us gaped like fish when her grace sent down to have me come up to the house. And with only a day's notice! But seeing as I've no more than one shirt, two shifts, one skirt, and two pairs of stockings, I'd not much to pack, thankfully." She tied off the braid with a ribbon and stood back, hands on her hips. "You look pretty as a picture, miss. That handsome Mr. Prince will like it, I think."

Eleanor swiveled on the chair. "Betsy, did the duchess hire you expressly to accompany me on this voyage?"

"Yes, miss."

She dismissed Betsy before undressing and waited. She listened for Mr. Fiddle's shuffling footsteps followed by the snuffling of dogs as he doused the lamp in the corridor. The light from his candle bounced along the crack beneath her door then disappeared to the fading patter of twenty paws. She waited another quarter hour, reading but not attending to the words, wondering instead what Taliesin was doing at his big house with which Fanny Upchurch was now thoroughly familiar.

When she hadn't heard a sound in the corridors of Drearcliffe for some time, she stole from her room with a lamp and tiptoed down the stairs to the door to the dungeon. Since this wasn't nearly as bad as drinking whiskey in a common room, she felt nearly sanguine about disobeying Sir Wilkie. This time she was actually dressed.

Taliesin had seen her in her nightgown.

He'd seen her in her nightgown when she'd been ill, as a girl, of course.

Not the same thing.

In the cramped corridor of books, the lamp illuminated a small radius. Setting it down, she drew a pile of books from a stack and lowered herself to the floor. *Cold*. It was a basement after all. A dungeon.

Taliesin had been in jails. Cold cells. Cold floors. Alone. She closed her eyes. Good heavens, why did it hurt so much now to imagine what he had suffered years earlier?

Taking up two books of poor quality, she set them under her behind and leaned back against a stack.

Dozens of books later, candlelight bobbed in the stairwell and her head jerked up.

"Miss Caulfield?" Robin Prince's hair was like an angel's, the blue dressing gown he wore over his shirt, cravat and trousers making his eyes dark in the night.

"Was I too loud?" Her voice crackled over the words. "Is your grandfather alerted?"

"You are silent as a mouse and he's still abed, deeply asleep." For a moment he seemed nonplused. Then he smiled. "You are tenacious, I see."

"I am. But I don't wish to cause you trouble. I will cease now." She set the book in her lap aside.

"No. Don't move, I beg of you. You look particularly fetching there. Would you like help?"

"Very much." The task was tedious and she'd been amusing herself by imagining what Taliesin might say about the scraps of paper passing through her hands: letters to parents from soldiers, to wives from sailors, to London bankers from their clients in the Americas or Spain or anywhere from which a ship might have come to the coast of Cornwall. But Taliesin wasn't here. He was in his house that he had purchased during the years he hadn't even seen fit to tell her where he was. Instead, a perfectly fine gentleman was here.

She could learn to appreciate Robin Prince. She could learn.

AN HOUR BEFORE dawn she found it. Hands stiff with cold, she turned it over and over again, as though the words might disappear and the world along with them.

She should have started searching with the large folios. But she hadn't known what she was looking for. That a ship's manifest would appear bound into a world atlas, and that at the top should be written "*Lady Voyager*, 18 October 1795," had never once occurred to her. It was too wonderful.

Smoothing the page on her lap, she sought the column of names, scrawled in a quick hand beside a narrow column of numbers from one to thirty-eight. Only thirty-eight. It could not be the entire manifest. But perhaps it was. Perhaps a cargo ship from a sugar company would not sail with more than thirty-eight people. She'd read somewhere that merchant ships ran heavy with cargo but light with sailors, and that passengers were an afterthought to make up some funds.

She ran her finger down the column of names, some Christian names only, some surnames with a first initial, some both. Her finger arrested. Scrawled on line twenty-three was a first name and initial only, "~~Grace T.~~" Beneath it, indented into the boxes for the names, on lines twenty-four through twenty-six, were "Eleanor (4 yrs.)," "Arabella (3 yrs.)," and "Rav. (6 mos.)." On line twenty-seven the clerk had written the name "Margaret Petite-Florie."

Their nurse. Margaret. Red-cheeked, with huge arms a girl could run into if she were being chased by dogs or a spider wasp. In a rush of memory, Eleanor saw her. Margaret, who had been with her every day of her life until the *Lady Voyager* sank beneath the waves.

How she could have forgotten Margaret, she hadn't an idea. But for years she had only allowed herself to think of the present moment—the anger and disapproval of the headmistress at the foundling home, Arabella's defiance of every restriction, Ravenna's free spirit that led her into trouble time and again. For years she had bandaged her sisters' work-wounded knees, elbows, and faces, and their backs and palms torn from the strap. She had kissed them, held them in her arms, and thought only of the present, closing her mind to memories of happy days that gave her pain to recall. And always she had prayed that God would deliver them.

He had. To Martin Caulfield, who had made them his own.

The name Grace meant nothing to her. She hadn't known her mother's name or their family name. But if this Grace T was their mother, she had initially intended to sail with them to England. The strike through her name on the manifest was clear. Why she had not embarked, it didn't indicate. But she had at least temporarily intended to sail with them.

Joy and relief and a deep, worn sorrow twisted in Eleanor's chest.

She'd no idea of the *Lady Voyager*'s destination. But she would search every port from Scotland to France if she must. She closed her eyes and breathed in dust and satisfaction.

"Miss Caulfield?" Mr. Prince's voice was scrubby with sleep. He had gone to Sir Wilkie's study earlier, from where she'd eventually heard soft sounds of snoring.

He came into the corridor. Manifest in hand, she started to stand and her leg buckled. He grasped her hand, then her arm, and helped her up. His hair was ruffled, his eyes a bit myopic, and his cravat crushed.

"There now," he said and released her. "I must have fallen asleep. I'm terribly sorry."

"I've found something." She offered it to him.

He peered closely. "Good God, the manifest of the *Lady Voyager*?" He looked up at her. "Is it—"

"It is. There. My name, and my sisters' names. Our nurse and our mother."

His smile spread. "Well, what a triumph. This must be celebrated. Then we will go straight off to my grandfather and inform him what a bloody genius he is to save everything."

She laughed and it felt glorious. "I must tell Mr. Wolfe. Will you ride with me to Kitharan this morning?"

"This morning? Why, what hour is it?"

Gray shone through the cell window nearby. "Nearly dawn, I think."

"And you've been awake through the night? I won't hear of it, madam. I insist that you take at least a few hours of sleep first." His brow furrowed. "You must preserve your health, Miss Caulfield, for the remainder of the search."

She didn't wish to sleep. She wanted to tell Taliesin. That he would want to know immediately, she had no doubt. That Mr. Prince spoke of preserving her health put a sour taste in her mouth. But he was adamant and finally she acquiesced.

TALIESIN HAD NEVER experienced this before. Not in exactly this fashion. He'd never lacked feminine company when he wished it, and frequently when he did not. But he had never been openly, actively pursued by a gentlewoman.

After setting off on his own at nearly eighteen, he had retained certain clear physical markers of his heritage as much as an act of defiance as to repel women with whom he had no wish to become entangled.

The women of the Prince family were apparently unaware that was meant to apply to them.

Both Mrs. Upchurch and Miss Prince arrived at his house a mere hour after he returned from his morning ride. With a brilliant smile, Mrs. Upchurch declared that after she sat for a bit with Mrs. Samuel discussing party plans she wished him to escort her riding. Henrietta would, of course, remain at the house with Mrs. Samuel, being shy of wandering too far afield on her horse after the unfortunate incident of becoming lost in the storm.

Unprecedented.

It had to be the house. And the four dozen horses.

He couldn't blame her. He still couldn't quite believe it himself at times. The house certainly proclaimed him a gentleman, as did his stable. But gentlemen didn't have calluses on their hands. Gentlemen didn't have family living under canvas either. What a study it would be when he invited his uncle's family to Kitharan. Then women like Fanny Upchurch wouldn't be quite so eager to call on him, he suspected.

Now, however, she pressed him for a private tour about the estate. He could not politely refuse and he found that he didn't wish to. She was pleasant company and it was a novelty. He'd had little commerce with gentlewomen and always in the context of business—except Eleanor. She hadn't yet returned to Kitharan, which must be for the best. The less he saw of her the less likely he was to do something they would both regret. Something *else*. Something more.

Mrs. Upchurch required a mount.

"You mustn't saddle the horse yourself, Mr. Wolfe," she said, draping the train of her gown over her arm. Long train. Riding habit. She had come in a carriage yet prepared to ride. He considered calling the stable hand to attend them on the ride. A wise man required a chaperone with women intent on mischief.

Except one woman—the woman he wanted to pull off her horse and kiss on a windswept hill—and on a beach—and in a stable—and anywhere else she would have it.

Except that he mustn't.

"I am a horseman, Mrs. Upchurch," he said as he fastened the girth on a gentle four-year-old gelding he'd been training as a lady's saddle horse. Nothing to compare to Iseult. "I was born on a saddle."

Her laughter was a gay cascade of light amusement. "You are too droll, sir."

He ran a hand along the gelding's flank. "You misunderstand. I was in fact born on a saddle. My mother gave birth to me on the road. A mountainside path. The saddle and cloth were the only furniture available." It was the one story he knew of his parents, told to him by his uncle, who vowed that he knew nothing else of his parents. A fantastical tale, but it suited him. A man born in motion must never become attached to anything, most especially not another person. He had learned that lesson well.

Mrs. Upchurch's bright eyes were wide. "How remarkably uncomfortable that must have been for her."

He laughed. "I suspect it was." He assisted her to mount. Settling herself in the saddle, she held on to his hand too long, then offered him a smile and urged the horse forward.

"Come, Mr. Wolfe," she threw over her shoulder. "I am eager to see all that you are lord of."

He closed his eyes and rubbed the back of his neck. Then he followed.

IN THE GLISTENING midday sunshine of late winter, Kitharan rose like a golden manse of fairy tales from the gentle emerald hills all about it. Eleanor paused on the opposite apex as Mr. Prince caught up to her.

"At last," he said bracingly. "I hope Wolfe will offer us luncheon. You must be weary after such a ride."

Not remotely. Rather, giddy in every nerve.

A pair of riders appeared below, walking along the winding drive toward the house. Fanny waved.

"Aha. I see my sister is busy planning the party," Eleanor's companion said wryly. "Do you mind it? That my sisters are behaving like such widgeons with Wolfe?"

"I don't know what you mean." It was not an answer, she knew.

Mr. Prince captured her eyes. "I think you do, and I hope that you would not mind it."

Fanny and Taliesin had turned off the drive and onto the hill to meet them and Eleanor pressed Iseult forward.

"Robin! Eleanor!" Fanny called. "How happy we are to see you."

We? He could still speak for himself, couldn't he?

Fanny's eyes twinkled, a jaunty little hat of burgundy velvet setting off her curls. Her habit, of the same color and fabric, cinched beneath her bosom and accentuated the tiny span of her waist and feminine swell of her hips. If Taliesin admired her, she couldn't blame him.

Stealing herself, she looked to him and met his gaze.

"Are you well?" No real greeting. He didn't care for the niceties. But his eyes upon her were intent. More than warm.

"I am. I—" The words stopped in her throat. He, Fanny, and Mr. Prince stared at her, but she could not speak. She could not share with him her news now, not in front of these strangers. "Yes," she said.

And that was all she said for some time. Fanny regaled them with plans for the party, and then launched into a rapturous account of Taliesin's lands and every one of his horses, it seemed, all the while casting him sparkling glances that seemed perfectly unobjectionable yet tied Eleanor's stomach in knots. By the time Mrs. Samuel offered them luncheon in the conservatory, she could eat nothing. Taliesin made no effort to speak to her alone or at all. By the time she departed with Mr. Prince, with the carriage carrying Fanny and Henrietta behind them, she wondered if she had imagined what had passed between them in the stable four days earlier. Perhaps she had. Just as she had imagined it eleven years ago.

After dinner, Fanny and Henrietta retired early. Eleanor sat by the fire in the drawing room with a cup of tea growing cold between her palms and an unopened book by her side.

Mr. Prince went to the candelabra on the mantel and

extinguished the fire. "You are pensive tonight, Miss Caulfield. Was the ride to Kitharan too taxing?"

"No." She set down the cup and stood. Part of her scolded silently, insisting that this was a childish game. The other part—the part that spoke in a voice that sounded remarkably like Arabella's—told her she mustn't be a fool. "Mr. Prince, if I were to ask you to kiss me now, would you?"

A startled deer stared out from behind his eyes. "I—I would not presume to impose upon you so."

She moved forward. "If I assured you it would not be an imposition?"

"Then I wouldn't know what to do, in truth. For I should like to kiss you. Very much," he said with a thick inhalation. "Yet I fear your traveling companion would object."

"My maid?"

His brow darkened. "Your escort."

Her stomach did an awful flip.

With determination, she took another step forward. "He is not my chaperone. I am twenty-seven and firmly on the shelf. What's more, I have been going about without a nurse or mother or chaperone of any sort since I became a woman." Since the night Taliesin had first kissed her in the moonlight.

Mr. Prince moved to her, took up her hand, and caressed the backs of her fingers with the flat of his thumb. He smiled gently. "That you consider yourself on the shelf is a misapprehension of which I would very much like to disabuse you. Allow me to call you Eleanor."

"I will allow it if you will kiss me."

"I should be a cad to do so without first begging for your hand."

Her stomach fell into her knees. "But— But—"

"Will you?" His face looked perfectly sincere. "Dearest Eleanor?"

"Mr. Prince." She dropped her eyes. Withdrew her hand. "You go too fast."

"And yet here you have asked me to kiss you. Which of us is more hasty?"

"A kiss is not marriage." Then she would have been married at sixteen, and deliriously happy about it. A pathetic, lovesick puppy.

"When I want that kiss as much as I do," he said in a peculiarly thick voice, "it recommends itself to marriage."

She had not expected this ardency. She turned away. "I don't—"

He grasped her arm and turned her about to face him. "I have seen you looking at me as though you wonder what to make of me. What have you decided, Eleanor? I've grown impatient to know."

"I don't know."

"Do you mean to test me, to test my honor with this request? If I assent, will it damn me in your estimation?"

"No. I would not play such a game with a man's sentiments." Yet she was playing it with her own. She felt nothing remarkable with him and yet she *wanted* to. She wanted to shatter the hold Taliesin had on her desire. "I promise you."

Mr. Prince drew her close to him by the taut cord of her arm. "Then I assent. Willingly. Ecstatically." He bent his head and passed his lips lightly over hers. Then he leaned in and, placing his hand on her waist, he kissed her.

Cool and curious. Interested. Assessing. Thoughts instead of feelings. Analysis rather than passion.

Destiny could not feel like this.

He looked into her eyes. "Tell me you were as moved by that as I," he said in a strained voice.

Was she to laugh or cry or tell him the truth? The

mere brush of Taliesin's gaze affected her more profoundly than the caress of this man's lips.

"Thank you for obliging me," she whispered weakly. "I know I should not have asked it." Perhaps the gossips whose words wounded Arabella were right. Perhaps their mother had been a woman of ill repute and Eleanor shared that blood. Asking one man to kiss her while wanting another seemed excellent evidence for it. Or perhaps she was simply like Guinevere, longing for Lancelot when she already had Arthur.

"That isn't what I thought to hear. God, Eleanor." He speared his fingers through his hair. His hand grasped her waist tighter. "Perhaps I should be clearer about my feelings." His mouth connected with hers and his arm rounded her shoulders.

Embraced, surrounded, drawn in. Desired.

His lips were soft, no longer tentative, coaxing now. Pleasing. He tasted of brandy and smelled of some subtle and masculine cologne. She curved her fingers around his shoulder. Closed her eyes. Felt the pressure of his lips, and the response inside her, the prickling of awareness in her belly. The warmth. Then in her breasts.

She gasped her surprise and broke from him. Her face turned away, hot.

"Eleanor." He was breathing hard. "You felt it. Tell me you felt it."

"I—" The truth jousted with denial upon her tongue. She forced her eyes to his. "I am confused."

Triumph crossed his face like a parade, but only for an instant. "Then I am taught to hope."

"I don't know what to do," she said honestly.

He gripped the mantel, as though to hold himself still. "I will not push you. I will wait for you to decide your mind. You need only time."

Her mind needed no time. It assessed his handsome features, his eyes vibrant with sincerity, her pleasure in his company, and she knew. Here was what her family hoped for her. Opportunity she would not have again. A good man who would give her a good life.

"I should go to bed." She went to the door.

She paused on the threshold. His face showed what her heart felt: desperation. Desperation to understand something that could not be understood, she feared. He truly cared for her, enough to offer marriage. Perhaps she could learn to feel something for him. Perhaps if she married him she would learn the truth of her family. Perhaps she would finally learn who she was.

"Good night, Robin," she said, and went to her room. She'd had little sleep the night before. Nothing sensible was ever pondered effectively while exhausted. She needn't make any decisions about her future tonight. After the party tomorrow, she would ask Taliesin to take her home as soon as he could tear himself away from his house and his new, deeply friendly neighbors. Then from St. Petroc she would write to Arabella and Luc and ask for advice about what action to take next. Perhaps they could contact the sugar company, or the shipping company. They might even place an advertisement in the London papers: "FOUND: Three lost daughters shipwrecked on the *Lady Voyager* in 1795. One of them happens to be a duchess. Inquire at Combe Castle."

She wasn't a fool. Robin Prince's financial security was dependent upon his grandfather's crotchety humor. He was impressed with her sisters' connections. Other gentlemen she'd met at Arabella's and Ravenna's weddings had been friendly too. Perhaps they imagined the Duke of Lycombe planned to settle a dowry upon his spinster sister-in-law.

But Robin's admiration seemed sincere, his eagerness to make her feel for him so honest. She could not reject such a man.

Chapter 15

The Truth

The day of the party at Kitharan dawned cheerfully clear. When Eleanor went down to breakfast she learned that Fanny had already departed.

Fidgety, she spent an hour riding and two hours reading, and all morning avoiding Robin.

At two o'clock Betsy fastened her into a gown of shimmering golden apricot silk sewn with beads across the bodice that Arabella had managed to tuck into the bottom of her traveling trunk. Affixing a triple-tiered pearl choker about her neck—also Arabella's secret gift—Betsy glowered at her in the mirror.

"Now, miss, you mustn't be so forward with *that*

gentleman as that Mrs. Upchurch is." She wagged a
finger. "She'll get herself in a pile of trouble with the
likes of him if she's not more careful." Then her face
brightened. "But don't you look pretty as a picture?
You should dress like a lady more often, miss. Those
plain gowns you wear hide all the pretty in you as if
you were the grocer's daughter."

"Don't be silly, Betsy. I am in fact a vicar's daughter.
I don't need ball gowns."

She thanked her maid and met Robin and Henrietta
in the foyer.

"I am dazzled," he said with a smile. The fervency
and desperation of the night before were absent from
his lapis eyes. But his appreciative perusal curled her
toes. Today, dressed in a fine coat and starched neck
cloth for the occasion, with his gold hair combed into a
fashionable arrangement, he was handsome enough to
catch any woman's notice.

The master of Kitharan, however, was simply handsome all the time, in every way, and not least when he
was dressed for his own hanging. For that, clearly, he
seemed to believe he was about to attend.

He wore nothing unusual, had not in fact altered
himself for the occasion, not any further than he had
altered himself over the past decade—dark breeches
and coat, a waistcoat of deep blue, and a grim mask on
his face. He hadn't even left off his boots.

Eleanor walked the long entrance hall of his house
to where he stood at the base of the stairs. She would
not be tongue-tied or afraid today. She had known him
since they were children. She would claim the privilege of family and friendship, even if she had the most
pressing urge to nibble on his jaw.

Still, when she halted before him, her face burned
and her stomach twisted with guilt. She had kissed
Robin Prince. She had liked it—*a little*. As if she had

betrayed Taliesin, shame heated her everywhere. Looking into his black eyes she knew her idiocy, and yet she felt herself fall another step into him.

"You are dressed as though you might leap onto your horse and ride away at any moment," she said quietly.

A slight smile. "I've been considering it."

"You won't die today, you know."

"Are you certain of that?" His gaze scanned her from toe to shoulder, then her face and hair. The gown bared her arms, and some bosom. On the chilly drive over she'd been wishing Arabella's modiste had been more generous with fabric. Now she wished the modiste had cut the entire gown away. She wanted the warmth in his eyes to burrow beneath the silk and set her alight.

"Fairly certain," she said. "Unless you throw yourself beneath the wheels of one of those carriages coming up the drive now. Will you, and end your misery?"

"Would you like that, *pirani*?"

"Yes. That would be delightful." He had abandoned her for days. "Ravenna would never forgive me for allowing it, and Arabella would bar me from her home for the remainder of my life. But certainly, on my account, yes, I think you should." She spoke because she wanted to be touching him, but she could not with guests descending from their carriages just outside the door. And he had warned her not to.

She moved behind him. "Oh, no. It is too late already," she whispered. "You must face the dragon."

He offered her a half smile and went forward.

It was the last she spoke to him all day. She had been hostess at the vicarage for years, but she was no longer that anywhere, and most certainly not in the house of the already infamous master of Kitharan.

The guests proved wonderfully diverting. A few were supercilious, with noses high and no evidence of humor or intelligence about them. But most of the people Eleanor met charmed her. Everyone in the county had been invited, from local gentry to farmers. When Fanny wrote out the invitation list, Eleanor had insisted on that. Fanny had laughed at her provincial ways, but obliged. Now they all enjoyed the delicacies Kitharan's cook had created, and Mrs. Samuel's tour of the house.

Kitharan's master alone seemed pensive.

Eleanor watched him. Surrounded by his guests, he spoke little, but they seemed to approve. Fanny was never far from him, laughing with delight, sparkling and gay. Mrs. Starch praised Fanny's management of the party to several of the neighbors, and Fanny's pretty cheeks grew rosier still. When finally she found her way to Taliesin's side she remained there. Like a hostess. Like *his* hostess.

"He seems taken with her."

Eleanor turned to Robin. "I beg your pardon?"

"Your friend Mr. Wolfe. He admires my sister. Funny that it should have begun with Henrietta's foolishness and now ends with Fanny's happiness."

Eleanor's heart stumbled. "Ends?"

"She has been alone too long since her husband's death. She isn't happy in solitude. I have often heard her speak of wanting children." He paused, looking carefully at her. "I am happy for her."

The room seemed to spin. It could not be. In so short a time?

In the same number of days Robin had proposed marriage to her.

But Taliesin was different. Taliesin was *hers*.

The air clogged with the truth, a hundred barrels of thick, cold comprehension pouring down upon her at once. Drowning her. She had never understood herself fully until now. She had never understood that in her secret heart she had always believed he would return to her. Why else hadn't she sought marriage? She wanted children too. A family.

Her papa . . . the safe comforts of the vicarage . . . *excuses*. In all these years she had been waiting for Taliesin. Waiting to begin the adventure again. With him.

But he hadn't waited for her. He had forgotten her. He had walked away from her years ago, and even so she hadn't understood the truth. Until now.

"Dearest lady," Robin said softly, close to her ear, "will you give me your answer? Your assent? Promise me your hand and I will make you the happiest woman imaginable." His eyes entreated.

"We are barely acquainted." Did she speak aloud? Her lips were numb.

"That hasn't proved a hindrance to Fanny and Wolfe." He smiled down into her face. "If you cannot answer at this moment, allow me only the hope that you might soon reply."

"I hardly know what to say." She couldn't think. Only feelings came, too quickly and too many. "I—I should like to have a breath of air."

"Of course." He took her arm but she tugged it away.

"No. Alone. I need . . . a moment." She fled, winding her way through the crowd in the hall to the kitchen.

"Oh, miss!" the cook said with a harried air. "You shouldn't be in here. You'll soil that pretty dress."

The kitchen let off into the winter garden. Eleanor hurried between beds of greens and turnips to a path that led to the terrace, wrapping her hands about her bare arms against the cold. Constructed recently, the terrace stretched the length of the building, integrated artfully into the house, from paving stones to balustrade. Above, the heavens shone with stars tumbling upon one another, each fighting to brighten the sky. She watched her own quick, desperate breaths make frozen clouds against the glittering night.

"*Y se alegre el alma llena*," he said behind her. "*De la luz de esos luceros.*"

She turned. He came toward her, limned in torch-light, silver glinting in his ears, as comfortable as master of this enormous house as he was of the open road. The Gypsy Lord. Not her Gypsy. Not hers at all.

"What does it mean?" she said.

"Something about stars, as I recall." But he wasn't looking up at the stars. He was looking at her.

"Why have you come out here?"

"I saw your abrupt departure. What did Prince say to make you run away from him?"

"I did not run away from him." The lie bruised her tongue. "How peculiar you are to think it."

He halted close and studied her face. "You turned white and then flew away."

"I must have taken a momentary chill."

"And you came into the cold to remedy that."

Her skin was prickly with gooseflesh. "Is this an examination? Am I to recite my letters and numbers to you as well?" She turned her shoulder to him. Then only his voice would turn her limbs to jelly. "Your guests are departing. You should return inside and bid them good night."

"I probably should." He didn't move.

"I rode here yesterday, with him, to tell you about something that I had found. A clue to my parents. A manifest from the ship with our names on it." She spoke to still her trembling lips, and because she wanted him to know. She needed to share it with him. "She was called the *Lady Voyager*. Isn't that curious?"

"That your quest should bring you to a ship so aptly named?" His voice smiled. "Yes."

He understood. She'd known he would. Perhaps it was their shared past. But perhaps it was because he simply knew her. "Arabella will be happy to hear it," she managed to say.

"Will you continue searching Drearcliffe?" In the

starlight his shadowed gaze upon her seemed so intense, focused.

"I don't know. I should probably return home now. To St. Petroc. But you must have matters to attend to here. I wouldn't like to force you to leave on my account."

"I am here on your account. This gathering of people at this house is because I am here in this country on your account."

"You are misrepresenting the matter. This party is because you own a house here." And because a girl just out of the schoolroom had forced herself upon him. And because a lady of spirit and warmth had chosen him for her second husband. The tight stays clamped around Eleanor's ribs and made her breaths short. "I . . ."

His eyes on her did not waver. A shiver rippled along her body.

"When I ran away from Mr. Prince just now, he had said to me . . . He . . ." She could not say aloud what she knew about him and Fanny. If she said it, he would confirm it as true, and she might very well cry. Or rip up at him. Or throw something hot and sticky. Or all of those.

But perhaps she should say it. Perhaps that was her next challenge, to speak honestly. To throw all scruples to the wind. Looking into his face—familiar, beautiful, so deeply missed for so many years—she wanted more than anything to fly.

"Yesterday I kissed him. He kissed me. I let him. I asked him to." Her tongue stumbled over the confession. "I enjoyed it."

His brow cut down. "Why are you telling me this?"

"Why not?" Her brittle nerves cracked. "Your interest is elsewhere."

He moved to her and she backed into the wall, her shoulders meeting the cold stone. "What are you—?"

He took her arms in his hands, grasping tight. *Touching her.* His eyes were sparks of black fire. But he was touching her and she was thoroughly, entirely, brilliantly alive.

His eyes scanned her face, swiftly, powerfully. "You believe in that penny fortune, don't you? You believe Prince is the man Lussha spoke of all those years ago?"

Her jaw fell. "You *know* about the fortune?"

"Ravenna told me. It is foolishness. Lussha trades in superstition. Don't tell me you believe in it."

"I don't know what to believe," she whispered, her heartbeats tumbling. "I only know that five days ago I think I propositioned you, and your reply was to disappear."

He dropped his hands but he didn't move away. "I have stayed away from you intentionally."

"How singular, then, that you agreed to escort me the length and breadth of Cornwall. Or is this merely momentary, and you simply fear I will demand an outrageous prize for helping you throw this successful party?" She tried to laugh; it caught in her throat. "If so, the prize belongs to Fanny. She did it all, of course." The widow arranging her future while the spinster searched for her past. "I don't blame you for it."

"Eleanor." His voice seemed tight. "I am trying to protect you."

"*Protect* me?" By abandoning her? It was happening all over again, but this time he had given her warning. He had goaded her, kissed her, made her want him, and now he would not give her what she wanted. The devastation of it was that she only wanted him. With him she tasted adventure. She was free. Truly alive. Until he left her aching for what she could never have. "Do you know," she said, "coming from the single person that has ever broken my heart, that assurance rings remarkably false."

Chapter 16

The Light in Those Lights Above

*I*mpossible.

But her eyes told him she spoke the truth.

"I—" He could not find his tongue. "I didn't know."

She slipped out of his hold. "Now you do. But you needn't concern yourself over it. I was little more than a child, with a child's heart still capable of mending whole and hale again, like my lungs already had. And as you've said, youth passes. Fortunately."

With the grace of a stalk of wheat bending to the wind, she smoothed her palms over her skirt, tucked a lock of spun gold behind her ear, and walked across the terrace and into the house.

Taliesin stood staggered, never having imagined she had felt that deeply. His memories had painted it one-sided, all the heartbreak his.

Ass. Fool. Young angry fool.

Eight months after that summer day at the pond, he had returned to St. Petroc, determined to defy all reason and rule to have her. On his way to the vicarage, he'd come upon a gig parked in the middle of the road in the shadow of tree cover. Thomas Shackelford had her in his arms.

He had loved her for a lifetime, and in eight months she had forgotten him. His ribs had only just healed entirely. Beneath the newly knit bones, in that moment his heart had finally given up the battle.

But it hadn't. Not in truth. He'd left St. Petroc during the May Day fair the next day, but he'd gone on angry and bullheaded for years after that.

Now he was no longer an angry boy. And she was offering herself to him. In the starlight her pale cheeks, glowing skin, and halo of golden tresses had bedazzled him. Her arms were bare, her dress caressing her slender curves, and the beads about her neck an invitation to touch her. She was beautiful, and he could no longer deny that he wanted her or pretend to himself that he only wished to tease her.

Carriages trailed away from the drive into the silvery-blue brilliance of the night. Bypassing the hall, he took the servants' stair to the upper floor. He knew where he would find her. He knew her.

In the empty library she stood before the tall, bare window, a silhouette against the moon and stars. He crossed the room and she heard him.

She turned to him, dropped back a step, and he pulled her to him and captured her mouth beneath his.

Her lips were pliant and welcoming, her hands moving to clutch his shoulders. *She accepted him.* He kissed her and knew he would never have enough of her, never enough of the flavor of her lips or the texture of her passion. When he allowed her a moment's freedom, her whispered *yes* undid him.

He dragged her against him, felt her hands in his hair, her slender, curved softness along every inch of him. Her mouth was hungry. He tasted her with his tongue and she met him with hers. A whimper of pleasure escaped her.

His hands consumed her. The arc of her back, the swell of her hips. All of her body his to hold now, to feel. The roundness of her buttocks in his palms was perfect beauty. Clutching his face she roamed his jaw with her mouth, arching her belly against his. Her hands tugged at his shirt, her fingers strong, frantic. Then they were beneath his shirt, against his skin, touching. Her hands on him, moving upward, exploring, making him insane. Her sighs came short and quick, desperate sounds that wrapped around his heart.

"*Please.*" She pushed at his coat, unfastening his waistcoat, and he was perfectly all right with that. He'd waited eleven years to get naked with this woman again. No time like the present.

She pushed his shirt up. He released her to pull it off, then took her into his arms. Her hands trembled as she put them on him now, her movements suddenly hesitant.

"Don't be afraid." He could barely speak. He closed his eyes and bit back his need, holding her waist tight to him. *God's blood.* Torture. Her hands skimming his flesh. Her hips nestling his cock. Torture he hadn't dared to dream. Real now.

"I'm not afraid," she whispered, smoothing her

palms over his chest, her glimmering eyes wide upon his body. "I don't think I'm afraid." She bent her head and her breaths brushed his skin. Her hands butterflied across his ribs. "I think I am in need."

He took her mouth and pulled her body against his, and her hands were everywhere on him—his chest, his shoulders, his back. Sinking his fingers into her hair, he kissed her again, and again, their tongues seeking, mating, her mouth a universe of desire. He plucked open the fasteners of her gown and the laces of the gossamer undergarments beneath. He tugged them from her shoulders.

"Yes, *yes,*" came from her throat. Her bare arms, beautiful in the starlight, circled his neck and her mouth sought his anew, then his jaw. Her fingers tangled in his hair. "Yes." Lips, soft and damp, branded his skin, her tongue hot upon his throat. "I never knew," she whispered, curving her hand along his neck. "I never knew."

She pressed to him, struggling against the barriers of cloth. Never close enough. Layers of fabric between her skin and his. He hadn't known gentlewomen were so vehemently protected. Against men like him. Her lips found his and her tongue ventured into his mouth, her hips rocking against his. Silken ribbons caught in Taliesin's fingers. Loosened. Broke free. He pushed the remaining garments down.

Sweet mercy. If he died now he would have no need of heaven. He stood before it already.

"*Y se alegre el alma llena,*" he uttered, and ran his hands to either side of her breasts. She shuddered upon a sigh of delirium.

"I never knew it would feel like this," she whispered wonderingly.

"I did." He had always known she would be beautiful. Ivory and pink perfection. The soft swell of her feminine flesh, the vibrant pucker of her arousal. He cupped one breast in his palm and circled the peak with his thumb.

"What—what are you doing?" she gasped against his cheek.

"Teasing you. I have always wanted to tease you, exactly"—he circled again, closer to the peak—"like"—he slipped the pad of his thumb across the bud—"this."

She moaned. "Do it again," she demanded softly, breathlessly. "And again and again." Then: "Please."

He smiled. And he did it again, and again, until she was panting and pressing herself into his hands.

"Tell me this is everything," she said upon a whimper, her fingers gripping his shoulders, "and I will be content."

She was thoroughly innocent. His beauty. His princess.

"I cannot. There is this too." He bent and brushed his mouth across her breast. She sighed. Then he pressed his mouth into her flesh, losing himself, breathing her in, his dreams beneath his lips now. Holding his need back, he trailed his tongue over her nipple and a shudder rocked him.

Her fingers were clamps on his shoulders. "*Ohh.*"
Eleanor. In his hands. In his mouth.

"And this." He sucked. He tasted. The soft fragrance of her skin, the bud between his teeth made him drunk. Sinking into his hair, her hands held him close. She tasted of honey. He had wanted her forever, her soft beauty, her fierce need. Her slender body shivered, froze, then writhed against him.

"It's too much. Too— Oh, *stop*," she cried. "Stop!"

He released her and she sprang back. In the silvery dark, with her hair cascading from its pins, her gown pushed to her waist and her breasts bathed in starlight, she was not an angel as he'd long imagined her. She was, quite simply, a goddess. His goddess. She had always been. He could lose himself in worship of her.

She crossed her arms over her breasts, like the battle armor of Athena. She lacked only spear and shield. "I think I have lost this challenge." Her voice shook.

"I'm quite certain you haven't." She had no idea what she did to him. Still.

"I-I look at you," she stammered, "at your chest and arms, and touch you—you are so beautiful—and I feel what you do to me—and it feels so good." Her throat worked, her eyes a storm of confusion. "Yet I feel like something inside me is . . . *wrong*. Like I might explode."

Ah. "Eleanor—"

"It isn't in my lungs, I think." Her chest heaved on fraught breaths under her arms. "But—"

He pulled her tight into his embrace. His hand explored her hip, the curve, the sensation of this body he had wanted for so long, and she pressed herself to him. He slipped his hand between her legs. "Here."

She gasped. "Yes." Alarm leaped from her eyes.

"No fear," he murmured.

She swallowed hard. "No."

He stroked the soft crevice of her womanhood, biting back his desire. "Allow yourself to feel it."

She remained stiff. "I w-want to. But—"

"Touch me, Eleanor. Now."

Her hand stole up to his chest, fingers spreading, burning fire into his flesh, then trailing across his ribs, his muscles contracting, hungry for this. Hungry for her, for her skin on his, feeding her need as it stripped him to nothing but need. Giving her pleasure, he forgot himself.

Her lashes fluttered down and a moan broke from her. "*Yes.*"

Bending his mouth to her delicate jaw, he caressed her with his hand as he had longed to for years, found her taut, sweet spot, and gave her what her body wanted. Passionate and eager, she needed no more encouragement. The rhythm of her hips sought him. She came swiftly, suddenly, shuddering into his hands with a cry that sounded like pain and shock and pleasure at once. She had never come before. He was the first to bring her release. The only. Heaven just kept getting better and better. And the abyss below him gaped.

Gulping in breaths, she wrapped her arms around his neck and put her lips on his, then teased his mouth with her tongue.

He ran his hands down her back and flattened her against him, seeking the satisfaction of her body against his hard cock. She kissed his jaw, then pressed her lips to his ear.

"I win," she whispered. Her laughter was like sin and sunshine.

He bracketed her hips with his hands and clamped her to him as her lips played upon his neck. He needed to be inside her more than he wanted air. To feel her now, to be one with her, he would give everything he had. Everything.

"What prize will you claim?" He sounded nothing like himself—whipped, alien, enslaved.

"Wasn't that it?"

Breathing her in, hoarding deep reservoirs of her scent of honeysuckle and passion like a thief, he prepared himself. "Then it is my turn to offer a challenge."

"That sounds fair." Her hands stroked over his chest. The urge to lift her up against the wall and make her take him—make her satisfy him—burned in his blood and his hot, heavy cock. But even that wouldn't be enough. Never enough.

"What will it be?" she murmured, sliding her slender palm across his nipple.

Commanding an effort worthy of Galahad, he set her off him and stepped back. "I challenge you to leave here." He dragged in air. "Now." He made himself say the words. "And to never return."

Her laughter died. Confusion filled her eyes.

Then betrayal.

Then, finally, pain.

He backed away. Took up his shirt and coat. Could not look at her. She didn't understand but he could not explain now. Not with her before him bare-breasted and tousled and sated in the starlight. Not with her in his house, the place he had thought she would never come. But always, always in the back of his dreams, he had wished it.

Tomorrow, perhaps, in the light of day, fully clothed, he would explain. Or perhaps never. Years ago he had made a promise to her. But he had made another promise to himself; he had built his life on it. No matter what the temptation, no matter what the loss, he would not break it.

Chapter 17

The Ring

T

*E*leanor awoke aching everywhere—in her head and body, especially between her thighs where the sensation of his touch lingered, that opulent gift he'd given her that she hadn't even known to ask for. She slid her fingers beneath her nightgown and caressed herself. She'd done it before, wickedly, sinfully, drawn to it from perplexing stirrings, and she had found mild pleasure in it. But she'd known only a piece of the picture, apparently.

Now she encouraged it with her fingertips. Eyes closed, she felt his hands on her, his body pressed to hers, and the throbbing began. She thrust her hips into it, imagined his tongue touching hers, his lips upon her breast, driving her pleasure higher, tighter. Then for a brief moment she allowed herself to imagine him between her thighs, possessing her. She convulsed in a shudder of pleasure, her body arching off the bed. A sob escaped upon her moan.

She gasped for air and slung her arm across her heated face.

That was what she had learned last night about wild adventures. That, and what she had already known: that he would hurt her again. And leave.

Slowly, the regular cadence of her breaths returned, the megrim somewhat relieved. But the ache in her chest clung like she'd clung to him the night before. She pressed her face into the mattress and refused to feel shame like some submissive medieval maiden chastised by churchmen for her desire. Or heartbreak. She'd felt every wretched emotion possible eleven years ago as a girl. A woman now, she was perfectly capable of doing incredibly foolish things without tearing herself to pieces about it afterward.

But she had liked challenging him. She liked all the challenges they had shared on this journey, albeit the last challenge the most. She would miss it.

At least she would win his final challenge.

Perhaps she would remain at Drearcliffe until the Prince siblings returned to Bath, and travel with them. But she would not be able to explain why she could not go to Kitharan, nor why Mr. Wolfe would not call at Drearcliffe.

She didn't know what to do about Robin. She could not possibly marry one man when she was finding such pleasure with another, even if only in her imagination and by her own hand. She could not marry any man who didn't make her feel the way Taliesin did.

Other women did. Other women married for the things she wanted: companionship, a home, children. Did those women settle for life without passion?

More than passion. She could not name it, but she felt it beneath her ribs like the tide's answer to the moon's caress. No lust or even heartbreak could feel so alive. The pain in her heart this time was a living ache, a storm she watched wide-eyed, marveling at its wild beauty.

She rolled over. Beside the garments that Betsy had set out were the shoes he had bought in Piskey to replace her ruined boots. A defiant tear dropped onto her cheek.

Swiping it away, she set her feet to the frigid planks and went to the grate to make up the fire.

Betsy had gone to sleep before their party returned to Drearcliffe the night before, but she had laid out Eleanor's brush and the apron she wore while searching through Sir Wilkie's dusty collections. Reaching into the apron pocket, she drew forth the ring and set it on the dressing table. The ruby winked like a sailor's sunset.

She blinked.

And reached for the manifest on the table beside the ring.

And found the air abruptly thin.

The T beside her mother's name—Grace T—had been scribbled poorly on the manifest, the pen catching the top right end of the cross bar and levering halfway down the vertical bar to curve, then merging into it. It had been drawn poorly because it was not in fact a T or any letter at all. It was the same symbol fashioned into the gold and buried beneath the ruby on the ring.

Dressing swiftly, propelled by urgency again, she snatched up her hair and tried to still her hands enough to knot it. She must ride to Kitharan. That he had exiled her meant nothing now. He hadn't any say over where she went. If he wished to call the constable to throw her off his property, she supposed she would relent rather than go to jail. Until then, she wished only to share this with him.

Pulling on her pelisse and buttoning it as she hurried down the stairs, the manifest between her teeth and the ring in her fist, she stumbled into the foyer. Surrounded by dogs, Sir Wilkie's manservant was opening the front door.

"Mr. Fiddle," she said, "could you bid Mr. Treadwell to saddle my horse? I must ride immediately to—"

Taliesin walked across the threshold.

"Kitharan," she croaked.

"Unnecessary now, perhaps," he said, his voice very deep, his eyes very dark, and his entire person very beautiful.

Here he was.

"Never mind, Mr. Fiddle," she mumbled.

Mr. Fiddle shuffled from the foyer, the dogs scampering behind him.

"Here you are," she managed to press through her lips. "I needn't lose this challenge after all."

It was possible—but she couldn't be certain in the shadow of the doorway—that the corner of his mouth lifted ever so slightly.

"You wished to speak with me?" he said. "Or perhaps I am presumptuous. Your purpose in going to Kitharan could be to speak with my stable master. Or my housekeeper."

"Or one of those other people that work for you, astonishingly enough." She swallowed over the heartbeats ricocheting about her throat. "Everybody there last night, by the way, was amazed that a Gypsy could be master of such a place. With such efficient servants too. They were all shockingly impressed. Shocked that they were impressed, that is. But I suspect you anticipated that. Rather, intended it. Did you enjoy your party?" She ducked her head and attempted the remaining buttons of her pelisse with quivering fingers. "That is, the earlier part?" They were misbuttoned from the top.

He came toward her. "What did you wish to speak with me about?"

He stood too close. If she lifted her head he would see her violently hot cheeks. Tucking the ring and manifest into her pocket, she crossed her arms over the lopsided pelisse and the breasts that he had kissed until she made sounds she had never made in her life before.

"Beside my mother's name on the manifest of *Lady Voyager*," she said a bit unsteadily, "appears a symbol I recognize."

He studied her arms across her chest and a muscle flexed in his jaw. He lifted his eyes to hers. "What symbol?"

"How much do you know about the fortune that Lussha gave to Arabella?"

"She gave it to all three of you." It seemed he had not shaved this morning. His jaw was more shadowed than last night when the scrape of his whiskers on her breasts and neck had made her weak with pleasure.

"We were all in the tent when she said it," she managed to say. "But Arabella had asked for it because of— When Ravenna told you about the prophecy, did she tell you about the . . . about our heirloom?"

"No."

"Our mother sent us to England with a small, valuable object that she said we must keep safe. It was so precious that rather than give it into our nurse's keeping, she tied it on a thick string around my neck. She told me to show it to no one until we reached our destination. It is one of the only memories I have— her instructing me in this. When they took us to the foundling home I buried it in a hidden place so it would not be discovered." During that first night, trembling with fear in the dark, she'd been determined to obey her mother. Then she'd believed her mother would eventually come to them. That she would not abandon them.

"What is the object? Do you have it now?"

"I cannot tell you what it is. And, yes, I do have it. Lussha said that we mustn't show it to any man until one of us wed a prince. Then we could reveal it to him and he would tell us about our parents."

His brows came together. "That's ludicrous."

"Of course it is." She curled her fist around the ring in her pocket, and the paper of the manifest crackled. "But that heirloom bears the same symbol that appears after my mother's name on the ship's manifest. I realized it only this morning."

"If it is her family's crest, its appearance on the manifest is not particularly remarkable."

"But it is the only clue we have ever had about her identity."

"You have now the name of the ship," he said slowly, "your mother's first name, and the heirloom with the symbol. Your quest has borne fruit. I know a man who can help us. He is in Plymouth."

She paused. "Us?"

"Have you suddenly become a travel-wise lady voyager yourself, able to brave the roads on your own?"

"No." She tightened her arms. "You told me to leave."

He bent his head and ran his hand over the back of his neck. "I cannot have you in my house." He looked up at her, a plea in his midnight eyes. "Eleanor, I cannot touch you."

Belated regret. She understood. Years ago she had regretted falling in love with him. It must be possible to regret kissing someone. And undressing her. And giving her extraordinary pleasure. She supposed.

It ached simply to stand near him and not touch him.

"I cannot imagine that you promised Arabella that too," she said.

Now she was quite certain the corner of his mouth lifted.

"No." His gaze seemed to scan her face, then swiftly he turned away from her to the door. "Can you be ready to leave here in two hours?"

"To leave for Plymouth? Only two hours? That will barely give you time to return to Kitharan, then return here. Haven't you a house you must . . ." Her words trailed off as the silver in his ears caught the light. House or not, he was a nomad. Free to go and come as he would. He could leave upon a moment's notice or none at all. This truce, rather, this cooperation he was offering her, would be brief. Leaving would happen again, inevitably.

"Taliesin, why did you come here this morning? To call upon Mrs. Upchurch or Miss Prince?"

"No," he said after a moment. "I came to see you."

He left her tongue-tied by her own confusion.

FANNY FOUND HER packing. She peered about the room. "Is your clever Betsy about?"

"She is in the kitchen preparing food for the journey. Fanny, thank you for the welcome you have shown us here. I am deeply grateful."

"Oh, Eleanor." She hung back by the door, averting

her face. "Your gratitude makes me ashamed, for I have been a poor friend to you, I think."

"You have not."

"But I have! Do you remember when I told you that I would do anything to ensure my brother and sister's happiness?"

Eleanor nodded. She had understood. Arabella and Ravenna's happiness had always been her first concern.

"That first night we were all here, Robin saw swiftly how it was between you and Mr. Wolfe. He asked me to distract Mr. Wolfe so that he might be able to capture your attention."

She was not so naïve that she misunderstood. "Your interest in him was not sincere?"

"Oh, no. It was entirely sincere. It still is. I think you are vastly fortunate to be the object of his affection."

"You misunderstand it, Fanny." Enormously.

"I don't believe so. But I should be a wretched friend if I did not apologize for attempting to monopolize his time so that my brother could be with you alone more frequently. Do you like him, Eleanor? Does Robin have any chance at winning your admiration?"

"I do like him," she said honestly.

Fanny clasped her hands at her breast. "Oh, I am relieved to know it! He admires you excessively. If I promise to never interfere again, will you forgive me?"

"I don't know how to assure you that you needn't apologize. But if you must have my forgiveness, I give it."

Fanny kissed her on the cheek. "I wish you great success in Plymouth. If you need me, you mustn't hesitate to send for me." She went to the door and offered a smile over her shoulder. "And, Eleanor"—her lips curved into a little smile—"if you ever decide that you haven't any need of Mr. Wolfe's devotion, do let me know."

GOOD-BYES WERE SAID on the drive before Sir Wilkie's house. Even the master himself emerged from his dungeon to wish her a good journey.

Betsy glared at Taliesin as she mounted the carriage steps. Then with a worried scowl, she tucked herself inside.

Mr. Prince followed Eleanor to her horse and helped her to mount. In full view of the carriage and the man on his stallion nearby, he grasped her gloved hand and held it tight.

"My thoughts will be with you every moment of your mission, Eleanor," he said quietly. "I wish you good fortune."

"Thank you. I am grateful for the help you have given me so selflessly."

"I won't have you imagining such a thing. It was far from selfless." He squeezed her hand and released her. Turning to Taliesin, he offered a stiff bow. "Good journey to you, Wolfe."

Taliesin said nothing, no word of thanks or farewell. Touching the brim of his hat, he turned his great black stallion about and spurred him onward.

Chapter 18

The Swordsman

*T*hey achieved the port town of Plymouth in two stages, with a night on the road spent at an inn tucked along the edge of the moor—a night during which Betsy physically barricaded the door.

"I'll not have you sneaking off in the small hours to drink spirits or read books again, miss. *That* gentleman has the most suspect sort of admiration for you. I'll not have you putting yourself accidentally in his way." She lay down on the cot stretched in front of the bedchamber door. "Nobody'll ever be able to say Betsy Fortnum let her mistress get into trouble with a swarthy Egyptian, no matter how fine a house he has."

"And his . . . horses," Eleanor mumbled. The ride had been long and uncomfortable, the sea winds cold and the wind across the moor even colder. Every bone ached. Yet still she could think of little else than the miraculous contours of his chest, the strapped muscle of his belly, and the strength in his shoulders and arms. "His horses are fine too." She fell asleep imagining touching him and dreamed of him teaching her how to ride.

PLYMOUTH SPREAD VAST and complex and like a living creature at the water, an array of houses descending the hill, some of great beauty and some squalid. Wind swept the scents of fish and coal fire smoke across the inlets. The tide was good, the keeper of the Lost Ship Inn told them. That meant that quays and boats were all afloat, a happy circumstance. Most naval ships had embarked upon exercises or to scout for privateers trawling the Channel for unwary merchant vessels. The shops and eateries were peopled mostly with women, old men, and small boys.

All except one tavern, it seemed. Close to the fishermen's wharf, the cobbles before it strewn with fish guts and bones and slime and circled by a flock of squawking gulls, the Siren's Lair was packed with men. Every one of them seemed to stop drinking, eating, and throwing dice the moment the door closed behind her and Taliesin. For the length of a second. Then conversation resumed.

As they crossed the crowded tavern, men tipped their caps at Taliesin. Most of them were seamen, clearly. Yet they seemed to know him.

In the farthest corner of the tavern, a tall man was bent over a chessboard, his coat stretched across square shoulders. Tucked behind his neck, his hand threaded through dark gold locks. Whiskers running close upon his chin and above his lip sharpened his profile.

His opponent, a small bald-pated man with equatorial skin, perched on the edge of the chair opposite. A folded handkerchief rested on the table before him. He took it up, dabbed at his upper lip, and set it down again in perfect parallel with the edge of the table.

"Well, look who's come calling," the blond man said without taking his attention from the game. "Taliesin Wolfe." Long, supple fingers moved his white queen a single square.

His opponent jittered.

The blond man chuckled. "There you are, Bose. Counter that." Every muscle in his face, hands, and wrists tightened as he turned to them, his coat gaping to reveal the hilt of a sword. "Wolfe, you thieving scoundrel," he growled. He stood with an unfolding of power, rising to Taliesin's height. His coat hung loosely on his lean frame, but the strength in his stance intimidated.

"Hello, Saint," Taliesin said, holding his gaze hard.

A grin that glittered like a sword split the whiskers on Mr. Saint's chiseled features. With his left hand he clapped Taliesin on the shoulder. "I am happier than I can express to see you, my friend."

Taliesin nodded toward the table. "Game almost finished?"

"I call a hiatus, Bose," the man named Saint said to his chess partner.

"You cannot call a hiatus in the midst of play, Mr. Saint," the little man said with pinched lips, his nostrils flaring. "It is simply not done."

"Of course it's done." He bent his head to Eleanor and lowered his voice. "At least it's done when I'm losing." A brow went up with supreme indolence. His eyes were deep emerald, rimmed with dark lashes, and sharply alert.

He gestured her forward. Men doffed their caps as she moved to the door, and a few nodded. Emerging onto the street filled with the sounds of gulls and a boat's ringing bell, she turned to the men behind her. "What sort of place is that?"

"The worst sort. My favorite sort." Mr. Saint perused her slowly. "Now, Wolfe, tell me how you happen to have the fortune to be in the company of this sweet lady. For, unless my eyes and ears deceive me—which they never do—this lady is a lady far too good for the likes of you."

"Pretty words, sir," she said.

"He likes to hear himself talk," Taliesin said. "Miss Eleanor Caulfield, this is Evan Saint. He knows every soul—"

"And soulless demon," he said without removing his studying gaze from her.

"—in Plymouth. He will be able to help you."

"How do you do, sir?"

"Better now that I have your acquaintance, Miss . . ." He cut Taliesin a glance. "Eleanor Caulfield, did you say?"

Taliesin's eyes narrowed. "I did."

"Eleanor." Mr. Saint drew out the syllables, as though tasting each one. "Lovely name. Lovely lady." Left hand on the hilt of his sword, he bowed deeply. "Enchanted to assist you in whatever manner I am able." He straightened his shoulders with great grace—a different sort of grace than Taliesin's confident strength. Mr. Saint's grace was like a dancer's, agile and fluid, his face and body so lithe that she forgot she stood before a very tall, broad-shouldered man.

A gull dropped the carcass of a crab on the cobbles beside him. He lifted a bronze brow. "Shall we remove to a more decorous location, madam? Wolfe?"

They walked away from the waterside and deeper into the city. The men remained on either side of her along the cobbles shining with dampness from the descent of mist over the port as night fell. Women turned their heads as they passed, some calling hellos to Mr. Saint, others eyeing Taliesin.

In the tavern, a cozy, fire-lit place that was nearly empty of patrons, Mr. Saint held her chair for her and sat only after she did. Taliesin came to the table with a bottle and three glasses.

"What's this?" Mr. Saint said. "No tea for the lady, Wolfe? Where are your manners, you motherless cur?"

Taliesin met her gaze. "Would the lady prefer tea or whiskey?"

She bit her lip.

Mr. Saint looked between them and his eyes narrowed.

Taliesin poured three glasses.

"Evan, Miss Caulfield possesses an object of some value which bears a curious symbol. This symbol could be associated with a family."

"A family crest, perhaps?"

"Or an abbreviation of a surname."

Mr. Saint nodded. "You believe this is a family of note."

Eleanor halted with the glass almost to her lips. "*No.*" She choked on the fumes curling in her nostrils. "That—that is, I haven't any notion that the family is of note. It is my family, Mr. Saint, and I suspect we are of humble origins."

"I see. What is the valuable object, Miss Caulfield?"

Like a man removed a coat, he had discarded his playful air entirely. Sitting as though relaxed, still he seemed watchful, not only of her, but of the room about him too. Only his left hand rested on the table around the glass. The contrast of his taut vigilance with Taliesin's assured, focused presence could not be greater.

"I have been instructed not to reveal it to anyone." Any *man*. Lussha had said nothing about showing it to women. And yet none of them had. Among the living, only Arabella's husband Luc and Ravenna's dear friend Sir Beverley Clark had ever seen the ring. Luc's discovery of it had been accidental, and Sir Beverley's temporary possession of the ring had been a necessity.

"Can you tell me its approximate value?" Mr. Saint said.

"Not its exact value. But it is very great, I think."

"I must assume it is a small object, and that due to its value you would not leave it at an inn with your maid. Perhaps you carry it on your person now."

"It easily fits in the palm of a hand. But where I have stored it needn't be of concern to you."

"I respect your wish to keep its location secret." He cut Taliesin a swift glance. "Miss Caulfield, I know a man that might help you. His name is Elijah Fish. His trade is jewelry. In the fifteen years I have known him, I've found his knowledge of trinkets to be extraordinary. He never leaves his shop except on the Jews' Sabbath, and then only to worship. Will you allow me to make you acquainted with him? Then you might reveal to him alone whatever information you believe would be useful for him to know to assist you."

"Yes. Thank you."

"After you have spoken with Mr. Fish, if you require my further assistance I will be glad to help. Have you any other questions for me?"

"I do," Eleanor said. "I seek answers regarding a ship that might have once been in these waters. When we were children, my two sisters and I sailed on a sugar merchant's vessel from Jamaica. It wrecked off the coast within two days' ride of here. We were the only survivors and our family was lost to us. We don't know who they are."

"Your trinket is the key to discovering them?"

"I hope so. But now I also know my mother's Christian name and the name of the ship upon which we sailed. Her name is written on the manifest, but is struck through."

"She intended the journey but was ejected from the ship before sailing."

"Why do you say that? It might have been her choice not to sail."

He nodded. "Perhaps. But not necessarily. What year did you sail, Miss Caulfield?"

"Seventeen-ninety-five, if indeed the ship I have discovered was ours."

"I lived on Jamaica at that time."

Her heartbeat tripped, quickened. "But you must have been very young."

"I was. But I remained there for many years. At that time, 1795, anything might have prohibited your mother from sailing. Ships, especially merchant ships, ejected passengers—" The tavern door swung open upon a blast of misty wind. His right arm shifted across his lap, toward his hip. A pair of sailors entered. Mr. Saint's shoulder relaxed.

Arms crossed loosely, Taliesin watched both the door and his friend without moving.

"Many ships ejected passengers for any number of reasons," Mr. Saint said as though he had not paused. "A soldier, for instance, might have demanded your mother's berth."

"But our nurse sailed with us. She perished in the wreck. If a soldier requisitioned the berth, wouldn't our nurse have remained on the island rather than our mother?"

He nodded. "Any other mishap of war or rebellion at that time might have precipitated it. But the likeliest candidate is yellow fever."

"Yellow fever?"

"I suffered through it when I was six years old, Miss Caulfield. It is a nasty affliction and takes more men and women than it leaves. If your mother had shown signs of it at embarkation, they would have refused to allow her to board. I once saw a ship sail into port with only one sailor left alive after a brief journey from another island. He grounded the vessel, of course, and was obliged to pay the harbormaster for the repair of the dock, poor sod."

"But why wouldn't my mother have canceled the journey altogether, until she was well again? Why would she have allowed us to sail without her?"

"Perhaps she hadn't any choice," Taliesin said.

She turned to him. "Choice?"

"Perhaps she parted with you of necessity."

What necessity would force a mother to abandon three tiny daughters?

"What was her name, Miss Caulfield?" Mr. Saint asked.

She dragged her eyes away from Taliesin's. "The name on the manifest is Grace."

"Grace . . ." He looked carefully at her now. "There was a woman named Grace who lived in the cottage near the officers' quarters in Kingston. She was young and very beautiful, I remember. My cousin was six years older than me and already liked pretty girls." His lips curved into a partial grin, then it faded. "I don't recall her husband, but I know she was married to an officer. A soldier, not a sailor."

Eleanor's hand gripped her empty glass, the whiskey in her blood softening her, making hope a tangible thing.

"What did she look like, Mr. Saint? That woman. Do you remember?"

"I do." His jaw beneath the whiskers was tight. "Her beauty was distinctive. Men—even boys—do not forget stunningly beautiful women."

"Distinctive how?"

"Her hair fell to her waist like a waterfall of brilliant copper. She wore it bound up when she went into town. But if a boy was lucky enough to see her on the beach with . . ." He sat forward and lifted both elbows to the table. "With her daughters, who were quite small at the time, he could see it flowing like fire all down her back."

Words stumbled to her lips. "My sister Arabella's hair is just such as that."

"Miss Caulfield, you should know something about this woman. It is the only thing I remember about her other than her beauty."

"What is it?"

"She lived in the cottage because she was not permitted to live in the officers' quarters with her husband. There were some who would not believe that they had wed. They said she was his mistress only, and mistresses were not permitted on the compound. To others it made no difference; they would have barred her from living amongst them either way."

"But why?"

"She was a free colored person, as they call people of mixed race in the islands, Miss Caulfield. A descendant of slaves."

Chapter 19

Temptation

They spoke at length, Saint trawling his memory for more about the woman Grace. When Eleanor's eyelids unwillingly drooped, Taliesin put an end to it.

"Thank you, Mr. Saint." She stood in the inn at the base of the steps to the bedchambers above and extended her hand. "I am grateful for your help."

Saint took her hand. "You needn't thank me, madam. It is my pleasure." He lifted her fingers toward his lips.

Taliesin cleared his throat.

With a slash of a smile, Saint released her. "Until tomorrow morning, then."

With a brief glance at Taliesin, she went up the stairs.

Betsy's voice came through the door of their bedchamber before it closed decisively.

Saint's face lost all trace of humor. He leaned against the wall but his stance was at the ready, his right hand casually loose. Taliesin had seen him move in an instant from this posture to skewering a man through the ribs. Evan Saint, master swordsman, never rested entirely. So little flesh hung on his bones now that Taliesin wondered if he ever ate either.

Now Saint's eyes were hooded. "What are you doing, Sin?"

Taliesin had anticipated this. "Come." He went toward the door. "I will buy you dinner and you can glower at me over a glass of wine if you wish."

"Make it brandy. Now that you can afford it." Saint pushed himself away from the wall and followed in long strides and they stepped into the night's mist. The inn sat at the water's edge. Years ago Saint had taught him that when a man lived by water, he should never sleep far from it. In need of a quick escape, a boat could always be found. And stolen.

By the looks of his lean cheeks, his days of living off the fat of other men's lands were behind him. Taliesin knew when the change had occurred years earlier. He did not know what had caused it.

Their boots echoed on the pier. A pair of molls standing in the shadow of a shuttered market booth called out to them.

"Not tonight, Martha," Saint threw over his shoulder in reply. "Though I thank you for the offer." He bowed. Then in a lowered voice said, "French pox, poor girl. But when the fleet returns, she'll earn a few pennies. The young fellows off the frigates are randier than schoolboys. It's like they've never seen a woman before. And, by the by, while I'm speaking of uncontrolled lust and imprudent blind spots—"

"Restrain yourself." Taliesin opened a tavern door. The sounds of fiddle and pipe spilled onto the pier, the aromas of cooked fish and ale spiking memories like the prick of a sword point in a winning fight: memories of a battle nearly won. Years ago, Plymouth had been his last stop before he'd left the past behind.

They found a corner table away from the musicians. Taliesin gave his friend the seat to the right. Space for the sword to dangle at liberty. That no one demanded Saint remove it spoke to the lawlessness of Plymouth when the navy was absent, as well as to the respect men in this town had for Evan Saint's blade.

A barmaid set a bottle of brandy on the table and two cups. Saint poured, and wrapped his hand around the tumbler. "Eleanor Caulfield," he only said. And that was sufficient, of course.

Taliesin did not drink. He'd enough trouble keeping his head clear lately.

His friend drained his cup and placed it on the table. "You fool."

"Probably," he admitted.

"What do you want with her now?"

More than he should. "I promised her sisters that I would assist in the search for their parents."

"Hire someone to do it. You have the money."

Arabella said she'd hired an investigator. But the records of that investigator's unsuccessful tour along the Cornish coast had not appeared before they left Combe, only a vague suggestion of the man's itinerary.

"Not loose capital," he said. "I've horses to feed and train, and people in my employ as well." And a house from which he had barred her.

For a moment Saint said nothing. "The horse you sent me is a superb animal. Thank you."

"What did you name him?"

"Paid." Saint's eyes laughed in the dim candlelight.

Years ago Taliesin had told him he would someday repay the debt he owed Saint for saving him from the living grave into which he had fallen after leaving St. Petroc for the last time.

A burst of laughter arose from a group of men across the tavern. Saint's hooded eyes went swiftly to the noise, and Taliesin glanced over. A woman wrapped about the waist by a seaman's arm slipped him a sly, welcoming smile.

Taliesin turned away and met his friend's assessing regard, as steady as his hand upon the hilt of a sword. Very slowly, Saint shook his head.

"You never used to warn me off women, Evan."

"You never used to escort Eleanor Caulfield about England."

"At one time you counseled me to make a new plan of attack."

His friend's eyes bent to the table. "Remarkably enough, it is sometimes best to let a woman get away." His hand was tight around his glass. "Watch your back, Sin. The way my luck is running lately, I might not be alive to salvage you from the aftermath of her this time."

"There won't be an aftermath." He had it under control. That he had ridden to Drearcliffe the morning after the party with every intention of finishing what they had started, despite his challenge to her—and that he had only been deflected from that foolhardy plan by her news—had no bearing on anything now. For two days he hadn't touched her. As long as he didn't get too close to her, he could manage it.

"I am handling it." He reached for his empty glass.

Saint took up the bottle and finally smiled. He poured. "She's prettier than you let on."

"I don't remember ever mentioning anything about her appearance to you."

"You didn't. Not once in two years. You told me that she read Latin. That she knew the names of every book of Holy Scripture—in order. That she could recite the first paragraphs of the *City of God* from memory. That she hand wrote a copy of the anonymously authored *Quest for the Holy Grail* for her father's birthday, including decorative capitals. And that she learned how to ride your horse with ease in less than a month. You told me that last bit, about riding your horse, at least four dozen times. Most often with a bottle in your hand."

Taliesin swiveled the brandy, sparks of gold dancing upon its rosy surface. "Did I?"

"You did. But you never told me that she was a beautiful girl."

"Perhaps she wasn't."

"I hope, my friend," Saint said over the lip of his glass, "that your Holy Grail doesn't turn out to be filled with poison."

"IT IS CALLED *The Book of Memory*." The jeweler hefted the tome onto the table littered with books and tools and peculiar gadgets. Wiry and quick, with whiskers to his chest, spectacles on the end of his nose, and a tiny circular cap attached to the crown of his head surmounted by a strap with a monocle affixed to it, Elijah Fish radiated energy. His workshop looked more like a trinket shop than a jeweler's, every surface covered with curiosities.

But when he opened the book, Eleanor's attention turned entirely to the page.

She moved closer and laid her fingertips on an image in the center of the page: a crested griffin backed by stripes of blue and yellow. Circling about it were objects that bore the griffin image in various forms: a painted shield, an embroidered banner, a wax seal, and a signet ring of gold. Words and phrases in Latin were scattered about, and at the bottom of the page several lines of text in a language she didn't know. Spanish, perhaps.

Her fingers strayed over the image of the ring. "What is this book?"

"A compendium of noble crests of all the world, Miss Caulfield." He turned the thick stack of pages to the first. "In the year 1504 of the Christian calendar, this book was commissioned to celebrate the joining of the Kingdom of Naples with Sicily, Castile, and Aragon under the great Ferdinand II." He nodded, his movements quick and compact. "Ferdinand himself ordered it made. He wanted to show the world his connection to all the great aristocratic houses of his day and thus all of history. There is nothing more important to a Spaniard than blood, Miss Caulfield."

She turned the page. An emblem of a bejeweled crown set atop a standard decorated with gold and red vertical stripes filled the center of the folio. Beneath it in Latin read: "Ferdinand II, King of Aragon."

"Why do you assume my ring came from a noble family?"

"Its quality, of course." He stretched out his palm and twitched his fingers nimbly. "The ring?"

Taliesin and Mr. Saint waited in the shop without, with Betsy sitting in a chair by the door. Now Eleanor drew the ring from her pocket and placed it in Mr. Fish's hand. Adjusting the monocle over his left eye, he bent to the worktable and affixed the ring in a clamp with the stone facing upward.

It felt right to allow this. Safe.

Eleanor's fingers trailed over the book. It was at least a thousand pages.

"How does one search through this? Has it an index?"

"No. The hubris of noble families of the time was in their confidence that everybody knew who they were. The crests begin in the lands of the Empire and wend their way through Europe and Britain then finally Iberia. After that are a hundred pages of Oriental and Arab insignia and a few fanciful native emblems from the Americas, though I suspect they were inventions on the part of the publisher. It took several decades for this book to be completed and by then American savages were becoming very fashionable, of course." As he spoke, he studied the ring through the glass.

Her nerves tingled with familiar excitement. She had shared this sort of studying with Taliesin for years. Driven to best him at every task Papa gave them, she had worked until her eyes were sore from reading and her fingers blistered from holding a pen. But she had not always won. Just as now, he hadn't let her.

She wished he were in the workshop now. He stood not five yards away on the other side of a door, and yet she missed him. If he were here, he would employ his strong hands with great care on the precious books and trinkets, studying them in silent concentration, and she would watch him and not be able to breathe. *She could not breathe when she looked at him.* If this was her penance for sinning with him at Kitharan, she could not regret it.

"Shall I begin at the beginning, and look at each page?"

"You needn't." Mr. Fish's fingers twirled a screw and the ring came free of the clamp to fall into his palm. He offered it to her. "I recognize this symbol."

Her lips whispered, "What is it?" She took the ring and held it toward the light from the window. The T symbol shone through the red stone quite clearly. On the ring it was more stylized than the scribbled symbol on the manifest, with an elaborate under-curl on the left top bar of the T, a flourishing up-curl on the right, and a sweeping diagonal line that curved inward toward the center of the vertical bar.

Mr. Fish shifted a thick section of pages toward the end of the book. "It is the symbol of the house of Torres."

"Spanish? But I thought my mother was English." She remembered her mother's voice, as clearly English as hers and her sisters' now. "I believe my father was English as well." She only remembered him in uniform, tall and handsome and kind.

The jeweler turned several pages deftly. "Yet the ring she gave to you is most assuredly of Spanish origin, Miss Caulfield. Look."

At the center of the open page was the T-shaped symbol: the curls at the upper left and right were precisely the same, and the curve of the diagonal identical, though the triangle it made was solid. Drawn in black and accented in gold, it sat atop a bed of deep crimson. Drawings of a shield, a banner, and a ring exactly like hers surrounded it.

"Mr. Fish." She touched a fingertip to the letters at the bottom, and her finger quivered against the page. "I don't read Spanish. What does this say?"

" 'The House of Torres, descended in the line of Ferdinand of Castile, lords of'— Ah, curious. It is written 'Al-Andalus.' That, Miss Caulfield, was the Arab name for the province which was conquered from its Muslim overlords during the Christian reconquest of Spain. The proper name is Andalusia."

"What does it mean that it is written Al-Andalus here?"

"Perhaps that the lords of the House of Torres traced their blood proudly through Arab lines as well as Spanish. Perhaps they wished to be recognized as such. Those Spaniards, you know, had a remarkable lot of pride. And well they should have. In that era, they were unconquerable." He shrugged. "Eh, but it needn't indicate that. It could merely mean that the scribe assigned to this page liked the Arab word better than the Spanish. Perhaps he was of Arab origin. There were plenty of them around at that time, of course, descendants of Muslims who had been in Iberia for seven hundred years, then forced to convert to Christianity or suffer exile during the reign of Isabella and Ferdinand."

Exile. A word reserved for gentlemen. Rather, in this case, *deportment.*

Pressing the ring into her palm, she felt its heat like the heat of Taliesin's skin beneath her hands. "I don't understand how this is connected to my family."

"That, Miss Caulfield, is another research project altogether, I suspect."

She slid her finger below the lines of names and titles. The artist had penned the elaborate T symbol again in black beside two words in bold red ink. But to the symbol, the penman had added three wavy lines radiating from the left side of the horizontal bar as well as a small, curled base to the letter. Highly stylized, still, it almost looked like the head and neck of a . . .

No.

She touched her fingertips to the thick red letters. "Mr. Fish, what do these words say?"

"Aha, yes, the modified crest." He said with a nod. "It says 'Horse Lords,' Miss Caulfield."

SHE DID NOT tell Taliesin or Mr. Saint what she learned in Mr. Fish's workshop. With Betsy she accompanied them to the satellite office of Lloyd's insurance company. There a clerk dug through records two decades old and found the receipt of the benefit payment to the investors of *Lady Voyager* upon proof of its disappearance.

"What proof was there?" she asked. "I was on that ship and only I and my sisters washed ashore the following day," and a captain's box now in the keeping of a peculiar old baronet.

The clerk peered at her imperturbably. "Its failure to appear at any British dock within a year of its anticipated disembarkation is sufficient proof, madam."

A year. Had the person who was supposed to meet them waited that long at port?

"What port was it intended to sail into?"

"I do not have that information." His brow pinched tighter as he glanced at Taliesin, then at Mr. Saint's sword. "Will that be all, madam?"

Outside the office, Mr. Saint curved his palm around the hilt of his sword. "How else may I be of assistance to you, Miss Caulfield?" His emerald eyes were unreadable beneath the brim of his hat.

"I've no other questions at present, Mr. Saint. Thank you for this help. I will always be grateful for it, as will my sisters."

"It has been my honor." He bowed then turned to Taliesin. "Wolfe, until next we meet."

They clasped hands. "You know where to find me."

Mr. Saint grinned. "For now, Gypsy. Always only for now."

The swordsman remained standing before the door to the insurance office as they walked away.

"Miss Caulfield, if you will?" he said behind them.

She turned around and he walked toward her. Leaving Taliesin and Betsy, she went forward. "Yes?"

"I like you," he said to her below the clinks of boat rigging and the clatter of cart wheels. "You are intelligent and forthright and deuced pretty, and it is admirable of you to have set off on this quest, however unlikely you are to find the answers you seek."

She frowned. "Thank you, I think."

"But allow me to make one thing clear to you. Taliesin Wolfe has saved my life several times. I love him as a brother." His emerald eyes glittered. "If you destroy him again, know that you will have me to reckon with."

Destroy *him*? The boy who had abandoned her?

"I think you misunderstand matters, sir."

"I hope I do. Godspeed, Miss Caulfield," he said, and strode away, the length of steel swinging from his hip like glittering splintered ice.

At the door to their inn, Betsy said, "If we'll be leaving town tomorrow, miss, I'll be off to fetch your linens from the washerwoman." She went, casting a puckered glance back.

Eleanor went into the inn and to the stairs, the rumblings of a strange thunder in her breast. Taliesin walked behind her.

"I suppose we should leave tomorrow," she said. Once he escorted her home, his promise to Arabella would be fulfilled. "I will pack now. Perhaps you could send word to Mr. Treadwell to prepare the carriage."

She mounted the stairs. She had already met with more success on this quest in a fortnight than she had dreamed of having in a year. She could not invent places she needed to travel merely to avoid the end of this journey. She did not want to return home, but had she any other choice? His words from the other night tangled in the thunder: *Perhaps she hadn't any choice. Perhaps she parted with you of necessity.*

If she remained in Plymouth she might learn which port *Lady Voyager* had intended to disembark. Or they could go to Portsmouth. Or Dover. Bristol. Inquire after the ship at those ports too. Not only insurance companies kept records. If it came to it, she could book passage to the West Indies and track down the sugar merchant. Arabella's investigator had proved useless in that, apparently, but he had only written letters of inquiry. Mr. Saint had mentioned that his chess opponent, Mr. Bose, often traveled in the West Indies. Perhaps he could help.

She was casting empty lures, but the idea of this quest coming to an end so soon made panic of her breaths. The finality of it bore down upon her.

At the door to her bedchamber she pivoted and walked two swift steps back to him. He halted and she laid her hand on his chest.

"Taliesin—"

He grasped her wrist. "Eleanor, don't."

"Mr. Saint said something to me about you just now." She watched her hand as she pressed her fingertips into his waistcoat and everything inside her awakened. She could not return to the sleeping half life of her existence before this journey. Not now. Not ever again. "I didn't understand it."

"Mr. Saint is the least likely man to deserve that name than any other I know. Whatever he said to you, I caution you not to heed it." His grip on her wrist was tight and he did not push her away. His scent of fine leather and wild kisses filled her emptiness. All her thoughts were of the smoothness of his skin, the contours of his muscles, and of how her naked breasts had felt against him.

"I want to tell you what I learned today from the jeweler."

"Unless you can tell me without your hands on me, I don't want to hear it." His voice scraped over the words.

She lifted her face.

Fever burned in his eyes.

Her heart stumbled. "Is—Is that an official challenge?"

His fingers slipped from her wrist to her hand, lacing with her fingers. "*Pirani*, you've no idea what this does to me."

"Tell me. Tell me now." Her tongue followed her heart. They were palm-to-palm and she wanted more. More of him. More of this mania of need and freedom inside her. "Show me."

"There you are, miss!" Betsy's voice boomed up the stairs.

Taliesin released her hand.

"I've fetched the linens from the washwoman, and paid her an extra penny for doing it so quickly. It's a fine thing to reward good work." Betsy clattered up the steps, her arms full, all energetic cambric and wide, accusing eyes. "A woman that does the best she can at honest work should be praised for it, no matter who's trying to make it difficult for her."

"May I assist you with your parcel, Miss Fortnum?" Taliesin said as Eleanor watched, her desire entwined with every note of his voice, every movement of his lips.

Sweeping past him, Betsy tipped up her nose and muttered to the ceiling, "Wouldn't *that* gentleman *like* to catch a glimpse of my mistress's linens? But I can carry any burden if it's in the service of modesty, no matter how heavy the load. No one will ever say that Betsy Fortnum wasn't up to the task set for her. Now there, miss, come along and I'll have a nice tray of supper brought up so we won't be bothered with that common room that smells like yesterday's fish and anybody that might happen to be taking dinner in it." She swung the bedchamber door open.

Eleanor covered her scalding cheeks with her palms and looked to Taliesin. But he was already moving down the stairs.

That was the last Betsy allowed them alone until Eleanor set foot in her papa's house in St. Petroc a day later.

Chapter 20

The Soothsayer

*T*aliesin made it easy for the girl. At times he'd been a servant, and he understood the difficulties that masters could impose upon their employees. Betsy was only trying to do what she believed the Duchess of Lycombe had hired her to do: protect her mistress's virtue. He understood her efforts.

That, and if Eleanor touched him again it would require less than a heartbeat to have her in his arms.

Emerging from the jeweler's shop in Plymouth, her face had been flushed, her eyes troubled. Confused. He wanted to wipe the confusion away and make them shine again. When she smiled he felt it in his gut. And when she laughed . . . He didn't even need to remove her clothes. His entire body ached when she merely looked at him.

He was spiraling. Directly into the abyss. The sooner he stowed her securely in her father's house, the quicker he would be free.

Throughout the remainder of the journey he allowed Treadwell to assist her in mounting her horse on every occasion. Once she was settled at the inn on the road, he left the building until morning. He'd bedded down in stables for most of his life anyway, and temptation was best savored from a distance. Damning himself for having provided a saddle horse for her and the pleasure he took in watching her ride—her straight back and easy seat and perfectly rounded behind that he'd had in his hands—he rode as far back as her safety allowed.

On the road to the coast they'd switched out the Duke of Lycombe's carriage team. Now they retrieved the horses, which put Treadwell in high spirits. Taliesin listened to him rhapsodize about the little termagant in the carriage and how he would name his next horse Betsy. He felt for the poor fellow; Betsy didn't seem to like the starry-eyed coachman any more than she liked him. Taliesin nearly smiled.

Then a turn brought him to a fork in the road—a place he could draw on a map in his sleep, with illustrations of every tree and hillock. Ahead, Eleanor had already taken the road to the right, toward St. Petroc. But the mare's stride seemed to lag now, the distance between her and the carriage closing.

Taliesin's heart beat a hard, uneven tempo. He hadn't ridden this road in eleven years. It seemed narrower now, the trees bordering it not as tall as he remembered, the fields to either side smaller.

At a slow walk, Eleanor passed the place on the road that was branded so deeply into his memory that he'd never managed to erase it. The last place he had seen her all those years ago.

Spring had just begun to turn to summer, the air still cool and bright. Knowing this countryside well from eighteen years of traveling through it, he'd cut across the field on the northern flank of the road to shorten the distance to the village. He'd sold the last of the horses his uncle had let him take north in September, as well as those he'd got on trade, and he'd made good money. He always did well when his uncle gave him the reins. From his years studying at Reverend Caulfield's knee, he knew how to speak with *gorgios* so they did not mistrust him. And he knew fine horseflesh.

With a purse of silver coins in his coat that he would use to prove to the vicar that he could make something of himself, he had walked all the way from Devonshire, sleeping beneath the stars on hillsides and haystacks, every moment anticipating the welcome she would give him after eight months.

Emerging onto the road with a spring in his step that he hadn't felt since before the squire's son had broken two of his ribs, he'd seen the carriage halted only a dozen yards away. Her shining hair cascaded over Thomas Shackelford's arm.

Then he'd seen red.

Then he'd seen Shackelford's crisp blue coat and brilliantly white neck cloth, the curricle's gleaming wheels and new leathers, and the fluttering skirt of her delicate dress the color of summer.

Then he'd seen the dirt beneath his own fingernails, the slashes in the knees of his trousers, the calluses on his hands that were dark as clay, and the hole in the heel of his shoe. And every word Martin

Caulfield had said to him eight months earlier had come back to him as clear as though he'd heard them that very day.

That night he slept in the woods. The next morning he went to the May Day fair, gave his uncle half the coins in the purse, and bid his aunt and cousins good-bye. Before the sun set, he turned to the northern road, vowing that the next time he set foot in St. Petroc he would be carrying a sack of gold. But he had never returned.

Until now.

Iseult had slowed to a crawl. Taliesin urged his mount forward and came beside Eleanor.

"What is amiss?"

Her attention jerked to him. "I don't think I should go home quite yet." Her eyes were overbright, her hands squeezing the reins. "Could we continue on to Combe? I should tell Arabella my news in person." Her lips could not hold the smile she attempted. A shrug, a tentative lift of her shoulders. "What trouble could three more days on the road be when at the end we will find my sister's luxurious mansion?"

What trouble? Three more days of torture.

"Your father's house is a mile down this road. If you wish to travel to Combe, there is nothing to halt you from it tomorrow or the following day. It is nearly nightfall now, and the horses require rest." And this was where he would leave her. He'd done what he had promised. His vow was fulfilled. In a day he would be on the road again. In a sennight he would be anywhere else but in the way of temptation, and he would continue on with his life.

"Of course." Her gaze slipped away. "Well then," she spoke to the road ahead of her. "Welcome home, Taliesin." She snapped the mare into motion and pulled away at a canter.

THE VILLAGE HADN'T changed in the weeks since Eleanor had left it. Except for the draperies in the window of the cobbler's shop, which the cobbler's wife changed out each month, everything was exactly the same. The high street was still ridiculously narrow given that there was nothing else around for miles, and caked with mud. Artie Shepherd's best ram rested in the middle of it, forcing everybody to move around it, as usual. The same pinafores and gowns decorated the dressmaker's window, and a carefully penned note affixed to the door of the tea shop boasted cream for a penny. The marquee at the door of the Lion & the Lamb was still cracked up the middle, right between the images of the lamb and the lion. And at the end of the lane the simple stone mass of her papa's church rested against the pale sky like a squat mountain, flanked on one side by the cemetery and a gate and path that led down to the creek.

Farther along that wall stood the barn, which served the vicarage as a stable too. In that barn Taliesin had slept every night of every September through every April from the day that she had first come to the vicarage to the festival night when he had kissed her beneath the old oak tree.

Tucked in the shadow of the church, the vicarage was a modest cottage of unremarkable construction and only some charm. But it had been home—a miraculous, safe home after the unspeakable years at the foundling home—and Eleanor had loved it.

She dismounted with the assistance of the rock bench at the gate and stepped down to face the house. Taliesin came to her side and took Iseult's reins.

"Well, miss," Betsy said, climbing from the carriage. "This isn't much to speak of, is it? Not like that fine house of Sir Wilkie's. That Drearcliffe was a fine house indeed. Compared to some." She cast Taliesin a narrow eye, conveniently forgetting that she'd been terrified of Drearcliffe's ghosts and dogs and creaking floorboards.

"This is my papa's house. He is the vicar of this village." She could not bring herself to unlatch the gate. Taliesin's silent presence behind her pulled at her. His absence from this house for so many years was a gaping emptiness inside her that she could acknowledge now.

Betsy folded her hands over her cloak. "Will you be going inside, miss?"

"Oh. Yes." She reached awkwardly for the gate.

Taliesin drew the horses away, across the yard.

Panic slipped through her. "Aren't you coming?"

He looked over his shoulder. "After I've helped Treadwell stable the horses."

"Oh."

Her horse, Saint George, was in the smith's stable at the other end of the village, where she had left him during her absence. She could go visit him now and . . .

No. She must do this. "Fine." Her voice sounded tight. Frightened. Why she should be frightened, she hadn't an idea.

You are a wild bird, caged too long and desperate to be free.

She lifted her chin and opened the gate.

Her papa answered her knock on the door. Wearing his spectacles and a loose coat, and holding a book in his hand as always, he smiled.

"Eleanor." His voice was warm and full of peace. "We did not expect you until next month."

"Oh. I— That is, I— I'm sorry, Papa." She had entirely forgotten that he was a newlywed. Perhaps he had hoped to have more time alone with his wife.

"Don't be. I'm glad for your early return. Of course." He peered behind her. "And who is this?"

"Betsy Fortnum, Reverend." Betsy curtsied.

"Welcome, Betsy." He gestured with his book. "Come in, both of you. Mrs. Caulfield will shortly lay dinner and I'm certain she will wish to hear all the news of your sister's house."

Eleanor gave her cloak and bonnet to Betsy. "Papa, I haven't come from Combe, actually." The deception weighed upon her. His lined face was so dear. He had cared for her more than anybody in the world along with Arabella and Ravenna.

"Have you been with Ravenna and Vitor?" he said. "Your stepmother will be just as delighted to hear about that, of course."

"Papa, I—"

"Martin," came Agnes's voice from the parlor. "Is that carriage in the yard from Combe? It bears the duke's crest." She appeared in the foyer and her face lit. "Eleanor!" She came forward, reaching out her hands to take Eleanor's snugly, affectionately. "Welcome home."

Home.

How could it be home now? How would her heart bear it?

"Betsy, would you bring the small bag from the carriage? The one with the gifts we purchased in Plymouth?"

Betsy bobbed her head.

"Plymouth?" Agnes said. "We thought you comfortably sojourning at Combe. Whatever took you to Plymouth?"

Betsy pulled wide the front door. In the opening, hat in his hand and black eyes as sober as Eleanor had ever seen them, stood the answer to her stepmother's question.

He had taken her to Plymouth. He had taken her on this quest. He had been her reason for the journey and her principal interest in it. He alone. The man who was about to break her heedless heart all over again.

TALIESIN DID NOT remain for dinner. Claiming an engagement with his family, he left the vicarage and the suffocating memories of the last time he'd stood in this house and heard his fate delivered to him by the man he had trusted more than any other in the world.

Leaving Tristan in the stable at the vicarage, he walked through the village. Most of the shops had closed, but the blacksmith lifted his head from his work, and recognition flickered in his eyes. He nodded.

Taliesin walked on, toward the Shackelford estate.

He saw the canvas-covered wagons clustered on the flank of the wood before he saw the people. Soon the campfires came into view through the deepening dusk.

He greeted his aunt and cousins, dug into his pocket, and distributed coins liberally among his nephews and nieces. His uncle, a head shorter than him, grabbed him in a bear's embrace as though he hadn't seen him in a decade. It had been less than a year, since the summer when he'd done business with several traders at the Rom gathering in Trowbridge. But he accepted the affection gladly.

None of them said anything about how he hadn't come to St. Petroc since he was eighteen. None of them cared, probably. The place meant less to them than the people. Only music, food, and song mattered when friends came together after long absences.

The children and women eventually went to bed, and he sat at the fire talking with his cousins and uncle until the moon appeared. Then he took his leave of them. They did not ask where he was going and he did not volunteer the information. He was no longer one of them. He had chosen that long ago and they had accepted his choice as though they'd long expected it.

He walked farther, past Shackelford's land, following the ribbon of the creek. When he finally grew tired, he found a pasture beside a wood far distant from the nearest farmhouse, and lay down on the grass. Propping his arm behind his head, he stared up at the stars that were ruled by none.

"*Y se alegre el alma llena,*" he murmured to the moon rising above the treetops of the wood nearby, where once he had loved a girl fair as sunshine. "And his heart is filled with rapture."

For the first time in many years, he slept in the night's cold embrace beneath the stars.

ELEANOR DID NOT wait for Agnes or her papa to wake. In the kitchen she cut a slice of bread, toasted it over the coals in the hearth, smeared it with clover honey, and ate it standing up, a cup of tea in her other hand. She almost felt like Ravenna, except there were no dogs about.

Then she slung her cloak around her shoulders and walked to the blacksmith's shop to recover her horse. Astride Saint George, she rode to the Gypsy encampment.

Two of Taliesin's cousins, both women, sat by a fire affixed with a tripod stand from which a pot hung, their youngest children playing with a ball nearby. Farther off two boys tended to a string of ponies just within the tree cover.

Lussha sat beneath a canvas awning, sewing black fabric. Eleanor had never seen the soothsayer wear anything except black. She'd also never spoken directly to her, only that once, on the day of the fair fifteen years ago, when Arabella sought their fortune.

Years later, when she had come to the Gypsy camp to find Taliesin for her riding lessons, Eleanor had felt Lussha's black eyes upon her. Always watching. Always a heat upon her neck and a prickling between her shoulders.

Children clustered about Eleanor's skirts now. The youngest girls, no more than three and four, tugged at her cloak. The boys stroked Saint George's dark coat.

"Good day," she said, passing the reins of her horse to the eldest boy. Reaching into her pocket, she drew out a handful of polished shells purchased in Plymouth, each inset with a sparkling bead. "I brought these for you from the sea." She placed one in each of the eager little palms, and two on the palm of the boy holding her horse. Not yet ten probably, he had black hair like all the other children, and golden eyes. None of Taliesin's family had black eyes. Among these Gypsies, only Lussha did. But she, like his uncle's family, did not look like Taliesin either.

Eleanor stared across the camp into her black eyes. Lussha spoke words in her language to the children and they scattered.

Eleanor climbed the scrubby incline to the wood's edge, nodding to the other women she passed: his aunt, three cousins, and two women she only knew as his younger cousins' wives. Taliesin was the eldest of his uncle's family, and she had long wondered how his departure had affected them. But she didn't know them to ask them. He had been a part of her world, yet she had never known his.

How ignorant she had been to have ever thought she knew him. How foolishly arrogant to have believed that he was hers.

The fortune-teller did not stand as she approached.

With a high brow and pockmarked cheeks, she was handsome and fierce. Unlike some of the villagers of St. Petroc, Eleanor had never feared the Gypsies. Papa had always said they were Christ's brothers and sisters just as surely as anyone else. And Taliesin was one of them.

But something about Lussha's eyes had always unsettled her. Black like Taliesin's, they held none of the warm intensity of his. Instead, the way Lussha looked at Eleanor made her feel like she was hiding a terrible secret, and Lussha was the only one who knew it.

Fanciful imagination. And perhaps guilt. She had hidden a secret from herself and everybody else for years.

"May I sit?"

"D'you wish your fortune read, miss?" She spoke with the double accent of her people and the Cornwall countryside, as all the Gypsies of St. Petroc did, except Taliesin.

"No." Eleanor uncurled her fingers from around the ring. "Do you remember a fortune that you gave to my sister—" Her mouth had been struck with a summer drought. "The fortune that you gave to my sisters and me fifteen years ago?"

The soothsayer bent her head to her needlework. A drape of her black veil obscured her face. "I can't be expected to recall every fortune I give. If you're wishing another, I'll read it for a shilling."

"I don't want another." Eleanor sat down on the folding chair by Lussha's knees. She spread her palm and the ring teetered atop it. "I want to know whether you invented what you told Arabella about this ring fifteen years ago."

The Gypsy lifted fearsome eyes.

"I mean you no disrespect," Eleanor said quickly. "But I am the daughter of a preacher. I know the theater required of certain professions, including his. And, I think, yours. I only want to know the truth."

Lussha's eyes bored into hers and Eleanor was sucked back to the foundling home, standing before the headmistress and shivering down to her frigid bare feet. Just as then, she remained silent. Waiting. Always waiting. Never doing.

Except with one boy. One man. He made her want to seize every desire in her soul and lift it to the sky.

"The fortune I read for your sister was true," Lussha said. "With Taliesin living in the vicar's house, how d'you think I could've invented a fortune for the vicar's daughters, hm?"

It was not what she had expected to hear. "He— Taliesin doesn't believe in soothsaying, you know."

Lussha's wide lips spread without smiling. "Of course he doesn't. Your father saw to that." She returned her attention to her sewing.

"Madam Lussha, do you recognize the mark beneath the stone on this ring? Do you know what it means?"

"I recognize the mark. I recognized it then." She didn't lift her head. "I told you. It's a princely ring."

"How do you know that?"

She shrugged and drew needle through cloth. "How does one know anything?"

"That isn't an answer." Riddles. Only riddles. She should not have come. She stood. "Thank you. I beg your pardon for disturbing your work." She stepped away from the tent.

"Have you found your prince yet, Miss Eleanor?" she heard behind her.

She turned around. "My sister looked for him. She didn't find him. Both of my sisters are wed now and they are very happy." She didn't know why she was saying this. "I do not believe in the fortune." Not any longer. Not now.

Lussha said nothing in response. Eleanor retrieved her horse from the boy and rode away.

SHE ENTERED THE vicarage through the rear door, removed her muddy boots, cloak, and bonnet, and slid her feet into thin house slippers. Then she went to the tiny parlor she had used as her sitting room.

Before departing for Combe, she'd told her papa that Agnes should now have the room, and she had begun to pack her books into crates. To be moved . . . where? To Combe where Arabella's library was already full to the ceiling? To Ravenna's house, which didn't even have a library?

She looked now at the half-filled crates, and at the cozy window seat in which she'd cuddled up with countless tales of bravery and daring, dreaming of someday having her own adventure. Less than a month's experiences had changed that. Forgiving her childish heart for believing that an adventure could fulfill her dreams was an easy task. Forgiving herself now for still longing for it—despite all—was not.

Her papa's footsteps came quietly behind her.

"Are you all right with this?" He gestured to the crates.

"I am. This is Agnes's house now. She must have a place to figure household accounts and write correspondence. This room will be perfect for her."

His brow creased. Sometimes when she'd been a girl and found his face drawn with worries, she had soothed away the creases with her little fingers and then brought him a cup of tea. Then she had read to him from whatever book he had given her, and sometimes from the books she chose from his shelves herself. Always the worry had disappeared from his eyes and her heart filled with joy. When he was happy, she had felt safe.

"She is concerned," he said now.

"About what?"

"That you will feel displaced here."

"I am displaced here. But she needn't worry over it." She sucked in courage. "I will move to Combe. Bella's house is far too big for her family, and I will like very much to see little Christopher grow."

"If that suits you." He looked at the crates again. "You will take your collection with you, I suppose?"

"Yes." There must be a parlor with an empty bookcase somewhere in the sprawling ducal mansion. If not, she could store them in her bedchamber. The empty bookcases in the library at Kitharan mocked her predicament.

She bent her head away. Closed her eyes. Drew in breaths to steady her tumbling nerves. She would give one last gift to the man who had given her his home: peace at her departure. That she felt like she was stepping off the edge of a cliff she would never reveal.

"I will leave you to the sorting of books, then," he said. "Anything you don't wish to take with you can remain here. The door of my house will always be open to you, daughter."

Tears prickled at the backs of her eyes, a thousand words wanting to be said. "Thank you, Papa," she could only manage.

He went out, but paused on the other side of the threshold. "I have an appointment with the curate at Trowtower this afternoon and must be gone for several hours now. My wife is closeted all day at the Shackelford place with the Ladies' Parish Commission. We hadn't realized you were to return yesterday or we would have altered our plans."

"That's all right. This will take some time, I suspect. You go off and enjoy the curate's erudition."

He smiled, but it slipped away swiftly. "Have you seen Taliesin today? I would have liked to say good-bye to him."

"Has he gone?" In an instant, she was in her papa's study eleven years ago, when she learned that he'd left without word, her heart plunging into a well of disbelief.

"Perhaps not," her papa said, "if he has not yet taken leave of you."

Her mouth opened, but all the words she knew were caught in the trap of her chest.

He nodded. "I must go now. I will see you at dinner."

Through the window she saw him ride up the high street. Then she went into the tiny parlor where she had spent almost every day for the past ten years of her life and knelt on the floor beside a crate.

A quarter hour into the project she found *Tristan & Iseult*. Hidden beneath a concordance of the Bible that she often used when correcting her papa's sermons, the slender volume was as worn and as tattered as the last time she had touched it. It belonged in her papa's study with the Malory and other medieval tales. It should have long since found its way back there.

But she had never returned it. Instead, she'd kept it close, shelved near her writing table. Yet she hadn't once opened it. After Taliesin had gone, she could not bear to.

More cowardice. Her life, it seemed, had been full of it. Quiet, modest, intelligent Eleanor, the vicar's perfect daughter, had been perfectly craven for far too long.

Cracking open the worn cover, she turned the first page and a scrap of paper fell onto her lap. Handwritten words crossed it, the ink of the final letters smeared. But nothing could disguise Taliesin's scrawl.

If you are ever in need, send for me. Wherever I am, I promise I will come.

For her. He would come if she sent for him. She could not doubt that he had written it for her.

She clamped her eyes shut and sought breaths, rational thoughts, justifications, anything to force back the surge of feeling. It hurt too much.

Her fingers traced the words, lingering on the smear of ink. He had written it in haste. When? Had he left the note this morning when she'd gone to see Lussha? Had he left her without word? *Again.*

She tucked the note back in the book, closed it, and set it down. Not pausing to gather her cloak or bonnet or to change her shoes, she practically ran to the stable. She swung through the door and her breaths stuttered out in jerks. Taliesin's great black horse stood in an open stall, haltered to the door. Tristan turned his handsome head and offered her an implacable stare.

An open stall for a mighty stallion.

Tethered by a single rope.

Tamed by loyalty.

Wherever I am, I promise I will come.

Blind, without direction, she walked across the yard and into the church, willing her heartbeats to slow and wishing he had already gone. In those months after he'd left, in this little gray church, with its pointed arches and clear glass windows that rippled the light as it bathed mellow limestone, she had sat numbly through sermon after sermon, hymn after hymn. All the while she had thought—*known*—that the women and men in the pews around her would be astonished to learn that the vicar's only good daughter—not willful Arabella or hoydenish Ravenna—but proper, modest Eleanor wished she were far away on an adventure with a wild Gypsy boy. She hadn't only wished it. She had *prayed* for it. On her knees. In this church. Not only for months. For *years*.

He had not returned then. Despite that, fool that she was, she had never stopped loving him.

TALIESIN'S KNOCK ON the vicarage door went unanswered. He opened it and entered. Today, in the light of morning, without Martin Caulfield staring at him as though he were a marauder intent upon rapine destruction, the house itself seemed unremarkable. Unthreatening. A place of countless memories, all good except for the last.

He found no one within, not even Betsy, who would undoubtedly beat him over the head with a broom if she discovered him wandering around the house uninvited. For he had most certainly been uninvited.

In the doorway to the small room that fronted the vicarage, where Eleanor had always stored her books and writing materials, he paused. Crates and books were strewn about the floor. Set on the top of a half-emptied crate was a book he recognized well.

He took it up, opened it to the first page, and found the note he had written in haste eleven years ago. The day his life changed forever.

On that day, after washing the blood from his hands and face, and binding his neck cloth around his broken ribs to hold them in place, he'd gone directly to the vicarage. As soon as the swelling started—*damn Thomas Shackelford*—his aunt would demand that he remain in camp so she could tend to his injuries. He'd had to tell

Eleanor not to expect him for at least a fortnight. He came into the house and finding no one, but in crippling pain and afraid of fainting, he'd written a short note to her. He'd been about to leave it in her sitting room when the Reverend appeared.

Distressed over Taliesin's wounds, the vicar demanded to know what had happened. With the pride of a seventeen-year-old, he refused to tell him. But Reverend Caulfield had known. Somehow. Or perhaps he only suspected. His gaze retreated. He accepted the letter for Eleanor and placed it on his desk.

"It is good that you are going away, Taliesin," he'd said as though taking up a conversation they had left off earlier. But they hadn't. Taliesin hadn't seen Martin Caulfield in four months. He'd just returned to St. Petroc for the autumn and winter. The Reverend knew that perfectly well.

"I have been thinking, son, that it would be best for you to spend less time here than you have been accustomed to spending. The girls are busy with their various activities, of course," he continued, as though each word weren't the blade of a knife digging beneath Taliesin's fractured ribs. "Now that Eleanor will be seventeen, fine young gentlemen will be coming around to court her. Her time will be occupied with dresses, ribbons, gossip . . . whatnot, women's interests. She will be too occupied to study all day. And you are a man now, not a boy to spend your hours researching obscure texts for me. It is time for both of you to be free of my scholarly yoke." He smiled self-deprecatingly, as though his demands were especially onerous, as though his students had not always been eager to please him.

But Taliesin's spinning mind had fixed on one part of the speech: Dresses? Ribbons? Gossip? *Eleanor?*

The vicar was lying. Or pretending. But he had never

lied to him. Never pretended. He had taught him the virtue of honesty and hard work and striving for better.

His ribs throbbed and his brow dripped sweat along his cheeks and he could still taste blood in his mouth. He swallowed it down.

"I don't understand, sir."

"Then I shall be clearer. For the respect you bear me, Taliesin . . ." He seemed to struggle to speak. "And for the affection you bear her, you must leave here. Today, son. You must make your way without my help now."

The floor seemed to fall away beneath him, a great abyss opening.

"And I ask you to do it far from St. Petroc," the Reverend continued. "As far as you are able to go. I should have demanded it before. I have cared too greatly for you, and because of that I have been remiss. But it is time now. It is past time, I fear."

Stunned, he had stood immobile while the vicar went to his bedchamber to collect what money he had. He was a poor man, but he would not send Taliesin away empty-handed, he'd said.

He stared at the letter he had written to Eleanor and knew her father would not give it to her. Tearing off a corner of the closest paper at hand, he grabbed a pencil and scratched two lines, then hid it in the single place he knew she would find it that no one else ever would.

Without waiting for the vicar to return, he'd left. Because in his heart carved open by betrayal, even then he knew that Martin Caulfield was right. That he had nothing to give her, except his life if she were to ask it of him.

Chapter 21

Strolling Amidst Ghosts

*E*leanor trod between the gravestones in slow steps, her slippers sinking into the soft moss. The grass that had grown up between the stones in spiky tufts had turned winter yellow, framing each gray stone slab in natural dejection.

She usually clipped them. Years ago when the Gypsy boy that Papa had hired to do such tasks disappeared without word, she had taken up the chore. But this winter she hadn't managed to find the time for it. Where all her time went was never clear; perhaps in trying to be good and useful and modest. Or perhaps she had finally grown weary of performing a chore that after eleven years still reminded her of him *every time*.

She would not have to worry about that at Combe. Her sister's house contained no memories of Taliesin Wolfe. What's more, she would live in sublime luxury. She would have the company of her sister, a fine gentleman, and their baby boy to dandle on her knee. And she could spend every day lounging in Arabella's library reading whatever she wished.

She should finish sorting her books now. Later, when Betsy returned from her daylong holiday in the village shops, they would pack up her belongings in preparation for leaving tomorrow. Aside from the books, she owned few things, since she had been a perfectly modest, poor, scholarly vicar's daughter for twenty years. A naïve girl waiting for a boy who would never come.

"Gathering wool?"

Taliesin walked toward her between the stones. His hair shone ebony in the sunlight and whiskers shadowed his jaw and he looked even more beautifully masculine than ever. No wonder she had undressed him in his house and was now eager for him to leave. A sensible woman mustn't spend all her waking hours swinging between ecstasy when she was touching him and agony when she was not.

She was no longer a sensible woman, however. She had dispensed with sensible weeks ago. For the next few minutes until he left, she would allow herself to swing.

"Rather, I should be gathering weeds," she said. "After you left here abruptly all those years ago Papa did not invite one of your cousins to take up your chores. Ravenna and I did them. When Ravenna left, it all fell to me. But you see, I am not very good with garden clippers." She could not quite meet his eye. "One would think the Ladies' Parish Commission would find a volunteer to see to these weeds. They find volunteers for nearly everything else. Last month they found a volunteer to repaint the narthex white."

If she continued talking, he could not tell her he was leaving. She already knew how that scenario felt. Familiar suffering at least had the advantage of no surprises. "Mrs. Shackelford did not like the blue," she continued. "She said it was not sufficiently austere. *Blue.* Can you imagine? And not a particularly secular blue either, but good old English stained glass blue." She gestured toward the church with a jerky movement. "We don't even have stained glass windows. She might have left the blue and allowed the church a little color."

"Eleanor."

"I think she is secretly a Methodist and hopes to convert us all, beginning with Papa." She could not allow him to speak. She could not bear to hear his voice, knowing that after today she would not hear it again. "You know, like all of those pagan queens of the Dark Ages that got converted by missionary monks from Rome. Then the queens converted their kingly husbands. Then their husbands ordered everybody else to be baptized because that's just what kings did back then."

"You are speaking nonsense."

"On the contrary. It is fascinating history."

"I'm leaving, Eleanor."

And there it was. "Of course you are. Arabella called you to help, and since you had promised to come if anyone needed, you came."

"She invited me to the wedding." His voice seemed quite low. "And I did not promise her. I promised you."

She met his gaze squarely. "You worked so that Papa

would not have to pay full wages to a manservant, because he could not afford it. That was good of you. And you studied. And after I was sick you helped me heal and become strong again. You were always here. Always. I don't remember when you weren't. Until you went away." Perhaps her heart had broken so hard because of that. When finally she had lost it to him, she'd had no doubt he would always be there, always hers, that no one would ever love her like he did. But she had been wrong.

"Your father offered me opportunity that I would have been a fool to refuse."

Oh, dear heaven, why couldn't he simply leave already? And why had she been such a naïve girl, even after the horrors of the foundling home? She should have known that his attachment to the vicarage had never been about her. She should have understood then. She *had*. Eventually. But now with his shadowed eyes and hot caresses he had blinded her all over again.

"Yes. True. Excellent opportunity." She sucked in a breath full of dissembling. "Well, then, you should be on your way before the day gets much farther along. Wherever it is you are going, it will become dark there too in about six hours. I shan't offer my hand to shake good-bye because of course I have been prohibited from touching you." She tucked her cold fingers into her skirt. "So I'll just say good-bye. Good-bye, Taliesin. Thank you for helping me."

His jaw looked tight. And edible.

She pivoted and slipped on wet moss and nearly fell over a gravestone.

"Eleanor—"

"I'm well!" She righted herself. "Quite well. I should have donned my boots before coming out." Her foot smarted. She'd twisted something. Wretched house slippers. She teetered toward the opposite end of the cemetery as swiftly as impractical shoes and sloppy moss allowed. It was in the opposite direction from the house. But she would not give him the satisfaction of thinking she had not intended to go in this direction. She pushed open the gate and started down the path that wended to the creek between holly bushes and laurel, as though she were merely out for a stroll. Limping.

"Oh, and—" She swiveled around. He was standing in the same spot amidst the headstones. "Thank you for the loan of Iseult. She was delightful. And congratulations on your stable. And house. And . . . everything." She turned and her foot found a rabbit hole.

This time no gravestone caught her fall. She went down in the grass. "*Ouch.*"

That he would come to help her now was a given. But she could not allow it. She struggled to stand, gasped upon pain, and plunked onto her behind again.

He grasped her arm and steadied her.

"I did not just step into that hole deliberately so that you would feel obligated to assist me."

"I know you didn't."

She struggled to untangle her skirts. A slipper fell off entirely. "Don't allow your arrogance to get the best of you and imagine that I did."

"I won't." His hand moved over her shoulder, then up the back of her neck, hot and intentional and like magic.

"What are you doing?" She tried to shrug him off. "Release me."

"I want more than a handshake." He caught her up in his arms.

She pushed at his chest. "No. Absolutely not. Not after—"

Then he was kissing her, and she wasn't pushing him away but pulling him closer as he dragged her onto his lap.

"Say yes," he growled, catching her lower lip between his teeth.

"Yes." She wrapped her arms about his neck and said yes again without speech. He tangled his hand in her hair and held her to him as their mouths devoured. As good-byes went, this was extraordinary. She was glad she hadn't settled for a handshake.

He caressed her cheek, his fingers trailing along her throat, and his lips stole her sighs. He stroked over her breast, touching, shaping his hand to the shape of her body. She allowed it. She sought it. Beneath her clothing her skin ached for him.

When his hand surrounded her calf under her skirt, and moved upward, she gasped. "You shouldn't do that."

His breaths were uneven. "I know I shouldn't." His hand climbed, saturating her with need. Neither of them stopped him. Instead, she met his mouth with hers, his tongue with hers, and found the heat of his palm around her knee unendurably sweet. She pressed tighter to him, wanting to imprint upon her body the hard beauty of his. Under the muslin, his fingers spread on her thigh.

"Stop me," he ground out.

"No."

His fingers moved upward. "Now."

"No." She tasted his perfect mouth, sank her hands into his hair, and drank from him.

His hand surrounded her hip. Curved around her buttock.

All pain, regret, doubt were forgotten. He touched her, caressed, intimately, securely, strength and roughness tempered to give her pleasure. He dipped between her thighs.

Her breathing ceased.

He stroked once, lightly. Both of them recoiled from

it—his hand, her hips. Their trembling breaths mingled in uncertainty.

Then he touched her again.

She moaned softly against his mouth and he called her *pirani* in a low rasp. Again. His touch. His caress. Her body arching to him. Longing swept through her—the longing to lay herself out in the grass and let him touch her like this forever. His mouth found her neck; her hands, his shoulders.

"How I have longed to be inside you." He kissed a line of pleasure to her lips, his fingers stroking, burning. "It is a constant ache."

She pressed to him, needing him. "I want that."

"God's blood, *pirani*. Don't invite me. There would be only regret, and I could not endure it."

Regret. He would regret making love to her. All those years he had stayed at the vicarage when he might have been elsewhere. She was that to him, memories and desire and regret.

"Was it I?" She grabbed his arm and pulled his hand away. "I must know. Was I the reason you left?"

His chest rose and fell hard, his eyes dark shadows of despair. "You were the reason I stayed."

Finally she understood. In the vicarage he had been a poor boy. In the world he had become a man. A gentleman. The slenderest tether had drawn him back now, and he was impatient to be free of it again.

She was shaking inside and out, her body rushing with heat and weakness from what he did to her so easily. But this time she must defend herself. This time she must break free by her own power.

She pressed her palm to his chest. "You were supposed to have left already."

"I'm leaving now." He stroked back her hair loosened by his fingers and kissed her there. Then her mouth. Then her mouth again, his lips soft, urgent, making her kiss him too. Making her ache so deeply she could feel nothing except how much she wanted him. "This very moment," he murmured against her lips.

She pushed against his ribs. Dragged her face away. "Then *go*."

A clatter of hooves and carriage wheels sounded in the yard. She clambered off his lap and squelched a gasp of pain. She'd forgotten about her foot, and modesty, and propriety. It was still broad daylight and she was within thirty yards of the church and street. She had learned to live adventurously so shamelessly well that she only thought of him.

She was a failure. Freedom from her cage was not a twisted stomach and agonized heart. Adventure? *Most of them failed*. She was Perceval, waylaid by lust.

But Perceval had learned from that episode. He had, in the end, vanquished the devil that tempted him.

Taliesin helped her to stand. She tugged away from him, smoothed her hair that had lost half its pins, and shook out her skirt that was now smudged with grass. With the slightest tilt of the corner of his mouth, he offered her the offending slipper.

She snatched it away. Turned from him. "Thank you. Now go."

"Eleanor—"

"Please, go. This good-bye has already lasted too long. I think I liked it better when you disappeared without word." She started back up the path, limping, biting her bruised lips against the pain in her every pore.

"I did leave word," he said behind her.

She squeezed her eyes shut. He had left that message in the book eleven years ago. If she had found it then, would she have suffered less? Would she have sent for him? Would he have come despite his wish to be free?

Grimacing and gripping the rail, she ascended the

steps between the cemetery and the stable yard. The carriage was an unremarkable traveling coach, the pair mere job horses.

She went toward it. A coachman climbed down from the box, put down the step, and opened the door. Fanny Upchurch's pretty face appeared in the opening. And behind Fanny, her brother.

Fanny's mouth split into a brilliant smile. "Eleanor! You won't believe it. We have found another clue for you!"

"ISN'T IT MARVELOUS?" Teacup poised below her rosebud lips, Fanny beamed. "We knew you would wish to know immediately, and I could not bear sending it by post and chancing that it would be lost. When Robin suggested that we bring it to you, I thought it the best idea imaginable."

Eleanor read the letter a fifth time. Then a sixth.

My dearest colonel,

Daily I go about my tasks with tears on my cheeks. I have lost so greatly that my sorrow is a living creature threatening to consume me. But this I vow: I do love you. You must never doubt that I love you.

Grace T

"Who could this mysterious colonel be?" Fanny said. "For this must be the same woman on the manifest."

Fanny and her brother sat across the table. Taliesin stood by the window as though he wished to be outside. To be gone already.

"This came from the captain's box of *Lady Voyager* too?"

"We don't know for certain," Fanny said. "But when Robin found it bound into that book"—she leaned forward—"for he could not halt the search for clues even after your departure"—she cast him a proud smile—"we knew it must have been written by your mother."

Eleanor's fingers slid along the edges of the page, creased from old wrinkles. Was this the writing of the woman who had abandoned her and her sisters twenty-three years earlier? But why would such a note have been stored in the captain's safe box aboard a ship her mother had not even boarded? A *love letter*? Had her father been a colonel in the army? Had she sent it on the ship hoping that he would receive it in England? But why had she needed to assure him of her love? And what had she lost?

"I found nothing else, I'm afraid," Mr. Prince said, his eyes sympathetic. "Though I searched through several hundred books. When I return to Drearcliffe, I will continue searching."

"Will you return with us, Eleanor? It is only a two-day drive and then we might renew your search and the labor of the three of us will meet with more success." She lifted speaking eyes to Talicsin. "Or the four of us."

"Mr. Wolfe has other plans," Eleanor said swiftly. "In fact"—she set down the letter and stood up—"he was just leaving St. Petroc when you arrived. Weren't you, Mr. Wolfe?"

"As you say." He looked at the Prince siblings. "Mrs. Upchurch. Mr. Prince." He bowed. Then he turned to her. "Give your father my regards."

Eleanor could say nothing. The cacophony of loss filled her throat and crippled her lips.

Mr. Prince rose to his feet. "I will walk with you to your horse, Wolfe."

They went from the room. Eleanor sat and took up the letter and pretended to read it again and pretended to listen to Fanny. But she saw nothing and heard nothing, only her heart as it shattered into pieces again.

THEY HAD BARELY stepped from the paving stones to the pebbled yard when Prince said in a strained voice, "I told her that you intended to offer for Fanny. At Kitharan that night. Rather, I suggested it to her."

Taliesin halted.

"I don't know if you had any such intention," Prince hurried to add. "Fanny never said so. She is a fine person—much finer than I am, in truth. I think she likes you very much. But she would never tell an untruth."

"Then why did you say it?"

"It should be obvious to you." Prince's jaw was hard. "I am in love with Eleanor, Wolfe. The fewer men I must contend with in this competition, the greater my chance of success." His mouth made a grim line. "She didn't like it. She . . . admires you."

"We have known each other many years." And he'd been a fool for her every one of them. He should not have kissed her. Touched her. Even now he could feel her in his hands.

"You are a clever man, Wolfe. I can see that. But I'm not a simpleton, whatever else you think of me."

"I think nothing of you at all, Mr. Prince."

His hands flexed at his sides. "I know it was you."

"What was I?"

"Almost as soon as we met at Drearcliffe I recognized you. But I refused to believe it. I convinced myself that my memory was mistaken. And you were so changed. But now—here—it's clear. Shackelford's house isn't two miles away. I visited it on several oc-

casions while Thomas and I were in school together."
His brow was low. "I know it was you, that day in the
woods. The fight. And now . . ." A hard flush colored
his cheeks. "Now I realize that Eleanor must have been
the girl. The vicar's daughter."

Taliesin said nothing.

"I expect it will mean nothing to you now." Prince
said. "But I'm sorry for what Shackelford did. I'm even
sorrier that I did not stop him from it. I could have. I
should have. Afterward, I regretted that I hadn't."

"For how long did you regret it, I wonder. As long,
perhaps, as it took my broken bones to mend?"

Prince's eyes flared. "If our positions had been reversed, would you have acted differently?"

Taliesin didn't even bother laughing. Prince had no
idea of what he spoke.

He started toward the stable. "Leave it be, Prince.
Some mistakes are better left in the past." She hadn't
been a mistake. Never that.

He entered the stable, took up Tristan's saddle,
and lifted it onto his back. The stallion sidestepped.
Taliesin stroked the ebony coat and his horse twisted
to nudge him on the shoulder.

"Where to now, my friend?" he murmured. He
would not return to Kitharan immediately, not if she
were headed to Drearcliffe. He had business elsewhere
he could see to. "Back to Plymouth, you say? To visit
Elijah Fish? I was thinking the same thing." Whatever
the jeweler had told her, he would learn it. Until she
had her wish to discover what had become of her parents, he would not give up the search.

He turned to remove the bridle from the peg. Prince
stood in the doorway. With a great breath that lifted
his shoulders, he reached into his pocket and withdrew an object. He stretched his palm open. Upon it
was a flat silver case.

"This belongs to her family. To her father. Last winter I found it in the captain's safe box from the *Lady Voyager*. It bears a family crest that was easy to trace."

Taliesin steadied his stance, every muscle tight as steel. "A moment ago, Prince, because of that apology, I admit that I had been thinking more highly of you than you probably deserve. But that you could have known this, possessed this, and withheld it from her, alters my opinion. I recommend taking yourself out of my sight now—to the vicarage with that, or to anywhere swiftly—or you will soon find yourself in need of a physician."

Prince stepped backward and his shoulders heaved. "You don't understand." He spoke rapidly. "At first I said nothing of it because I didn't know if she was truly who she said she was. Traveling alone, with only a Gyp— *you*. What was I to think of her? When her character became clear to me, and I could see what this search for her family meant to her, I intended to give it to her. I did. But she departed so swiftly, I hadn't the opportunity to . . . to . . ."

"To admit that you had lied to her?"

"To explain to her the situation," he said firmly. "I haven't lied to her in the most important matter. I have told her how I feel about her. I want to make her happy. I don't believe that meeting her real family will accomplish that."

"Perhaps you should allow her to make that decision."

"I would, but— For God's sake. You don't understand. It's not a simple matter. I went there. To her family's house. Her father's. I met him. That is, I was *shown* him." He seemed to choke. "The family did not want it, but I was in possession of this case and I insisted. When I saw him I understood why." He shook his head. "Wolfe, her real father is a madman."

Chapter 22

A Proposal of Marriage

Prince walked toward him. "I want you to have this."

Taliesin made no move to accept the silver case. Prince placed it on the ledge of the open stall. "I owe it to you, for not defending you all those years ago. It's too little too late, I think, but it's all I have to offer you."

"You haven't the courage to tell her yourself?"

"No. That isn't it." He straightened his shoulders. "You aided her in this search until she came to my grandfather's house, and then afterward in Plymouth. I want her. Make no mistake about that. And I intend to have her. But if finding her family helps her decide where to rest her favor, then you deserve her."

"I don't trust you."

"You shouldn't. When Fanny told me she admired you, I wrote to several friends of mine in London. One of them discovered that the new master of Kitharan has a checkered past. He provided me with details." Prince looked him up and down now, as though Taliesin still wore the threadbare clothes and fight-blackened eyes he'd worn then.

"That life is behind me."

"But it needn't be." Prince's bright eyes were hard. "If you tell Eleanor that I found that case in the captain's box—or if you tell my sister, who doesn't know anything of it—I will make your criminal past known to your neighbors at Kitharan. And to your servants. Many of them are having trouble enough accepting you. If they learn this, you'll be damned there. You'd be as well to sell the property, if anyone would buy it from you. Baron tried for a decade to rid himself of it before you took it off his hands."

"I've never been particularly fond of threats, Prince. How do you know I won't simply walk into that house now and tell her all you've just said?"

"Because you want her happiness too." Prince's lips were tight. "I'm sorry it's come to this, Wolfe. I think you must be a decent man. She wouldn't trust you if you weren't. But I intend to win this competition. She deserves a man who understands her. A man of her own kind."

WITH THE SILVER case in his pocket, Taliesin rode to London. The Adler family's emblem was etched into the case and easily identified. Nearly a century had passed since, lacking an heir, the title had reverted to the crown. But the Bridgeport-Adler branch of the family still held property in east Devonshire. A modest estate, it nevertheless spanned acres in two shires.

The tavern master in the village told Taliesin where to find the lane to the main house. All the while he assessed Taliesin with suspicious eyes. Taliesin had long since grown accustomed to such assessments, and he hadn't broken any furniture or split anyone's lip in this tavern in particular. But nine years ago he'd spent plenty of time in this county, enough to be escorted from it by the law. And he supposed that a Rom who spoke as a gentleman and didn't try to sell anything was a memorable enough stranger, drunk or sober.

The house of the Bridgeport-Adlers sat at the top of a gradual rise from a lake, a brick building of relatively recent construction from the look of it: rectangular from the front and subtle in its classical adornments. Settled amidst clustered evergreen shrubs and flanked by a formal garden enclosed in a hedge, it bespoke modest prosperity. The absence of any view of outbuildings from the curving drive suggested the family cared for appearances; vulgar barns, brewery, and other buildings in which work occurred were hidden out of sight of approaching guests. Only the carriage house could be seen peeking out opposite the garden.

Taliesin dismounted before the house and waited for a stable hand. None appeared. He walked Tristan to the stable and startled an old groom awake.

"Sir! That is . . ." The groom peered at him, then scratched his head. "Er . . . What can I do for you?"

"You can stable my horse while I call upon your master."

The groom tugged his cap and took the stallion in hand. Tristan never failed to impress men who knew horseflesh. The groom was whistling by the time Taliesin rounded the house again.

The front door was open. A man in neat servant's garments stood in the doorway. "Your business here, sir, if you please?"

Taliesin considered that perhaps he had become too accustomed to doing business with the same breeders and traders who knew him well. He hadn't been so keenly assessed in years, not even at Kitharan when they'd come to gawk at the Gypsy landowner—the Gypsy landowner who would no longer be welcome when Prince spread the news of his past.

He would not hide the truth from Eleanor. But he didn't trust Robin Prince. He'd come ahead to ensure the truth, to protect her from unnecessary hurt. In that, Prince had pegged his man.

"I wish to speak with your master. Is he in?"

The manservant's nose inched higher. "Who, may I ask, is calling?"

Taliesin offered his card. The servant studied it, then studied him again. Taliesin waited. He'd waited like this hundreds of times before, scrutinized by servants from the lowest stable boys to lords' secretaries. *If their positions had been reversed.* He wondered if Robin Prince had ever waited for a servant to do anything. But he was not a wealthy man, rather dependent on his grandfather. Bound to his family. To his sisters as well.

He had once enjoyed bonds like that. Then he learned that a man who trusted in such bonds could have it all swept away from him in an instant.

Easier to remain unshackled.

The manservant turned Taliesin's card over and read the words he'd written there. His eyes widened.

"If you will wait here, sir," he said swiftly and went inside the house, leaving the door open. Taliesin had often been told to wait on door stoops. On occasion when doors closed at this moment, he liked to imagine a bevy of servants rushing about and hiding all the small valuables.

Now through the open door he saw a high-ceilinged foyer paved in costly stone, with intricate crystal wall sconces and, above the landing at the break in the stairs directly ahead, a full-length painting of a uniformed soldier.

Taliesin crossed the threshold and walked to the foot of the stair. The young officer in the painting was Eleanor and Arabella's father. Or a very near relative. Without doubt. The portraitist had perfectly captured the curve of lips, cast of brow, and shape of eyes that two of the three Caulfield sisters shared, and the white Burgundy flavor of Eleanor's hair.

In London he'd learned that the head of the Bridgeport-Adler family had the name Edward Bridgeport, and that he had spent time in the West Indies many years ago. Taliesin took the stairs two at a time and came to the painting. The bronze plate attached to the bottom of the gilt frame read "Capt. Edward Bridgeport-Adler."

"Sir! You must come away from there at once," the manservant insisted from the base of the stair. "The master is not receiving at present. He kindly asks you to leave."

Taliesin turned away from the face of Eleanor's father as soft footsteps pattered and a woman hurried into the hall. Her features were more delicate than Edward Bridgeport-Adler's but almost identical. She was perhaps forty years of age.

"No, Stoppal." Her voice vibrated with agitation. "You mustn't do this. The baroness is wrong." She held Taliesin's card between the fingers of both hands, as though she were praying with it. "Mr. Wolfe, thank you for calling. I wish very much to speak with you, but I—" She looked over her shoulder. "My aunt is coming." She hurried to the base of the stairs. "She will make you leave now," she whispered. "But you *must* return. And bring them with you. She cannot deny *them* entrance into his house. I beg of you, return as soon as you are able." Straightening her shoulders, she glided through the doorway she'd come from, saying loudly, "Stoppal sent him away, Aunt Cynthia. You needn't fret."

Stoppal stood at the open front door. "Sir?" he said sharply.

Taliesin descended the stairs and went to the stable. He had sufficient proof. And whoever the woman was, Eleanor and her sisters had an ally in the house. The master might truly be mad, as Prince had said, but at least one member of the Bridgeport-Adler family wanted to know Edward's daughters.

Leading Tristan out, the groom looked him over appreciatively. Then he looked over Taliesin again.

"Fine animal, sir."

"He is indeed."

"Master Edward used to have a black horse a bit like this one. Gelded, a'course. The master was just a boy at the time. Couldn't handle a stallion." He patted the stallion's rump for emphasis. Tristan bore it with disinterest.

"I suspect Mr. Bridgeport-Adler became a . . . bruising rider." Taliesin stroked his horse's neck and withheld his smile. "He must have a fine mount now."

"Aw, no, the master don't ride these days." The groom wagged his head sorrowfully. "Not since they sent him home with his head all in a muddle. He likes the horses, you see. But between you and me, sir, I think in that prison they mixed up his noggin a bit. A shame, I say. A man don't deserve to be locked up in a dark hole for so many years he forgets what he knows, no matter what wrong he did all the way across the ocean years ago." He slapped the stallion's rump again. Tristan flared his nostrils and grunted.

"No doubt you're correct about that." *Prison.*

"But, you watch, I tell you: he'll be back in the saddle before the season's out. Came around here just the other day telling me he wanted to drive. Drive, if you can believe it! And him not even climbing on a horse's back since I've seen him. Well, I said, I'd be glad to teach him how to drive if he'd like, but that I didn't know that her ladyship'd be having any of it. She likes matters arranged her way, you see. But he said he already knew how to drive, that I'd been the one to teach him years back when he was a boy. I told him he sounded right like young Master Edward before he went off to war, and he said as that was a good thing, being he was one in the same. We had a good laugh over it. Yessir, mark my words, he'll be riding come summer."

"I'm pleased to know it."

"I won't keep you now, sir, and I've got my work to do. Fine animal you've there. Mighty fine animal."

WHEN A MAN went to his knees to offer marriage to a woman, she should feel something, if only gratitude for his willingness to scuff his trousers.

Eleanor felt more than gratitude. With his strong jaw and brilliantly blue eyes full of sincerity, Robin Prince was an attractive man. In the fortnight since he had appeared in St. Petroc with his sister, he had proved to be everything she'd thought him at Drearcliffe: amusing, good-humored, well-mannered, and intensely interested in her.

Fanny, in whom Eleanor could truly see no fault, adored her brother. She had confided in Eleanor that if Sir Wilkie gave Drearcliffe to her, she would sign it over to her brother without hesitation. Her husband had left her nothing, yet Robin kept both her and Henrietta comfortable on an excessively modest allowance from their grandfather. Robin had plans to restore Drearcliffe and was eager to be busy and useful.

Looking down into his handsome, hopeful face, Eleanor felt a weight upon her breast more painful than she had expected.

Her papa liked him. Agnes liked him. Betsy liked him. Even the squire's wife liked him. Everybody in St. Petroc liked him. Only her knee-weakening desire for a Gypsy horse trader stood in her way of this.

"Robin," she whispered. "I cannot."

"Eleanor." He grasped her hand in both of his. "Dearest Eleanor, do not refuse me with such finality. Tell me only that you must have more time to consider. We have known each other a short month. Allow me another sennight—a fortnight—as many weeks as it requires to win your affection."

She bit down on her lip and for an instant the discomfort of it smothered the discomfort in her chest. "More time will not alter my response."

He smiled gamely. "Since ladies often spend an hour choosing a hair ribbon, you will not convince me that you can decide on a life's partner in the space of a month."

"I am sorry, Robin. I know my mind on this."

He came to his feet but kept hold of her hand. "Your mind is formidable, indeed. But what of your heart?"

Her heart. Empty. Full. Confused. Furious. A jumbled bag of contrary emotions she'd been struggling for a fortnight to set in rational order. With no success.

"I cannot assure you with complete finality that my feelings will never alter," she said honestly. "But I do not believe they will."

"Then I am content. Even a small lack of certainty allows me to hope."

She drew her hand away. "You are generous," she mumbled.

"My constancy has nothing to do with generosity. I am simply a man in love."

Of all the expressions of admiration he had offered her over the past weeks, this statement made her heart thump with excruciating force. A man in love was, apparently, a directed and definite creature. Like her brother-in-law Luc, he would pursue the object of his affection the length of countries and seas until she succumbed to him. Like Ravenna's husband, Vitor, he would relinquish the life he had known for her. Like her papa, he would remain alone for decades until she appeared. And like Robin Prince, he would smile when she offered him even the slimmest ray of hope.

A man in love did not abandon a woman. Twice. But Taliesin's love had been calf love only, and after that no love at all. Only lust. She wished she could separate the two as handily as he did.

Robin bid her adieu with a fervent kiss on the back of her hand. She went into her bedchamber and opened a hollow book in which Ravenna used to store dried frogs on occasion. Now it contained only a man's gold ring with a glowing ruby set over a peculiar T-shaped symbol. Closing her palm around it, she gathered her cloak and left the house.

The spring air was fresh against her cheeks. She would leave for Combe tomorrow. She had already instructed Betsy to pack her traveling trunk. Like Robin and Fanny, Mr. Treadwell had also lingered in St. Petroc, with the reason that the duchess had commanded him to remain in her service as long as Eleanor wished. But Eleanor suspected he didn't want to leave without Betsy.

It suited her. St. Petroc was no longer her home. She had remained in this place overflowing with memories she now wished to discard only because of Fanny and Robin. Fanny would not hate her for refusing her brother; she was too kind. But if Robin truly intended to repeat his offer, she might as well leave now before he got in the habit of it.

She saddled Saint George, acutely aware of the bay mare with four white socks in the adjacent stable. Taliesin had left Iseult. He could not possibly intend her as a gift; the mare was far too fine and he must know that the vicar of St. Petroc could not afford to keep such an animal. Eleanor could not help seeing Iseult in the same vein as the message he had left in the book eleven years ago: as a consolation.

She didn't want a consolation. She wanted freedom. Freedom from pain and regret and doubt and wanting what she would never have. She wanted to begin again, not with a temporary adventure, but forever. This time on her own terms.

Drawing Saint George from his stall, she mounted and rode to the squire's property. Then she rode past it. Finally she reached the wood where she hadn't gone in a decade, not since she stopped crying on her pillow every night.

One final deed must be done before she would begin anew entirely. Now that she had refused her prince, she could do it.

Reining in her horse at the edge of the wood, she peered into the shadows. Budding with spring green, it looked entirely different than it had that sweltering summer day eleven years ago. Now it seemed pale and passionless.

She reached into her pocket and palmed the ring.

Lifted her arm.

She froze.

If she were going to do this right, she mustn't see where it went. Closing her eyes and turning her back on the trees, she prayed it wouldn't bounce off a trunk and right back at her. She squeezed her eyes shut.

Arabella would murder her for this. But Arabella had already wed her prince charming, and Ravenna hers. She already knew what she must about the symbol for Arabella to continue searching for their family if she wished. The ring itself was now only a burden, bound to a ridiculous fortune it was high time she discarded.

There would be no prince for her of any sort. There would instead be eccentric maiden Auntie Eleanor who occasionally hared off on larks and possibly, hopefully, got herself into dreadful trouble. Adventures needn't involve half-naked men to be exciting, and she had many places she wished to explore, many books yet to read, many plays to see, many monuments to visit. She would not have children of her own, which surrounded her soul with a bottomless ache. But she would enjoy her sisters' children, and she would never again lack courage now that her life was hers to determine—not her papa's or her sisters' or some foolish prophecy's.

She lifted her arm again, this time with determination. Hoof beats sounded in the distance. She opened her eyes and her heart fell into the soles of her boots.

Taliesin rode toward her.

Desperation clawed at her. *This* was not part of her plan. If she were to start anew, to live life on her own adventuresome terms, he had to disappear. Forever. *That* was the plan.

"How did you know I was here?" she shouted, shoving the ring back into her pocket.

He reined in the stallion. "Nice greeting."

Her heart broke through her ribs. "I don't have to greet you nicely. I never have."

"I saw you leave the village. I followed you."

"At a covert distance? I didn't see you."

"I wanted to know where you were going."

"You could have caught up with me and asked."

"Then you might have altered your course." He glanced at the trees. "Have you come for a dip in the pond?"

The breath left her. Jogging her head to free it of the madness that was him, *here*, the one thing she had not expected ever again *and did not want*, she pivoted and went to her horse. She yanked his lead free of the shrub and dragged Saint George away from the copse. "I do not wish to know why you are here. I asked you to go away. Please do so."

"Eleanor—"

"This time, take your horse with you."

"She is yours."

"A fine pair of shoes is one thing. A very fine horse is another altogether. And as you can see, I already have a horse."

"Then sell her. I will not take her back."

Sell Iseult? Never.

She looked frantically about, scouting for a rock to mount. Taliesin was following her on his giant horse. The stallion could outrun Saint George, but at least in the saddle she wouldn't feel quite so powerless. *Vulnerable.*

A tree stump jutted from the ground. She headed for it.

"I will help you mount," he said.

"I don't want you to touch me." She led Saint George beside the stump. "How does it feel to hear that, Mr. Wolfe?"

"Not so good, I admit."

She hefted her foot into the stirrup and threw her leg over. Her skirts caught and she tugged at them to cover her calf. It was a gown she'd sewn with a wide skirt for riding astride. That it misbehaved today in front of the one man who had touched her legs was her curse.

He came beside her. "I must tell you why I have come."

"Must you? Well, it will have to wait"—she pressed her knees into her horse's sides—"until after you have tasted my dust. *Hui!*" Saint George took off.

She didn't expect Taliesin to ignore the challenge, and he did not. Tristan's hooves thundered at Saint George's flank and the field disappeared behind them, then the next field and the next. The wind tearing at her hair and cloak, the powerful creature between her legs, and the man on the massive stallion just behind drove her on.

When everyone else in St. Petroc had barely believed she could walk on her own legs, across these fields Taliesin had taught her how to gallop.

When tears stung her face she knew that they did not come from relief at his return, or frustration or pain in knowing that whatever had brought him here now, he would certainly leave again. Beneath relief and pain was a peculiar, unfamiliar sort of hope. Life must be lived. Casting away the old shell of careful self-control, she would gallop into life as she had done years ago when she recovered from her illness. But this time she wouldn't hide it from everyone except him. She swiped at her cheeks with her sleeve and rode.

At the final hill before St. Petroc, she pulled up and Taliesin slowed.

"You could have beaten me," she panted. "Why did you let me win?"

"I didn't let you win."

She leaned forward and stroked Saint George's neck. "Tristan is the stronger runner."

"But you are the better rider."

She snapped her head around to him. Wind-tousled,

and commanding the mighty stallion with the hands and thighs and muscles she craved, Taliesin was not smiling.

"Eleanor, your father is found."

RIDING BESIDE HER along the path to the village, he told her about a manor house and a portrait and a story that a groom had candidly shared with him.

"Edward Bridgeport-Adler." She tested the name on her tongue. It did not sound familiar. But neither had the name Grace. "A captain in the army?"

"According to the plate on the portrait."

"But the letter that Mr. Prince found at Drearcliffe was addressed to a colonel."

"Perhaps your mother did not write that letter."

Or perhaps Grace had loved another man.

Her father. In Devonshire now. Injured, perhaps. And weak-minded after years in prison. She had never really believed they would find him. Yet during all these years he had been in England.

"How was it that you went there? What took you there?"

"Prince suggested it to me."

"*Robin?* But why did he say nothing of it to me?"

"You must ask him." They came to the high street and he halted his horse. "The woman at the house was eager for you to call on her. Do you wish to?"

"Yes, of course." She could return to Combe and perhaps Luc and Arabella would go with her. But she didn't want to wait. "Will you take me there? Or have you fulfilled your promise to me already?"

He hesitated only a moment. "I will take you there."

"Eleanor?" Fanny came from a shop. "Mr. Wolfe! What a fine surprise to see you here again so soon."

He bowed from the saddle.

She dimpled. "Dear Eleanor, how very adventuresome you are to ride astride. I've never had the courage."

She dismounted. If anyone saw her ankles now, she hoped they spread the news far and wide. She would be Eccentric Miss Caulfield and revel in it.

"Fanny, I am sorry to abandon you, but I must leave here this afternoon, as soon as the carriage can be prepared."

"Goodness! Have you come to carry her away, Mr. Wolfe?"

Too many of her dreams had looked exactly like that. "I am to pay a call on family, I think. In Devonshire."

"Family?"

Eleanor's throat tested the word. Then her lips. "My father."

"Why, Eleanor!" Fanny exclaimed. "This is most wonderful!"

"I will depart this afternoon."

"Robin has just gone off too today, although he said he would return within the fortnight. But of course you must already know that." She offered Eleanor a smile of confidence. "Oh, how I wish I could stay here so that when you return I can hear everything about your visit with your father. But I suspect it's high time I leave here too. I do so like St. Petroc. Now that Henrietta is happily settled in with her friends in London, I have half a mind not to return to Bath. I may let that adorable little cottage by the draper's and live here. Robin would be thrilled." She laughed with genuine happiness. "Now, Eleanor, wouldn't that be splendid?"

Chapter 23
The Leaving

*T*he house was not as large as either Drearcliffe or Kitharan, but it was modern and elegant, and the grounds neatly kept. From the length of the drive and pastures around, the estate seemed extensive.

"I'll wait in the carriage, miss," Betsy said stiffly.

"Betsy, I have told you a dozen times today that I must do this."

"You trust what *that* gentleman's told you if you like, miss. But I won't be leaping into it like a foolhardy girl myself."

Swallowing back her nerves, Eleanor climbed out of the carriage. A groom was leading Tristan away.

Taliesin came to her. He had spoken little to her during the long day of travel, and only as necessary.

"Are you well?"

Three little words. He had said the same three words to her after he hadn't seen her for days at Drearcliffe, before he had kissed her like he would consume her.

"Of course."

A servant in a neat suit opened the door.

"Hello. I am Eleanor Caulfield. I would like to see Edward Bridgeport-Adler. My father."

THE WOMAN WHO came into the cheerful little parlor in which the servant left them was Eleanor's height, with blond hair smoothed into a tight chignon and a face so much like her own, but delicately lined with age, that Eleanor gasped.

"Good gracious," the woman said from the doorway, her hands busy in the air in agitation. Her hazel eyes were overbright. "My dearest niece." She flew across the room. Taking up Eleanor's hands, she squeezed them in a fierce grip. "Dear, dear girl." Her eyes blazed with mingled joy and disbelief. "What is your name, child? Tell me at once."

"Eleanor." It came out as a croak. "Eleanor Caulfield."

"*No.*" Shock slashed across her face. "All this time . . ." Her hands clasped Eleanor's face and she pressed their cheeks together. "No, you are *not* Caulfield. You are Eleanor Bridgeport-Adler. Finally," she whispered into her hair. "Finally you are found."

When she released her, she turned to Taliesin.

"Mr. Wolfe, you did not tell an untruth. I have waited in distress these three days, wishing against hope for what you wrote on that card to be true. But I should have had faith." With an agitated timidity that was etched into the lines at either side of her mouth, her eyes scanned Eleanor's face again. "For this is my brother's daughter that he wrote to me of years ago and of whom he sometimes still speaks. It could not be any other. You are in his image, Eleanor. I never had the fortune to know Grace, nor to see her. But my brother said she was accounted a beauty by all. Love sees beauty where there is none, I think. But it is clear that it was not only his love that made Grace beautiful." The etchings curved into a smile. "You are prettier than him by far."

"They were . . ." Now she found it difficult to speak. "They were wed? My father and my mother?"

Her aunt's eyes popped wide. "But of course. It was not—" Distress colored her face. "You know nothing of it all, I think? For it was secret at first, and then we lost you, and . . ." Again she seemed overcome.

"Was my father in prison?"

"For four years."

"Is that why he did not come to meet our ship? Is that why he did not search for us?"

"Your ship? Oh, no. No, dear child. If he had known . . . Oh, my dearest niece, he never knew your mother sent you to England. If only he had . . . If only I had known then . . . But there is so much to tell. I hardly know where to begin."

"May I see him?"

"I would have it no other way." But she hesitated. "Now?"

She squeezed Eleanor's fingers until they hurt. "She . . . Our aunt . . . The dowager baroness . . ." She glanced at Taliesin worriedly, then at Eleanor's face as though searching.

"Miss . . . ?"

"Mary. I am your Aunt Mary." Again she curled her palm around Eleanor's face, gentle now.

"Aunt Mary," she said, "May I see my father? Please?"

"I would have you see him immediately. But the baroness, our aunt . . . You will have to meet her first."

"I should like to do so."

She turned to Taliesin and seemed to study him. "Mr. Wolfe, I cannot . . . That is . . ." Her eyes were fraught again, almost afraid. She grasped Eleanor's hand tightly. "No. *No*. We *will* go. All of us together. There is strength in numbers," she added with a spark of defiance in her retiring eyes.

She led them into the foyer and to the stairs, pointedly averting her attention from the servants. But her hand shook around Eleanor's.

Eleanor halted before the full-length painting on the landing.

"Your father," Mary said. "My brother, Edward. Wasn't he handsome in his regimentals?"

The butler stood before a double set of doors at the top of the landing.

Mary's fingers were like a claw around Eleanor's. "Mr. Stoppal, open the door."

He looked down his nose. "Her ladyship will not approve."

"Stoppal, open that door at this moment, or I shall see to it that my brother turns you off without a reference."

With a narrowed glance at Taliesin, Mr. Stoppal opened the door.

Furnished with austere elegance and bathed in early spring sunshine, the room was inhabited by five people: two young women, two young men, and an elderly woman, all of them dressed as though to attend one of Arabella's fashionable parties, with lace and intricate coiffures and jewels. The ladies' gowns were exquisite confections of silk, beads, and embroidery. The gentleman's coats had large lapels and their shirt collars and stiff cravats brushed their chins. Their conversation ceased as Mary led Eleanor toward them.

"Aunt Cynthia, cousins, here is a wonderful surprise come to us today," Mary said tremulously. "At long last, I have found Edward's daughter."

In her sisters' homes, Eleanor had been introduced to duchesses and countesses, barons and earls. She had never been perused with quite such blank shock.

She curtsied. "I am pleased to make your acquaintance."

"You have not made my acquaintance until I have said so," the baroness said. "Stand up so that I can see your face." She lifted a monocle on a satin ribbon. Lips like raisins pursed. Powdered skin wrinkled around them in tight folds. "At least she looks like him," she finally said.

"She is not brown or frizzle-haired at all, Mama, but quite pretty," one of the younger women said, lifting her nose as if to smell Eleanor across the room.

"She is passable," the baroness said.

"Eleanor," Mary said hurriedly. "This is your great-aunt, Lady Cynthia Boswell. And these are our cousins, Harold, Seraphica, and Miriam, and Seraphica's husband, Mr. Custer. Cousins, won't you welcome Eleanor to our family at long last?"

The gentlemen bowed stiffly. Harold's eyes narrowed. The younger ladies stood to curtsy. Eleanor wished herself in the carriage with Betsy, or back at the vicarage, or anywhere else than in this place with these people. But she hadn't come for them.

"I would like to meet my father," she said.

"What you would like, girl, has nothing to say to anything," Lady Boswell said.

Girl?

"You might be my nephew's issue. Your appearance is so near to Edward's and Mary's that none would doubt it. But the blood of that mulatto whore in your veins does not make you an equal here. You will speak when spoken to."

"Good gracious, Mama," Seraphica said. "Look at what she has brought with her." Wide-eyed, she gawked at Taliesin.

"Has he come to read spurious fortunes to your maids, Mother?" Harold chuckled.

"After the peddlers come to the village each year," Lady Boswell grumbled, "those silly girls are forever complaining that their futures look brighter than their present lot. Can you imagine the insolence? How on earth did Stoppal allow him inside? But those persons are despicably ingratiating. They will say anything for a shilling. Be off with you, now, boy. Stoppal! Remove this person from the house."

A sick chill lapped at Eleanor. "You are mistaken."

"Mr. Wolfe is with our Eleanor, Aunt Cynthia," Mary said.

Lady Boswell's penciled brows ticked up. "How original of you to keep a Gypsy manservant. I have never seen the like."

"I'm certain it will now become all the rage, Mama," Miriam said snidely, sweeping Eleanor's simple traveling gown with disdain.

"Mr. Wolfe is not my manservant. He is a friend of my family and has assisted me in finding you."

Lady Boswell's nostrils flared. "I admit myself unsurprised."

"The apple, and all that," Harold said with a smirk. "Hm, Mother?"

An explosion was building inside Eleanor's chest. And yet Taliesin stood as calmly as though he hadn't a care in the world. But perhaps he was accustomed to this.

She *was not*.

"I will make certain to tell the Duke of Lycombe that you said that, Cousin Harold," she said between gritted teeth. "Since his son and heir is my nephew—that is, Edward's grandson—he will be interested to learn that you consider my mother's mixed blood contemptible. I'm certain my other brother-in-law, the son of the Marquess of Airedale, will be equally intrigued. For while the duchess and I are quite fair, our sister, Edward's third daughter, is quite as brown as a berry." An exaggeration, to be sure. But Ravenna wouldn't mind it.

The faces of the five people before her had gone white as the vellum medieval monks used to make books.

Mary grasped Eleanor's hand, a grin twitching the corners of her mouth. "It will be delightful to meet my other nieces and their families. What a wonderful day it is. Edward's daughters are found, and they are grand ladies! Aunt Cynthia, you must be in alt." She stepped forward. "Now, Eleanor mustn't be made to wait to meet Edward another moment. Please, Aunt . . ." She drew a deep breath, as though filling her meager frame with courage. "Give me the key."

WITH A LARGE bronze key clutched in her spider fingers, Mary led Eleanor up another stairwell to a door in a narrow corridor. Taliesin had left the house. But that was for the best. He needn't remain to be further insulted by her horrible relatives.

"When they released Edward from prison," Mary said, "Aunt Cynthia was mistress of this house for three years already. She did not allow any of us to speak of him, and she allowed me to see him only once a week." Her voice crumbled. "He was . . . unwell, Eleanor. For many years. He seemed not to know us or anything about his house. In the first year, I inquired into the conditions at the prison in which he had been held, but no one would tell me anything. I think it must have been horrid, and that he was isolated from others. It disordered his mind."

"Why was he imprisoned? What was his offense?"

"Desertion and treason. He had abandoned his regiment and joined rebels fighting for abolition in the mountains of French San Domingue and Spanish Santo Domingo, one island divided into two colonies. He was to be executed in the West Indies. Aunt Cynthia's husband, the baron, made a special request of the crown that he be transported to England and imprisoned here indefinitely instead. His sentence was reduced and he was allowed to keep his property, but it was all done in secret. It was the last thing Lord Boswell did before he died. It saved Edward's life, and yet no one was to know of it, not even his wife."

Desertion and treason.

"You said he was in prison for four years. Has he been here, in this place"—she looked at the door— "since then?"

She nodded gravely. "My aunt has kept the key." The furrows in her brow deepened. "I am sorry for what they said about your mother."

"You seem unlike them. Why do you live here?"

"Because of Edward. I could not leave him alone to their horrible . . ." Her voice trailed away. Then her eyes brightened and her gaze darted about the corridor. "Eleanor, he is *better*," she whispered. "These past ten months he has come out of the prison in his mind that trapped him. He speaks lucidly most of the time now, and while he seems to recall nothing of his life before he purchased his commission, he has begun to remember his years in the West Indies with your mother and you and your sister Arabella. And I believe I know why. It began with a visit late last winter by a young man. Mr. Robin Prince."

Eleanor's eyes flew wide. "Robin Prince?" *Robin* had been here.

"I had never seen him before and Edward has little memory of the visit itself. But it seemed to lift the cloud from his mind." She reached for the door. "When I sat with him yesterday afternoon he was well. I cannot imagine what seeing you will do to his temper, but I cannot keep you from him, nor him from you now, as my aunt would have it."

"She disapproved of his marriage so much?"

"She wants this house. After word came from the West Indies that Grace perished and my brother's daughters had disappeared, Aunt Cynthia imagined this house and estate were hers. She was the baron's second wife. When he died he left her son Harold nothing. They live here only because Edward has not told them to leave. Miriam has not wed, and Mr. Custer has no fortune or profession, so Seraphica lives here as well. Aunt Cynthia is terrified of being thrown out."

"Why haven't you done so?"

"Before he was imprisoned, my brother wrote a will. Eleanor, you and your sister are his legal heirs."

"Sister? But I have two sisters."

"Oh, my dear child, it will all be clear soon. You will see." She squeezed her hand. "But you must promise me one thing before you go in."

"Of course."

"You must not mention the name Caulfield."

TALIESIN WALKED TOWARD the Duke of Lycombe's vehicle where Betsy waited.

"Your mistress is becoming acquainted with her family. She will want you shortly, I suspect."

Jutting her chin away, silently the girl went toward the house.

"Sir?" Treadwell said. "What shall I do with the girls and Pendragon?" He gestured to the carriage team.

"I think you will have some time before departing. Await Miss Caulfield's instruction." He went to the stable where he had spoken with the groom three days ago that seemed peculiarly like a year. The stable was long and well kept, like the stable at Kitharan, except empty.

He would return home. She would not return to Drearcliffe now, and he would go on as he had before Arabella had called him. How, he wasn't quite certain. But he'd done it once before. Wasn't that how he had become who he was now, free and unfettered? Unbound.

Betsy returned after some time, her freckled face wreathed in glee. A servant from the house followed her.

"My mistress has been invited to stay the month!" she proclaimed like a king's trumpeter. "Mr. Treadwell, you must unstrap the luggage now and help carry it inside." She saw to the task with triumphal efficiency. With a final lifted brow at Taliesin over her shoulder, she marched inside with them.

Taliesin went to his horse and, like a vagabond, prepared to take to the road.

EDWARD BRIDGEPORT-ADLER WAS emaciated and pale, the flesh hanging on his frame and his hair gray. But his eyes focused on her in wonderment.

"Grace?"

Eleanor's tongue tripped over her hope. "No. I am Eleanor."

He blinked. Twice. "Eleanor?" In a whisper: "My daughter?"

Her eyes filled with tears. She nodded.

He came forward, touched her cheek, and a tear fell down each of his cheeks. "I am redeemed."

MARY SAT WITH them. His memories came in pieces, some solid, others like mist.

"What of your sister? What of Arabella?"

"She is well, Father." To say the word *father*, to believe it, was a sweet struggle. "As is Ravenna."

His eyes emptied. Mary's face worried. His hands clutched at the tail of his coat.

"Ravenna was an infant when our ship wrecked, father. Only six months old." Eleanor glanced at her aunt.

Mary's eyes were keen upon her brother. Expectant, it seemed.

"Ravenna . . ." He stood and shuffled to a table across the room that was strewn with papers. His chambers were comprised of a dressing room, sitting room and bedchamber, all neat and clean except for piles of papers and maps. He leafed through the folios, his movements growing jerky, agitated.

"What are you looking for, Edward?"

"Hmn, Mary?"

"I asked what are you looking for?" She spoke gently, as if encouraging him. "Eleanor and I would like to know."

He swung around. "Eleanor. I am remembering," he said with abashment. "It helps, you see, to jar the memories if I look at my records."

"Your records?" Eleanor said.

"Records of those years. Documents. Letters. Grace sent letters. And Alejo. They were avid correspondents. I would not allow her to come to the mountains with us, of course. The battles were too fierce, everything unpredictable. She was safer on the coast, safer there with you and Arabella. But after I was captured, Alejo left immediately, to take her the news of my execution . . ." He returned his attention to the papers, lifting one then another, and studying them.

"Edward," Mary said. "What happened after Alejo told Grace of your execution?" It seemed to Eleanor that Mary knew, that she only wished him to remember.

He lifted his head and peered at his sister. Then he returned to his chair and pulled it close to Eleanor's knees.

"Your sister's name is Ravenna," he said with more certainty now, as though confirming it to himself by saying it aloud.

"Yes. It is an odd name for an English girl. Did my mother choose it?"

His lips cracked into a smile. The confusion in his eyes retreated entirely. He looked clearly at her. "Do you know it? The city of Ravenna?"

"I know that it was once a capital of the Roman Empire." She looked at the maps strewn on the table close by, like the maps her papa stored in bookshelves at the vicarage. Once, when Taliesin and she had discovered those maps, they pored over them, sitting on the floor, shoulders nearly brushing. "Have you been there? To Ravenna?"

"No," he said. "Alejo had. He told me many times, many times, that of all cities in the world, he loved Ravenna the greatest. A city of a thousand mosaics sparkling like jewels, he said. Once he likened them to your mother's eyes." He smiled. "Alejo was a horseman, a warrior, and a rebel. But he was also something of a poet."

A frisson of energy rippled up Eleanor's neck. "He was your friend?"

"The best friend a man could have. We fought together side-by-side in the mountains, a band of rebels battling for justice alongside escaped slaves. I trusted him with my life. And with my wife. When they seized me and took me away to execute me, I told him to protect her."

"What happened to him?"

He placed three fingers upon his brow, above his eye. "I read about it some months ago," he said quietly. "There." He gestured to one of the tables covered with papers. "As though I had never known it before."

"You hadn't, brother," Mary said. "I only discovered these papers when that young man came calling last spring and I went into the attic to search. It was only then that Aunt Cynthia revealed to me the truth: how, before she perished, Grace had sent your personal belongings to me, including the letters she had written to you before your capture, and to Alejo after they believed you dead."

He nodded. "Yes. He told her of my execution, then he returned to the mountains to continue the fight we believed in so fervently." He lifted his eyes to Eleanor. "Alejo was a great revolutionary. We met on Jamaica the year you were born, when I was quartered there. After I left my unit and took your mother to San Domingue to aid in the struggles there, he and I were like brothers. He never said it, and he never betrayed me, but I knew he loved her. When I was captured, I knew he would protect her and my daughters with his life if it came to it."

"They didn't know you were still alive." As Eleanor spoke, the image of her youngest sister's black eyes and black hair and olive skin—so unlike hers and Arabella's—was before her. "They didn't know you were in England, that you had not been executed after all. Did they? It was a secret, what Lord Boswell had done to save you, bringing you back to England. Wasn't it?"

"Alejo and Grace married, Eleanor," Mary said quietly. "Before he returned to the mountains. Their letters to each other in those months speak of it."

Her father studied her eyes. "Your sister, Ravenna . . . What does she look like? Does she have your appearance? Mine?"

Eleanor's throat was thick. "No, Father."

"Are her eyes black? And her hair? Is her spirit untamable?"

"Yes. Who was he, Father?"

"Colonel Alejo Torres, son of the feuding horse lords of Andalusia. Royalty." His smile was soft, and proud. "If I had been executed as my wife and dear friend and all others believed I was, if I had not lived and made their marriage invalid, Eleanor, your sister Ravenna would be a princess."

WEARINESS CAME UPON Edward abruptly, and Mary hurried Eleanor out of his apartments. But he insisted that Eleanor remain at the house, and grew distressed when she demurred. After she agreed to it, he calmed.

"I cannot impose upon you," she said as her aunt showed her to a bedchamber. "Yet I have so many more questions."

"You must stay, Eleanor," Mary insisted. "My brother spoke more clearly just now than I have heard him in decades. Stay, I beg of you."

"But Mr. Wolfe has been insulted."

"No need to fret about *that* gentleman, miss," Betsy said. "Seems to me he was fixing to leave when I came inside."

"You must stop him from leaving if you wish it, Eleanor," Mary said. "Then hurry back and I will tell you all that I can."

Eleanor ran to the stable. Her father's groom and

Mr. Treadwell greeted her. No black stallion stood in a stall. She gripped the door.

"Where is Mr. Wolfe?"

"Well, now," the groom said, "he took that fine horse and said he'd best be on his way."

She had prepared herself for his departure. But now the air went from the surface of the earth entirely. No air. No breaths. She left the stable, dizzy, telling herself that she was strong and free, because all she could do was insist upon it until it became true.

By the lake at the bottom of the hill, Taliesin was leading his horse toward her. Heart careening somewhere between the sun and the moon, she walked swiftly, the damp wind whipping at her skirts, her fist bunched around the pouch containing her family's ring in her pocket.

He released the stallion's lead and came to her.

"You have found what you sought," he said. "I am glad for you."

She grabbed his hand and pressed the small pouch into it, then closed his fingers around it.

"Take this to Arabella. I pray you. I will write to her and explain all. My father is well—well enough that he knows himself, and me, and has told me more than I ever expected to learn. And my aunt is kind. But I don't understand everything yet, and I need to know. I will remain here until Arabella can come. But I want her to have this immediately, and I cannot entrust it to anyone else." She could not look into his face. *Strong and free.* She would not weep now, not today of all days. "Will you do this last for me?"

"Of course." Without looking at it, he tucked the ring in his coat.

"I am sorry for what those evil people said."

"Eleanor, I don't care—"

She put her fingers over his lips. "Allow me to say that I am sorry. For everything. Forgive me. I don't think I could bear it if we parted on poor terms."

A pause. His eyes were shadows of distance. "There is nothing to forgive."

"Thank you for what you have done for us." She stroked his jaw, stealing a final memory of him into her senses, imprinting him upon her flesh.

He grasped her hand, slipped it to the back of his neck, and bent his mouth to hers. His kiss was good-bye. She felt it in the touch of his lips like the end of summer, of childhood, of all that they had been—companions, competitors, friends, and, if she allowed herself to believe it, lovers. A sob gathered in her throat.

"Good-bye, *pirani*." His voice was rough.

She watched him mount, then turn Tristan about in an arc. Without looking back, he spurred the great horse away, as though leaving any time and not the last. She ached, bottomlessly, hopelessly. Nothing could relieve it. But life must be seized now, she told herself. She mustn't waste another moment pining over what had never been.

FOR THE FIRST time in years Taliesin rode directionless and without awareness of time. Eventually his horse's steps slowed and dusk thickened. He found a bridge spanning a creek, went beneath it, and slept.

It was over. Finally. Forever. He would not return to St. Petroc and she would not call on him again. The darkness had returned but this time deeper, more desolate. Now he could see that always before he had harbored hope.

She had said good-bye with great finality—thrice.

He should count himself fortunate that she left nothing to question.

Over.

He should continue to Combe without delay, but despair curled about him like vines. Forgetting would not be found in a luxurious mansion in the company of those who loved her, but in the hard ground beneath his back and, above, the diffident stars that never felt pain, and the moon that watched him with silent sympathy.

After several nights of such vagabondage, however, Tristan complained. He was a gentleman's mount, weaned on oats and warm stables. He did not appreciate scrubby spring grass as much as a Rom's horse should.

Taliesin rode to an inn and found lodging for the pampered beast. The innkeeper served him ale brusquely, as though he hoped he would leave soon. He didn't. He considered drinking the entire contents of a bottle of whiskey and then breaking furniture. He decided against it. Years ago he'd had the excuse of youth and hard treatment.

Now he had no excuse. He'd made his choice, and she was well, not only a gentlewoman but the daughter of a man with considerable means and aristocratic connections. No longer a poor vicar's daughter. If he hadn't been such a blind idiot a month ago he might have considered the potential disadvantage of helping her find her real family. But a month ago she'd been the sister of a duchess already. And he had believed himself impervious.

He wanted for her what she wanted for herself. He wished only for her happiness. After delivering the heirloom into Arabella's hand, he would continue with the life he had made for himself. If they summoned him again he would not go.

Settling back into the shadowed corner of the tap-room, he reached into his pocket and withdrew the object she had given him. A ring. A man's large gold ring, set with a costly gem. She wanted Arabella to have it. Wise, of course. Her father's family had made no attempt to find his daughters. They were not to be trusted. Eleanor wished this ring safe elsewhere.

He leaned forward over his glass of ale and held the ring to the light of the candle. He turned it over in his fingers. What symbol had intrigued her so? And what had she learned about it in Elijah Fish's workshop? Mysteries she had not wished to share with him. Mysteries . . .

Through the flat gem shone a clearly etched insignia. Taliesin recognized it. He never saw it, but he recognized it well, and a pounding, haunting heat filled him from his fingers to the back of his throat to his gut. He sought breaths, blinked hard. But the symbol did not change, blood red in the flickering candlelight.

Still, he could not believe it. This was the object the girls' mother had sent them to England with? This was the symbol written beside Grace's name on the ship's manifest?

He scraped back his chair, dropped coins onto the table, and headed for the stable. He could go to Plymouth, but that was three days' ride. He could return to Edward Bridgeport-Adler's house and question Eleanor. But if she hadn't told him about this, she didn't know. She would have told him. She *must* have.

One person would know. One person much closer than the jeweler in Plymouth and infinitely more opaque than Eleanor. He opened the door to Tristan's stall and roused the stallion.

"Come, my friend. It's time to leave. We are going to see Lussha."

Chapter 24

The Captive

It began innocuously enough. After several sleepless nights punctuated by megrims, Eleanor asked Betsy to procure from the housekeeper a simple sleeping draught.

She hadn't taken such a draught in ages. Far too many years being dosed with medicines had soured her on remedies that muddled her head. But she must sleep. Her father wished for her company during the days, and she wanted to be with him.

Some days he was contemplative. On those days he told stories of his past, of the revolutionary fervor of the era, the dangers, the excitement, and sometimes of Grace, his stunning wife that every man desired. He never spoke of prison or of his life before he went to the West Indies with his regiment. A few vibrant years captivated his mind, fed by the letters he showed her, like the letter Robin Prince had brought to St. Petroc.

Robin had lied. He had not found Grace's letter to Alejo in a book at Drearcliffe; he had taken it from this house without her father or Mary's knowledge. It didn't matter how many more letters he had taken. She knew the truth now: that he had discovered an object belonging to Edward in the captain's box at Drearcliffe; that when he'd come to return it to its rightful owner, his visit had led Mary to discover a collection of letters stored in the attic; and that these letters had given Edward's beleaguered mind a window onto his past.

Written by Edward, Grace, and Alejo, some had been sent between Jamaica and San Domingue, and others between Port-au-Prince and the mountains where rebels gathered and planned for a glorious day when all men would walk as proud equals. Her father had drunk of the fervent brew of revolution and risked his life for that glorious future.

Some of the letters conveyed only news, instructions, concern for the safety of Eleanor and Arabella. Other letters spoke of love. None of them mentioned Ravenna by name, and only one spoke of both "the baby" and "the Fever that is taking children in the city as well as soldiers and sailors"—a single letter written by Grace who was on the coast to Alejo in the mountains, scant months before a ship with her three daughters sailed toward England.

All of the letters she'd sent to Edward's family resonated with the turbulence and passion of their lives. It wasn't to be wondered at that they inspired her father's memory.

At times he grew restive and suspicious. On those days he spoke in short phrases, sometimes words only, and a sheen of sweat coated his skin. He would clutch his head and complain of pain. When Eleanor sympathized with his discomfort, telling him that the sleeping draught improved her sleep but her megrims persisted, his eyes ringed with distress like a wild horse's. But a walk to the lake would soothe him.

Arabella did not respond to her letter, or to the return of the ring. Perhaps she had gone to London for the social season that had already begun. The letter would take time to find her. Carrying the ring, Taliesin would be swifter, Eleanor knew. But time seemed to pass slowly now, her days taken up with her father's memories, and her nights full of dreams that troubled her but which upon waking she could not recall.

Eleanor avoided her great-aunt and cousins, taking breakfast and lunch with her father. But at dinner she suffered through their company, with only Mary to relieve the unpleasantness in her own timid fashion.

"My maid tells me that you require a special draught for your megrims, Miss Caulfield," Lady Boswell drawled one evening. "She says that you are well accustomed to such medicines."

"Well accustomed?" Eleanor stared. "No, I— That is—"

"She says you suffered quite a lengthy illness."

Eleanor set down her spoon, wondering what Betsy had heard in St. Petroc and promising to chastise her maid for flapping lips. "Years ago. A—"

"You must allow me to send to London for my physician."

"No. Thank you, my lady." The megrims would pass. The lassitude had only to do with the content of her heart, not the muscle. After her adventure and the revelations of the past weeks, it would be remarkable if she weren't a bit weary. Soon she would throw off this humor.

"I have written to assure Mrs. Caulfield that she needn't fret for your comfort here," the baroness continued with a hard eye.

"Aunt Cynthia," Mary gasped. "I told you that you mustn't write to the Caulfields."

"I was certain the Reverend and Mrs. Caulfield would wish to know their delicate flower is well. But we shan't let our dear, fragile Eleanor fall ill under our watch, shall we? No, no. Not our little mulatto. We will see her well so that she can inherit my nephew's entire fortune." She laughed.

Only the soup had been served. But Eleanor stood, apologized to Mary, and left the dining room. Behind her one of her cousins whispered, "Mama, today the maid said she saw Eleanor embracing that Gypsy by the lake last week."

Let them whisper. It meant nothing to her. Only let her heart stop aching like this.

She went to her father's rooms. He stood in the middle of a pile of old papers in his stockings, his face drawn.

"I cannot find it, Grace," he said to her. "I cannot find him."

She hurried to him. "Father, what can't you find? Who?"

"He is lost. I have lost him." He slumped onto the floor. "I have lost him." He sobbed.

Mary rushed in, shushed him, and led him to a chair.

"He will be well," she whispered to Eleanor. "You must go to sleep, dear niece. Your face is drawn. I will see to my brother."

Eleanor left the house and walked to the lake. The evening had turned chill and a misty rain crisscrossed the hill, whipping up her skirts and pressing her hair wetly to her cheeks. She wrapped her shawl tighter and walked until her anger and grief were once again pressed down and she could think. Good Eleanor could be useful sometimes, she thought. Wild, free Eleanor needn't rule her every moment.

She returned to the house, climbed into bed, and for the first time in years, wept herself to sleep.

She awoke in the darkness, her lungs poked through with a hundred sharp holes, her limbs heavy. Her hair and nightclothes were sodden with sweat. Betsy came.

"Water, please, Betsy," she mumbled. Her lips were like raw dough. A glass was pressed into her palm.

"Drink this, miss. Her ladyship's maid says it'll help."

A sweet smell made her throat tight. "No. Water only."

The glass went away. Eleanor put her head on the pillow again and waited, and her mouth grew dry, her tongue thick. It seemed all night she waited, her heartbeats shallow and fast, her skin cold beneath the damp linen. The night went on and she could neither sleep nor wake fully.

When Betsy returned, she struggled to lift her head from the pillow. Betsy put the cup to her lips. She gulped it down.

Relief. Thirst gone. Longing satisfied. Like wanting him and touching him.

The sweetness curled in her throat. *Laudanum.*

"*No.*" She sputtered and pushed it away. "No. Water."

"Her ladyship's maid says this'll help you sleep," Betsy whined.

"No." Her head was too heavy to lift. Her cheek touched the mattress again.

Silence.

Sleep and wicked dreams. Kisses. Bodies entwined.

Tears.

Heaviness.

Thick, dead shadows, so unlike his living eyes.

Pale gray lightened the room. Through eyelids like cracked bricks she saw the furniture. The draperies, she thought, were closed. But it was day. She must rise and go to her father.

She pushed herself from the mattress. Her limbs twisted and her foot bent beneath her. She fell to the floor. There was sudden fire, and darkness. Her head ached. Her jaw. The flavor of metal filled her mouth. Dampness on her chin and in her hair.

No sound but the labor of her breaths. Sleep.

Betsy was beside her again. "Oh, miss!"

Someone dragged her soggy limbs onto the bed. Thoughts came and passed, short and eternal at once. It seemed all dreams, some restful, others wrong. She begged for water. Her tongue could not feel her lips, but she knew her lips were sore, cracked. She smelled blood. Her arm ached, the life sucked from her in droplets. Thirst. Fierce aching, and her chest felt cold. They could not be bleeding her. She was not ill. Not now. Not for years. He had healed her. He had saved her.

When they brought her a glass, she drank the sweet wine and asked for water again. They left. She dreamed again. Black night. Gray. More sweet wine. She insisted to Betsy that she must dress. Go to her father.

"He's gone, miss."

"Gone?" No. He was ill. Not clear-headed. Mary would never have allowed it. She was dreaming now. "Mary . . ."

"Miss Bridgeport-Adler's gone off too. I don't think anybody knows where. I overheard her ladyship say to her maid he took the carriage."

Who took the carriage? The doctor? Had the doctor come? He would give her medicine but it would not make her better. Only Taliesin knew how to make her better.

"Taliesin."

Betsy said nothing now. She had gone too. The room was black again.

Night.

Thirst.

A cup at her lips. Sticky-sweet. Fingers fumbling as she pushed it away, tried to close her lips. The lips brushed against each other, open, swollen and dry.

"They won't let me give you anything else to drink, miss." *Whisper.* "They've said I'm impertinent. And I am, I know. But she said her ladyship's bound to turn me off if I don't make you drink it. Please, miss. Do this for me. Then I'll think of something."

Her mouth screamed for the cup. Her tongue. Need hollered in her like a demon, grabbing at her throat, making her want it. Temptation swallowing her. She turned her face away.

Light streamed through her eyelids. Jolting. She was sliding.

"For the love of th'Almighty." *Hushed voice.* "Don't let her fall off it. Don't want to add broken bones to her troubles. Poor miss. And just when she'd found the master, and he gone missing."

"A tragedy, to be sure. But her ladyship'll find him and bring him home."

Light speared her eyelids. Warmth on her hands and face. Sunlight?

"Here, miss." *Shadow.* Dark. A cloth over her face. A pall? She wasn't dead. Not yet. But they were trying to kill her. Had they tried to kill her father too? Had they drugged him for years and locked him in an attic?

No. Penny plays. Lending library novels. She was ill. Again. Dying of fever or whatever fragile, innocent maidens died of in the storybooks. Broken hearts, she supposed.

The jingle of harnesses. The scent of newly cut grass. Wind. She tried to open her eyes.

"Betsy?"

"I'm here, miss." By her ear, a tight hand around her fingers.

She squinted. Tried to lift her hand. Pushed away the veil.

Treetops. A carriage. "Where are we going?"

"They're taking you to a cottage on the other side of the estate. Her ladyship says it's quiet there and you'll be able to rest better than in the house with all the comings and goings. Also, she says if you stay, the fever might catch on in the servants' quarters, and make everybody sick. But I don't feel any fever on you now, though for a bit there I was frightened."

A cottage? "No. My father."

"He's gone, miss. Nearly a fortnight now. I've told you that a dozen times. Oh, miss, I can't see you leave. It's tearing me up."

The pain in her head was like a smith's press, crushing. "Mustn't go . . ." Her breaths were so shallow she couldn't force words.

"I'm not going, miss. They're keeping me here. Her ladyship's maid will be caring for you—"

"No." Had she spoken aloud? How could this be real?

Perhaps she *was* ill. She recognized this weakness. This hopelessness. So long ago. But then she'd been a girl. Had she been sick again for months? No. He had saved her then.

Thoughts alighted. Swiftly flew away.

Confused.

The only certainty: he was gone.

"Come," she whispered. "I need you."

THERE WERE MORE days of thirst and befuddlement. The draperies in her little room in the cottage remained drawn, the daylight only peeking through, shafts of pale sunlight cutting deep into the dragon's lair.

Each time she entered to bid Eleanor drink, Lady Boswell's maid said nothing else. Eleanor refused. The weakness swallowed her. It was a battle to open her eyes. The maid did not offer her food.

Perhaps there was only one endless day.

She woke, opened her eyes, and saw the ceiling. Painted white. A tiny spider's web in the corner.

She thought for many minutes, perhaps, or hours, about moving her head to the side. With a mighty breath that tore at her lungs, she finally did.

Green flowered wallpaper. A small table beside the bed.

An open door.

Beyond the door, pale light crossed a corridor.

Her thoughts came one after another, brief but cleanly now. A new, sharp clarity.

An open door.

She could escape.

Light.

She would be noticed. In the darkness of night she might find success. Had they placed guards on her?

Ridiculous. They imagined her ill, only. Then why hadn't they given her food? All those years ago, Ravenna and Papa had spooned broth into her every hour, especially in the early months. Taliesin had brought her fruit from the garden.

Her eyelids closed against the unfamiliar light, against the pain of memory, against her helplessness.

She forced them open again. She mustn't sleep. All she'd done her entire life was to sleep. Except with him.

She could call for Lady Boswell's maid and ask to return to the house. But if they did have malevolent intent toward her, the woman would know the drug had left her entirely.

Her limbs would not hold her upright. She let herself slide from the bed to the floor. On hands and knees, sometimes on her belly when the effort exhausted her, she crawled to the door. Her knees knocked over the bumpy threshold.

A few endless yards to the corridor.

There were stairs. Narrow and steep. *Good heavens.* She would kill herself.

At the bottom was an exterior door.

No one heard her bumps and grunts as she slid down. No one came. It seemed a miracle. But perhaps living a good, modest, poor woman's life had some positive effect. God was merciful to sinners, and she had certainly sinned. Countless times in thought. Twice in deed. She had sinned *after* being good. But perhaps that was all right. She had a bank of goodness to draw upon. And sinning with Taliesin felt like heaven anyway. Perhaps the preachers and theologians had got it all wrong.

Her fingers slipped on the door handle. She grappled for it again. Got purchase. Turned it.

No lock. It cracked open.

"Thank you, God," she whispered, but no sound came forth. Exhaustion dragged at her and she sat in the doorway searching for air. Her limbs were lead. Bags of old seed. A hundred barrels of uselessness. How many days had she been ill and drugged? For how many days had she not eaten? Her tongue stuck in the desert of her mouth. Her lips would not close. In her head, wool and cobwebs fought for dominance.

With her back against the door, she slept.

Pain roused her soon enough.

After some time, she worked herself into the crack of the door, pushing it wider with her head and shoulder.

She dragged herself across the scrubby grass. Each inch acquired was an agony and a triumph. The day was new, too new for bright sunlight but late enough that someone would surely discover her. But this was not the front of the house. A small garden lay untended by the wall, and thirty feet away, a barn. There would be water in the barn. If there were animals, there would be food. Raw hope propelling her ravaged muscles, she crawled.

She fell into shade.

No odors or sounds of animals came to her. The stable was clean-swept. Empty.

Except for a bucket at the opposite end.

Madness seized her then, giving her strength. Stumbling to her feet, she lurched forward, grabbing the doors of empty stalls. She fell and pain shot across her knee. Blood. Plenty of it. Soaking through her shift and spreading across the linen already stained with grass and dirt. She crawled and her hand met the bucket. Her fingers plunged into water.

She drank until her belly could hold nothing else, and still she needed to drink. Pressing her back against the wall, she swallowed and forced her throat closed, struggling not to retch.

Slowly her stomach settled. Weakness devoured her. She sat without moving. The sun tiptoed higher, slanting through the open doorway in pale beams like the sorts one saw on medieval paintings of angels bestowing blessings upon humans. Her vision was a fog of gray and black.

There was no strength in her now, only will. With that will she gripped the bucket and pushed. Lifting an arm like wet peat, she reached upward. Cool iron met her hand. She curled her fingers around the bar of the stall door and heaved herself to her knees.

"*Uh.*" She gulped back pain. Her ragged knee oozed through the matted linen. No more crawling. She must walk.

Pulling, straining, aching everywhere, she dragged herself to her feet, struggling to catch besieged breaths. Her lungs protested. The floor tilted. If she fell, she would not rise again. Her hand slipped on the bar, her fingers without strength, giving way. Her sob of desperation had no sound.

No. *No.*

Willing her body's obedience, she lifted a head heavier than stone.

Taliesin stood in the doorway silhouetted by sunlight. His body. His stance. She must be dreaming. But she would know him across miles and lifetimes. She had called for him and he had come. Just as he had promised.

"I am . . ." Her tongue stuck, thick in her mouth. "In need."

He came swiftly and caught her up in his arms.

IF HE'D BROUGHT a carriage he could conceal both of them. But speed mattered most. After a night of running already without rest, the stallion now seemed to feel his urgency. Gathering his muscles beneath him, Tristan flew.

They would both be ruined by this—Taliesin and his horse.

So be it.

In a month she had become a shadow of the woman he'd left at her father's house. Betsy and Treadwell had found him just in time. If only there weren't so many miles of this county to be ridden though, he would believe fortune to be with him. Closing his mind to fear, he held her securely against him and rode.

The stallion's gait faltered. Taliesin rode him limping into a village—one of the several in this county that he remembered well, including its jail. He didn't even have a hat to shade his face. And he had a sleeping woman wearing no more than a bloodstained undergarment in his arms. A woman for whom he would risk much more than exile if she needed him.

Turning Tristan from the road, he walked him into a wooded area and lifted Eleanor from his back. She stirred, her hand curling around his coat.

"You came," she whispered, and burrowed her face against his chest.

"Of course I did." He lowered her to the ground. He'd nothing to place beneath her; the soft pine needles must suffice. "I must leave you now briefly. Tristan can go no farther and I must find another horse." Or a carriage. He'd money, but taking the chance of being recognized would be foolish. A horse like Tristan could be easily traded. A carriage would take time. "I will bring food."

"Water." Her hair was lank, the gold dull. He must tend to the wound on her knee that was bleeding again. She looked like she'd been starved and stripped, a woodland maiden ravished by the wicked wolf. To anybody who might come upon them now, that wolf would be him. No one would believe it if he said otherwise, not in this town from which he had been barred, or any other.

He stripped off his coat and tucked it around her.

"I will return soon." He stroked her cheek.

Her breaths were shallow, her skin prickled with cold. "Kiss me," she said like the brush of a fingertip across paper. "So I know that you are not a dream."

Then, like sunshine, her lips curved. "But perhaps that would only prove that you are a dream."

He kissed her, holding the treasure of her face in his hands. Her lips were desiccated and cold. He had nothing more than his coat, nothing to warm her. All of his gold and lands now, yet he had nothing that could save her.

"I will return," he said again, but she was already asleep.

No one recognized him. At first.

At a blacksmith's shop he completed the trade of his prized stallion for an animal of vastly inferior quality. Taliesin did not speak to Tristan or look at him when the stallion snorted as he walked away. *No fetters. No bonds.* No heart to break at partings.

All the while the smith watched him with suspicion. Fearing to spend any more time in the village, Taliesin went to the well, filled his flask, and in his shirtsleeves walked with the hack as though he hadn't a care in the world, to the end of the high street and onto the road. The first stand of trees on the road was almost a quarter mile away. He drew the horse from the road and across the pasture, then doubled back to where he'd left her.

The first glimpse of the white of her shift stained at the knees with blood, and then her face set peacefully in sleep, nearly undid him. Lifting her into the saddle and mounting behind her, he wrapped her in his arms again. Two men walked toward them across the pasture.

"There now, sir," one of them said. "We'd like to welcome you to Normanton correctly now. We don't get many peddlers and we'd be interested in looking over your wares." It was an excuse to approach him. The man's eyes were fixed on Eleanor. She had tucked her face against his chest and wrapped her arms around his waist.

The other man hadn't looked at her. He was studying Taliesin's face.

"I'm not a peddler," he said, and tightened his arm around her. "I'm a horse trader." He dug his heels into the horse's sides and it bolted.

The animal could not match Tristan for gait, but it had some strength and, more importantly, speed. The villagers pursued, but he went off the road and lost them in the fields. At the edge of the county they caught up with him again and drove him hard. Again he evaded them. He'd done so plenty of times before. He'd never done so carrying a woman, but she proved no burden in his arms. He had been born to hold her in his arms.

After that, he made no pretense of hiding, but rode the most direct route, across fields and creeks and farms he knew so well he could describe them in perfect detail if interrogated. There were some advantages to being a rogue for life, a wanderer who knew trees and rocks and barns better than polite company. He could not get lost in this country. They would be in Exeter by midnight. If no one forced them to a halt before then, she would be safe. It was all he wanted, all he had ever wanted except her.

THE MOON ROSE bright, leading him into the city. The streets lay quiet, the buildings of stone and the medieval spires of the cathedral rising into the darkness. He lifted her from the horse standing with its head bowed and sides heaving, and carried her into the house.

A small house that shared walls with the houses on either side, it didn't look like the home of a gentleman. Which was precisely what Edward Bridgeport-Adler wished when he had escaped his family a fortnight earlier.

Taliesin went up the steps with Eleanor pressed to his chest. She hadn't stirred in hours. But he knew she was alive, just as he would always know, even if separated by oceans, whether she was well or not.

Treadwell opened the door. "Lord almighty, sir!"

In the flickering glow of Treadwell's lamp, Taliesin carried her within. Betsy hurried forward.

"Miss, oh, *miss*! Look what I let happen to you! I'll never forgive myself for it. Never!"

"Miss Fortnum," he said, weary in every limb. Even a vagabond had his limits. "A bed for her. And water. Fresh garments. Then food. Swiftly. And when you have done that, rouse her father."

"Her father is already roused and has waited anxiously for your arrival," Edward Bridgeport-Adler said from a doorway, eyes wide upon Taliesin's face.

Beside him, the Reverend Martin Caulfield said, "Both of us."

Chapter 25

The Rogue

T

"*Y*ou mustn't stay, sir," Betsy said. Like the opening of a tight bud into a flower, the girl's scorn had turned to blushing apology overnight. Literally.

Taliesin crossed his arms, spread his feet, and settled deeper into the chair in the corner of the bedchamber. He let his heavy eyelids close to the sight of Betsy tending to her mistress, who lay on the bed.

"I will stay here until I see her drink a cup of tea." His voice sounded slurred. Drunk with relief. And exhaustion. He could not sleep yet. The men in the parlor below awaited him.

"I've got to change her night dress," she said tartly.

"Ah, the old Betsy returns. And so soon. I'd hoped the

new Betsy would last more than a quarter of an hour."

"Sir." She harrumphed, but relief colored her voice too.

Two days ago she'd been frantic, standing on the open road beside the Duke of Lycombe's carriage, explaining in a tumble of words how she had come to be there: how twelve days earlier, without anything better to do and sensing subterfuge, Treadwell had secretly driven Mr. Bridgeport-Adler and Miss Mary to Exeter by their request; how after Eleanor was taken away to the cottage, Treadwell told Betsy they'd best send news to the duke and duchess; how Betsy had refused, insisting they must go in person, but afraid to leave her mistress.

That Taliesin, finally on his way to deliver the ring to Arabella, had crossed their path on the road had been less happenstance than inevitable: Betsy had gone back and forth, demanding that Treadwell turn the carriage around a half dozen times, frantically undecided whether to return to Eleanor's side or to seek out help at far-distant Combe. When Taliesin came upon them, they'd been traveling the same stretch of road back and forth for nearly a day, Treadwell dutifully obedient to the girl he admired.

Some men would do anything for a woman, Treadwell had said with a wise eye. Then he'd recommended that if Taliesin managed to remove Miss Caulfield from Lady Boswell's keeping, he could bring her to Exeter. To her father's house.

"My eyes are closed," Taliesin mumbled now. "I won't watch." But he did. While the maid removed Eleanor's filthy garment and replaced it with a fresh garment, he saw through shadows and candlelight that the beauty of her body had become far too slender. In pain, he traced her still limbs with his eyes, and the weight of loss bore down upon him.

When the maid bathed and dressed the wound on her knee, Eleanor grimaced. Her eyes fluttered open.

"Betsy." She sighed. "How good it is to see you."

"Oh, miss," Betsy blubbered. "I'm so sorry. Terribly sorry I let them—"

"Miss Fortnum," Taliesin said quietly. "Fetch for your mistress tea with milk, and biscuits if they can be found. Now, go. And be quick."

She sniffled and hurried out.

Taliesin sat on the side of the bed and gathered Eleanor into his arms, and she laid her head on his shoulder.

"I think you saw me dress," she whispered.

"You did not dress." He pressed his lips to her brow. Like paper, her skin held a mark from the caress. "You were dressed by a maid, like a great lady. It isn't the same thing."

"Great ladies . . ." Her words tickled his neck, her lashes a flutter against his jaw. "Are not dressed by their maids in front of . . ." Her next breath came upon a quiver that shook her slight frame. "Rogues."

He reached for the cup of water and tilted her chin up to make her drink. "It is my understanding that great ladies can do whatever they please. A good thing for you, as you seem to be making a habit of that."

She sipped, then leaned her face into his shoulder again. "I have only undressed in front of one rogue."

"Probably best to keep that number low, it's true."

She slept and he held her. There were not enough hours in eternity to satisfy his need to hold her, and this hour would be his last.

When Betsy entered she glowered, but there was no real feeling behind it. Contrarily, she promised to tell him if her mistress's condition changed, and she thanked him again.

He made his way down the stair, stiff from even the few minutes he'd sat, needing a bath and twelve hours of sleep. But he could not tarry here long, and this conversation must be had.

What Lussha had told him amounted to little, only

what he already suspected: that years ago she had been astonished to see the symbol on the ring Arabella had put before her. But when he pressed her to admit that cruel whimsy made her give that fortune to the sisters, Lussha refused. The Sight did not lie, she said.

Taliesin had ridden away from St. Petroc angry, heading north, but slowly. He was not yet ready to give over the ring to Arabella, but neither did he wish to speak with Elijah Fish in Plymouth.

For Lussha had also spoken of a man—a man with gold hair and hazel eyes. An English military officer. The man in the painting who now waited below for him.

"She is well," he said as he crossed the parlor's threshold. "It will be some time before she is strong again. She is not ill, but weak from starvation and the drug." The drug Lady Boswell's physician had forced Betsy to feed her. "And it seems they bled her. But she will recover." She had an indomitable spirit, his angel-goddess.

Edward Bridgeport-Adler stared at him, eyes like his daughter's wide and still.

The vicar of St. Petroc came forward and grasped Taliesin's hand. "Thank you, son. I know not how to thank you sufficiently."

Taliesin pulled back his hand. "Tell me how it is that you are here now. Did her maid send for you? Or Treadwell?" But he already knew that Martin Caulfield could not have ridden to Exeter from St. Petroc in so little time.

"My old friend sent for me last week." He looked at Edward. "Finally, he remembered me."

Taliesin's throat closed. "Old friend?"

"We knew each other well at university," Martin said.

Taliesin swallowed. "How well?"

"As well as two hot-headed young idealists could,"

Martin said soberly and turned his face to Edward. "In the heady days when revolution stirred men's spirits, those of us with hearts devoted to liberty and minds trained for debate were rarely found apart from each other." He looked back to Taliesin. "But until yesterday I had seen him only once in twenty-six years. Twenty-six years ago, Taliesin, when he left you with John Wolfe and asked me to watch over you."

Taliesin's lungs struggled, the air packed into disbelief.

"You are cast in his image," Edward said, his eyes wide. "And yet there must be something of her in you, for I don't remember him as such a tall man." He seemed to study Taliesin's face, as though searching. "I never knew her, of course. He said she had been a beauty."

The room seemed to reel. "Of whom do you speak?"

"Of your parents."

His tongue was numb, his hands cold. "You know my parents?"

"I knew your father only. Alejo Torres was a great man. A warrior and a valiant defender of liberty. I understand that you are a fine horseman, like he was."

"Where is he?"

"He perished of fever in the West Indies. The same fever that took my wife, I believe, shortly after she sent my daughters across the ocean to Martin."

His wife. Eleanor's mother. "What of my mother? My . . . family?"

"Your mother died in childbed. Alejo found himself in danger in his home of Andalusia. Rivals contended for his lands. He believed the death of your mother was subterfuge, disloyalty within his own court. He was desperate to protect his only son. He took you across the ocean in search of allies in the Spanish territories of the West Indies where he had many friends."

Edward's brow pleated. "But matters in the islands had grown too dangerous. At that time my father perished, and I was given leave from my regiment to see to matters of my inheritance. When I left for England, Alejo asked me to bring you here and hide you until he could come as well."

"I don't understand. He told you to take me to St. Petroc?"

"He told me to ensure that you would not be found," Edward said, spreading his palms. "I knew John Wolfe. His skill with horses was renowned. And no one would think to look for you among the Gypsies. Your father approved. I believed that with my friend Martin watching after you, you would come to no harm. It was to be temporary only. A year, perhaps eighteen months until Alejo could sail to claim you. We didn't know then that fate would destroy those plans."

Taliesin turned to the vicar, a hot thrum working its way from his chest into his limbs. "You agreed to this?"

"I did, but I had no idea who you were. For your safety, Edward had told me nothing of your identity. Then he returned to war in the West Indies, and the next I heard he had been executed. It wasn't until four years later when his sister, Mary, wrote to me that I learned he had actually been imprisoned in England. She remembered we had been dear friends at university and she begged me to visit him, to encourage his memory. But when he saw me it only distressed him further. She feared for the thread of sanity he still possessed, and barred me from communicating with him again." His hands clenched at his sides. "You were still a child, and I owed it to him to continue to keep you safe. If it hadn't been for me, Edward would never have even joined the army. I had encouraged him—"

"Martin," Edward said, looking at the floor. "You mustn't blame yourself."

"He hadn't an idea of rebellion until I put it in his head," the vicar pressed on. "I encouraged him to use his wealth for a grander purpose. I urged him to do the work of God."

"You stood on a bench in that tavern and preached the equality of all men to an enthralled crowd. How could I have ignored that call for justice?" Edward said with a soft smile. "And if I had not gone to fight in that battle, I would never have known Grace. I would never have known your father, Taliesin."

The vicar stepped toward Taliesin. "Perhaps you will be angry with me. Perhaps you will not understand. But allow me at least these words: I have spent the past eleven years agonizing over whether I did right by both you and my old friend. With his mind gone from the tragedies of the struggle that my words had sent him into, I knew only that I must continue to live by my promise to him."

A slow, searing disquiet crept over him. "Eleven years?"

"I did not drive you from my home for Eleanor's sake, Taliesin. I did it for you. For your future."

"You told me to leave." Martin Caulfield had been like a father, treated him as a son. The betrayal had destroyed him. The violent tearing away of all he had known. Of the girl he loved. "You sent me away allowing me to believe that . . ." Years of vagabondage, jails, grief. He had rebuilt his life from nothing. "It was a *lie*? I was—"

"You were a young man of honesty and intelligence, and unafraid of hard work. I could not have wished a better man for my daughter."

"But . . ." The truth rocked through him.

"I knew only that you were destined for much more than a wagon and a barn. And I knew that I could not give you what you needed. If I had allowed what you wished, and you had remained in St. Petroc, with John Wolfe's family, you would never have become anything else."

Anger like spitting stars crackled. "I was not ashamed of my uncle's family."

"That in itself was a marker of your character. But your anger to prove me wrong drove you to become who you are now, I think. Still, I am sorry that it had to be as it was."

It was the truth. He had never wanted anything but Eleanor. If he had been allowed to have her then, he would never have left his uncle's family or the vicarage. He would have had no reason to.

The clack of the door knocker sounded throughout the house. In the foyer, Treadwell peered out.

"Do not open it, Mr. Treadwell," Edward said, his eyes abruptly feverish. "It will be my aunt."

"Not in the middle of the night, I think, Edward," the vicar said gently.

Taliesin went into the foyer. The knocking came again.

"Seems like it might be the law, sir," Treadwell said, "seeing as those two in the rear are wearing uniforms and they've got lamps. P'raps they saw you bring Miss Caulfield in here looking like a damsel in distress."

And he, the villain.

It wasn't far from Normanton to Exeter. It would not be difficult to track a galloping rider carrying before him a bloodied woman wearing nothing but a shift and a man's coat. He hadn't been particularly careful. He had only wanted her safe.

He unbolted the door and stood before his destiny. One of the men who had chased him from Normanton pointed.

"That's him. That's the one."

"Good evening, gentlemen," Taliesin said. "I've been expecting you."

Chapter 26

The Dragon's Flight

*E*leanor had never had such dreams. Always before, her dreams of Taliesin had ended in frustration and grief. In her dreams now he held her and told her of his love with caresses that made her mad for more. More of his hands. His mouth.

Upon waking, she found the bedclothes tangled about her legs. Then Betsy would make her drink, eat, and she would descend into sleep again, and perfect dreams.

When finally she roused enough to remain awake for longer than the moments it required her to swal-

low a cup of tea and a custard, she looked about the
room. A small bedchamber and simply furnished, it
boasted only one chair in which Mary sat, an embroidery board and needle in her hands.

Her aunt rose and came to the bed. "You are better.
There is color in your face but no fever. I am relieved."

"Where is this place?"

"My brother's house in Exeter. Reverend Caulfield
is here. Betsy has been tending you. Mr. Treadwell is
here as well. We have sent word to your sisters. You
are safe." She placed her hand atop Eleanor's on the
mattress.

Eleanor struggled to understand. "Papa? Did you
send for him? Have I been here long?"

"Only two days. My darling girl, you mustn't weary
yourself with unnecessary—"

"I must." She pushed up to sit. Her limbs were like
wet wool, soft and heavy, not obeying. She leaned into
the headboard. "Why is Papa here?"

"He came to see Edward before we even knew that
you were in trouble. I am sorry we left you with Aunt
Cynthia, Eleanor. If I had known to what lengths she
was willing to go to cut you from your inheritance,
I would never have left you, even to help Edward
escape."

Eleanor's eyes rounded. "Escape?"

"This is not the time for that. You are still weak—"

Eleanor grabbed her fingers. "Tell me. I beg of you."

Mary dipped her head. "They drugged my brother
for years before I discovered it. For you, whom they
hate because of your mother's blood and the threat you
pose to their home, I think they would have gone to
greater lengths to control you."

"That is preposterous." The words felt like sand on
her lips. "My sister would have inherited after me."

Mary's smile was full of pity. "You have an honest

heart and a fine mind. You cannot imagine the simple evil that lurks in others, can you? You must always understand matters rationally. But greed and hatred have no reason except themselves."

"How is it that Papa came to see my father even before I came here?"

"Edward sent for him."

"At his house, you led me to believe that the name Caulfield was anathema to my father. I didn't question it because I hoped you would explain someday. Now you must."

"When my brother was released from prison, his mind was deeply disordered. He remembered so little of his past, only battles in a vague manner, and prison. In hopes of reminding him of happier days, I searched his mementos and correspondence from his years at Oxford, and I discovered your father—rather, the man who later became the Reverend Martin Caulfield. At university he was a fiery preacher, rousing other students with his speeches about justice and the rights of men."

Her papa, a street preacher? It seemed incredible.

"Desperate to bring back my brother's mind," Mary continued, "I searched for the Reverend and found him in St. Petroc. I begged him to visit. He arrived swiftly, and for many hours he remained secluded with my brother. When he came from the chamber, he seemed devastated. I went in to my brother and found him unable to speak. Edward did not say another word for two years."

"Of what . . . Of what did they speak?"

"I don't know. Edward has never spoken of it to me and I have not asked Reverend Caulfield."

Eleanor's fingers clutched the bed linen at her waist. "When did that happen? What year was it?"

"It was the autumn of 1798. I remember because I

did not hear my brother's voice again until the new century."

Autumn of 1798. Six months before her papa discovered them in the foundling home. They must have spoken of her and her sisters. Or Grace. Something that would have sent him searching for his friend's daughters.

"When he found us, why didn't Papa tell you?"

Mary stared at her hands in her lap. "He did. He wrote many letters to me, Eleanor. Without reading them, I cast them all into the fire. Finally he wrote directly to Aunt Cynthia. She replied that she would not take orphans into her home, that Martin could dispose of Edward's bastards as he wished. She refused to acknowledge that my brother and your mother had ever been wed, and Martin had no proof to contest her denial. She told me nothing of his letter then, nor of her reply."

"But . . . My mother sent me and my sisters from the West Indies to *Papa*?"

Mary nodded. "I only learned of it all when I confronted my aunt a fortnight ago, after you took ill Aunt Cynthia finally admitted that Grace had sent a letter to her after your ship departed, begging her to go to St. Petroc and claim Edward's daughters. Grace had grown very ill, and Alejo had already perished of the yellow fever. She was desperate to ensure your safety."

"Lady Boswell must have confronted my father with my mother's letter even before you wrote to my papa. Then Father told Papa, and Papa went searching for us. But why did my mother not send us directly to Lady Boswell in the first place? Why did she send us to a man she had never met?"

"Perhaps Edward had told her to trust Martin Caulfield more than my aunt." She shook her head. "But this is enough storytelling for today, dearest niece. You mustn't weary yourself further. I will ring for Betsy to bring dinner." She went to the door.

"Mary." Eleanor had no appetite. She wanted only one thing. "Where is Mr. Wolfe? I know he brought me here." That had not been a dream. "Is he here?"

"He departed the night you arrived."

Eleanor's cold hands unclenched on the coverlet. "He does not mean to return, does he?"

"He cannot return, Eleanor." Mary's voice fell. "He is in jail."

TALIESIN HAD SEEN far worse. For a sizeable town, Exeter had a well-kept jail. Since dusk he'd heard only two rats scuffling in the straw that kept the cold damp of the stone floor from sinking a man into hell. Jails near waterways always featured plenty of cold and damp.

He hoped they sent him to New South Wales. He'd heard New South Wales was covered with dry, hot places. America would do too. Plenty of land to keep horses.

If he could ever afford a horse again.

They stripped a man of his possessions before they deported him. Kitharan and the herd would go to the crown. Except Tristan. Of all his recent losses, the loss of his stallion cut next to the deepest. He could admit this now, on the verge of the end. To a man abruptly alone, fetters and bindings suddenly looked remarkably appealing.

He did not allow himself to think of his deepest loss. She was safe. Cared for. Among those who would protect her. He could ask for no more.

Unless Edward Bridgeport-Adler was entirely insane, Taliesin supposed he might own some property in Andalusia. If they ever removed the shackles from his wrists, he could request a berth on a ship heading in that direction. There must be some advantage to having an actual family, after all. Spain was closer to England than America or New South Wales. Closer to her by thousands of miles.

Footsteps clopped on the stone pavement. A ring of keys jangled. Taliesin lifted his head.

"You." The guard spoke through the bars in the window of the cell Taliesin shared with three other men. Actual criminals. *Recent* criminals. Earlier, the two that were conscious had eyed his coat as though it were made of gold.

"Wolfe," the guard grumbled. "The magistrate wants to see you."

The magistrate. This couldn't be good. The bailiff of Exeter had no jurisdiction over his case. He had summoned the rural law to make certain of a conviction.

But Taliesin had anticipated this.

He climbed to his feet, exhausted and filthy and sore in every muscle and joint. They took him from the cell in manacles, like the rogue that he was.

"Della!" In the foyer of the courthouse, Eleanor threw her arms about her sister. "You are here!"

"The Reverend sent for me. He said you found our father. But Ellie, you are—" Arabella held her shoulders and her brilliant eyes swept her body. "You are terribly changed. Betsy told me some of it in the carriage coming from our father's house just now. But—"

"There is no time to explain. Taliesin is to be sentenced within minutes. Why didn't you respond to my letters? And why did you not come to our father's estate after Taliesin brought you the ring?"

"I received no letters from you. He did not come to Combe."

"Then you don't know all that has happened?"

A tall, strappingly large man in a long black robe and scrolling white wig entered the corridor. Dwarfing the two uniformed men that flanked him, he crossed purposefully into another chamber with long, powerful strides.

"Oh, no. It is to begin now." She gripped her sister's hand. "Come."

"Proceedings pursuant to the arrest of one Taliesin Wolfe of Kitharan, upon the charges of roguery and vagabondage, as well as destruction of property in the parish of Normanton, will now commence," the bailiff intoned as they entered. The chamber was high-ceilinged, crescent-shaped with rising benches, and sparsely populated: the magistrate filled the principal chair with the sheer authority of size; a clerk, the bailiff, and two guards stood below; and in the benches were her father, Papa, Betsy, Mr. Treadwell, Mary, several men she did not recognize, and Robin Prince.

Robin?

He tried to hold her gaze, but she had attention for only one man.

Taliesin stood on a platform at the base of the benches surrounded by a waist-height wooden barricade, his hands behind his back. His jaw was dark with whiskers, his coat wrinkled, and his shadowed eyes upon her. Only Arabella's hand holding her elbow tight kept her from running to him and throwing her arms about him.

He turned his face to the man ensconced in the throne-like chair.

The lord magistrate peered at Taliesin. "Kitharan, did he say?" he boomed. "Are you that Gypsy my father sold the place to? Wretched old drafty house. The whole thing should have been torn down a century ago. How do you find it?"

"Suitable for my needs, my lord."

"Hm." The lord magistrate looked about. "Bailiff, who are all these people?"

"Bystanders, my lord, I think."

"All right," the lord magistrate said. "As this is only a sentencing, I am allowing the condemned and accusators to speak on their own behalves. Nobody needs a roomful of prosy wigs to clean up old business after all. Bailiff?"

"My lord, the court calls Roger Tanner of Normanton."

One of the strangers stood up. "Good day, my lord. My name is Roger Tanner. Me and these men"—he gestured to the other three strangers—"have come from Normanton. Nine years ago this man, Wolfe, caused harm to property of considerable worth in the parish. Your lord father, may his soul rest in peace, gave him a suspended sentence on the condition that he never again enter the parish. Well, my lord, he came through five days ago, and we've the horse he rode into town on as proof."

"You have a horse as proof? How singular," the magistrate said with steepled brows. "What would you say if he denied it was his?"

"I wouldn't deny it." Taliesin's voice was deep and a bit rough.

The lord magistrate looked at him. "Mr. Wolfe, you are not to speak until I have called you to do so. Do you understand?"

Taliesin nodded.

"Now, why wouldn't you deny the horse is yours if that is the only proof they can furnish? Do you have a wish to be deported?"

"I've no such wish, my lord. But that horse is the finest animal I have ever bred. I'd no more think to deny him than fly to the moon."

The magistrate pursed his lips thoughtfully. "Well said."

"My lord," Tanner said. "We've other proof. A witness." He pointed at Eleanor. "The Gypsy—that is, Wolfe—was seen absconding from the county on horseback with that woman. She was . . . well, she wasn't dressed in a ladylike way, my lord, rather, wearing nothing but nightclothes. Not even shoes."

The magistrate's eyes widened and he peered at Arabella. Recognition came into his face. "Duchess." He stood to his considerable height and bowed from the waist.

"My lord." Arabella curtsied.

"I have a mind to arraign *you*, duchess," he said as he settled back into his throne. "That likeness Lycombe had painted of you, the one hanging in your house in town, is the envy of my wife and her friends. Since we dined with you at Christmastime I haven't heard the end of it. She insists on having a picture done of her now. Pesters me about it every day."

"Thank you, my lord."

"It will cost me three hundred guineas. But she knows I cannot deny her," he said with the comfortably resigned air of a man thoroughly under the thumb of the woman he loved. Like Arabella's husband, Luc. Like Ravenna's husband, Vitor.

Eleanor stared at Taliesin's hard profile and her heart beat raucously.

"Duchess," the lord magistrate said, "have you been absconded with lately by that man?" He gestured to Taliesin.

"No, my lord," Arabella said. "I believe Mr. Tanner was pointing to my sister."

"Aha." He turned his attention on her. "And what is your name?"

"Eleanor Caulfield, my lord."

"Is what that man"—he pointed to Mr. Tanner—"said true?"

"Yes. But—"

"See there, my lord?" Mr. Tanner looked smug.

"But, my lord—"

"Well, is it true or isn't it, Miss Caulfield?" Lord Baron demanded. "I've no patience for dithering in my court. And I've a house party I've just left to come here, which I'd like to return to swiftly. Rather, my wife wants me there. Something about making even numbers at the table. Did the accused abscond with you from the county five days ago?"

"Yes, my lord. But we were only riding through. I—"

"Whether you were riding through, commenced, or ended your journey there, the terms of the penalty are clear. I suspect Mr. Wolfe was fully aware of that at the time. Were you, Mr. Wolfe?"

"Yes, my lord."

Eleanor's heart twisted into ragged pieces.

Lord Baron lifted his gavel. "Bailiff—"

"No! Arabella, *do* something."

"Miss Caulfield," the lord magistrate said, "Lycombe's magistracy is far distant from mine and as such he has no sway in matters of my court. My interests must be for my constituents and the rule of law, of course."

"Of course, my lord, but—"

"Clerk, let it be recorded that upon the testimony of these two parties, the accused is sentenced. Bailiff, read the sentence."

The bailiff lifted a parchment. "For entering the parish of Normanton after legal prohibition set upon him by the court of Caesar Augustus Baron, Lord Magistrate, in the year 1809 due to crimes thereafter forgiven—"

"What crime, by the by?" the lord magistrate asked Taliesin.

"I broke several chairs, my lord."

"Chairs?"

"And Mr. Tanner's arm."

"The accused, Taliesin Wolfe," the bailiff boomed, "is sentenced to perpetual incarceration in England, commutable upon recommendation of the judge to deportment to the Antilles at which time he will be at his liberty, effective immediately or, in the event of deportation, the securing of whatsoever mode of ship passage can be arranged within seven days from this day, 17 April of the year 1819. All the accused's goods, chattels, properties, and monies are to be seized forthwith by agents of His Majesty, with a portion to be reserved for payment of jail fees or ship passage, and fees of this court, etc. etc. This sentence is hereby undersigned by etc. etc."

"No." It came forth as a strangled whisper. Eleanor's throat locked. She forced sound through it. *"No,"* she said more loudly. "You cannot punish him for rescuing me from harm."

"Miss Caulfield," Lord Baron said, "it is clear from Mr. Tanner's testimony, as well as yourself, that you've lately traipsed about the countryside with a Gypsy on the back of a very fine horse. Have I misunderstood the matter?"

"I did not precisely traipse, my lord."

"Then what would you call it, Miss Caulfield," he said with an unsympathetic wag of his finger, "when a young lady puts on die-away airs and insists on being carried on horseback in her nightclothes across the countryside?"

"I—"

"I knew a girl like you in my youth, come to think of it. Pretended to be frail so all the young bucks would swoon over how delightfully delicate she was. Well, I said rubbish to that, and let them waste their time swooning. A lady with spirit, I tell you, that's the sort of girl a man can admire!"

Die-away airs. Frail. Delicate. All uttered with disdain.

"I understand, my lord," she said. "But you see, when I was residing at my relatives' house, I took ill briefly. My relatives used the occasion to dose me with laudanum—"

"Aha, splendid stuff! My grandmother has taken a spoonful every night for the past forty years. Sleeps like a baby. She's ninety-four, by the by." He narrowed his eye. "Your relatives sound like clever people, Miss Caulfield. But what that's got to do with the business of my court today, I haven't an idea."

Eleanor's heartbeats were thick and hard. This big, powerful man would never understand what Lady Boswell had tried to do to her, how it could take so little effort to drag a woman into helpless dependency, and how little power a woman like her truly had.

Unless she fought back.

"Yes, well, as I was recovering from my illness I was obliged to go on a journey, and Mr. Wolfe came along as . . ." Her stomach turned. "As a deterrent against thieves upon the road."

"Had you hired him as a guard?"

"No." The magistrate's words rolled around in her mind. *A lady with spirit . . . The sort of girl a man can admire . . . She knows I cannot deny her.* "But it was understood that the protection he offered was in exchange for certain . . ." Her cheeks flamed. She forged on. "For certain *benefits* during the journey. You see, my lord." She softened her voice. Made it deeper. "Mr. Wolfe and I have a long acquaintance."

Her papa's face was white.

Chains clinked and she realized they came from

where Taliesin stood. She saw now the chain hanging down the back of his legs. *Manacles?* Her chest ached.

"My lord," Taliesin said. "What Miss Caulfield has said is untrue. There was no such agreement or exchange. I escorted her as a favor to her family. Apply to the duchess for the truth, if you will."

"Mr. Wolfe," Lord Baron said, "I repeat that you will speak when I bid you do so and only then."

The chamber door opened and Ravenna and Vitor came into the room.

"Now, who are you?" Lord Baron demanded.

"Vitor Courtenay, my lord." He bowed. "Good day."

The magistrate's brow screwed up. "Airedale's son?"

"The very same, my lord. And this is my wife."

"My other sister," Arabella supplied.

"All right, all right." The magistrate scowled. "Sit down, Courtenay. I'll not have you disturb these proceedings either." He returned his frown to Eleanor. "Miss Caulfield, it seems to me that you are playing a lovers' game that has no place in this court. Or anywhere in polite company, I daresay. But I am intrigued. Explain how it is that Mr. Wolfe came to be in Normanton despite the prohibition that he knew would put him in the way of breaking the law."

"I am playing no game, my lord. I am only stating the truth." Her stomach churned, but he was listening to her lies now when he had not listened to the truth. "I knew he would come if I summoned him. He had said so years before, when he was my father's servant and infatuated with me. He wrote it to me in a letter. I will gladly produce that letter for you if you require, my lord. After I accepted his assistance traveling, I saw that it was the same with him now as it had been years ago. I depended upon it. You see, as I said, I was residing with my father's family at the time and found myself in an unpleasant situation. I was desperate to escape it, really. They were horrid. Truly."

"How so, Miss Caulfield? Other than the laudanum," he said with a dismissive wave of a large hand.

"They . . . They were trying to force me to marry where I don't wish to marry." She trained her voice to subtle complaint. "My cousin, Harold, you see, wants my father's inheritance."

"Aha. Well, it's a good thing to keep the property in the family."

"But I don't wish to marry my cousin. He . . . He has warts."

"Warts?"

"All over his hands." She shivered dramatically. "And a cowlick," she added quickly. "And he smells of compost."

"I see."

"I said I would not marry him, but they locked me in a room and told me they would not release me until I accepted him."

Arabella gasped.

"They *locked* you in a room?" Lord Baron exclaimed. Eleanor nearly sighed aloud in relief.

"Well . . . That is what I wrote to Mr. Wolfe. I told him to come swiftly and rescue me in the middle of the night."

"In the middle of the night?"

"I was obliged to leave on a moment's notice, of course, or my cousins might have discovered my escape. Also . . ." She paused. "It was much more exciting that way. And Mr. Wolfe obliged. In the past, he has liked to see me in my nightclothes, when I have allowed it." She let a wicked little grin curve up the corner of her mouth. Good heavens, this gamble had better work. She felt like retching.

But Lord Baron seemed rapt. The nonchalance on his

features when he had proclaimed Taliesin's fate had turned to fascination.

"But I knew he might not have sufficient funds to carry me away," she continued, "so I told him I would bring my family's heirloom to serve as proof to anyone on the road that I am who I said I was. Did you find a gold and ruby ring in his possession?" *Please, God.*

"Bailiff?"

"Yes, m'lord. We did."

"I want to see this ring. Bring it."

The bailiff approached the magistrate. Eleanor could not look at Taliesin or her sisters. Shame burned like coals in her cheeks.

The lord magistrate studied the ring. "Duchess," he said, "does this ring belong to your family?"

"It does," Arabella said tightly.

"Have you any idea of how it came to be in Mr. Wolfe's possession when he was arrested five days ago?"

"I do not." She set a hard eye on Eleanor. "I have no reason to disbelieve my sister's word. In this."

The lord magistrate stared for a long moment at Arabella, then at Eleanor. "Who is your father, Miss Caulfield? Who is the man who ought to have put you over his knee and taught you a lesson in propriety years ago?"

"I am Captain Edward Bridgeport-Adler, her father." He stood, frail and gaunt, with round, sunken eyes ringed with gray, but the aristocratic cast of his features and his military stance was unmistakable. "I take full responsibility for my daughter's immodesty, my lord. I have been a negligent parent in the past. But I promise to see to it that she is suitably controlled in the future."

"I should think that this nephew of yours, Harold, has had a near miss," the magistrate said with asperity.

"And how *you*, miss," he said, pointing at her, "came to be such an immodest troublemaker when your sisters are ladies, I cannot imagine. It is a travesty." He turned to Taliesin. "As for you, Mr. Wolfe, I commend your loyalty, if not your thorough stupidity for giving it to a woman of lax morals, however pretty she is. I am also impressed with your bravery. She manipulated you and you ought to be ashamed of that. But show me a man who hasn't made a foolish mistake because of a woman and I'll eat my wig. I've a mind to waive the penalty for breaking the old injunction against you."

Eleanor's blood raced.

"But I'll only do it on the condition that you cease all connection with Miss Caulfield at once."

"I cannot agree to that, my lord." He spoke so calmly. "Miss Caulfield has just told you a tale that I cannot corroborate." He swung his black gaze to her and everything inside her melted, her courage, her hope, her last shred of resistance to loving him. "She seeks to protect me from the consequences of my actions," he said, "but I need no such protection."

"Well," Lord Baron said, "that's nicely said. But you are sealing your fate, you understand?"

"Of course he understands it, my lord." The vicar of St. Petroc stood. "He speaks only as honor allows him to speak. He is that rare example of a man born into an inferior station who, nevertheless, with education and good rearing, has risen above his lot. And admirably so. If only we Christians extended our charity to all races less civilized than ourselves, England would never be obliged to jail or deport its hardworking sons. We ought not to punish men like this, but to applaud them for the challenges they have overcome and the struggles over which they have triumphed."

The earl's shaggy brows disappeared beneath his wig. "A reformer, eh? And you are . . . ?"

"A poor country vicar, my lord." Her papa folded his hands. "Only here at the request of Mr. Bridgeport-Adler, and prepared to take this wayward woman into my home as a pupil."

"As *your* pupil?"

"Rather, my wife's. She is eager to teach Miss Caulfield the maidenly modesty she lacks."

The earl sat back in his chair and looked at Taliesin. "Hm. Mr. Wolfe, what say you to that?"

"I could not imagine a better tutor than that gentleman, in truth," he said.

Sinews strained in her papa's folded hands as he looked at Taliesin.

The lord magistrate drummed his fingers on the arm of his chair. "I've heard all you've argued." His eyes scanned them. "But who's to say this isn't simply an elaborate scheme to convince me other than the truth, which is that you, Miss Caulfield, would say and do anything to save this man from jail or deportation because you are in love with him?"

The room seemed to tilt back and forth. She opened her mouth.

"I am to say so, my lord," rang a clear, masculine voice throughout the chamber.

"Robin?" she whispered.

"Who now are *you*?" the lord magistrate demanded.

"My name if Robin Prince," he said firmly. "And I know for certain that Miss Caulfield has no real interest in Wolfe."

"And how do you come to know that, Mr. Prince?"

"Because I myself would have wrested her from her cousins' home if I had known of her trouble. A month ago I left her there in order to travel to my home to prepare it for her. You see, my lord, five weeks ago I asked Miss Caulfield to marry me, and she accepted."

The lord magistrate swung his satisfied gaze to Eleanor. "Aha. It becomes clear now. This wasn't really about cousin Harold, was it, Miss Caulfield? Had yourself a final hurrah before the vows are said, did you?"

She could not speak. She nodded.

Mr. Tanner sputtered. "But, this is preposterous!"

"Merely the typical folly of young lovers." Lord Baron lifted his gavel. "Let it be declared that the condemned is forgiven his imbecilic misstep on behalf of a woman, with the understanding that he cease any further connection with her. And if Miss Caulfield bothers Mr. Wolfe again simply because she gets the whim for a bit of adventure, I'll throw *her* in jail the next time. You too, Mr. Prince, for your poor choice of a wife. I maintain that spirited fillies are the best sort. But a man can't let himself be minx-led, now can he?" He smacked his gavel on the table beside his chair. "This court is adjourned. Now I'm going to return to Lady Baron's party before she decides to serve *my* head on a platter for dinner." He stood.

The bailiff called out, "All rise!"

Pulse pounding, head awhirl, Eleanor pushed herself to her feet. A black fog crowded her. Her legs wobbled. She grabbed for her sister's arm. "Bella—"

Chapter 27

The Princess

A scratch came at the door to the tavern's hired bed-chamber. Taliesin opened it. Betsy stood in the dim stairwell.

"She's well, sir. Much better! She's just had dinner." She pinched her lips together. "I've said it already: I think you should come to the house. The vicar hasn't stopped talking about you since you walked out of that courtroom. And I know my mistress would be pleased to see you, after all she did to free you from—"

"Miss Fortnum, I have appreciated your assistance. But I have truly had enough of your harangues."

"Well." She set her fists on her hips. "If that's the thanks I get for keeping secret that you've not left town yet, I don't know what to say."

"A first, I daresay."

Her freckled nose crinkled. He took her hand and pressed a small purse into her palm, then released her. "Thank you for your assistance. I will not be requiring it again."

"Then you'll be leaving town *now*? Just when she's well? You're a queer one, Mr. Wolfe, and I'm saying that honestly." She turned and started down the stairs. She paused. "But if you ever need a maid in that ramshackle old house of yours, you just send for Betsy Fortnum."

He managed a smile for her. "I shall."

She left and he paid his bill, found his horse, and rode away from the other half of his heart.

HE HAD GONE. *Again.*

She stared up at the canopy above the bed. "He might have at least stayed long enough to thank me."

"You insulted him and revealed intimate secrets about him," Ravenna said, nabbing the toast from Eleanor's breakfast tray and crunching it. "Then you said you were going to marry someone else. How would you expect him to react?"

"With the intelligence God gave him." She had hoped he would understand. But perhaps he had. Perhaps he simply didn't want her. It seemed certain, in fact. After all that had passed, she knew it was time to finally accept that his loyalty to her family determined his actions toward her. And some lust. But he would never be only hers.

Knowing this with such finality drove an ache so deep inside her that she could only lie on her back and stare blankly into her future.

Oddly enough, that future did not look dark and gloomy. It looked tentatively bright, a sort of peach color with shimmering edges. This was unaccountable. Her heart was in ten thousand pieces, an anguished collection of shattered bits. And yet the future looked like . . . spring?

Like May Day.

"Robin Prince calls thrice every hour," Ravenna said. "He is smitten."

"I don't know why. I haven't given him any encouragement." Except the kiss. A kiss she had enjoyed. A kiss she barely remembered now. While every touch, every caress she had ever shared with Taliesin was carved on alabaster in her soul.

"You never showed Tali any encouragement either," Ravenna said, "and yet you've had him wrapped around your little finger forever."

It hurt to hear this. But her sister didn't know everything. "I haven't."

Ravenna set down the half-eaten muffin. "Why haven't you showed him encouragement? I've always thought you loved him. But even now the two of you circle around it like vultures over a fresh carcass."

"Charming, Venna," she mumbled.

Ravenna brushed her palms against each other, scattering crumbs on the bed. The gesture struck Eleanor forcefully.

Her sister stood and went to the door. "I will send up Mr. Prince the next time he calls."

Eleanor stared at the canopy, then closed her eyes and prayed for dreams.

Sometime later Betsy roused her from sleep and

made her sit up. "The gentleman is here to see you, miss. Let me put this shawl around your shoulders. Lud, we've got to put some meat back on these bones. I'll bring up tea and cakes."

Betsy left, and Robin entered. He pulled a chair beside her bed.

"Good God, it's a relief to see you well," he said upon a rush of breath. He took her hand. "Do you mind it? What I claimed without your permission?"

"I think you know that I am grateful for it. It convinced the lord magistrate. Thank you, Robin."

"Will you marry me, Eleanor? In truth?"

She withdrew her hand. "I cannot."

He ducked his head. "I am here," he said to his empty palm. "I have remained, with hope and determination." His gaze came up to hers. "He has gone, Eleanor. He doesn't care about you. Why can't you see that?"

"Robin . . ."

Spring stirred the filmy draperies at her window, the pinkish light of morning steeling in and tickling her skin. She breathed it into her lungs.

"I have lived my entire life thinking that if I pleased people, they would give me what I wanted—what I needed—safety, a home, family, love." A ghost of laughter stole from her throat. "Even adventure."

"I can give you those. I *will.*"

"I don't want them from someone else. I want to find them in myself." She turned her eyes to him. "I want to be the heroine of my own life."

His chin dipped. He did not speak immediately. "If you ever have a change of heart, you need only come to me."

He left. But Eleanor's heartbeats would not slow.

I will come.

She had waited for years for Taliesin to return to her.

She could acknowledge this now. She had stayed in one place for a decade, not moving, barely living, in the hope that he would return. In her heart she had known he would come if she truly needed him.

He had. Even when it hurt him, he had come.

But she had never gone to him.

Rather, she had gone to him once. One cool September day when she was fifteen, after the Gypsies returned to St. Petroc for the winter, she had tied boots onto her soft feet, threw a cloak about her bony shoulders, and without anyone's knowledge walked ten times farther than she had walked in two years.

Standing by the string of his uncle's horses, one hand wrapped around the handle of a tin water bucket, the other stroking a horse's neck, he must have heard her coming. Felt her. He turned his head, smiled like the sun had taught him to, and she had fallen into his eyes for the rest of her life.

She had demanded that he teach her how to ride a horse. All the great heroes of legend knew how to ride. So she should too.

And he'd taught her.

Sliding from the bed on quaking legs now, Eleanor went to the clothespress.

"Miss!" Betsy exclaimed from the door, porcelain jittering on the tea tray in her hands. "Why aren't you in bed?"

"I am going on an adventure." She tugged a stocking over her foot.

"Well, you'll collapse in a swoon if you don't eat first."

Eleanor swallowed the tea and biscuits, and a pile of little sandwiches too. "Is Mr. Treadwell still here? With my sister's carriage?"

"Yes, miss. What are you thinking?"

"Pack my portmanteau."

"You're weak as a kitten and I've nothing to pack. You've only got the one gown I got at the shop before we went to court."

"That's fine. I don't need gowns." She only needed to tell a black-eyed Gypsy what she should have told him a lifetime ago.

TALIESIN WALKED THE length of his property as rain and dusk fell, Tristan following along behind as if they hadn't been parted for a sennight, and he wondered how long it would be before Kitharan seemed like home to him. But perhaps no place ever would. He had no Rom blood, but he'd lived with them long enough to have adopted some of their wandering spirit.

No.

He could not blame it on nomadism. No place would ever be home without Eleanor. Wherever she was—on a frigid beach, in a sultry wood, or on the back of a horse—his home would always be there.

Kitharan was merely a house. A ramshackle, falling-down house. A house that might someday be habitable if he continued breeding and selling superb horses. Which he would. That, apparently, was in his blood. Just as a golden girl was in his heart, no matter how he tried to shut her out of it.

He paused on the hilltop upon which he had seen her weeks ago after too many days apart, comfortably seated on Iseult, her hair shimmering in the sunlight. At that moment he had wanted only to mount the hill in an instant, if necessary to ascend to the heavens to have her.

He'd had it wrong for years. Giving himself to her was not to fall into an abyss. It was to surmount the stars.

"Tristan," he said. "Prepare for a journey. When the sun rises tomorrow, we're going home." To battle a prince for the woman he loved.

SPRING COATED THE road with mud and the carriage crept the last mile to Kitharan as daylight failed.

"They'll be frantic by now," Betsy said darkly, staring out the carriage window at the green shrouded in falling rain.

"I left a letter."

"You'll swoon and die, and me and Mr. Treadwell will be turned off."

"I've done nothing but eat and sit in a carriage. I'm well rested and I won't swoon." Unless he touched her, perhaps.

The drive appeared from the mists in the darkening dusk, winding gently around low hills to the house. She couldn't catch full breaths. The thrill of this adventure was overflowing inside her and she was dizzy. Anxious. Hopeful. Desperate to see him and finally *to know*.

The carriage drew to a halt before the house. She stumbled from it and to the door. It was unlocked, the hinge loose. She slipped inside and pushed back the hood of her cloak. Her breaths were the only sound in the cavernous hall.

"Eleanor?"

She swung around. He stood at the other end of the longest expanse of uneven floorboards ever. Perhaps six yards away. But it seemed miles.

"Why are you here?" she demanded.

"This is my house." His deep voice sounded tight. "Still. Thanks to you, of course."

"You needn't have made me travel across half of England to speak with you."

"I'd no notion that you wished to speak with me." It seemed in the shadows that his mouth curved up at one side. "Did you mishear the part of the acquittal that stipulated that you were not to seek me out, upon threat of imprisonment?"

"But . . ." He could not be serious. "I must say something to you. I am sorry about what I said in the court. How I did it."

His smile vanished. "It served the purpose."

"Arabella and Ravenna are furious with me."

"Why should they be? You told the truth."

"They understand why I did it, but they think I have betrayed you. It was not the truth. Not entirely. You know that."

"Do I?"

"Of course you do. But perhaps you don't know everything." She stepped forward.

He remained still, his shoulders rigid.

"I am sorry for my behavior toward you all those years ago," she said. "I have only recently understood why I taunted you when we first came to Papa's house. I always thought it was jealousy, that I was afraid he would love you more than he loved me. But it wasn't only that. The foundling home was never far from my memory, the work and cruelties. I wanted nothing of those thoughts, nothing that could mar the paradise I had been granted after so many years of sadness and abandonment. I wanted no more toil and labor and reddened hands. I was unkind to you because I hated the work you did in Papa's home."

"That work won me a place there each winter."

"You came despite my unkindness because you wanted the money and a warm place to sleep."

"I came despite your teasing because I wanted you. I would have endured much greater hardships to be with you."

A tear slipped onto her cheek. "Eleven years ago, the last thing you said to me was that you would do what I wished. And I believed you. I was young. We were young. Still, I find that after all of this, or because of this, I must tell you now, finally . . ."

"Tell me."

"Since that day there has not been a night when I did not wish upon the stars that you had given me what I wanted. I was always afraid to say it to you. I believed that I could not want something so much and have it, for it would certainly be taken from me. Every summer when you left it only proved my fears, like now, when you have gone again. But I can no longer be silent. If the heavens opened up and offered me one wish now, I would wish that you loved me as I have loved you." She heaved in air and looked down at the ground. "I have said what I came to say. If you—"

Hard, swift steps crossed the chamber. Her head jerked up.

He grasped her arms. *Touching her.* Holding her tight. "What of Prince?"

"How, with your astounding arrogance, can you have imagined that I could ever want any man but you?"

He enveloped her in his arms, and his mouth found hers. He kissed her crushingly, completely. A sob of pure joy escaped her.

"You may not marry him," he growled against her lips.

"I never intended to marry him. I want to marry you."

"You are mine."

"I have always been yours." She was laughing and crying at once, clinging to him, her hands taking possession of his back, his waist, his shoulders, claiming him finally, entirely. "And you are mine."

He kissed her mouth, her cheeks, her eyes as though

she were air and he needed her to exist. Again, her mouth. "I am yours."

She dragged herself from his arms. "Not yet." She clamped her fingers around his. "But you will be." She pulled him toward the door and shoved it open.

Upon the threshold in the rain, Betsy and the coachman stood side by side. Mr. Treadwell twisted his sodden hat in his hands. Betsy's face was stern. She swept them with a sober perusal.

"Another minute, miss, and we was—"

"Betsy, Mr. Treadwell, you must stand witness now."

"Witness, miss?" the coachman said with raised brow.

Eleanor's grip tightened around Taliesin's hand. She looked up into his face. "Mr. Wolfe and I will now say our wedding vows and you will be our witnesses."

Taliesin's mouth crept up at one corner and his black eyes shone. Her heart turned over.

"But—" Betsy sputtered, "neither Mr. Treadwell or me is a churchman!"

"Well, now, I'm thinking Gypsy folk don't need a churchman to wed," Mr. Treadwell said with a thoughtful nod.

"They need a broom," Betsy declared. "I once heard a peddler say he'd gotten married over the broom. When I told Mama, she said her cousin got married over a broom too, and she married a blacksmith who'd Gypsy kin."

"Should I fetch a broom, sir?" the coachman asked.

"No, Treadwell," Taliesin said. "Miss Fortnum, you needn't have concern. A church wedding will follow shortly."

Eleanor threaded her fingers through his and traced his beloved face with her eyes that would never cease hungering for him. "Taliesin Wolfe," she said upon a quiver of ecstatic nerves, "I want to be your wife. In truth, I long to be your wife. I give myself to you in marriage."

"Eleanor Caulfield Bridgeport-Adler," he said quite clearly, "My heart is already yours. With its every beat for twenty years I have given it to you. I offer my body and soul to you now. I offer all that I am and all that I have as your husband."

"I accept," she whispered, dancing up onto her toes. "I accept. I accept."

Smiling, he drew her hands to his mouth and kissed them.

Betsy burst into tears.

Mr. Treadwell beamed and sniffled, then pulled out his kerchief and tucked it into Betsy's hand. "There, there, miss. It's all right. Everybody's happy now."

A gust of cold mist swirled about them. Taliesin swept Eleanor up into his arms and carried her across the hall toward the stairs.

She laughed and wrapped her arms around his neck. "Where are you taking me?"

"So that we haven't any misunderstanding about the matter, I intend now to put action to words."

"Do you?"

"I do. And then some."

Heat flew into her face. "But Betsy and Mr. Treadwell, and your servants, they will—"

"Let them. I don't intend to give you up. Not even for a moment. Not for anyone ever again." He brought her into a bedchamber furnished simply with a canopied bed and woven rugs.

"Give me up?" She gripped his neck. "For anyone? *Again?*"

He set her on her feet, cupped her face in his hands, and tilted it up. He kissed her softly, then deeply, brushing her tongue with his, and she felt it every-where in her body.

He drew away only enough to meet her gaze. "Did you truly believe that eleven years ago I left of my own will?"

"What else was I to believe?" she said with the little breath she still possessed.

"You found the message I left in the book."

"A month ago."

"A month ago only?" He released a long breath, stroking a lock of hair back from her brow. "Eleanor, it is time we leave the past behind."

"But—"

"I did not go willingly. Not then. Not ever."

"Not ever?"

"Every time I left Cornwall for the past twenty years, I left my heart behind me. Since the moment I first saw you." He kissed her lips, her cheeks and throat with slow kisses now, and with each caress of his lips on her skin, she grew warmer, then hotter, longing for more. He drew her close and his hands shaped her body to the hard length of his.

"Taliesin? I'm frightened." Quivering with need but terrified.

He placed a kiss behind her ear and she heard him inhale deeply. "Never be frightened of me."

"Of disappointing you. Now." She glanced at the bed. "There."

"I'm fairly certain that's impossible." His voice smiled.

"But you know I haven't any experience at—at *this*."

He held her in the shadows of his eyes. "Then we are well matched."

She stared, disbelieving. "I cannot believe it. In all these years, you *must* have . . ."

"I have never made love to the woman I love," he said quietly.

Starlight lit the air.

"But what if I disappoint you," she whispered.

"Feel what you do to me, Eleanor. What you have always done to me." He placed her hand on his chest, and his hard heartbeats thrummed through her palm, his breaths deep and trembling. Then he moved her palm downward. Her fingertips shook as she traced the tight contours of his belly. She knew what he intended and could not contain her impatience. She covered his arousal with her hand. His intake of breath against her cheek fueled her confidence. Through his breeches he was thick and hard. Touching him, holding him, made her hot again, and peculiarly faint, the longing she had denied forever escaping from her heart and pouring into every crevice. Her body wanted him.

His words caressed her cheek. "Now, love, let me make you feel it too."

By the bed, he undressed her. And he kissed her. Everywhere. On her throat and neck and breasts. Especially her breasts. Over and over until she was weak from it. Then on her wrists and belly and buttocks. She had not known that men did such things to women. She wondered if only he did. Then she became so lost in the pleasure of his tongue and lips stroking the inside of her thigh that she didn't care as long as he never ceased. Her body became the landscape upon which his hands and lips traveled, his nomadism her pleasure.

Urging her onto her back on the mattress and bidding her spread her legs, he told her that this was what Perceval must have wanted to do to the seductive succubus that tried to destroy his chance of finding the Grail. For nothing could hold him back from such temptation.

She laughed and said that would make her the devil in disguise. Then his mouth on her most sensitive flesh shocked her into silence, then made her whimper in need, then cry out in desperation as she rocked her hips and begged him for more.

"It feels too good." Her gasps came frantically. "But I want . . ." She clutched the bedclothes. "I want more."

He moved up between her legs, his lean, hard body glorious, the candlelight bathing his muscles and sinews with gold. "You want this." He fit himself inside her, a shocking, wonderful, breathlessness of intimacy. "You want me."

He allowed her only a moment to adjust, to become accustomed to the revelation of his size and to begin to feel the pleasure of his possession of her. Then he thrust into her. Then again. Surrounding her jaw with his hand, he turned up her face so she looked into his eyes as he took her. Fierce and black and full of passion, his eyes spoke of his love and the years apart that were now forever in the past. He held her hips and drove into her and she wrapped her arms around him and urged him closer still, until she felt him everywhere. Snarls of his male pleasure tangled with her moans. He gripped her knee, drew her closer, tighter, and forced himself deeper, making her mad for him, for *more*. The tender lover had gone. This love was wild and powerful and real. With every touch, every caress, every interlocked cry of pleasure, he took from her and gave of himself to fill her empty spaces.

He laughed, an exultant sound from deep in his chest. "Not frightened any longer?"

"This is heaven." She threw her head back and her hair cascaded as she closed her eyes. One hand gripped his shoulder tight, as though she would never release him. She cast her other arm to the side to clutch the bed linens, and her delight drew him in until he was drowning. He kissed her arched throat, swallowing her flavor and drunk on it.

"How foolishly we wasted time when we might have been doing this," she said upon a brilliant smile.

"We have forever now, *pirani*."

"I love you, Taliesin. I love you."

Again and again she said it, her lips parted in ecstasy, her hips moving with his. With some magic of her body she was working his cock inside her, and he drove deeper, to take more of her, to have all of her. She moaned and sought him, crying out upon his thrusts until she gasped and gave a strident shout of triumph. He spent himself in her—his heart, his body. "*Eleanor,*" he choked, consumed with feeling her and knowing finally that she was his. "My love," he whispered against her cheek.

"I love you," she said again, her fingers tight on him, her breaths shuddering. "I love you."

He stayed with her, tracing her lips with his fingertips and loving the rosy flush on her face and breasts that he had put there. When her hips moved against his, testing the sensations that lingered in her body, he gave her what she needed. She undulated beneath him and gasped again, her eyes flying open.

Then she relaxed entirely. Her lips curved. "Nice," she whispered.

He smiled. "That's all you have to say?"

She turned her face so that her lips brushed his palm. "We." She sighed. "Win."

He kissed her neck, her soft lips. The cushion of her body beneath him was too slender. But he would remedy that. He'd done it before.

He drew away and covered her with the bed linen. Then he took her hand into his and laced their fingers together. Palm to palm.

They lay beside each other for some time without speaking. The shadows had deepened into night, the room lit by a single candle by which he had been writing instructions to his staff when she appeared in his house—miraculously, like countless dreams he'd had and denied.

"I have acquired a new skill tonight," she finally said.

He laughed and angled an arm behind his head, closing his eyes. In the perfect silence he heard her stir. A soft fingertip skimmed along the muscle of his arm, her touch sweetly tentative now.

"I don't think I will ever be quite as good at it as you," she said with a breathless sound.

He curled her fingers around his palm and brought them to his lips. "You are quite good enough at it already. Exceptionally good."

"The bother of it is that I will not be able to improve myself without your assistance."

He smiled. "It's not a competition, *pirani*."

"There must be books that will help me. The ancients were routinely scandalous. The medievals too, although they seem to have glossed over the most interesting bits."

He shook his head in wonder. "How you ever doubted that I loved you . . ."

"You loved me then because you could not have me." She spoke too quietly.

He turned his face to her. Flecks of candlelight lit her questioning eyes.

"I loved you then because you were an angel and you saved me," he said.

"I was a plague on you. You said so more than once."

"If you had not come to St. Petroc, and if you had not fought to best me at every letter, word, phrase and page, even at riding, I would not be the man I am now. I wanted to impress you and I wanted to be good enough for you."

"You are saved," she said. "You do not need that inspiration from me any longer." Her throat constricted in a swallow of uncertainty. "Now that you have had me, will you abandon me again?"

He turned onto his side and propped an elbow beneath him to look down at her. "Did you come here imagining that after I took you to my bed I would throw you off in long-awaited righteous triumph?"

"No."

"Then what do you imagine?"

"That I will wake up and this will have been just another dream," she whispered. "I have had so many."

For a moment, he could not speak. "Do you believe that you are the only one who fears waking up?"

"Then let us never sleep." She trailed a fingertip down his chest.

He kissed her lips with great tenderness. "For a decade I tried to cease loving the girl you were, and I failed. I will never cease loving the woman you have become."

Eleanor curled into him like a kitten begging to be stroked. He obliged.

"I'm glad I decided to seek adventure."

"As I am. Immeasurably glad." His hand stilled. "Married to me, Eleanor, you will not be received by your father's family, and few others in your society."

"It is not my society."

"It is your sisters'."

"Then let it be theirs alone. They will always welcome us, for they love you. The others matter nothing to me."

"Are you certain?"

"Do you think that in all these years in the vicarage I have been pining for fashionable soirées?"

He grinned. "Haven't you?"

"I have not. I have been pining for . . . No. I won't say it again. You are sufficiently arrogant."

"Yet I long to hear the words that you will not say again," he said quietly.

"I have been living a simple life. Reading, writing, translating texts for Papa, keeping house, shopping at the market on Wednesdays, recording minutes for the Ladies' Parish Commission meetings, taking tea with—"

"I fear I'm nodding off."

"I said it was a simple life. And you aren't nodding off, unless that thing you're doing with your hand is something you can do in your sleep."

"I cannot keep my hands off of you." He nuzzled her neck. "I cannot get enough. I have never been able to get enough of you."

"I like it, so you're quite welcome to never get enough. I like this house too. I like the room at the top of the stairs for the library. Perfect . . . walls." Walls against which he had made her feel things she had never known, like he was doing again now.

"Mm." He brushed the coverlet aside and kissed her breast. "Perfect."

His mouth upon her breast robbed her of words. Thoughts. She smoothed her palm over his shoulder, feeling the power he had used for her so many times.

"Can we live here or have you someplace else that you must go to trade?"

His tongue traced a languid circle. "We can live wherever you wish."

She moved into his caress. "I am sorry you lost Tristan."

"You needn't be. I recovered him. He is here."

"Oh, I am so glad." She stroked her fingers through his hair. "Is that why you left Exeter so swiftly? To retrieve him?"

"No." He raised his head and looked down into her eyes. "I believed you were to wed another. I left because to be near you and prevent myself from loving you was a challenge I could no longer meet." He pulled her up and onto his lap, settling her knees to either side of his hips. His hands spread on her back. "Also to escape the temptation of doing this at first opportunity." He kissed her neck and she leaned into it, wrapping her arms around his shoulders. Nothing was between them now, not miles, not years, not a single garment.

"What exactly is it you are doing?" she said.

"Making you mine again."

She kissed his jaw that was rough with whisker growth. She wanted to feel the scratchiness on her skin again. On every inch of her skin. "How many times will you do so tonight?"

"Until I am convinced it's true."

"It?"

"This. You in my arms. In my bed." He brought their lips together. "Your love."

"I am torn between convincing you immediately that it is indeed true and allowing you to come to it in your own time." She worked her way to his ear, tasting the depression below with her tongue. His scent made her hungry for him, his skin smooth and hot against her lips. "The latter has certain obvious advantages."

"If you choose the former," he said huskily as she licked again, his hands clenching around her behind, urging her tighter to him, "I vow to not alter my current course of action."

She drew aside his hair to kiss his neck. "Then I will set about convincing you in all ways. My heart is yours, Taliesin Wolfe," she whispered in his ear, as though she hadn't already told him a dozen times as they'd made love. "I have loved you forever and—"

She stilled and brushed satiny black locks away from his skin. Her lungs could not capture air. "What—?"

She clambered off his lap and behind him. With her fingers she framed the dark mark at the base of his neck, a letter burned into his skin like a scar: a T with a diagonal line from the top right to the center. The symbol on the ring.

Her body trembled. "What does this mean?"

He turned his cheek toward her. "Your father did not tell you?"

"My *father*?" She traced the T on his skin with her fingertip. "No."

"Long ago my uncle told me that I came to his family already marked with it. He said he did not know what it meant. But another did." He removed her hands from him, kissed them, and went to the desk. He drew the ring from a drawer.

"Lussha knew what my uncle did not. When Edward left me with the Gypsies and the vicar, he told her my father's identity so that if he and my father should perish in war, someone would know. She never told another soul. Twelve years later, Arabella appeared in her tent with this ring."

"But . . . What Lussha said that day . . . The fortune about a prince . . ."

"Some Rom have the Sight. Schooled to mistrust magic by the Reverend Caulfield, I never believed it. Until you gave me this ring."

"Edward . . . ? My *father* brought you to St. Petroc? To Papa?"

"To hide me from my father's enemies. After Edward's mind deserted him, no one knew the truth but Lussha."

"Why didn't you tell me this before? After I gave it to you?"

He sat on the bed beside her, turned her palm over and enclosed the ring in her fist.

"Because it meant nothing to me. If I wasn't to have you, I did not care what a ring or my blood or anything else said about me. In my entire life I have only ever wanted you. No prophecy or far-distant crown would ever change that."

She put herself in his arms. He held her tightly.

But her eyes flew wide and she broke from his embrace. "Your father was Alejo? Alejo Torres?"

He nodded, lines cutting the bridge of his nose. "How do you know this?"

"Before I fell ill, my father told me of him. And of my mother."

"Your mother, Grace?"

Wonderment constricted her chest. "After they believed Edward dead, Grace and Alejo . . . They . . ."

Taliesin's handsome features creased into uncertainty. "They what?"

"They loved," she said simply. A smile broke over her lips. "Taliesin, Ravenna is your sister."

Ebony eyes shone and a slow, crooked smile slipped across his mouth. "Of course she is," he said quietly. Then he took Eleanor into his arms.

She nestled into his shoulder and uncurled her fingers. "After Alejo died of the fever, she must have sent us to Papa rather than Lady Boswell because she wanted you to have this." Ruby and gold winked in the candlelight. His family's symbol was dark and bold through the crimson gem. "You must take up your inheritance. You must go fight for it."

"Must I?"

"Yes."

"Eleanor, after eleven years apart, we are now together again. Yet you wish me to immediately travel hundreds of miles away?"

"With me. I have always wanted to travel."

"With you," he said. "Into a war?"

"Whatever we find in your father's lands, I will go with you, Taliesin. I won't be without you again, even if it means facing danger."

He kissed her brow softly. "And the magistrate who has prohibited you from dragging me into your lust for adventure ever again . . . ?"

"He'll never know. Not until you are presented at court as a visiting prince, at least. But then I suspect I might be forgiven. I've heard it's terribly difficult for women to resist a prince. I wouldn't know about that, of course. I have only ever loved a rogue."

"Have you, *pirani*?" He bent to the curve of her neck, making pleasure on her skin with the lightest brush of his lips.

Reluctantly she pulled away from him. But she must know, finally.

"Ever since I remember, you have called me that name. I always suspected it meant something horrid."

"You might have asked me at any time," he said quite seriously.

"I hadn't the courage." She stroked a fingertip down his neck, then spread her hand on his chest. The beats of his heart caressed her soul. "Now I do. What does it mean?"

He drew her forward and placed a soft, perfect kiss upon her lips. "Beloved."

Epilogue

Love, Triumphant

T

"*T* invited Taliesin to the wedding with the sole intent of throwing you two together." Draped in a pink silk mantua accented with white lace, Arabella reclined on a divan, suckling her infant at her breast. This portrait of maternal leisure smiled like a cat that has feasted on Dover sole.

"And Papa wanted his wedding at Combe because he knew Tali wouldn't come to St. Petroc," Ravenna added, lounging beside an enormous white mass of fur. "It turns out that he hadn't visited St. Petroc in so many years, Papa felt certain nothing could entice him to go there, not even an invitation from me or Arabella." She stroked the fur and a tail thumped on the sumptuous carpet that lined the floor of the duchess's dressing room. "I told Papa and Bella I thought that was the silliest part of it. I said you were far too intelligent to believe that Papa would require everybody in St. Petroc to travel to Shropshire just for a party. But apparently you aren't too intelligent after all. Who would have thought it?"

Wearing a gown of white silk threaded with gold embroidery that made it shimmer, a string of milky pearls around her neck, and a delicate circlet of pearls in her hair, Eleanor sat quiet correctly in the straight-backed chair at the dressing table. Hands in her lap, she looked for all the world like a demure, virginal bride mere hours from her own wedding. That she had spent the night skin-to-skin with a black-eyed prince was their secret alone.

"You might have simply told me what you thought," she said to her sisters.

"We tried," Arabella said.

"For years." Ravenna rolled her eyes.

"You always walked out of the room whenever we said his name."

"Even Agnes connived with us," Ravenna said. "Since we knew Tali wouldn't go to St. Petroc, she devised the plan of throwing you at her son in order to make you desperate to flee the vicarage."

Eleanor gaped. "Frederick connived too?"

"He's wonderfully charming." Ravenna grinned.

"And conveniently eager for a lark on occasion." Arabella's eyes glittered.

"Bella devised his costume, but he did the rest himself. He said that no matter what he did, you hid your repulsion so valiantly that he began to despair of success. He told us he'd never had such fun."

Arabella lifted a staying hand. "He only agreed to it because he understood how desperate we were and how much we love you. He did not wish you to be hurt by it."

Caught between dismay and laughter, Eleanor groaned. "I don't know whether to thank him or never speak to him again."

"You cannot imagine how thrilled I was when you fell in with my plan so effortlessly," Arabella said. "I'd thought I would have to spend months convincing you to set off looking for our parents."

"*Your* plan? Searching for our parents?"

"As soon as Ravenna married, I decided that you and Taliesin were destined for a quest."

"Travel can be remarkably eye-opening," Ravenna agreed.

Arabella bit her lip. "I never hired an investigator."

Eleanor's eyes widened. "My manipulative sisters. Did Taliesin know that?"

"No! Good gracious, with his pride?"

"He would never even speak your name," Ravenna said. "That's how we knew."

Arabella drew her sleeping infant from her breast. "Will he be piqued with me when you tell him?"

The warmth that had remained with Eleanor since dawn when she had slipped from his arms lapped at her now. "I don't think he will be piqued with anything for quite some time, actually."

"My brother is a very good man," Ravenna said with a sparkling smile. "And he awaits you at the church." She jumped up, took the babe from Arabella, and set him easily on her shoulder. "Bella, you must straighten your gown and we will go now, so that Tali and Eleanor can finally do what they should have done years ago."

Arms linked, the three sisters walked together down the stairs of Combe Park and onto the drive. Among the family and smattering of other guests standing by the carriages that would take them to the chapel a small distance from the house, only Taliesin was absent. *Awaiting her at the church*. It seemed at once unreal and the only reality Eleanor had ever imagined.

She allowed her father to hand her into a carriage with her aunt. In the three weeks since her return from Kitharan, Edward had grown ruddier and his eyes had lost much of their agitation.

"You seem well, Father."

"With daughters now that I thought I had lost," he said, "how could I not be well?"

"Eleanor," Mary said with bright eyes. "It is done. Aunt Cynthia and her children are gone from Edward's house."

"They will not be invited to return," he said.

Eleanor grasped their hands. "I am very glad for you both."

"And I for you. That my daughter would wed my dearest friend's son is a blessing for which I could not have hoped."

They came to the chapel. Arabella, Ravenna and their father only remained in the narthex with her as the others took their seats. Then the violinist began to play, her sisters went forward, and she stood still and ready. So ready she could sing. Dance. Make love to a rogue all night, every night.

Impatient to commence this bliss, she peeked around the edge of the door. Arabella and Ravenna hovered mid-aisle, fiery head bent to black locks. Standing on the stair to the altar, simply robed and with a book between his palms, Papa waited.

Taliesin was not present.

Eleanor's heartbeats slammed against her ribs. She did not believe what her eyes told her. Not again. *Never* again.

"Daughter?" Edward said, extending his arm.

Her head shook as though attached to a weather-vane, the wind howling between her ears. "He is not there."

"Taliesin? Not there?" He went forward into the nave.

She pressed her back to the wall and tried to breathe. To think.

Betsy appeared and hurried to her. With a grin and a curtsy, she placed a folded paper on Eleanor's palm, and went into the church. Eleanor opened the paper. His scrawl:

Come outside

She pushed wide the door. Before the church, re-splendent in a black coat and snowy neck cloth with silver glittering in his ears, he sat upon his great ebony horse that was decorated for the occasion with silver and gold chest piece and breeching like the steed of a medieval knight.

Taliesin smiled and her heart lurched again to life. He urged the stallion forward.

"My bride," he only said.

"That I am," she said.

He bent and lifted her up onto the saddle before him. Wrapping her in his arms, he kissed her deeply, soundly, until her hands clutched his shoulders and the pearl circlet in her hair was askew.

"Where are we going?" she asked with what little remained of her breath. "Do you not intend to marry me today?"

"I do. As soon as it can be done."

"Then why are we mounted?"

"I want you in my arms when you promise yourself to me. I could devise no other acceptable means of assuring that."

She laughed. "Acceptable? Riding a horse into a church?"

"Feasible, rather."

"Feasible?"

"I am a horseman, *pirani*." He cocked a brow. "Medieval knights did it all the time."

She stroked her palm over his cheek and kissed his lips. "I have promised myself to you with every breath I have drawn for years. I do so again now, with all my heart."

He looked at the church door, then into her eyes. With a smile of utter confidence he said, "Prove it."

A Word About Gypsies, Rogues, and Revolution

There is an overwhelming fascination about them and their mode of life. It is the fascination of freedom. We think that we are free: indeed we boast that we are. But of our civilisation we have made a tyrant.

BRIAN VESEY-FITZGERALD,
The Gypsies of Britain (1944)

The word Gypsy evolved from the word Egyptian. Lore had it that when the first Romany people entered Europe in the later Middle Ages, they claimed to have come from Egypt. The name stuck, eventually becoming the most popular in English: Gypsy. Today the word is often considered a pejorative. My characters—all but Taliesin—use it because it was the typical terminology of the era.

The early nineteenth century saw increasingly strict

laws across Britain against vagrancy. Tinkers, peddlers of all kinds, disabled war veterans, and "lunatics" were often lumped together in anti-vagrancy laws with "Gypsies" or "Egyptians" as "rogues" and "vagabonds." A resolution passed at the quarter sessions of Norfolk in 1817, for instance, indicated that "all persons pretending to be gipsies, or wandering in the habit or form of Egyptians, are by law deemed to be rogues and vagabonds, punishable by imprisonment and whipping." (Mayall, 258) Most of these laws were reiterations of centuries-old legislation against vagabondage that penalized "rogues," fortune-tellers, and "Egyptians" with crippling fines, imprisonment, and forced removal from their homes, including deportation.

The struggle for domestic tranquility in the shifting social landscape of early-nineteenth-century England after the end of the Napoleonic Wars led reformers in and out of Parliament to seek solutions, including "domesticizing" England's Romany. Many of the reformers, some of whom were religiously motivated, perceived Gypsies as lawless, irreligious creatures of an inferior nature to "civilized" man, who could nevertheless be educated to become moral, law-abiding subjects and integrated into mainstream society. I drew Martin Caulfield's comments about Gypsies—those in Eleanor's memories of childhood and those he speaks in court for the benefit of the magistrate—directly from the writings of contemporary reformers. With Martin I hoped to paint a portrait of a common type of reformer of the era whose heart and actions were directed toward justice and equality, but whose notions of culture were nevertheless still essentially racist. Scholars have done exceptional work on attitudes towards Gypsies in British history, including David Mayall's *Gypsy Identities, 1500-2000: From*

Egipcyans and Moon-men to the Ethnic Romany (quoted above) and Deborah Epstein Nord's *Gypsies and the British Imagination, 1807-1930*, among others.

A word on deportment is in order here. While deportment was a punishment for Gypsies for hundreds of years in Britain, by the beginning of the nineteenth century English law was more likely to prohibit than require it. Hefty fines and imprisonment were the most common punishments for those identified as "rogues," including Gypsies whom many lawmakers considered threats to the proper order of society. Since Taliesin's years of vagabondage included many episodes of incarceration, some for acts of violence, and since local lord magistrates in this period still had significant autonomy, I allowed the elder Lord Baron to lay down an especially severe threat.

Across an ocean from England, the West Indies (today the Caribbean) in this era was a bubbling cauldron of abolitionism, revolution, and rebellion. Despite popular ideas that included liberty for all men regardless of race or ancestry—and rebellions by slaves who were forced to live as property and labor in unspeakable conditions—the European nations that had long since claimed the islands refused to relinquish the bases of their vastly lucrative sugar industries. At war both at home and across their empires, they switched alliances swiftly according to the complex politics and dangers of the moment. The French Revolution, which created warring factions within that country, complicated alliances further. At the time Edward Bridgeport-Adler deserted his regiment to fight with Spanish and French rebels in the mountains of Santo Domingo (today the Dominican Republic), which bordered French San Domingue (today Haiti), English military forces were supporting the French plantation owners on San Domingue. England's leaders perceived their greatest threat at the time to be the French Revolution. Since the plantation owners were fighting the revolutionaries, who were abolitionists, in order to keep slavery alive and prosperous, England briefly defended those plantation owners. That years after his incarceration Edward was quietly forgiven his briefly rebellious past reflects the swiftly shifting waters of British domestic and foreign policy. Many in Britain sympathized with the horrifying plight of slaves, and Britain's abolitionist movement during these decades was fierce. In 1807 Britain forbade the slave trade from Africa and in 1833 become the first colonial nation to entirely and permanently abolish slavery. I also take up these themes in my novels *Swept Away by a Kiss* and *Captured by a Rogue Lord*.

Real history is a complex and intricate creature. I thank my husband, Laurent Dubois, one of the world's foremost experts on the Caribbean in the age of revolution, for helping me create the story of Martin's fiery preaching that inspired his friend to sail across an ocean to fight for justice; Edward, Grace and Alejo's love triangle during these years of tumult; and Grace's sacrifice that sent her daughters away from danger to what she hoped would be safety. In the time since I began planning my Prince Catchers series, my husband and I have spent countless hours pouring over the details of these events that happen decades before the stories in the three novels occur. But such is history: while it appears comfortably in the past, its effects never fail to impact the present profoundly.

For readers of a geographical bent, you will not find Piskey on any map of Cornwall. It is an amalgamation of several coastal towns in Cornwall and Devon that I adore. In the Cornish dialect I named it after the fairies ("little people") who inspire me to write fiction. Normanton is also fictional, mostly because I couldn't bear to populate any one charming historical Devonshire village with bigots. I fell in love with Devon and Cornwall while researching and writing these books, and will return to them in future books without doubt. The small, independent Andalusian principality of which Taliesin is heir is also a creation of my imagination.

And so we come to the end of my Prince Catchers series. I hope you enjoyed the Caulfield sisters' adventures. You can find another glimpse of the prince-catching sisterhood in my novella *Kisses, She Wrote*.

Once a character appears on the stage of my nineteenth-century Britain, he or she is likely to appear again. Master swordsman Evan Saint returns in the fourth book of my Falcon Club series, featuring Lady Constance Read, also known as "Sparrow." Evan's fastidious chess partner, Joshua Bose, appears in the second book of that series, *How to Be a Proper Lady*.

For more about my books, including extra scenes from *I Loved a Rogue*, I hope you will visit me at www.KatharineAshe.com.

Thank-yous

For their angelic influences on this story (some knowingly, others not), I thank Mary Chen, Erin Knightley, Melinda Leigh, Lisa Lin, Caroline Linden, Helen Lively, Teherah Mafi, Mary Brophy Marcus, Jennifer McQuiston, Miranda Neville, Lydia Olander, and Maya Rodale. To the good people of Saladelia Café, without whose welcoming haven this book would not exist, I raise a glass in thanks. For their inspiring title ideas, my gratitude goes to Amanda Banks, Nova Conover, Angela Daffern, Melody B. May, Tin Ong, Joanne Pall, Ashley Seamon, and Celia Wolff, with special thanks to Celia for coming up with *I Loved a Rogue*.

Thanks to my assistant, Cari Gunsallus, who is all that is good and patient and industrious when I am at my most scattered and frantic, which is, in fact, always. And to my Princesses, the best street team in The Entire World.

Georgie C. Brophy and Meg Huliston's reading and

suggestions shaped this book meaningfully. For their generosity and wisdom I am deeply grateful.

Thanks to artist Jennifer Wu for the Torres family symbol that graces the first page of each chapter in this book. She rendered it perfectly.

Copious thanks to all the fabulous people at Avon who make publishing each of my books look so easy, especially Gail Dubov whose gorgeous covers make me sing, Eleanor Mikucki whose copyediting is superb, and Eileen DeWald whose patience astonishes me, and to Nicole Fischer, Pam Jaffee, Shawn Nicholls, Megan Schuman, and everybody in Sales & Marketing. Thank you most especially to my wonderful editor, Lucia Macro, who makes all my books so much better and especially this one.

To my agent Kimberly Whalen, a hundred, thousand, million thank-yous.

To Mary Buckham, who once told me to be the heroine of my own life, my most sincere thanks for mentorship which has sustained me ever since.

To my readers, for your open, generous hearts and your thirst for goodness and joy in this world. I wish that I could wrap each one of you in a bear hug and imprint stars upon your brows.

To my mother and father, who gave me both the permission and the privilege to write fiction, I am eternally grateful—really, beyond words. And to my husband, son, and Idaho, whose love and companionship and support sparkle in my heart like the heavens, thank you, beloveds.

Don't miss

THE ROGUE

the first book in a brand new series

THE DEVIL'S DUKE

by KATHARINE ASHE

Coming Spring 2016

Read on for a sneak peek!

EVAN SAINT TOOK what he wanted when he wanted it. Whether by the tip of his blade or the finesse of his words, he rarely lost a battle.

Yet when he stood within reach of her, his tongue faltered.

"You were staring at me." Blanketed in the brilliant blue of her eyes peeking out from ivory silk, he could contrive no other words, no empty seductions for this girl.

"You were staring at me," she replied, her voice a whisper of satin or cream or something equally pure and rich. Unmistakably aristocratic, with a lilt of Highland music. She was not one of the hired women in this den of hedonism tonight.

"One of us must have begun it," he said.

"Perhaps it was spontaneously mutual." Her lips like generous rose cushions curved. "Or coincidence and both of us imagined the other began it."

"How mortifying for us both then."

The beautiful lips smiled again, an arc of delight. *And mischief.* She knew of him. Of his reputation.

"Dance with me," he said.

From within the mask, her eyes darted into the dim ballroom beyond. "I cannot."

"Or you will not?" he challenged, but his heartbeats were quick. "With me?"

She caught him in her wide, brilliant gaze. "If I could, I would only with you."

Then Evan knew, with the certainty of a warrior, that what they had begun so innocently, so easily now, would ruin them both . . .